The Prophecy—and the Promise…

In his dream—and he knew that he dreamed, though the grass was cold and wet beneath his bare feet—he arose and went under the rustling eaves of the oakwood, to the well in the clearing where a bubbling spring led from the rockface into a channel down the slope.

Brendan looked up swiftly…between him and the well stood the Goddess Herself, gowned in green, unearthly fair. Reaching up to the oak branch above Her head, She broke off a sprig that turned to green leaf and white blossom at Her touch, then bending plucked a shamrogue from the grass; and held out both to Brendan, who took them wonderingly but without fear.

"You have the Oak-strength, the Sky-strength," She said then. "Your brother—and he is your brother—will subdue to his own ends the power of the ground, and great sorrow come of it. You will be unfriends all your lives for what you believe—the great Rift between you. But also you will be linked forever: as the Branch of Gold rises from the crown of the oak, never to touch the earth, you will rise out of Éruinn; and though bondage be behind you for the Gael, freedom for the Kelt is in the stars."

A BOOK OF THE KELTIAD

THE DEER'S CRY

PATRICIA
KENNEALY-
MORRISON

HarperPrism
A Division of HarperCollinsPublishers

🔥 HarperPrism
A Division of HarperCollins*Publishers*
10 East 53rd Street, New York, NY 10022-5299

ISBN 0-06-105927-7

HarperCollins®, 🔥®, and HarperPrism® are trademarks of
HarperCollins Publishers Inc.

Cover illustration © 1998 by John Ennis.
Cover design © 1998 by Saska Art & Design.
Maps by the author.

A hardcover edition of this book was published
in 1998 by HarperPrism.

First paperback printing: August 1999

Printed in the United States of America

❖ 10 9 8 7 6 5 4 3 2 1

TO

AULTAIN AERON MAEVE

Acknowledgments

This one is for Patrick O'Kinealy, my great-great-grandfather and immigrant progenitor for whom I was named, and his sister Ellen who came over with him, and all the millions of other Patricks and Ellens who left Tir Gaedhil not in starships but in coffin ships, driven from their homes to seek another land; to the ones who reached it, and the ones who did not, warriors all—an mhuintir a tháinig rompu—fáilte romhat!

Praise and thanks also to Willie Yeats and Walter Scott and Alfred Tennyson, they know why.

And all glory, love and honor to the highness that was, and is, and ever will be, Diana, Princess of Wales, whose royalty owed nothing to anyone but herself.

BRENDAN'S IRELAND
425 C.E.

N

To AULBA

WESTERN SEA

CREAVANORE

FANAD

ULIDIA

TIR
GAEDHIL
(ÉRUINN)

TARA

CONNACHTA

SINAN RIVER

KNOCKFIERNA

BLUESTACK MTNS.

EASTERN SEA

THOMOND

LAIGHIN

To GWALIA →

To CORNOVIA

To SULYONESSA

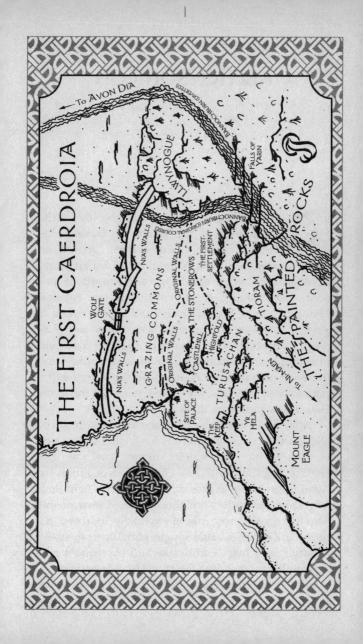

THE FIRST CAERDROIA

To AVON DIA

BANNOCHBURN (DIVERTED)

LLWYNOGUE

FALLS OF YARIN

BANNOCHBURN (ORIGINAL COURSE)

NIA'S WALLS

GRAZING COMMONS

ORIGINAL WALLS

THE STONEROWS

THE FIRST SETTLEMENT

WOLF GATE

NIA'S WALLS

ORIGINAL WALLS

CASTLEHILL

HIGHFOLD

TIORAM

THE PAINTED ROCKS

TURUSACHAN

To NI-MAEN

SITE OF PALACE

THE KEEP

YR HELA

MOUNT EAGLE

N

KELTICHRONICON

Twenty thousand years before the start of the Common Era, the Tuatha De Danaan, the People of the Goddess Dâna, arrived on Earth as refugees from Núminôrë, a distant world whose star had gone nova. They settled without incident, establishing great city-realms at Atlantis, Lemuria, Nazca, Machu Picchu and other centers of energy. It was an age of high technology and pure magic coexisting—lasers, powered flight in space and in atmosphere, telepathy, telekinesis and the like—and there was only minimal contact with the primitive Terran native inhabitants, who, awed, regarded the lordly Danaans as gods from the stars.

After many centuries of peace and growth, social and spiritual deterioration set in: faction fights, perversions of high magical techniques, civil war. The Danaan loyalists withdrew to the strongholds of Atlantis, or Atland as they called it, there to fight their last desperate battle with those of their own people who had turned away. Atland was finally destroyed in a fierce and terrible battle fought partially from space, resulting in a huge earthquake and subsequent geologic upheaval that sank the entire island-continent.

The evil Atlandeans, the Telchines, seized the

secrets of interstellar travel and headed off back into space; their descendants would later be heard of as the Coranians, and they were to trouble all starfaring nations until Aeron Imperatrix made an end at the battle of Nandruidion. But the Danaan survivors found their way as best they could over the terrible seas to Ireland and to the other sea-countries on the edge of Europe. There had long been Atlandean outposts in these lands, and they made a likely refuge.

But the refugees had yet another battle to fight: with the Fir Bolc and the Fomori, the native tribes currently in occupation of the island. Atlandean technology, or sorcery, prevailed, and the Danaans settled down to rebuild their all-but-lost civilization.

After a long Golden Age, the Danaan peace was shattered by invasion: the coming of the Gael, Milesian Celts from the mainland. The Danaans, at first victorious in defense, were defeated, and shared possession of Ireland with the new race; the two peoples found they had much in common, and the coexistent amity between Danaans and Milesians lasted many hundreds of years. But suddenly, for some reason they would not tell, the Danaans began to withdraw, to live apart in their hollow hills, and the Gael now prevailed.

But four centuries after the beginning of what would come to be called the Common Era, a slave was bought in Ireland who would enslave the Irish, and a boy was born in Fanad who would free the Gael...

THE LEAVING OF FANAD

What do you build with sails for light?
A ship I build for sorrow.
Shall you depart on Samhain night?
Nay, on Beltain's morrow.

Where do you lay her rib-keel down?
In fields of stars and sunlight.
Where were her mast-trees felled to ground?
In caverns dark and unlight.

Why do you leave your land so fair?
We go as we are driven;
the names of snake and serpent there
forever to us are given.

For an outland god seeks magic's death—
Exiles at home we find us.
To keep alive our ancient faith
we leave our world behind us.

Who shall go with you when you sail?
Hearts never known to falter.
We would sooner in death and darkness fail
Than bow at the stranger's altar.

Who stands behind you on the shore?
One who is stone to reason.
But the lie he proclaimed for evermore
shall die in its own dead season.

For foreign creed and foeman's gain
Our honored ways were bartered.
The magic wrought to serve and sain
Rome's cowherd now has slaughtered.

What do you take for cargo hence?
Souls and swords and glory.
What will you find when you come thence?
A new and greater story.

What winds those sails of silver shake?
Winds from the sun's heart sending.
What roads your starry dragon take?
Paths that shall have no ending.

For we sail a ship whose helm is hope
And I shall stand commander.
A thousand thousand worlds before—
I think it be a wonder.

> *—from* 'Brendan's Voyage',
> *by Séomaighas Douglas Ó Morrighsaun*

There is hope from the stars.

—Nia the Golden

THE DEER'S CRY

FORETALE

t would not be called Ireland for centuries to come, and before that day dawned it would have many names—and many masters. But those who dwelled there in that time called it Éruinn: more simply still, An Tir, the Land; or, if pressed, or speaking with those who visited from afar, An Tir Gaedhil, the Land of the Gael, for that was the name of their race, and the land was indisputably their own.

It had not always been so. Others had dwelled there long before the Gael had ever dreamed of riding westward to the double water, and they too had thought the land their own. Indeed, it still belonged in part to those first folk; and even they had not been first, they had displaced others in their turn.

With the coming of the Gael, the land had passed again, in the ways that all lands pass everywhere in all times, through marriage and friendship and purchase and work, and not infrequently at the point of the sword: in great swift leaps and wrestings, and in small goings so slow as to scarce be seen. But though it passed, it had never passed entirely, and the two mighty races that now shared the lovely green island between them did so in what it pleased them alike to call peace.

He belonged to them both. His mother was a lady of the High Danaan kindred, the magic race that had come out of that other doomed island in the west, and who had fled to the sea-countries on the continent's sunset fringe when their homeland was whelmed by the ocean that now bore its ancient name; his father was a lord of the Gael, a chief of the Laighin tribe that dwelled in the south.

But far in the northwest he had been born, in Fanad, a rough mountainy country where his father had grazelands and his mother's kin held sway beneath the hill. At his saining, his grandfather, a prince among the Danaans and one who had the long Sight, beholding the spirit that was in him and the fate that was on him named him Brendan; and so he would be known in the history of many worlds besides his own.

But in the High Tongue of his mother's people, that name is turned as Brandoch—and, either way, its meaning is 'torch'...

BOOK I

TIR GAEDHIL

CHAPTER ONE

hat day on the hill of Slemish the sheep were most contrary, and perhaps that should have given him the clue right there. They jigged and poked when he would drive them, or ran away with leaps and goat-jumps, or else they simply stood there and stared at him, and what they were thinking behind their mild affronted faces he could not guess.

He was seventeen years old that Beltain past, tall and lithe of build, with brown-red hair and dark eyes and the fair, fair skin of his mother's people. He was clad as a shepherd: a kilted plaid of summerweight wool fixed on his left shoulder with a bronze brooch, a full-sleeved leinna of yellow linen, hill-shoes of oak-tanned leather to spare his feet from the knife-sharp gorse and bracken—though the plaid had long since been unwound and set aside in the heat of the day, and the long tails of the leinna knotted up loosely between his legs for coolness and ease.

The hills among which the balky sheep disported were quaratz scree, rough and blocky, not more than two thousand feet at their highest point. Prevalently chill and gray, wreathed with the clouds that roll in off the nearby ocean, they were green and lush now, the brief northern summer full on them; though that day's heat-haze was rare weather indeed for this far north-western corner of the island, cooled as it is by onshore winds and the currents that wash the rocky coast.

This lovely, lonely, empty country was called Fanad. His father was its ruling lord—a reality rather less grand than the splendid-sounding title—and had his seat at the dún of Creavanore, 'Branch of Gold', named for the Holy Tree itself: a comfortable and rather grand brugh well built of dressed cut stone. Those less inclined to compliment, or more to envy, had been heard to call it a jumped-up farmstead, and that to its master's face. But Fergus Tinne fo Brega—Fergus Fire on Brega—of the tuath of Aoibhell, only laughed when they did so, and cheerfully agreed.

On the other side of the hills, down the well-wooded valley of the Davan Water, lay the lands of Fergus's dearest friend, the chieftain Coll, of the Clann Morna, who dwelled in a place no whit less agreeable, together with the wife he had carried off from her home in north Britain—gossip had it that no sooner had Beirissa of the Brigantes set eyes on Coll mac Gréine naked on the battlefield (though other, more waspish tongues said naked elsewhere) than she her-self had arranged the carrying off—and with the six sturdy children subsequently born to them.

But apart from Creavanore and Magheramorna, and a handful of other, lesser maenors, the tiny settle-ments here and there throughout Fanad were mere clusters of shielings and cotts, wherein dwelled the sub-tigerns and lieges dependent upon the greater estates; in all that far-flung district there was no town of size to speak of. The Gael have ever been a solitary race, not a great folk for clustering together hard by their neighbors; their ways are not cast in cities and towns but in apartness. If one craved close society—a cashel-town or river settlement or shoreport—it required a journey of a week afoot, and little less ahorse, to come by it, over rough wild country to the south or the east; and in those days the island boasted very few such precincts.

It was a fine life and a pleasant one, if sometimes a little lonely; but even for a lord's son there was no calling that was not open as well to any Gael who suited. In his boyhood Brendan had thought to train for a Fian, one of the warrior fellowship; the other high crafts—bardship, brehonry, druidry—seemed far beyond his gifts or graces. And it might yet be Fianship for him, he had not been forbidden it; but they were short-handed that year on all the western maenors—a plague had carried off many in Fanad, even the Fian healers had not been able to save them—and where other lords had bought from the sea-reivers sufficient captive backs to fill the empty places, Fergus Aoibhell had ever found that expedient unacceptable. So everyone at Creavanore, himself and his son first among them, redoubled their labors wherever they might—and Fergus's lady also, after her own fashion, or the fashion of her people.

But all noted very well indeed how, with fewer workers and no bondslaves, somehow more seemed to get done, and was better done, and more thrivingly and lastingly and beautifully done, at Creavanore than anywhere else in Fanad; and whether or not that was the work of Nia the Golden—wife of Fergus, mother of Brendan, princess of the Sidhefolk—none could say; or would say…

*   *   *

So it fell out that Brendan mac Fergus was a herder for the nonce. He liked it very well: the sheep were placid, if deeply stupid—horses, though he loved them and had great affinity with them, would have been considerably more trouble—and save for the necessary twice-daily milking by the young maenor lads and lasses, the shaggy lyre-horned red cattle that were the real wealth of the tuath took care of themselves.

And to be out alone on the Fanad hills in high summer was by no means a hardship. The short season was warm and bright; but a few times each year, between the Swanmoon and the Ottermoon, there would come tundish clouds that hung like skyhooks out of the giant thunderhelves rolling in from the sea to build their silent towers into the blue. The air would smell chokingly of flint, a wind begin to rise; then the rain would move across the hills, lightning stitching cloud to earth with bluefire threads and the wind louder even than the wrathful sea. These storms, however ferocious, were things of the moment, tearing themselves apart in a matter of minutes, hurtling east to vanish over empty moorland, and the cool seawind swelling in behind.

But this one particular time was different, a new note in the wind gave it away: Brendan, who did not like the feel of the air and was already anxiously chivvying the sheep to shelter, looked up to see a fat white snake of spinning wind, half a lai wide, casually stretch down out of a dark cloudbelly and fasten itself like a sucking mouth to the green ground. *A cam-anfa, a crooked-storm...* He had never seen one before, though he had heard plenty of tales of what their appalling power could do; but despite the danger, for a moment more he stared at it, rooted in simple wonder. *Goddess, the majesty of the thing...how mighty it is—it can drive a straw through a shield, pluck a goose alive, rip the eyes out of one's head...*

No time even for fearing: between one heartbeat and the next the sky went black and green and yellow as a week-old bruise, the air cooled so quickly it hurt to draw breath; snowstones began to drum down with enough force to flatten the grasses. In the blinding rain that came at him from all quarters at once, he saw the cows sensibly bolting for their shielings, or down for safety into the swales, as the tundish, with a roar like a million stags, plowed across the grazeland. But most of the sheep, though bred to this stretch of hills, were not so wise: in their terror they followed not the sagacious yowes who headed calmly for shelter but the yearling taggets who dashed headlong, and in their panicked flight they were stampeding straight for the cliff where the hill of Slemish fell sheer away to the river, a hundred rocky feet below.

Brendan began to run, in his desperation and helplessness whistling and calling to his hound Luath to head them off; wiping the rain from his face, to his great surprise he saw blood mixed with the rainwater—the hail had cut his scalp, he had not even felt it. The dog was a brown streak now, belly low to the ground, racing between sheep and rocks, intent on his job, knowing the danger and doing his best to obey his master's command. *Gwenhidw help me! They are slowing, I think; but Luath is only one, he cannot turn the whole flock when they are so feared, they will go over the cliff like a tide, and alone I cannot...*

Then, in the rain and the endless roar of the camanfa, he was not alone. Another youth was suddenly by him; out of nowhere, seemingly—Brendan could have sworn there was not another soul for ten lai round. More importantly, the newcomer had two sheepdogs with him, and at a sharp whistle from their master, 'Away to me!' they went long and sweeping out to each side, racing to join Luath, and together dogs and youths succeeded in turning the flock.

The whole thing was over surprisingly swiftly; already the storm was miles away inland, the watery gray light broadening and sparkling as the sun broke through the clouds, though winds still buffeted. The rescued sheep milled round, vaguely distressed but the terror already receding in their dim brains, the unlovely scent of wet wool strong in the air.

Brendan—wet, draggled, exhausted, but deeply relieved—made much of all three dogs, who had bounded over, well pleased with themselves, to receive their due praise, then turning to the stranger he held out an eager hand and spoke with passionate relief.

"My thanks, m'chara, and all gods bless! The sheep would have been lost if you and your hounds had not been by to help." Then recollecting (for the custom among the Gael is to name oneself and one's dúchas to a stranger, not to rudely demand the other's name): "Brendan, of Creavanore; my father is Fergus, lord of Fanad." Even so, he said it diffidently, lest the other should think him boastful.

But that did not seem to be the reason that the stranger youth, every bit as soaked and draggled as Brendan and much of an age with him, turned a shuttered face away, and kept his own hand at his side, nor why his voice came harsh and tight in reply.

"Aye, I know—I have seen you, though you have

not seen me. And it is not fitting that you address me as 'friend', though I am glad your sheep are saved. I had put my own flocks into the shielings an hour since, by the grace of God, and was on my way—" He broke off abruptly.

"Home?"

The voice tightened another twist. "To my master's home."

"Ah." Brendan felt discomfortable; not because the other youth was no freedman but a slave, but because he himself had required him to admit it, and thus embarrassed them both. It was a thing Brendan almost never did: he had that rarest grace of the inborn tact that sees what others do not wish to be reminded of—and, even rarer, the compassion that then does not remind them. And he was sorry that he had done so now, and all the more to one who had saved his sheep… "Still, any deed deserves proper thanks to its doer from the one it benefits."

"That may well be—in a more perfect world than this—but not many think as you do."

"What is *your* name?" asked Brendan point-on, since the knowledge was plainly not going to be offered.

The other gave a short surprised laugh, as if this were not a thing he was often asked. "Ferganam I am called."

'Nameless'… "Truth! That is no name for a man!"

"No man am I, but a bondthrall of the chieftain Coll mac Gréine."

Brendan's surprise overrode his chagrin renewed. "Mac Gréine! He is my father's dear and longtime friend; they have been swordbrothers since their boyhood."

Ferganam looked away. "And one could find worse masters far—if one must be unfree."

Though he would have gladly spoken more with the stranger, Brendan saw well the distress he was causing, and knew too that it was up to him to end the encounter—thralls, however incautiously frank of tongue they may be in a strainful hour, nonetheless may not leave a freedman's presence until they are dismissed. So with a word or two more of warm thanks, and a blessing as warm for the road home, though he himself was shivering now in his soaked clothing and the cold wind, Brendan turned away from Ferganam, and followed the chastened sheep down from the hill. When he turned round again, thinking to wave, the slopes of Slemish were empty behind him.

When he had been a very little lad, Brendan had loved nothing more than to hear the tale of how his father had met his mother. In his innocence, he was burstingly proud that no other child of his acquaintance had parents who had found each other in such a way of high romance, and he hugged the knowledge to him like a cherished treasure. It seemed to him to come straight out of the legends he already loved to hear the bards recount: how, one summer day, a young warrior of an undistinguished chieftain-grade kindred had been walking and singing to himself in the Fanad hills near his home, when all at once a beautiful red-cloaked golden-haired maiden, with three singing birds hovering round her head and bright silverwork at her throat, had suddenly appeared upon a gold-maned white horse. She seemed to have ridden right out of the green hill side, though neither door nor gate could he see, and she was riding straight for him.

"And no mistake, she was a lady of the Shining Folk, Brandoch, one of the People of the Star. And I fell in love with her on the instant, and she with me. So entranced was I that I could not stir hand nor foot nor eye nor breath till she had passed by. Then I leaped upon my own horse, and rode after her like a bansha, but could not catch her up; though her horse went a slow easy pace, she seemed to go away from me like the moon. Thrice I saw her so, and never catching her I called out at last in despair, that she might rein in and wait for me. She turned at once and did so, and smiling said, 'Better for your horse had you asked that sooner!' And she rode home with me to meet my kin, and we were wed."

It was not until Brendan was older, and grew aware of the way folk watched his mother, or stared covertly after her when she went by with her straight-backed stride, or spoke of her in her absence in low and secret tones, that he began to realize the import of what his father had told him: just how it was that his mother was not as other boys' mothers, nor as other women of the Gael, nor indeed was she a Gael at all... He told the tale to Ferganam, one afternoon upon the hill—by now they had become friends, or as much friends as Ferganam would allow—but the slave-youth merely made a sour mouth and said no word.

Brendan persevered, though he did not understand the palpable disapproval, and was hurt and sorry he had spoken—as if he had given away something he was not yet ready to part with.

"It is by no means so uncommon as you might

think. Indeed, the warrior queen Aoifa of Galloway herself did wed a faerie lord, and even the prince Connla, son of great Conn the Hundred-Fighter, fell in love with a ban-sidhe. Aye, truly! He sailed away with her to Avilion in a crystal ship with sails of silver, and they were seen never again by Gael or Gáll."

"Like as not because God's own clean storm sank their devil's craft, claiming their sinning bodies and their impious souls alike!" Ferganam burst out. "As for the woman Aoifa, the less said the better; she lived by the sword, and, good quittance, she died by it. Thus perish all who have such dealings with the Unensouled."

Brendan looked startled, as well he might; he had never before heard such naked venom in anyone's voice. "The Sidhefolk have no souls? How can that be? They are creatures like all the rest, and subject to the One Who is above all gods forever; more than that, how could there be sin in love—"

And was startled yet again, by the fierce, freighted gaze Ferganam suddenly bent upon him. There was a new judging consideringness in the bond-youth's look, as if he saw a potentiality in Brendan that he had not noted sooner. *He looks at me as a woodcutter eyes a likely tree, or a horsebreeder a promising mare: seeing not me but what might be made of me for others to use—a chair, a colt— and I do not think I like it much...*

"If you speak of the One," said Ferganam after a while, "there may yet be hope for you. But for those beneath the hill, no hope, not even if—" He broke off. "Well. The fault and blame are not yours; you are only ignorant. But perhaps another time you may wish to hear more of what the true and only God has given me to tell you."

"If ever I do," said Brendan, and now he was entirely chieftain's son speaking to slave, "be sure you shall be the first to know of my so wishing."

Nay, thought Ferganam, watching him walk away, *God knows first, and already. Though that too you may come to know, in God's good time—*

But dán, that had been long time at work upon them both though they did not yet know it, had other plans.

CHAPTER TWO

hat summer Brendan and Ferganam met often on Slemish to graze their flocks, as if by arrangement, though neither would ever admit that they had been rather lonely for company out on the hill, and were glad of each other's presence—and, each in his own way, eager to keep hold of it.

For the sake of that companionship, they had unspokenly agreed to steer clear of such disputable matters—ancestry, rank, faith—as might raise a weal on sensitive areas, but for the rest of it they were no different than any other two youths of their age, and comported themselves so: they ran races, swam in the lochans or in the Davan Water itself on hot days, taught each other crafts and skills—carving, wrestling, leatherwork, herb-lore. In the long nights on watch there was laughter and eager converse: Ferganam spoke more easily now of his home in Britain the More, yearningly recounting the beauty of his native lakes and mountains—and awakening for the first time in Brendan the wistful desire to travel beyond his own country, to see new lands—the history of his family and tribe, their links with Rome. For the first time Brendan heard of the great warrior queen Buadicca of the Iceni, whose name meant 'victory', who had struck back hard against the Empire and died just as hard for her struggle, and that other queen, Cartimandua of the Brigantes, whose name meant 'sleek pony' and who betrayed the Gwalian king Caradoc and all his family to her Roman masters—though the two youths inevitably differed in opinion as to which queen was the true hero.

There were no more cam-anfas, but now came unbroken days of blazing heat, a waterless blue sky overarching a land more 'customed to mist than drought. In the shimmering noons the sheep and cattle crowded eagerly at the lower springs to drink deep and long, and their guardians threw themselves panting down beside the stone coping of a deep-watered well, higher up the hill, where an ancient hazel spread boughs thick as a man's thigh, and shed its gray-shaled nuts into the waters of the pool.

Scooping a double handful of the icy water, Brendan let it spill through his fingers onto the sheep-cropped turf, murmuring a prayer to accompany the libation, as his mother had taught him from his childhood was only polite. The ground drank eagerly, and only when the water had sunk from sight did he lower his face to the pool; when he raised it again dripping and refreshed he looked curiously at his companion, who despite the brutal sulter and his own obvious thirst had not stirred to follow Brendan's example.

"The Gael does not love heat, not for us those Fomor-summers! But you do not drink?"

Ferganam's voice came colder than the water itself. "This is a well unclean and accursed; sooner would I drink seawater."

"Not so! It is a good natural spring of the Goddess, the holy tree of Fionn himself grows beside it—" A thought struck Brendan then, a speculative assess-

ment, born of all the odd things he had noticed over
the summer, the sour words he had only half-heard.
"Are you a Christling, then? Of the Christom faith—
those who follow Iosa Crann-draoi—the Tree-druid?
We have heard of such folk dwelling across the Eastern
Sea in Britain the More; there are even some of that
suasion in the southlands of Tir Gaedhil. I did not
know any had come to Fanad."

"Only one, so far, and that much against his will...
But I follow the true and only Word." It was as if a flame
had suddenly kindled behind Ferganam's eyes. "As you
must do, and indeed all your people, turning from the
old ways, if you would save your soul from fires worse
far than summer heat."

Brendan looked curiously—and with a certain faint
wary distaste—at the glittering eyes, the fervent face
working with passion.

"Even Iosa of the Tree, who from my own understanding of the Christom holy book seems to have been
a teacher of rare plain sense, would not have
begrudged a drink to a thirsty man on a hot day, no
matter the god or goddess who owned the well; and the
Shan-vallachta, the Old Ways, *are* old ways for a very
good reason... As for true words, there are as many
truths to sound as there are ears to hear and tongues to
speak and souls to cherish—and not one syllable is
more true or less true than any other."

Ferganam's passion redoubled, until it seemed that
he would shake himself apart with his own zeal. "You
cannot believe that; nay, you must not! There is but
one God, and Christ is his only begotten son." In his
agitation he laid a hand on Brendan's arm, a punish-
able offense in a slave; Brendan did not stir, but his still-

ness communicated much, and at once the hand fell
away. Presently Ferganam spoke more calmly. "You are
a chieftain's child in your country, and I but a slave in it
who am civis in my own, but we are all children of the
One True God. You have said that we are friends; for
friendship's sake I beg you, let me show you the right
and only way to worship."

Brendan let it pass, and the silence trembled
between them like the heat. There seemed nothing
more to be said, so nothing was, and still in silence they
shared out their noonmeal rations between them as
was their custom: fat grilled sausages wrapped in soft
bread, thick slices of a sharp gold cheese, some of the
fresh green herbs that grew wild roundabouts, a burnt-
sugar sweet made of the sap of the maple. In hall it is
far otherwise, where bardic law decrees who shall have
which cut of meat, and who may sit where, and when
who shall be served their dinner and by whom they
shall be served it; but out upon the hill, a lord's son
dines no better nor in greater pomp than does a
thrall—and strange though some might think it, it
pleases both that it should be so.

"Tell me, then," said Brendan quietly, in a tone that
both soothed and invited, his willingness to listen plain
to even the dullest hearer. They had finished their
meal and now were sitting replete beneath the hazel
tree; Ferganam, who refusing the Goddess's spring-
water had contented himself with a few mouthfuls of
blood-warm ale, was apparently not too proud to
accept the gift of shade Fionn's tree conferred. "You
called yourself 'civis'; that is the word a Roman citizen
uses of himself. How came you here, and as you are?"

Ferganam drew a long breath, looking into the

blue distance, deeply moved by the sincerity of the other's tone, though he would not admit it.

"I am not an educated man, not learned like mac Gréine's poets or even yourself, but neither was I born a slave... When the reivers took me, in my sinful pride I scorned to name myself to such as they, and therefore they called me Ferganam, 'man who is nameless'. I am glad to be called so, it never ceases to remind me... But I have a name of my own, an old name and a high one—a *Roman* name." The voice rang with unquenchable pride. "In the common tongue of my folk I am called Maughn; but in the Latin we speak in my home, Patricius Calpurnius; in your tongue"—and, his whole being conveyed by the perfect lack of inflection, a far more barbarous one—"Pátraic mac Calprin. I am a Roman Brython, and civis indeed; my home is in west Bryneich, what some call Rheged, just south of the great Wall."

"I have never seen the Wall," said Brendan, interested. "Though I have often heard of it, and Coll mac Gréine has been there many times to visit his wife's kin, who come from thereabouts."

"Aye, well... My folk live some leagues to the south and west, a country of peaks and lakes and forests, very fair; we have a place called Bannaventa, a villa near the northern end of the Long Lake. My father is a decurion—an officer of Rome—and a diaconal of Holy Church; my grandfather was a priest. I have a sister and a brother, and many cousins, or did when last I saw them; my mother is a lady of the Brigantes tribe from the other side of our mountains."

Brendan looked even more interested. "The Lady Beirissa, Coll's wife, is a woman of the Brigantes."

"And so it was that Coll's raiders were near Brigantian lands that day, though for their lady's sake they
reive ever shy of her tribe's borders. I had gone to visit
my mother's kin, and on my way home to Bannaventa
the raiders came upon me. Nor was I the only one they
carried off that day—or other days. We were taken to
their longboats, which were drawn up on the shore a
few miles away, and then conveyed to this country as
slaves. I was not sold in the eastern shoretowns as the
others were, but brought overland and bound into the
service of Coll. I was sixteen years old, or nearabouts,
when I was taken, and I have been three years now in
this place." He broke off, busied himself with the ale-
flask.

A shadow crossed Brendan's mobile face. "It is the
way of the world, right enough, and of my people very
surely," he said after a while, "but I daresay all nations
put on Erith shall know slavery soon or late—and from
both sides of the iron collar. Your folk too keep slaves,
and the Sassanaich that your lord Vortigern has let
creep onto your Eastern Shore do so as well— We have
all been slaves; or if not yet, then we will be. We who
have kept slaves shall be enslaved in our turn; and all of
us have found our freedom, or shall find it—freedom
from slavehood and enslaving alike. But for myself I do
not hold with the practice. My father does not keep
bondfolk, but if he did, upon my succession, hear me
Goddess, I had freed them all myself. I would see a day
when no nation is in chains to any other, no man or
woman bent as thrall beneath a yoke of any sort."

Ferganam—Pátraic mac Calprin—Patricius Calpurnius—looked at him amazed; but seeing truth upon
Brendan's face to match the words, he nodded grudg-

ing respect, and even managed a smile; a real smile that warmed all his countenance—a surprisingly engaging one, with his black hair and tanned skin and the small gap between his two front teeth. And all at once he seemed in Brendan's sight truly the lad he was, or had been...

"At least the status of slave is something less harsh among the Gael than with the Romans—for one thing, there is the chance under brehon law to buy one's freedom, and I have not yet lost hope of doing so. The only Roman way to liberty is by death, or by the master's whim."

"Britain the More is still part-Roman, and may be for yet a while—a generation, no longer. And I am thinking that those who dwell upon that island, those who are cousin to the Gael—the Brython, the Aulbannach, the Cornovians, the Gwalians—will never take back their own again where once the legions trod; even you must know that the Sassanaich will triumph in the end, as they do now where Vortigern so foolishly—or treasonously as some say—did let them in. The sun has set on their Empire as it did on their Republic— Yet you bear a Roman name."

Ferganam drew himself up proudly. "My gens—my tuath, my tribe—has long history with Rome, and honor from her too. We live at home like Roman Christians, not—" He gestured round him; the meaning was clear, if impolite—and impolitic.

Brendan, unexpectedly stung, responded more sharply than he had intended; indeed, with more of the air of his father's son than he had ever yet permitted himself. *I try to bespeak him kindly, I see us being friends—but he makes it so very hard. Then again, I have*

*never been a slave—well, in no lifetime I can recall—perhaps
if I were I would be as prickly as he. But even so...*

"We also have stone brughs and heated baths and
beautified pavements, you know, if that is how your
people measure civility; and remember, though Rome
may once have swayed all the world in arms, she never
did so here. Our druids and ban-draoi raised mighty
magic to keep the legions on the far shore of the Eastern Sea; Môn in Gwalia was the nearest the Rómanach
came. Doubtless they cast longing looks over the water,
but they never tried to cross. The power of Draoíchtas
kept them out, and well they knew it always would."

"A black and evil power," said Ferganam clearly; the
other's abrupt coolness had stung his pride in turn. He
knew he had overstepped not so much the bounds of
his thralldom as what truly mattered to them both—
the bounds of their friendship; and he was suddenly
afraid lest the chief's son should now think less of him
than he had so far, astonishingly, proved himself willing to think. But there was still defiance in his tone, as
if he cared not a whit for it—or so, at least, he wished
Brendan to think. "The wicked work of devils and darkness—"

Brendan shrugged; he was at all times good-natured,
and in truth he was not much offended now. *I might well
be snappish and untrusting myself, were I a thrall and someone
began suddenly to treat me as a man— But he has no right to
speak so of our faith; and that is a lesson he must learn—and
better it comes from me than from another...*

"The faith of the White Druid of the Tree is a very
new one. And new faiths have ever sought to establish
themselves by wrapping the name of Darkness round
the older, wiser ways they crave to displace. Do not you

Christom say that your god Iosa mac Mhúir was born of
a virgin mother, in a cave while angels sang and beasts
knelt and spoke with words, and that as a man grown
he died on a tree to save all folk and rose again to life?"

"Truly, but it is not we who say so; it is the word of
God which tells us."

Brendan grinned. "Then how comes it that Coll
mac Gréine, a soldier and a well-travelled man, tells the
identical tale of Mithras, who—as you surely know,
good Roman Brython that you are—was the chosen
god of Roman soldiers? Many gods in many lands seem
to have begun so: the Hellenes have the same story of
Diníosas, the Éigipteach of Ósirais, the Síreach of Attis
and Tammuis and Bâl. And do not the warrior Northings chaunt of the Allfather, who died as a sacrifice to
himself on the World Ash Tree, to get knowledge for
the people, and came again to life after nine nights?
That is thrice as long as your Iosa spent in the Otherlands after he hung on his own tree; maybe Othinn
then is thrice worthier, or loves his people thrice as
much, but then Iosa is only one god in three so perhaps it all comes out equal—".

He had meant only teasing discourse, not mockery,
but the thrust had been taken as a real one: if Ferganam had been angry before, now he was white with
fury.

"A trick of Sathanas, the Evil One! He knew that the
Christ would come, and took care to cast doubt beforehand."

"A neat trick," said Brendan, bored now. "Powerful
indeed must that evil one be—more powerful than
your Iosa—to have made something false before ever it
even existed. Talk about an-da-shalla!"

After that Ferganam did not talk to him about any-thing at all, not for seven whole days together, save for the bare minimum exchange of words that their shep-herding tasks required. But Brendan, repenting of his taunt, was troubled enough to take the matter to the ban-draoi of the tuath, a wisewoman, who smiled when she heard his aggrieved outpouring.

"Only a very young soul needs such rigidity in belief, Brandoch, one who has not been through the Circles more than a very few times. It may be that the way of the White Christ has been made for just such souls, who are yet too inexperienced to face Arawn and judge themselves in Annwn, too green to learn aught from the contemplation and calm of Moymell—too simple and childlike to deal with more than one god at a time and too feared to deal with the Goddess at all. Now *our* faith holds that one does not grovel or plead or bargain with the gods: one speaks to them as equals, as one chief to another; each has differing powers in different spheres, and they need us as much as we need them. Perhaps the Christlings find it easier to speak to one god rather than all the High Dânu, and if they do then that is their business, not ours; but that they deny the Lady, and put scorn and shame on women, nay, that is only wrong. Honor his beliefs, amhic, for that he believes them, and respect his god; but never fail to seek and be sought by the gods that are your own, as you are theirs. That is the way of the Shan-vallachta: the only Path with heart, for you or for anyone, is the Path with heart for you, however indulgent or demanding it may seem—or even be."

Brendan followed her good advising; and though after a tense day or two more, he and Ferganam ceased to be unfriends, their quarrel over, or at the least tacitly ignored, it was not forgotten; and it would seed a long and bitter harvest for more than those two alone.

It was the pleasant custom of Clann Morna to feast all of Fanad for the winter Sunstanding each year, as Clann Aoibhell did every Midsummer at Creavanore, and Coll the chieftain went about it with all the magnificence he could muster. Bards, players, harpers, games of skill and chance, even friendly sword-contests, all brightened the Longest Night in the dún of Magheramorna; as for food and drink, the laden boards groaned no louder than those who stuffed themselves thereat, and ale and wine and mead flowed faster than the Sinan.

That night everyone in the household, slave and free alike, worked hard to make the banquet go smoothly. It was Ferganam's indoor duty, in the winter months, to serve at the high table, and so harried was he with extra duties for the feast that he did not notice the entrance of the chief of the district, with his lady and his son, and the folk of his tail standing proud behind.

But his ear, tuned as a servant's must be to gauge need of service by nature of din, noted a sudden dramatic lowering of voices, and he turned to the hall doorway to see what might be the cause.

"The Lady Nia," whispered one behind him, in a voice that held at least as much fear as respect. Ferganam looked at the tall golden-haired woman who stood beside the lord of Fanad, her white hand resting on his arm, and did not know that he gasped aloud,

though he had long known of what kindred came the
wife of Fergus Fire on Brega...

"The Lady Nia is of the High Danaan blood, the
Sidhefolk as some call them," came a different voice,
calm and amused, and Ferganam turned to see that it
was his master Coll who had noted his attention, and
who now addressed him. "Does that trouble you, lad?"

Ferganam looked again. And as if she had heard,
from down the length of the hall Nia turned her glance
upon him. Oh, fathomless are the eyes of the Sidhe, as
any who have gazed into them will tell; but the gaze of
Nia the Golden had depths that no mortal, and few
even of her own folk, could sound. She was the daughter of Calatin, a high prince; her mother was the sorceress Súlsha, sister of Síoda and daughter of great
Maeve; she was true heir to them both. The step of a
mountain doe was on her, and she held her head high
beneath a silver fillet set with clear gems; but cold
haughtiness was never Nia's way, and she treated all
folk as equal, and as her equal, until they proved themselves otherwise. Tall and fair and willowy in her red
gúna she stood there that Midwinter night, her neck
circled by a torsade of river-pearls and rough-polished
rubies. A faint silver light clung to her as closely as her
gown, and every eye followed her as she came down the
hall with Fergus and Brendan, to greet Coll and
Beirissa who were their friends and hosts.

Ferganam, watching that greeting narrowly, noted
the warm affection that was plain among them all,
though he would not meet the eye of Brendan, who
stood behind his parents, vainly endeavoring to catch
Ferganam's gaze. *One of the Unensouled—ensnared a mortal to her unclean lusts, the evil one! When the true Way comes*

*into this pagan land, all that will change—pray God I may be
the instrument of its enlightenment, and of her destruction
and all her kind alike...* But the feast was beginning, and
with a start he hastened to attend his master.

The seating was arranged according to the strictest
bardic procedure: Coll and Fergus side by side at the
center of the high table, their ranking guests down the
table's length, their ladies presiding one at each end of
the board; at the two tables set at angles sat the bards
and sorcerers and captains. The rest of the hall, hung
with garlands of fragrant pine and fir wreaths studded
with bright-berried holly, was filled with trestle tables
and benches, which this night held most of the folk of
the province. Some too had come from far beyond
Fanad's borders, up from Ossory away in the south, or
down from Ulidia to the northeast—guests of the high
blood of Uí Néill, even, who sat with the rest of the
mighty at the head table, even as their great kinsman
Niall Nine-Hostage sat as king at Tara—and those who
served in the hall were kept busy indeed.

There was little serious converse for some while, as
harpers played at their stations and feasters attended
to the serious appetites they had brought with them—
Coll mac Gréine being far-famed for his table's liberal-
ity. Going silently about his duties, Ferganam stared
straight ahead, and handed round the laden chargers
heavy with pork and beef and bread. But Fergus, holding his quaich to be refilled, looked up to thank the
one who served him, and seeing who it was smiled cor-
dially.

"Ferganam, is it not? Pátraic, rather—how is it we
have never come across you before? Certain it is we
have heard no end of you, from Brandoch."

Ferganam poured the ale and spoke coolly. "In this place I answer best to Ferganam, athiarna… As to that, it is only in winter that my master makes a housethrall of me. I have been a shepherd these three years past; so it was that I met your lordship's son."

Though Fergus would have questioned him further, he sensed the youth's discomfort, and with a nod sent him along the table. While he poured for the others, Ferganam stole covert glances at the Lady Nia in her great carved guestchair at the table's far end—the long hair like a gold veil, the silvery eyes of her people—not wanting to admire, fearingly forced to it. *Sinful even to look at her: she is of the race of air-devils, the Soulless, a bansidhe from under the hill—her lord as pagan as she, aye, and the son they got between them. Yet those two I might save even now, and others like them…*

So long he stood there considering that Coll mac Gréine, who had risen to offer the customary libation to the God—the Cabarfeidh, the antlered King of Winter, Who brings back the sun from the south as a white flame between His mighty horns, and so paired antlers decked the pine-hung tables where precious tallows were now being set alight—himself noticed, and called down along the table, "All here, free or bond, may drink to the return of the Light— Do you so then, lad!"

Ferganam shook his head, and spoke to be heard throughout the hall. "We of my faith do not celebrate such a dark pagan thing, but rather the birth of our lord and savior Jesus Christ—who *is* the Light."

Coll gave a laughing sigh and shook his head, as one who had heard it all before and does not want to be hearing it again. *Nevermore do I let my reivers bring away a Christling for a thrall! They are biddable and humble to a fault—which is why they are Christlings to begin with, I suppose—but in their tiresomeness they can be pests of hell...*

"The Light was there long before your Christ was, lad... Well, if you will, drink to him, then, or to whomever you please. But only drink!"

As if it were some other who spoke, Ferganam heard himself from a very great distance. "Nay, athiarna, by your leave I will not drink, but I will rather offer good blessing for all here, in the name of the season, over the water and the wine and the loaves, in the fashion of true believers." And he stared straight at Nia as he said so.

And if she is the Devil's creature I know her to be, surely she will fly out the window at the holy words, or blister her hand at the touch of holy water and blessed bread, the wine will burn and choke her...

Coll roared with laughter. "As you will, priestling—on Midwinter Night all right order is reversed! The chief shall be thrall, the vassal lord! Be it as you will have it."

Before he could lose his nerve or Coll change his mind, Ferganam stepped forward and took bread and water and wine from the table. Muttering a word over the untouched loaf and the two half-filled quaichs, he made a pass or two over a dish of salt, then poured the wine and water together; and, taking a deep breath, offered the quaich and bread and salt to Nia, first of all those present.

All through the feast the Lady Nia had given Ferganam not so much as a sidewise glance, or so any in the hall would have said if asked. But in the manner of her people, she had been studying him all the same... Over the months since summer, she had heard of this slave from her son more than enough to disquiet her, and—again in the way of her folk—she had sensed more beside; and she had longed to learn if what she had come to fear was truth. But the proper opportunity had not until this night presented itself.

So that now, with the glint of a smile flickering, and a tiny warning headshake to her frowning lord who had already pushed back his chair a little from the table, Nia took the quaich and drank deeply of the watered wine; then breaking a piece of bread from the blessed loaf, she dipped it in the consecrated salt, and, her calm gaze fixed on the young Brython who knelt by her chair, ate it neatly and quickly. Though Ferganam watched avidly, visibly trembling in his eagerness and zeal, to his great disappointment she neither burned nor fled nor choked.

Worse, far worse than I feared! So great is her evil that she is proof against even the blessing of Holy Mother Church... So Ferganam thought, as Coll, who had not foreseen this, and whose face was now dark with anger at the public insult a slave of his had dealt his friend and guest, with a jerk of his head dismissed him from the table.

Hugging himself against the cold and his own excitement, Ferganam went out into the windless night, crossing the gort to the midmost of the dozen clochans that were the quarters of the humbler souls who labored in Coll's service, free and slave alike. Within its thick stone walls he had his own bed and clean soft bedding of bracken and ferns, with sheep-skin coverlets and even a precious feather pillow, all tucked away in a snug imda, a sleep-nook big enough for bed and wooden clothes-kist and low rush-seated chair. He shared the little beehive-shaped house with

only two other bondslaves, and for all his understandable resentment at his state, he thought himself most
fortunate: gruff and hot-tempered as he could be, at
heart Coll mac Gréine was a kind and generous master;
many freedmen born, even, did not dine so well nor
dwell so comfortably as did Coll's meanest thralls.

Now, gathering up a soap-slab and other small arti-
cles, he headed to the bath-house, where a slow fire
kept water always on the bubble, heating the stones
upon which water could be thrown to make steam, and
snibbed the door behind him.

Washing his linen and hanging it on the drying-
pegs provided, Ferganam soaped himself all over, then
climbed into the deep stone-cut bath and submerged
to the chin in stinging hot water. As he flung a few dip-
pers of water onto the hot bath-stones by the fire a few
yards away, and steam rose hissing to cloud all the little
chamber, he closed his eyes in bliss. This was one of the
few things he found totally admirable in the Gael: their
passionate devotion to the bath. *Indeed, it is more even
than Roman, such regard for cleanly habit; though as good
Christom man I should not have such a care for the sinful
body's comfort...* It was actually a chargeable offense in
law if a guest arrived and a host did not at once offer a
ready bath. Even a slave got a bath a day; more, if he
wanted it—among the Gael, filth was no virtue. But he
was thinking now of more than baths...

*I expected no more, truly; it was but a start at a start—still,
one day...one day these people will know the true Light that
enlightens the world. God has told me: I do not yet know how,
but I shall be the one to bring it them—God has promised...*

So Ferganam luxuriated in the bath, head and
heart as warm with dreams of godly mission as the rest

of him with heated water, glad to be free of the pagan revelry that went on unabated behind him in the dún; and never did he stop to consider that, just possibly, a greater Mother still than Mother Church, and certainly an older, might hold Her hand above those who so rejoiced.

CHAPTER THREE

hen Ferganam awoke next morning, at an hour somewhat later than usual—though judging by the unbroken silence round him everyone else on the maenor lay even later abed than he—his thought fled back to the events of the previous night. Though it could not be said that he regretted, perhaps—with the clearer head dawn ever brings to bear on rash behavior—he now repented a little, for after his usual prayers he washed his hands and face, attired himself and hastened out to the sheepcots.

Out on the winter pasture, the air calm and cold and bright, he crossed purposefully to where Brendan already stood watching the grazing flocks. Lambing began at Brighnasa—not so far off as it seemed—and both youths made sure these days to keep a careful eye on the gravid ewes. Storms came short and sharp in this season, without warning, and even on these protected lower slopes the shepherds must be at hand to drive the flocks on a moment's notice to the shielings.

"I did not mean to insult the—the lady your mother," said Ferganam by way of greeting. "I meant only—well, I do not *know* what I meant, it was, I do not—did not—"

Brendan did not look at Ferganam as he made this

faltering contrition, but kept his gaze upon the middle distance, where the sky showed gold above the hills.

"A thing of nothing," he said at last. "My mother took no offense."

Ferganam shot him a long unbelieving glance. "None? Mac Gréine said he will sell me into the galleys for it… Though that is not why I seek pardon, I would not mind for myself, you understand; I am a wretched sinner, and deserve to do penance for my manifold sins—whatever is God's plan for me, he will make it come aright."

Brendan drew a deep breath and let it out in one puff as the repentances flowed anew. Since their acquaintance had begun, he had come to sincerely like Ferganam—and as he very well knew, better than Ferganam liked him—but all this abasing oneself before deity was most tiresome to one reared in a very different tradition.

Mighty Dâna! Who would worship any god who demanded that you grovel, and what god worth the worshipping would ever demand it? Now, we respect our gods, right enough, but we are equals before them, on our feet to meet them, and they respect us back again; we require their belief in us as much as they require ours in them. That is how it should be, between god and folk; and they would have it so as gladly as do we…

"I do not hold with incivility," said Brendan aloud, when the spate of breast-beating seemed to have at last abated, "nor indeed with the plans or ways of foreign gods, whatever; but neither do I hold with that pleasant custom of chaining folk to an oar until they drop or starve or die beneath the whip… I will speak to my mother, to Coll himself—well, more to the point, to Beirissa. She will not have a countryman of hers sent to

the galleys, even if he *is* an uncivil thrall, and she rules
Coll; for that matter, no more would my mother see
you sent there."

"But it was against her that I offended!"

"I have said it is no matter." Brendan grinned at last,
and turned to look at him. "*She* has said it is no matter;
bread and salt and wine and water are sacred to far
more folk than the Christom alone, you know... What
does your Iosa tell you in that book of yours—'Do as you
would be done by'? Even the druids do not fault that
teaching; it is but good dán, and good manners also, no
matter whose god says so. Accept the gift with grace, and
let be."

The Brython flushed, then paled, then flushed
again. Brendan watched the changes with interest. *He
looks as if he would swat me given half a chance—but that
would mean the galleys for certain, if not worse. More importantly, his white godling would be cross with him... Still, he is
by no means so perfect a Christling as he likes to think, you can
see where it would make him feel so very much better to strike
out— I would gladly bat him around a little, if I thought it
would do him any good; but he would only repent, with
prayers and lamentations and signings of himself with the
cross, and beg my forgiveness, and his god's forgiveness, and
be ten times more tiresome than before...better to leave it as it
is. But he makes it very hard to be his friend...*

True to his word, Brendan that day spoke privily to
the Lady Beirissa, who was amused, if more than a little
exasperated with her husband; and, as Brendan had
predicted, most forgiving of her fellow tribesman's
lapse. So, far from being sold into the galleys, Ferganam remained on the hill, though for all his sullen-
ness he might as well have been sent to the ships—and

if truth be known, the thought still idly crossed Coll's mind from time to time.

But, though he hardly knew it himself, or could have put word or reason to it if he had, Ferganam's attitude to Brendan had begun to change: he was properly grateful—and not as a slave is grateful—for the intercession; civil and cheerful too, more often now than not. Still, on three things only he remained forever implacable, however altered their fellowship. Never did he inquire after the Lady Nia, and never did he join in the revels and observances of Draoíchtas, but stood ever aloof and apart.

And never once, no matter the thirst or the wish or the desperate parching necessity, did he drink from the waters of the Goddess's cold clean silver spring.

"Tell me how it came to be, that you are Christling."

Late summer again. These cool nights Brendan and Ferganam slept out on Slemish, on the edge of the oakwood called Voclut, their flocks peacefully settled in the warmer, sheltered swales below; the time was near when the flawless blue weather would break, the autumn storms begin to roll in. They had been friends, if what was between them could be called friendship, two full years now; and that day Brendan had at last asked the question he had never before asked straight out.

It was more command than invitation; but to the surprise of them both, Ferganam answered eagerly.

"My family have long time been believers. My grandsir was a priest, as I have told you—in Britain the More, we faithful are yet few, but the faith grows strong.

Even the High Lord of Britain, Vortigern, encourages
it, I am told, though he follows not the way himself...
But though I said the holy words and performed the
deeds, I tell you, I did not yet know God. I had to be
brought here as a thrall, where I could learn to hear his
voice, before I could know him as I have come to know
him, to become *his* thrall—it was all his plan and doing,
greatest glory be to him."

"I think you have surely come to know deity here,"
said Brendan, after a long pause, and very gently. "But
you would have found it regardless, for you are a
seeker—that is the true nature of your questing soul...
As for what name you put on it, it makes little differ. It is
all the Divine Family: the Holy Mother and Her Mate,
Their Daughter and Their Son—male and female in
harmony and balance, doing and being, the Shaping
and the Making, the Wisdom and the Word. And
beyond that Triplicity, above all thrones forever there is
the One—Yr Mawreth to the Kymry, Artzan Janco to the
Danaan, Kelu to the Gael."

Ferganam's face had darkened as Brendan spoke,
but it was a measure of the feeling of friendship that
had grown in him that he did not fly as of old into one
of his fervid passions; and when he replied, it was not as
an outraged follower blind to any view but his own, but
firmly, as one who knows he has the truth and will not
be denied.

"There is no Goddess, and there is but one God;
God the Father, whose only begotten son is Jesus the
Christ, true God and true man, and God the Holy
Ghost. God himself has told us."

To his own surprise, this time Brendan was the one
whose patience went up like straw. *Name of Fionn! He*

provokes me beyond all enduring... He heard his own voice—amused, courteous to the point of mockery.

"Oh aye? No Goddess? Let you tell *that* to the women and the ban-draoi, and see what pitiful rags of you are left when they are done showing you Her power!" Beginning to enjoy himself now: "If the Father has no Mate, pray then how did he even get this much-vaunted son of his? On himself? Even a god might well boast of such a feat... But nay, your Tangavaun, your own holy book, says that Mhúir, a mortal woman, wife to the carpenter Joussef, was mother to your god Iosa; well enough. So—do not speak, not until I am done speaking! I only wish to be sure I have this correct, in my pagan unenlightenment—your god may get a divine son, who is man also, on a mortal woman, but not with a goddess; and then, still denying she is a god-dess, you honor that mortal as high as any goddess, being the mother of your god as well as his mate—or is it his father's mate? Most confusing! And I believe there is a third one too, but let us not even get into *that*... Now. *Now* you may speak."

Ferganam did not know where to begin, so out-raged were all his sensibilities, at the attack no less than what he perceived as the blasphemy.

"The woman is not God's mate! The very *thought*—" He struggled to control himself, wild in his eagerness to refute. "It is but metaphor, the Word got her with child, as the angel told her, she stayed ever virgin after, not even her own husband—"

But Brendan seemed of a sudden duergar-ridden, for he wished now only to goad.

"Ah, I see! You claim to be a poor unlettered thrall, Ferganam, but I say you can chop logic with the best... So: after lying with a god—or rather not lying with one—your Mhúir would have no mere man after; understandable, and most praiseworthy. Though why you insist she was yet virgin after having given birth to a divine child—great Ísais Herself is Mate and Mother, and Sister also... You can find no answer to this, because it makes no sense and well you know it."

"It is *faith!*" Ferganam all but shrieked. "It does not *need* to make sense! Pagan magic, now *that* makes no sense—"

Gods, does he even hear *himself?* Brendan laughed, and shook his head.

"Our faith is the magic of the seasons, of the land and waters; right and ordered, nothing makes more sense than that—it is there, you can see it and feel it and touch it and know it. Whereas *you* say the Tangavaun is but metaphor—when it suits you that it should be so—and yet you also claim it to be the word of your god, set down to his instruction, most literal and correct; and must be believed in every particular either way! The laziest druid, son of Calpurnius, will tell you you cannot have it bothwise."

Ah, it is too easy, no sport in it; not fitting, too, to mock that which a bondthrall must clutch at, a slave-faith, all he has to give him hope when hope is gone...

But, sulky now, Ferganam would not see it, or would not admit it if he did.

Sooner would he die torn apart by lions, a martyr for his creed—or, more like, to it. Well, perhaps that can yet be arranged; the Rómanach may have had the right idea with those arenas... Brendan, in whose nature there was nothing of malice or cruelty, was by now beginning to repent of his tormenting; but in that one instant of Ferganam's uncontrol he had sensed something else behind the thrall's obduracy, something that the rote piety had hidden until now, and, liking not its scent—a trace of foumart on clean hill air—he pursued it anew, as a hound will chase a streaking rabbit.

"Still, there must have been dark times when you doubted, all folk doubt— Have you never wondered whether what you hold to is true and real?"

And Patricius Calpurnius, all earths stopped, turned not like the rabbit but the stoat, and lied for the first time before his own chosen god, and said, "Nay. Never. Not once. Nay."

Summer was gone now; on the edge of Voclut wood, Brendan huddled down luxuriously into the pieced-sheepskin bunting he slept in on the hill, and stared up at the autumn stars. In those days, sailors kept the star-knowledge close among them, and as a landsman he knew the names of only a few—the Warrior, the Wain-light, the Eye of Fire. *If history is to be given credence, my mother's people came to Erith from those very stars, though the one they left behind is long destroyed; and these days, many among the Gael have forgotten that high origin, and have even ceased to believe. Still—*

He settled down comfortably inside his sheepskins, so that the fire-warmth was at his back and his face was cooled by the night air. Just as he was on the falling-edge of sleep a distant howl echoed in the next valley over; he smiled at the sound, and took comfort, as at a good omen. There had always been wolves in the Fanad hills; they came down in late autumn from the higher mountains to the east and south. No Gael

grudged them a sheep now and again, in hard winters
when the hill-deer were scarce and the packs hunted
close to the haunts of men; wolves were royal beasts,
sacred to the Goddess and the God, not to be harassed
or harmed. For their part, the wolves seemed to appreciate the courtesy; certain it was that they exercised better discretion than poachers, for never in greed did
they slay more than they could use, or raid one flock or
herd above another.

As was their way after quarrelling, Brendan and Ferganam were friends again, though this time each had
pushed the other too far, and both knew it, and had
learned from it, so that nevermore did either broach
between them the subject of faith; Brendan performed
his Draoícht rituals, and Ferganam his own Christom
ones, neither of them commenting one way or another.

Though on the hill they were 'customed to sleep
light, one ear tuned for disturbance among the flocks,
that night Brendan slept deeper than his wont, for it
seemed that he came slowly up to wakefulness like a
swimmer to the surface of sunlit water, limbs heavy
against the water's weight, up from beneath, breaking
through to light and air. *Yet am I dreaming still...* In his
dream—and he knew that he dreamed, though the
grass was cold and wet beneath his bare feet—he arose
and went under the rustling eaves of the oakwood, to
the well in the clearing at Voclut's heart, where a bubbling spring led from the rockface into a channel down
the slope.

As in a dream within his own dreaming, he saw the
making of the well: saw a young brown-haired lass
come into the wood—long ages since, to judge by her
attire—and at the Goddess's commanding, she knelt

down and dug at the stony earth with her bare hands, digging and scraping until her hands bled and the water came out of the ground, flooding round her fingers and making a path for itself down the green hill side. From that day the well of Voclut had never failed; indeed, its water held healing properties for folk and beast alike, and many made long journeys thither, to drink of the spring and to be healed by the Goddess's power, or to take away some of the sacred waters for those who could not come themselves. *And none who drinks in faith has ever failed of healing…*

"At My will she made the well; all the wells were made so."

Brendan looked up swiftly, back at once in his first dream, still asleep without. The girl was gone; before him now, between him and the well, stood the Goddess Herself, gowned in green, unearthly fair, Her bare feet white where She stood upon a fire of roses. Her long brown braids were bound off just above Her knees with golden apples that swung and chimed; round about Her broad smooth brows was a chain of stars. Reaching up to the oak branch above Her head, She broke off a sprig that turned to green leaf and white blossom at Her touch, then bending plucked a shamrogue from the grass; and held out both to Brendan, who, bowing to Her, took them wonderingly but without fear.

"You have the Oak-strength, the Sky-strength," She said then. "Your brother—and he is your brother—will subdue to his own ends the power of the ground, and great sorrow come of it. You will be unfriends all your lives for what you believe—the great Rift between you. But also you will be linked forever: as the Branch of

Gold rises from the crown of the oak, never to touch the earth, you will rise out of Éruinn; and though bondage be behind you for the Gael, freedom for the Kelt is in the stars."

Brendan came bolt upright, heart pounding, hearing round him only the small natural noises, the quiet of the night. He sat there for long minutes, trying to remember as much as he might—*What was that strange name She did say?*—shivering with suppressed joy and something that felt like fear, though fear was the last thing it felt like. Then crawling over to where Ferganam lay motionless upon his back, he saw starlight shining in the other's open eyes, and a track of tears upon his cheek. With a start, Ferganam sat up, and clutched at Brendan's cloak, and spoke like a stream in spate.

"I have seen an angel— Tall and fair, a light about him of holiness—I could see no wings but I knew him for what he was, a messenger of God... He said his name was Buach, which in my language is Victoricus; we spoke! And then it seemed that a great darkness came, and a huge stone fell upon me, crushing my limbs and stealing away all my power. With the last of me I cried out 'Eirias!' A word I do not know, whence came it into my mind to call it? But upon my calling the sun arose, and the weight was gone."

"'Eirias'—it means a sacred blaze, a holy fire, of the kind lighted at the times of festival, on the Hill of Tara, by the king and the king's druid, or the queen and her ban-draoi..."

"It was no dream of pagan evil!"

"Nay," said Brendan, patiently unfastening the

clutching fingers from his cloak, "it was a dream of the Shan-vallachta. I have had a dream also—"

Ferganam looked long upon him. "I have seen an angel—but you have seen the Mother of God, I see her in your eyes—"

"I have seen the Mother, right enough."

After silence and a sigh, Ferganam broke. "A vision of the Holy Mother—she might have come to me if I were not the sinner that I am. Instead she would liefer show herself to a pagan... That is my lesson, and my penance— Well then, know that once I sinned shamefully, and my sin was a great one. It was in my home lands, five years since; because of it God permitted the reivers to take me, my punishment to be thralldom in this land. But because of that sin and punishment, I have found my way to the true God, and I will never turn from that way again."

"I have read in the Tangavaun book," said Brendan at length, "where once your god commanded a man to sacrifice his own son, then at the moment of the knife's descent said nay, hold, not so, only a jest, or a test, to see if the man would obey. No Gael would ever thole that! If any god of ours should try that on with us, very soon they would have no one, and they would *deserve* no one... No matter your sin, surely it cannot have merited such punishment of any divinity who claims to love—"

But Ferganam would say no more, only gathered up his gear, and, clucking and whistling, sent his dogs to part the flocks of Magheramorna from the ones belonging to Creavanore, and ran to follow.

"Never try to teach a pig to sing," said Brendan then, aloud and meditatively, watching the fleeing fig-

ure diminish in the distance. "It is a waste of your
time—and it only annoys the pig."

But when he came back to his own sleeping-place,
to shake out the sheepskins to the morning air, two
small things fell out of the folds: a wilting shamrogue,
and a tiny blossoming sprig of oak.

Later that day, as he drove the sheep down Slemish for
the noon watering—Ferganam and his flock were
nowhere in sight, he had likely gone to the grazing on
the far side of Magheramorna, undoubtedly to avoid
another encounter—Brendan saw his mother walking
on the hill. Knowing that she sought him, and saw him,
he sat down in the grass and watched her approach,
looking upon her not as a son would see her but as a
stranger—the tallness of her, the air she carried with
her of the halls beneath the mountain, those halls he
had never yet viewed with waking eyes.

*I have heard many say that the Sidhe look most unhuman
when they are among mortals. And perhaps that is so, but it
seems to me they are most unlike us—most themselves—when
they are alone in their natural places, on the hill or in the wood
or by the shore of the sea... Though I have known very few of
my mother's Folk—yet they are my folk also...*

She greeted him soberly, and sat down a little way
away, laughter on her face for the sheep who clustered
round to stare unblinkingly at her, all their simple
souls in their adoring eyes.

"Go, silly things, eat grass... I know what you saw
last night," she said then to her son, and now her smile
was gone. "Or Whom..."

"Ferganam says he saw an angel," remarked Brendan after a while. "An angel called Victoricus, which is to say, in our tongue as it may be, 'Buach'?"

Nia's face did not change; though it might be said that the corners of her mouth quirked, they were as swiftly stilled.

"One called Buach, right enough. Very fair"—Brendan looked up sharply at the note of drollery in her voice, but her mien was grave as before—"but no angel."

"Ah," he said as dryly. "Buach your kinsman, it would be, then. But why?"

Nia said no word for some moments, but watched the cloudshadows chase down one hillside and up the next.

"My folk have long had a prophecy of one who would come with a master-word, to bring great grief to the Gael and to many another people; the Tangavaun, that word was called."

Brendan looked sharply at her, startled. "But that is the name of the Christom holy book! It means 'white tongue' or 'white speaking'; as fair words or a fine speech."

"It can mean so; but in the bardic usage, it means 'Word of Death', and also the messenger who carries it. When first we heard what this word was called that the Christlings brought with them to Tir Gaedhil, we felt the need to know a little more—as you might well imagine. Donn himself, king under Knockfierna, was troubled, and Buach offered to find out; no more than that. But the Goddess came to you," said Nia then, and it was not a question.

Her son stirred uncomfortably. "Ferganam is jealous for it, says I saw the Mother of God—"

"And so you did. What else did you see?"

"I saw what the Tree-priests will do to our land, and all the lands," said Brendan at last, and his voice shook a little. "She showed me... Not the word of their Christ, but the will of the Christlings, shall prevail. War, and hatefulness, and other things that the Crann-draoi would love not at all; of his own teachings, little, and that bent—a harsh unlovingness, that will set kindred against kindred in this island for many hundreds of years."

Her voice was soft and quiet as a stream. "And what more?"

He turned to look her full in the face. "You have taught me to See—but I cannot say, it seems traha even to think it—"

"Tell me..."

After a long painful hesitation, and not looking at her but out across the hills: "I saw myself—a ship with sails of silver—you were with me—leading folk out of Éruinn, many thousands, oh, a great immram!—to a world that hung like a golden ball in a black sky, and the world had rings round about it. But how can such things be?"

At last Nia spoke, and he noted that she did not answer his question; or at least not then. "Pátraic and you have dán together, that is plain enough. But how it may fall out, even those of my folk who See the farthest and deepest cannot say. That is why Buach came to Pátraic, to put the thought on him that it need not be as he thinks it must be. And if that thought should blossom into deed, the people of Tir Gaedhil may be spared great grief thereby."

And Brendan also noted, as for the first time, though he had long been aware of it, that never did Nia speak of Pátraic save by his correct name; never once had she named him 'Nameless'. It was a courtesy the Brython youth would have never accorded her—indeed, he never spoke of her at all, by name or otherwise—but there it was.

"What you name folk is what they are, or what they shall become," she said, perceiving his thought. "Names have power—as I have taught you, as I know you have learned; in your power that is to come, do not use that power lightly."

"What must I do, then? Mathra"—he reached a hand to her, as he had not done since he was a little lad, caught it back, then reached again—"tell me, for I am sure I do not know!"

Nia rose with fluid grace and brushed the dead leaves from her skirt—gently, as if she did not wish to hurt the poor crushed things any more than they had been hurt already—and looked down at her son, seeing the questions in his face; the other, deeper questions that lay behind, that never would he ask aloud. *Young shoulders, to be a bridge between so many worlds—and they must now begin to grow strong enough to serve so, for more to cross upon than himself alone... Oh, the strength is there, right enough—his father and I both have Seen it, and others also—but if it is to grow at all, I cannot spare him—my son!—not ever, and not now...*

"What you must do, you know already," she said at last. "And because you know, it is already done."

CHAPTER FOUR

Ferganam startled awake, glancing wildly round the imda—the bednook built into the clochan's stone walls. Only pitchy darkness within, outside no sound but the rain that had been falling steadily since sunset, no moon: it was perhaps a month after that night of visions in Voclut wood. *It must be long gone middlenight; what then…* But the voice that had awakened him still echoed in his ear: "It is well that you fast, for soon you will go to your own country."

He was alone in the clochan, his own imda the only one occupied of the four the little house contained. The two other slaves who shared the clochan with him slept away that night, having ridden with Coll mac Gréine on an errand into Ulidian lands; they would not return for a fortnight. He had taken advantage of the rare solitude to pray openly, to fast in penitence, to flail himself with knotted thongs while none were by to mock him.

Yet when he lay down again, heart racing, to attempt a return to sleep, another voice came, a different voice—"See, your ship is ready"—and again he shot up in his bed.

What in the name of blessed Mhúir— "Is it devils?" he asked loudly. "Know then that I am not afraid." Confused, nervous, for all his words of challenge very much afraid indeed, he did not lie down again, but kept motionless in the darkness of the imda, to see what he might see. *If it is Corcc or Flann playing tricks on me...*

Then the door of the clochan opened quietly and surely, and Brendan son of Fergus slipped in. He was muffled in a dark hooded cloak; gloves covered his hands, and a fethal-mask concealed all but his eyes. *So that the whiteness of face and hands cannot be glimpsed in the night, and his presence betrayed... But why? The son of Crea-vanore has guest-right here, to come and go as he pleases—why sneak like a common land-thief past the maigen?*

"What I do is an offense against the law of my own people," said Brendan, knowing that Ferganam wondered mightily but dared not ask, and handed him what he had carried over the hills from Creavanore: the thick-woven travelling-cloak with its rain-shedding fringe and deep hood, the leather backsack stuffed with food for a journey—bread and cheese and dried sausage—the small purse heavy with Roman coin. There was no sword included in the gift—defiance of the law, or perhaps just prudence, went only so far, and slaves might not bear such weapons—only a sgian, the little black-handled dagger of many uses that everyone in Tir Gaedhil kept about them.

"But—"

Brendan held up a warning hand. "To my mind, their offense is the greater, though the law is on their side— To keep folk slaved—well, as of this moment, you are free. Nay, do not thank me, either: I do not *know* why I do it, not entirely. I only know that I do it for myself as much as for you, maybe even more so... It will not be easy, this escape—very hard on you, and I will be called upon to make reparation for it after—but it is on me that I must help you make it. This is the perfect only time: such a chance you have never had before, and as good a one may never come again. So—will you take the chance?"

Ferganam had begun at once to gather up the bits and bobs of his meager possessions, desperate to believe, still doubtful of what was being offered and too staggered even to give proper thanks—but Brendan knew he was thanked even so.

"Aye, indeed, I will, but—how am I to go?"

Brendan made a small impatient gesture. "What would you have, an escort in triumph out of Fanad? Mighty Macha! Listen to me: in the house they are all asleep; no one will see you leave. Slip round past, get well up into the hills, then travel east as quickly as you can. Keep to the high tops, hide in the woods, sleep rough; stay as far as you can from the places where folk are, at least until you are well out of Fanad and into districts where none will know you."

"And the Lord Coll?"

"Coll is away and most of his guard with him, my father has told me so; your disappearance will not be discovered for many days. If anyone asks, I will say you are out on the hill and cannot come down; that is no lie, I simply will not say which hill, or why you cannot come! Any road, they will not doubt my word, and even if they do find out there are none who can be spared for pursuit. By the time they realize what has happened you will be long gone, and safe, and I will have declared my hand in setting you free. When you reach the coast no doubt there will be a ship to take you where you wish—back to your homeland, or to Rome, or wherever. This is the best that I can manage; the rest is up to you."

Ferganam stood up now clad for travel, and turned to fetch his crómag, the man-high blackthorn staff he carried on the hill, from where it leaned in the corner by his bed; Brendan did not forbid it.

"Why did you speak to me, and then not answer when I gave challenge?"

"When?"

"Now. Well, before. Before you came in."

Brendan cast up his eyes to the clochan roof. "How could I speak to you before I was even here, and why would I be silent about it after? Nay, of course I did not speak to you! Perhaps it was one of your holy angels, heralding your glorious deliverance—"

Ferganam ignored the barb; in his pride he had already thought much the same, and he would for no sake that Brendan saw.

"You are a better son of the Word than you know," he said then. "You lack only the teaching and the naming. I have often thought and dreamed of escape, but I could not have done it without your help and aid. When I return—for I shall—I will gladly repay your gift with the greater gift of the true faith."

Brendan laughed shortly in the darkness. "I said I would help you escape! Leave it at that, and do not press... As I have told you, I do not hold with enslaving of any sort—body or spirit or mind. It is plain that we have dán between us, you and I, which now this deed only furthers. But no more are you 'Nameless' to me— Pátraic mac Calprin."

*   *   *

A fortnight later and a hundred miles away, on the island's mist-hung eastern coast, a ship raised sail from a small port town, having loaded a cargo of wolfhounds bound for the games in Rome—beasts bred by the Gael not to hunt wolves but in admiration of them, to have a little of that wild strength and power as a friend dozing nose on paws by the hearth.

The ship was open-decked and clinker-built, with two rows of oar-ports, her painted sails full-bellied now with wind; the Eyes of Gwenhidw, that goddess who is mate to Manaan Boundless, lord of oceans, looked out from either side of her prow. Her sisters sailed the waters from Phoenicia to Aulba—had brought the Pictoi yelling down from the north and ferried the Sassanaich to the Eastern Shore; a familiar sight in many seas. Her next call would be in Sulyonessa, to ballast her hold with tin from Lúndaigh and Cornovian copper and Gwalian blue-stone; weeks earlier, she had put in to northern ports, for pottery and baled furs and sacks of amber—the great trading circle of the ancient world. All these things now would be taken through the Pillars of Herakles: some to be offloaded on the way in ports of Hispania or Portingale or northern Afferic, some sent on to Ebbrow and Grecaia, or north overland to Alemaenna; the rest was destined to An Róimha—great Rome itself.

As was the tall quiet youth who spoke good Latin with a north Brython accent, who worked an oar for the price of his crossing: his back paid the toll of his passage, but in weariness only—free rowers, or at least those tacitly assumed to be free, are not whipped as slaves are to make them pull, though neither are their voyages beds of ease—and both rower and captain thought the price well worth it.

And as the ship slipped away southeastwards on her track, and one white morning the Pillars loomed out of the mists to herald their arrival on the glass-calm Inland Sea, he gave prayers hourly—fervent thanks to his god for his deliverance from slavery and the difficult flight therefrom, and prayers, no less fervent, for the one who, pagan though he was, nevertheless had given him the gift of freedom to do that god's own work.

But in the hall at Creavanore, Brendan stood proudly and silently before his father, and offered his unrepentant self for punishment. That morning the news had come to Fergus that his son had abetted the escape of a slave—news delivered by Coll, just now returned home to discover his thrall fled, and who, though unarguably the aggrieved party, was predictably more entertained than wrathful. But Fanad's lord had been furious, and as chieftain of Clann Aoibhell he had ordered up justice swift and sure.

So now Fergus looked upon his son, who gazed serenely back, and at the bard and brehon of the tuath, who had been summoned there to see justice done but who now struggled vainly to suppress their own smiles, and then turned to Coll who stood openly grinning.

"It is no laughing matter, mac Gréine," he muttered reprovingly.

"Nay, nay, to be sure, it is not!" came the hasty and insincere assent. But the amusement did not leave Coll's bearded face, and once when he thought Fergus did not see he winked at Brendan.

"Still and all," continued Fergus, who had seen very

well but thought best not to mark it, "the lad must be punished for his hand in the slave's escape."

"Oh aye," agreed Coll dutifully. "It shall be even as you say."

Fergus sighed. "The offense was against you and your dúchas; therefore you, not I, must determine. Propose now what honor-price you will have of him; I myself and Garalt, brehon here present, will deem if it be either too lenient or too stern, and the bard Thure Strathaquin, whom you know, will record it."

Coll laughed. "I am more inclined to think you will reckon it the former—but, as you will. Brendan Aoibhell mac Fergus ac Nia, of the line of Erevan"—Brendan drew himself straighter still—"as enech-clann for the abetting of the escape of the slave called Ferganam, you will give me the Goddess's half of the year in service. At Beltain you will leave Fanad, and go south to the country of the Laighin, to labor for me until Samhain on my maenor at Dromore, in the Bluestack Mountains of Corca-Vaskin. There you shall do such work as my rechtair shall decree, your labor buying the place of the slave you unlawfully did loose. That is my judgment."

When Brendan had bowed to Coll, and to Fergus his father, and to the brehon and bard who praised Coll's wisdom and justice, and taken silent dignified leave, Coll turned smiling to Fergus, but his smile died away to see the trouble upon the other's face.

"My thanks, old friend," said Fergus at length. "That was fairly done—and gently."

"Aye, well enough, the law, the law—but why did you make me requite it so hard of him? Slaves go missing every day; I promise you, the Christling Brython

was no great loss! Brandoch made no offense that I
would not have blown away like a windpuff; or, if you
still insisted, that a cow or two could not have bought
him free of—" Coll gently shook his friend's arm, to
make his point. "He is a good lad, Ferghallach! Well-
grown, skilled in war and lore—there is great kindness
in him, and thoughtfulness also, and by no means is he
dull-witted or slug-spirited. We have had no trouble out
of him before now, and neither did they complain of
him when he was away in fostering. He is your son,
right enough, and I see where an example must be set;
but why do you fear not to be seen to punish?"

Fergus did not reply at once, but dismissed with
thanks for their services Garalt and Thure, who though
feigning disinterest seemed to be listening a bit too
hard; when he was alone with his friend, he sighed and
motioned them to two chairs by the fire and the ale
keeve that stood on a low chest between.

"Because he is not *my* son only."

"Ah." Coll poured out two quaichs, drank deep
from his before he spoke, pondering what he would
say. *I have long wondered how her share in the boy would show
out, and when—perhaps now it makes itself known at last...*
"Well," he ventured then, "Corca-Vaskin is not so distant; he was fostered there, after all. While he works at
Dromore, I had the thought that his father's kin may
keep an eye on him—and his mother's also?"

"When two strains of mountainy sheep are cross-
bred," said Fergus presently, "the lambs lose the hill-
knowledge both strains have long been bred to,
through sire and dam alike. We breed the sheep to our
home hills so that they have the instinct for their own
ground, they know where to return if they are lost or

strayed—it is why we do not barter away or buy-in the breeding stock, they have no inborn knowledge of another's range—"

"He is no wetherlamb, Ferghal!"

"I know he is not; but neither is he entirely a Gael... Have you never wondered, then? About us? About— her?"

Coll shot him a glance, decided candor was best. "Aye, often. But one need only look at you together—"

"She is my life," said Fergus simply, and Coll lowered his eyes before the look upon his friend's face. "From the day she rode out from under the hill of Tallaght and into my heart— When we wed, I thought there could be no higher happiness in all the world. Even Brandoch's birth, great joy that it was to me, was not in it; but dán will not be denied, and it is on me that we are doomed to die apart, my lady and I."

"Everyone dies apart."

Fergus shook his head. "Not as apart as we shall die; another age, another world—and the darkness that lies between the stars. I have Seen it."

"She is of the High Danaan blood," said Coll gently. "She will outlive you any road, by many lifetimes. This you know."

"True; but at least I would have gone out with my head in her lap. And that would have been more than enough."

Coll laid a hand on his friend's shoulder. "And so it may yet befall. Tomorrow's dán to tomorrow—let be. But Brandoch?"

Fergus ran a hand over his beard, and shook his head again. "Will go south for the Goddess's halfyear, as you have deemed upon him... Though what I am going to say to his mother, I am sure I do not know."

But Nia, when she heard of it, only smiled enigmatically. "Give a man a sharp enough blade, sooner or later he will cut himself." Though whether she spoke of her son, or of her lord, or of Coll, or of another, even Fergus could not be certain.

The covin-tree that stood on its own little raise in front of Creavanore was a yew-tree a thousand years old; it was said that beneath its branches Fionn himself had found shelter from a storm. Ancient it had already been when Iosa Crann-draoi hung on his own tree in Ebbrow far in the eastlands of the world; in its seedling-time perhaps it had trembled hearing Othinn Allfather cry out in pain, when he reached for the holy runes where he hung from his place on the sacred ash; barring axe or fire, flood or borer, it might live a thousand years more.

The day after Beltain, clad for his southern journey, his backsack at his feet, Brendan stood before the ancient yew and laid a hand upon its bark, feeling the slow steady life deep within. The covin-tree had been one of the first things he could name, as a tiny lad; a little older, when sad or chastened, or merely wanting to dream in peace, he had often run to hide himself deep within the tangled branches, breathing in the tree's own peace as he inhaled the clean scent of its needles. *My dear and oldest friend—do not die before I return—nay, nor for long years thereafter*…and smiled as he sensed through the bark the tree's long slow many-syllabled answer.

He lifted his head then, feeling a gaze as palpable

upon him as his own hand on the tree—*Never would I not know that gaze!*—and, still smiling, turned to see his mother. And saw her again as he had seen her that day on Slemish: the pale oval face, the dark-gold hair, the eyes of her people that some believed could see the wind...

He knelt then for her blessing, raised his forehead for her ritual kiss, then after a few unremarkable words, the usual in such circumstances, a young man to his mother on leaving home, he turned away and headed down the valley; he did not look back. *It is on me that when I return here again, all things will have altered; for better or worse, I cannot say, but they will have changed...and so will I.*

But behind him Nia stood like a tree before a thunderstorm breaks, white and still, watching him go; and though Fergus, who had come up silently to join her, laid a consoling hand upon her shoulder, and her fingers went up to clasp his, hard, she did not turn to him, and they spoke no word, not until their son was lost to their sight; and even then they stood there, close together, until darkness came upon the hills.

Fanad in Éruinn's far northwest is a harsh place, if a beautiful one, lean as a mountain wolf; but Corca-Vaskin in the southern country of the Laighin is a fat land—where elsewhere abundance may go hidden, there it is all plain to be seen, the opulence and ease of it. But appearances are as usual deceptive: even lushness can harbor strength unguessed at; and those who thought to make an easy conquest of the people of Corca-Vaskin are now whitening bones upon those pleasant slopes.

A month Brendan spent on the road south, by Coll's private good-humored order taking his time of it, interested in everyone and everything he saw. He fared on foot, eating travellers' food when he could cook it—craivahans by choice, those tastesome cakes of beef chopped with porrans and cannauns and browned to crispness over the fire—meatrolls and bannocks and cheese when he could not.

He was often entertained as welcome guest in the houses he passed on the way, by folk high and humble alike, and he lost no chance to make acquaintance of his hosts, nor they of him. In that time the law of the coire ainsec, the Undry Cauldron of Guestship, still prevailed, and no stranger passed unfed of the best at hand, unhoused of the warmest shelter, unrested in the softest bed, anywhere in Éruinn. That hospitality was repaid in kind, with news or song or story; and the hosts were as eager to hear as guests to tell.

One morning many days out from Fanad, having crossed the mighty Sinan at a ford of raked white gravel, Brendan saw the Bluestack Mountains rising up like a low stone wall. A week later, coming through a belt of trees that clothed a small hill—na hAorai, it was called with exquisite if uninspired logic, the Rising Ground—he halted to look down into the valley that lay open before him, and found that he looked on it as a stranger.

I was fostered in this country until I was twelve years old; how is it I remember so very little of it, or of those here dwelling who are mine? Why does the land not call out to me? Do I have no claim here, do not my bones and blood have history in this place?

Strangely troubled, he turned his eyes to the south, and was at once reassured. Halfway down the vale of

the Lannabrachan, where the Tioram Water comes
down off the hills to join the broader stream, stood a
prosperous-looking dún that he well remembered, a
sprawling place of whitewashed stone, with thatched
outbuildings and solid shielings, full pastures and
planted fields: Killary, the home of his father's parents,
Domhnall Avarcagh and Aoifa Fínneachta.

*Not only my grandsir and granddam, but I have cousins
there, and aunts and uncles, fosterns too... Nor is even this
the end of my journey: Coll mac Gréine's place of Dromore lies
just ayont the hills, another half-day's walk...but here there is
kin to me, dear and near, and tonight I shall be again with
them.*

Almost against his will, his gaze moved northwards,
lifting, following the white ribbon of the Tioram along
the rising line of the Bluestacks, until his eyes rested
upon a great smoke-colored peak at the far end of the
valley; standing behind a low range of foothills, the
mountain shut off the openness of the lands like a
fallen shield. Even to his eye, and from this distance, it
seemed clothed in eerie remoteness; and well it might
seem so, for deep beneath that forbidding hill-flank
was delved a hall of the Sidhe.

*Drumnadarroch, 'Ridge of the Oak Trees', is that moun-
tain called—beneath which lies the palace of Rinn na
gCroha...* He lifted his head, in pride or defiance he
could not have said, and stared long at the distant hill.
And I have kin there also.

CHAPTER FIVE

hat summer in Corca-Vaskin was a fine and fair one. On Coll mac Gréine's pleasant and well-run maenor of Dromore, Brendan did such tasks as were assigned him for his reparation—haymaking, herding, thatching, harvesting—putting into them such eagerness and energy that the rechtair, an easygoing southern man called Guaire, could find no fault with him even had he been so inclined.

From time to time, straightening from the baled hay or the sheaves of thatch, Brendan would look round him, weary, aching, proud with the honesty of work—and smiling to himself he would take a deep breath or two, and bend renewed to his labors. *If Ferganam—Pátraic!—could only see what honor-price I am paying for his freedom! Now he would call it penance, that tiresome concept the Christlings have of guilt and forgiveness: as with so much else, our way is the better; we earn our forgiveness ourselves, we do not have it handed to us merely for saying sorry…*

Despite the duties he owed Coll, Brendan had all the time he wished to spend as he pleased, and he chose to spend it most often at his grandparents' maenor of Killary, just over the high pass of the Stile from Dromore—to Domhnall and Aoifa's delight.

Among families it often goes that the chick least seen is
the chick most cherished, and so it proved here, the
master and mistress of Killary never tiring of their
favorite grandson's visits, nor he of visiting. They were
fine folk, full of wit and the long wisdom they had
learned: Domhnall was a Fian healer now retired from
practice, while Aoifa had ridden with Niall Nine-
Hostage on that raid already legend, when he threw
down Emain Macha of the Ultonians.

Apart from that, Brendan went about renewing his
acquaintance with his southland cousinage—a fairly
extensive proposition—and with the friends and fosterns of his childhood. Of those last, Amris mac an Fhiach was chief and dearest—Amris Son of the Raven,
named so by his Welsh sire who came to the Laighin
from Gwalia long since, for love of the swordmaiden
who became his wife. He had followed her home to
Corca-Vaskin, where she had borne their son, and
together they had raised him, but both were dead
now—perished a year or two since in some plague;
Domhnall and Aoifa, for love of his dead parents, and
of him also, had taken the lad into their house and
hearts.

Seated on a natural rock seat up in the high pass
called the Stile, where the Tioram bubbled and chuck-
led to itself in its rocky bed, the blue vale of the
Lannabrachan stretching away before them, Amris and
Brendan would often talk long and earnestly together—
of their pasts as much as of present or future. They had
rediscovered an affinity of spirit, which doubtless had
had much to do with their childhood friendship in the
first place: early on in their reunion, Brendan had
recounted the reason for his coming to the Laighin,

and Amris had been both amused and annoyed.

"But you know, Brandoch, the Christlings have made inroads in this country also; so far small comings only, stealing over from Britain the More in twos and threes, but still they are here. Aye! Down along the coast there are holy places they have made for themselves, we might ride over to see them one day—stone nemetons like little tiny beehives, all roofed over against the Goddess's own natural weather…"

Other times they spoke of their kindreds: Amris talked much and lovingly of his father's folk in Demetia, whom he went to visit every other year; and Brendan of the Danaan connections he had never yet seen, though with the exquisite courtesy common to Gwalian and Gael alike, each waited for his friend to bring up such tender topics rather than broach them himself.

"Our mothers both came to their mates as outlanders," said Amris one day, with a sigh of admiration, after Brendan had recounted yet again the tale of how Nia and Fergus first had met. "Yours from beneath the hill, mine crossing the seas to fight in Gwalia—and our fathers loved them for their difference."

"Not to mention their daring! They knew what they wanted when they saw it, and claimed away their men like proper young reivers." Brendan grinned. "I have heard mighty tales of the blade-hand of the Lady Vevin, my dama-wyn has told me; two decades apart in age, but they were swordsisters even so…"

Amris laughed with shy pride, and his voice took on something of the song-lilt of his father's folk. "And from what *I* have heard, the Lady Aoifa was no feather-arm either… They were on a raid in Demetia, Aoifa and Vevin, with the war-band of King Niall, only he was

not yet king then, and one of the warriors they captured was Brân, the son of a prince of the province. My
mother, liking well the look of him, offered him his
freedom if he fought her for it."

"And did they fight?"

"Indeed they did; and he won, though barely! But
so taken was he with his opponent that he refused to be
released. And neither of them was free of the other
ever again, nor wished to be—he came back here with
her to wed, and I was born a year after…" Amris
stretched out on the rock in the sun, was silent for a
while. "I am glad we met again, you and I. Not long am
I for the Laighin." Then, with pride, sitting up again,
eagerly explaining: "Through my mother I am close-
cousin to Laoghaire, son of great Niall who sits now as
High King at Tara. I will go there soon, to enter his
household; it has long been arranged. Come with me,"
he added, as if the thought had just occurred to him.
"As you know, Niall is the son not of a chief-wife but a
ban-charach, the Lady Cairenn. Because of that, there
were difficulties when Niall came to the kingship, and
there may be more for Laoghaire. He will need friends
about him—friends who are chiefs—when, or if, he
becomes king. Join me at Tara to help him—oh, but
perhaps you must hold here at Killary instead?"

Brendan shook his head, flattered by the suggestion—and tempted also. *To go to the court of Niall Nine-
Hostage! To see the warriors and poets, men and women alike,
and the very Ard-rígh of Tara himself, already legend; to serve
his son in his own days of rule…*

"Nay, Fanad for me," he said, with a twinge of
regret—and concomitant disloyalty—that he had
never before felt at the thought of his destined dúchas.

"I shall follow my father as chief; my cousins, my father's sister's children, will have rule here. But my thanks for the thought—and, you know, we yet may meet at Tara, you and I."

And they spoke no more of it for that time. But as Brendan had noted that first day atop na hAorai, the folk of Killary were not the only kindred he could boast in those parts...

Crossing over the Stile alone one day of late summer, on his usual way to Killary from Dromore, Brendan heard the sound of bells in clear air; remembering the oft-told tale, and sensing with a flash of an-da-shalla what he was about to encounter, he halted to wait. But what came through the granite defile of the pass was no gold-tressed maiden upon a gold-maned mare.

Calatin, prince in Rinn na gCroha, and Súlsha, his princess, rode up on tall gray horses. Behind them were arrayed their attendants, each of them fairer than the next, or more beautiful than the last. They drew rein before Brendan, and gazed upon him, and Brendan stared back, as if he could never tire of the looking.

Never in my life have I seen so many of the Shining Folk all together—and they too are my people...

The eyes of Súlsha regarded him with love; his granddam though she was, she looked barely older than her own daughter. Then Calatin spoke; his voice seemed to Brendan both deep and warm, dark gold-brown like a cairngorm in the sun.

"We are your kin—mother's mother, mother's father. Though you have been a stranger to us, you are ours as well as the Gael's. And we do not quit our claim to you."

As for Brendan, he looked upon his folk and kindred, and found his heart was stirred; a tide of rightness rose within him, as if he had come home to a home he never knew was his, and yet had always known was there.

"I know you—or should have known you, long since."

"Indeed you have, amhic, and more often than you know," said Súlsha; great Maeve's daughter she was, sister of Síoda who was queen at Aileach in the west, beneath the hill of Tallaght. "We have kept watch beside you on Slemish, more nights than not, lest harm befall; we even sent the wolfclanns to keep you company when we could not come ourselves."

"From here to Fanad is more than fifty leagues—"

"We have swifter means of travelling at our command," said Calatin, "and so also, one day, shall you."

Though Brendan, courteous as ever, looked his question, his grandsir offered no explanation; and though Súlsha's bright face clouded a little, she said no word.

This first encounter was of necessity a brief one; as Calatin went on to explain, they were on their way to visit Donn, who was high king of all Sidhedom in Éruinn's isle, at his great palace of Knockfierna to the north and west, and so they could not tarry; and Brendan himself was due at Killary within the hour. But before they parted, they had embraced him, and their companions had greeted him as honored kin, son of a princess and therefore prince himself among them, and he had been warmly bidden to Rinn na gCroha.

My mother's home long since—if not yet mine...

"The Goddess's half of this year I owe as honor-price," he had told them. "But when my service to Coll mac Gréine is paid and done with, I will come."

Calatin had smiled as the company gathered rein to ride on. "You will always find us at home."

On the day before Samhain, his term of reparation now completed, Brendan received his quitleave from Guaire; excusing himself from the merrymaking at Dromore, and from all those who urged him stay, he gathered up his gear, and bidding warm farewell to all at the maenor he took horse over the Stile. He was riding north to Rinn na gCroha, to accept the invitation of his Sidhe kinfolk for the Samhain feast, and Domhnall and Aoifa were to meet him there.

Súlsha and Calatin, well pleased to have their grandson with them for the great festival—which is at least as important to the Sidhefolk as it is to the Gael—were pleased as well to entertain their mortal counterparts, whom they saw less frequently than either kindred wished. Not only was there cliamhan kinship between them—through the union that had produced Brendan as a grandson for them all to have share in and to love—but long history of friendship also, and the rulers of Rinn na gCroha hosted all their guests with greatest honor.

Brendan himself looked handsome indeed; it seemed that on that Samhain night the best beauty of both his bloodlines made itself known in him. His hair glowed like a dark garnet where it fell upon the shoulders of a fine new green tunic; he had worn his grandest jewels for the occasion—the heavy topaz-studded gold torc of the Heir of Fanad, a pendant black pearl in his left ear, matching wristlets of gold and silver stags with antler-racks intertwined.

He greeted his grandparents with love and gladness, leading out the Princess Súlsha, as his hostess, for the first dance, and the Lady Aoifa for the next; but though many lasses shyly sought to catch his eye as partner, for the next few reel-sets Brendan stood out.

"How do you like our musicians, then?" asked Calatin, curious as to why his grandson did not dance.

"They play well enough."

"But—?"

"I have danced with the two fairest ladies in the hall, lord grandsir, and I have no complaint! But I might love the music better," said Brendan with mock sorrow, "had I a true partner for the dancing. I have no acquaintance here, so if the master in the hall could remedy such lack—"

"Trivially." Hiding a smile, Calatin exchanged a quick glance with his lady, then raised a hand in princely wise, and across the dancing-floor a tall girl turned at the summons.

Brendan saw, and stared. She was slender as a white birch in winter, and looked like one: her curving form gowned in clinging white siriac, at her throat a huge and sparkling crystal like a tear of ice; her eyes were amber-gold seen through running water, her black hair fell loose and past her knees.

So it was that Brendan Nia's son met Etain the daughter of Gwastor: as she came toward him across the great hall of Rinn na gCroha, with the walk of a panther and a bearing as proud as any queen's, and stood before him, more than a dance was determined, and greater dán than their own was set thereby.

And dán did not delay: long before the winter Sun-standing, they were deep in love, and well resolved to wed. Yet though they had already given pledges in token each to the other, they had told no one of their intention, least of all their dearest and nearest kin.

"Well," said Brendan one day at Rinn na gCroha, when they had been thrashing the matter over for hours and a solution was no whit the nearer, "if my grandsir denies us, though I do not see why he should, we will go to Donn Midna, who is king over Calatin and all other princes, and seek *his* leave to wed. He is ruler of all our people"—never did he notice how naturally came that 'our' now to his lips—"in this isle, though Maeve of course has precedence at the western end."

Etain brightened. "His son, the prince Kelver Donn Midna, and I have long acquaintance—nay, not *that*, we are childhood playfriends, only! But if I ask him, I know that he will plead our case to his father. As to my parents, and yours—that may prove a harder matter."

But in the end the matter did not require much special pleading, though all concerned considered the young couple far too young to wed—or at least that Brendan was too young. Domhnall Avarcagh thought privately that his beloved grandson could perhaps have looked higher for a bride among his mother's folk, or indeed his father's, than the daughter of Gwastor—however fair she might be or noble her spirit ("A dancing-partner is one thing, Brandoch, a mate is something else!")—and for his part Donn who was king at Knockfierna was perhaps not best pleased to see so rich a jewel as Etain wed one whose blood was after all half mortal ("A dancing-partner is one thing, Tamhna, a mate is something else!").

But Nia the Golden was respected among the Gael, and Fergus Fire on Brega was by no means unknown or unbeloved beneath the hill; and though neither kindred was pleased entirely, in the end both were reconciled and even well disposed to the match, and wished to see it celebrated in suitable fashion.

And so it was that Brendan of Fanad and Etain of the Sidhe were wedded that next Brighnasa, the February snows deep on the mountain above them, the cold biting like a white wolf in the valleys without. In Donn's great thronehall at Knockfierna they stood forth to be married, Brendan tall and splendid in worked leathers, a torse of gold-wrapped silk upon his brow, Etain in sumptuous furs white against the darkness of her hair, but not whiter than her skin, her winter jewels of gold and garnets glowing bright, but not so bright as her eyes. Donn himself, with Aobhinn his queen, presided over the ancient rite of handfast marriage, as sacred a binding among the Danaans as among the Gael; and all close kin of bridegroom and bride were in attendance.

Indeed, Fergus and Nia had journeyed down from Fanad, with Coll and Beirissa, and as many members of their households as could be spared to attend, and the folk of Killary and Dromore, all expectant of a long guesting; and by the time Brendan and Etain had made the last of the Three Cuts, and had drunk the consecrated wine, and spoken their vows, even those

who had been most averse to the match were shedding
tears of joy.

For tinnól Brendan gave his lady a collar of pearls
and dark sapphires wrought in silver knotwork, and
she gave him a ring with a pale-gold adamant; though
many had offered the use of brughs set in romantic
lakelands or hill-crowning maenors by the sea, by their
own choice the bridemoon was passed beneath the hill
at Rinn na gCroha.

The room that was their bridal chamber, in which
they chose to live thereafter, had once been Nia's own.
For its beauty, rare and lovely even among her beauty-
loving people, Etain had early claimed it for Brendan
and herself, and it was fair indeed: tiled floors, silk car-
pets, a wide bed hung with gold silk. But the greatest
splendor could be seen surrounding: the chamber's
walls of hammered silver—a commonplace in the
dwellings of the Sidhe—were covered with a pavement
of pearls, pearls set so close and thick that only the tiniest diffused gleam of cool metal could be seen between
and behind them—pearls of all pale lucent colors,
cream and white, dove-blue and blush-gray, pink as a
spring sunset and water-gold as the summer moon.
The soft orients blended into one lambent mosaic; the
light of day, when gone from above, lingered in the
pearl walls, so that neither sconce or torch was needed
to illuminate the chamber, and darkness never held
sway.

Yet even beneath the hill, time passes: by the time Brendan began to think of returning to Fanad, he had been
five years away. Though he and Etain often spoke idly

of going north to make themselves a real home, as yet
no step had been taken in the way of such a journey.
Looking back, he could not have said upon what
endeavors those first blissful years had been spent—
they lived, they loved, time passed—but the days had
been full even so. All his instruction heretofore had
been in aid of his future needs as lord of Fanad; but at
Rinn na gCroha he learned very different things
indeed. He was taught much that he had never before
known about his mother's people, their history and
lore, how they dealt in war and lived in peace; faerie
bards rehearsed him in saga and chaunt, and trained
him in the harp and the art of poetry, a gift that was to
stay with him all his days. The healers educated him in
their own calling, and sorcerers gladly instructed him
in such magics as might prove useful. He proved most
apt and competent to all the work, if brilliant at none
in particular.

But one butter-soft May morning he looked out to
see the white mists drifting in the spring-green hollows
of the hills, and he knew in that moment that it was
time for them to depart. His grandparents all four,
and his mateparents Gwastor and Liriagh, protested
against the leaving, but Etain sided with her lord, and
against such an opponent even Calatin, prince though
he was, could not prevail—indeed, having come in very
short order to respect and adore his grandson's mate,
he had not the heart to even try.

On the side of the mountain Strivellin that lies
between Killary and Drumnadarroch, there was a holy
well, near-twin to the one on distant Slemish: a well
where water seeped from the granite cliffside, then
leaped spouting to fall into a small pool hollowed out

in the stone. Never had that spring been known to fail, not even in times of direst drought, for Nia herself had once called it forth, to aid the Laighin in a year of terrible water-famine. In the days when Calatin's daughter had dwelled at Rinn na gCroha, so long ago that no mortal now remembered even the tale, she had been besought by the local priestess in the tribe's desperate need—their crops were dead, their cattle and their children dying—and pitying them she had gone to the hill and struck the living rock with an alder branch, and the water came.

In a deep-cut niche in the stone three stone cups always stood, put there by the grateful tribe, as they had vowed to Nia they would do forever, and replaced whenever necessary by others, always in varying materials and style. Two—just now one was of carved bloodstone, the other of plain black jade—were for the use of any who passed and chanced to thirst, for by Nia's command the water was free to all. The third cup was always made of polished clear rock crystal, clear and cold as the water it held—the cup of the Goddess, the cup of the spirit of the spring; none who drank there would dream of drinking without first pouring out libation from the crystal cup, in thanksgiving for the water's gift.

When Brendan went to the well early one morning, to draw water for the rites to bless his journey home with his bride, he found that he was not alone. A red-cloaked woman was standing by the stone coping of the pool; her garb was neither rich nor poor, and her brown braids were tied off with carved wooden acorns. Brendan gave cheerful greeting to her, and she replied the same.

Then the woman took one of the cups—the one of polished crystal—and dipping it into the flow just where it sprang from the stone, she filled it and raised it to her lips.

Brendan startled in shocked protest. "But that is the Goddess's cup—"

The Woman smiled. "And so I drink from it."

For a long moment Brendan did not stir; then, there on the green hillside, he made deep reverence.

"Get up at once, these knee-bendings drive me mad, I would forbid them if I thought anyone would heed—" But the warmth of voice and smile told him that the Goddess mock-scolded only.

"What may I do for You, Lady?" asked Brendan humbly, too awed to be set at ease by the Goddess's jest, but rising at once as he was bidden, gazing upon the face before him—a face that was not of any unearthly beauty, though pleasant enough to look upon, square of shape and strong-featured, lined here and there; a countrywoman's face, fresh-colored, of a robust vibrant strength. *Not here the glory I beheld on Voclut; but the Goddess even so. She puts on mortal form as a garment, whatsoever form may suit Her holy purposes...* "Is there somewhat that You wish of me, Lady—of us?"

"Much; and I mean to have it. But later for that; lives later. Now we must speak. So you are Nia's lad..."

In due course Brendan returned with the water he had gone to fetch; but when Etain asked him, purely in chaffing, had he met some secret lover at the well, so long had he tarried away, though he gave her a level look, as one who wonders what lies in truth behind an innocent-seeming query, in the end he made her no answer, and she did not press him.

*   *   *

They had spent their last night in the south at Rinn na gCroha, in the chamber with the walls of pearl. All that evening Etain had been unwontedly silent, though when he taxed her gently she shook her head and smiled and said there was no trouble.

But before the sun dawned on their departure she woke, and shook him awake also, and after he had clad himself as she was clad—a mantle hastily flung round his bare self, no time allowed for anything more—she led him through the silent brugh and out onto the hillside, still and blue-shadowed, loud with the dawnsong of birds. And deep within the oak woods that clothed the slopes, she turned to her mate and flung off her cloak.

"I know you," he said, and the Goddess burned like a white flame through her nakedness and her being alike, the air brightening round them as the sun leaped above the horizon-line, far eastaways where sea met sky. Upon her he knew only her motion beneath him to match his, they moved in the dawn as two waves of the sea that rolled in splendor against the land.

"First and last in Laighin," she whispered in his ear. "Next and last in Fanad; after that, and ever, in the stars."

CHAPTER SIX

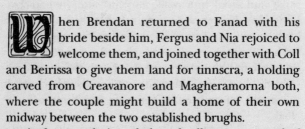hen Brendan returned to Fanad with his
bride beside him, Fergus and Nia rejoiced to
welcome them, and joined together with Coll
and Beirissa to give them land for tinnscra, a holding
carved from Creavanore and Magheramorna both,
where the couple might build a home of their own
midway between the two established brughs.

And presently, in a sheltered valley near a stand of
oaks and elms, a stone-built maenor rose, and Nia herself sained and sealed its maigen, naming it Clanadon;
but most folk in Fanad, if they thought about it at all,
suspected that the young pair lived as much beneath
the hill of Aileach as in their own dún. And if any idly
wondered why Brendan mac Fergus could not have
found himself a nice warrior lass of the Gael to wed,
but had chosen to follow his father's example, and take
to wife instead a maiden of his mother's people, they
never wondered so aloud.

Three Midsummers later, a daughter was born to
Brendan and Etain, Fionaveragh, with flame-colored
hair and a temper to match; two years after that, at
Lughnasa, a son, Rohan. And when Rohan was a sturdy
six-year-old in Fanad, dark-haired like his mother, blue-
eyed and merry of heart, his father having taught him

to ride and his mother just now teaching him the sword, far across the Narrow Seas, in the land of the Prytani that was sometimes known as Less Britain, a Brython priest, a little stooped, a little thin-haired though yet young, was making his way on foot through rough country toward the rock-fanged coast, and the two great isles that lay beyond.

'Nameless' was he no longer: it was Pátraic now, not Ferganam, who had taken the roads from Rome up the spine of Italy, passing into all three parts of Gaul divided, and now traversing the sea-fringe lands that thrust their fingers into the foam of northern oceans.

In the years of his absence from Éruinn, much had befallen him: after his escape, he had come safe to Rome on the trading galley, and in superb physical condition too, after all that rowing and ocean air. In short order he had found himself lodging in a monastery guesthouse not far from the imperial city's center, and also a small employment, with equally small but sufficient stipendium, as translator and copy-scribe in one of the great libraries—he was often heard to boast, afterwards, that his back had gotten him to Rome and his brain had kept him once he got there.

Attaching himself to various mentors and masters, he had worked his way upwards, each of his protectors more powerful than the last—a chief copyist, a travelling scholar, a papal ensign. Through those and other contacts he had been priested in Rome as his dearest wish had been, and by the pope himself.

As civis—even of a fallen Rome—and priest together, Pátraic could have stayed and advanced further still;

but he had declared his destiny long since, if only in his own mind. So that now, armed with a commission from that very Celestine, pope at Rome, whom the Gael derisively called the Tassans, 'little-father', he had passed through Gaul, where he had been consecrated bishop by the venerable Amathorex, chief apostle of the Christom faith in that defiantly heathen land. And now he was on his way back as he had promised long ago, to convert by the pope's own command the habitants of Tir Gaedhil—or at least the human ones—and to end for all time the pernicious pagan influence in that island, and the Unensouled who wielded it.

The prospect comforted him as he crossed Less Britain's endless salt flats and rocky barrens, scuttling fearfully past those serried ranks of standing stones that march like enigmatic armies into the sea. *They are as snakes and serpents, those in Éruinn whom I go to destroy, aye, even as the ones who raised these iniquitous stones—their kindred all across the isles no better! Indeed, their sorcerers make boast of mastering the Serpent Power—but I and those who shall come after, in Christ's holy name we shall drive those serpents from the land...* And as he went he chanted hymns of praise to his god.

Crossing the stormy Sleeve, sick as a pig all the while, at last he unsteadily decanted himself from the fishing smack that had borne him across, and found himself once more upon the sands of Britain the More—which after a considering moment he forbore to kiss, but sketched a blessing in the air instead. *Home at last, home; after all these years...* To his very unspiritual pride, he had landed not as a fugitive slave, or even as the respectable son of an official family that he had been before his captivity, but as a bishop, a priested man bearing the pope's precious commission. And, as such, there was one place to which he knew well he must betake himself, and one man of whom he most humbly must seek leave...

"So the sons and daughters of the wood of Voclut are calling you," said Vortigern politely, from his seat in a vassal's hall at Londinium, and his hearers nearby at table dutifully smiled. But it was no smiling matter as far as Vortigern was concerned: and though he had just listened courteously to Patricius Calpurnius's lengthy account of his slavery and escape and priesting, no sign of what the High Lord of Britain might be feeling at hearing of the boresome—and, he suspected, highly edited—tale had been allowed to flicker across his dark bearded face.

But best listen always: you never know when a pigeon may turn hawk, or a hunting owl drop a plump coney at your feet; always wiser to listen... Now Vortigern shifting in the painted wooden high-seat gave Pátraic a keen glance and a small smile, and spoke again in the deceptively sleepy voice that had lulled so many to their doom.

"So the pope of Rome sends you into Éruinn; but I am told that one Palladius has been there before you?"

Pátraic blinked, surprised. *How well informed he is; but then, he is High Lord—if a traitor lord, for that he invited in the godless Easterlings to settle and hold for him, and now they turn on the Brython like the mange-bit curs they are...*

"Aye, lord, a fine preacher of our faith. He converted a few in the southeastern corner of the island, but, sorrow to tell, he met with mockery and rebuff, and the folk would not leave off their pagan ways." Pátraic seemed aggrieved at the thought. "He is gone north now, into Pictavia, the country of the Crúithin... I trust I may have greater success than he in Éruinn, if of course it is God's will—"

Vortigern made table-talk a while longer, then with a courteous word to the uninvited guest dismissed him to his own host's care—and the humble dorter reserved for folk of the lower rankings.

Pátraic noted the snub, and chose not to mark it, offering the insult to his God, a gift from his own humility. In truth, the wooden palace, elaborate as it was, brought a faint smile to the lips of one who had dwelt for years in the splendors of that Rome which the mighty Augustus had found brick and left marble. But it brought back memories as well... *What of my own home, far in the north—the lakes, the hills, the Wall? My family— Shall I not go there before going on to Éruinn? Doubtless they think me dead, I have been gone from them so many years now— Have I not earned the right to a reunion?*

But not all the memories he had of home were such as might lure him north, and in the end he did not go, but pressed on instead westward. Indeed, he had travelled to the capital only to go submissively before the High Lord Vortigern and seek his permission to convert in Éruinn. His request was as calculated as his dismissal had been, and no one was fooled: Pátraic did not need such permission to do his work, and Vortigern had no slightest writ that ran beyond the seas that girdled his own island.

Nor, for all that he was called High Lord of Britain the More, since the incoming of the Sassanaich to the eastern shires, did he hold much real sway far outside his old lands in Gwent. Certainly Tir Gaedhil was no dúchas of Vortigern's, and he had small use for the irritant Gael who dwelled there; but it never hurt to give the illusion of power if power was not to hand, and if a little flattery eased his way and Pátraic's alike, well enough. *It may serve as warning also to the Gaelfolk, that Rome and Britain alike are not uninterested in the internal affairs of Éruinn…*

But if it suited the far-off Celestine's purpose that the Gael should turn Christom, it suited Vortigern's also: in the years of Pátraic's absence from Éruinn the great king Niall Nine-Hostage had gone to the Goddess; his brother Fiacha and Fiacha's son Dathi had had brief rule by the laws of rígh-domhna election, but now Niall's son Laoghaire sat at last in the throne at Tara. Sat there however uncertainly: none yet knew if his arm in war was as mighty as his sire's; or if, as son of the son of a ban-charach, who had been her king's beloved but not his queen, the nobles would follow him, or seek instead to overthrow him and promote another to the kingship from among the rígh-domhna, another more to their liking—or their ruling.

Vortigern and his 'invited' Sassanaich were by no means the only ones who watched these developments with careful interest: and if the writ Britain's master now gave to the priest from the North was not his own to give, naught else that was his—save a rather generous purse of coin—was given either. And that too did Pátraic mark.

So it was that Patricius Calpurnius came to be crossing south Britain wearily, if steadily, on foot. One whole day was spent passing the tremendous White Horse cut

into the living chalk on a green hillside in the heart of
the land; it grew before him as he walked, looking
more like a great horned dragon than a horse, and he
cursed it for heathen with every step he took, uneasy
under its single eye that gazed enigmatically down the
broad vale. That same night, a dark wild night of rain
and wind, he hastened past Welland's Smithy along the
old straight track edged with trees, head bowed, crossing himself every nine paces, listening half-believingly
for the hoofs of the horses of the Wild Hunt riding the
storm, or for the sound of the hammer echoing off the
huge blocky stones of that chambered souterrain, as
the Smith-god shod those hoofs with silver before and
gold behind. And he cheered himself the while with
tales of how these evil pagan things, and all others
like them, were not long for this world or indeed any
other...

Turning his steps south, he went past Stonehanger,
the Giants' Dance, standing alone upon the empty
sweep of the Great South Plain—the huge inscrutable
bluestone trilithons and sarsen dolmens, visible for
miles, were company only for ravens that cold gray
day—then straight southwest along the old Roman
roads that ran out of Aquae Sulis, stopping for vails one
evening at a hill-fort in the misty green country not far
from Isca Dumnoniorum, where a brilliantly gifted cav-
alry commander still a few years shy of twenty was
beginning to make a name for himself against the Sassanaich, and not just in his native westlands. Even Vortigern had spoken of him respectfully.

But since the youthful warlord was unregenerately,
devoutly, publicly pagan—if also expediently unaverse
to lip-serving Christery where and if such served his

needs—and his warriors the same, Pátraic did not deign to enter the visit, or even a list of the young commander's stunning victories, into the account he kept of his journeyings; and, much later, when he was in a position to do so, he would forbid mention of him in any history that monks had a hand in—which in those times was to say all.

So passed a chance that never would come again: and in his own lifetime not even the name was ever to be set down of Ariothamus, Arithor as the tribes called him—some of them had even begun to put 'king' before it, and not in mere cheap flattery. And when, later, the legends would begin to attach themselves to his deeds, and the great, the astonishing prophecy was made, the name was not his that would cling to those deeds, that foretelling, and so it was that all the confusion began. Even so, it was a name that would be writ in letters of flame upon the walls of legend—the name of Arthur.

If any had been standing atop the shore cliffs on the northeast coast of Éruinn upon a certain summer day, they might have seen this sight: a youngish man coming ashore from a fishing boat, weary with journeying and as usual vile sick with the sea, but looking exalted by some unknown purpose. His hair was shaven clean across the top and front, ear to ear, and left long in back, down upon his shoulders—a strange new tonsure. On his feet he wore Roman army sandals, the best shoes in the world, though his looked as if they had seen many miles and hard ones. A rough-spun shirt and trews, only, covered his lean body—no soft linen

undergarb for him—and a sheepskin mantle, no more
than a large tanned hide with a slit for his head, roofed
his shoulders tent-like, wool side in to keep off the driz-
zle and the chill; a small backsack held his few possessions and necessities, while a well-stuffed flat purse was
wrapped tight against him by a leather sash beneath his
shirt. In his right hand was a book-satchel, well laden
from the look of it; his left clasped a crómag, a shepherd's tall crook of use-hardened blackthorn—his grip
upon it was light and loving, as one who well knew its
use, and who planned to use it to drive more than
sheep, or different sheep...

All in all, in itself not a picture to tempt road-
thieves, or to inspire fear or conjure dread in any who
might cross his path. Yet though Rome's armies never
came to Tir Gaedhil in might, this lone invader, and
those who followed after him, would conquer it for
Rome in a way the tribunes and centurions could never
have dreamed of, and more completely, more lastingly,
than ten thousand legions could have done...

And if any had been standing two days hence atop
the beacon hill of Knocklong, they had seen this same
stranger, a good strong pace on him now, journeying
along to the west and north, the Hill of Tara far on his
left, low against the sky. And if they had heard his
thought that was prayer and threat and promise all in
one—*I shall be claiming that royal hill for royal Christ, before
I am many days older!*—they would have cut him down
before he had taken another step into Éruinn and
buried his body in a bog where none would find it for
twice a thousand years. If it had been done, it would
have been well done—and it could have been done,
most easily.

But it was not done, and so he walked on into history; and the sorrow caused by that slaughter foregone would be felt among the very stars.

And as he went, upon that same royal hill of Tara which he had gazed at from a distance, in the pillared banqueting-hall of Midhcuartaigh that great Cormac had caused to be built, hard by the palace of Rath na Ríogh, a young man and a younger woman sat side by side like well-behaved children in the midst of their court, to listen to what a master-druid had travelled many miles to tell them.

Laoghaire, king at Tara these three years past, sat in his high seat, one hand to his bearded chin; his queen, the darkly glowing Duvessa, was enthroned upon his right in no less state, his grandmother the Lady Cairenn at his left. He was son of the mighty Niall Nine-Hostage of song and story, but he had not succeeded his father directly. His uncle Fiacha, Niall's brother, had been elected to follow Niall, and had died almost at once; then Dathi mac Fiacha had claimed from right of his dead father, and when Dathi too was slain in battle the succession of the rígh-domhna had fallen at last upon Laoghaire mac Niall.

Many had protested his election, citing his youth, his inexperience of war, his lack of entirely acceptable royal descent. Though his grandmother Cairenn Chasdubh, 'of the dark curling hair', had indeed been a king's daughter, still she was an outland one, born in Britain the More—and any road, she had been bancharach, not chief-wife, and therefore not queen. But for all that, Laoghaire was indisputably rígh-domhna, and he had been voted to the throne in the teeth of all objection, though those who had protested most vociferously against his taking the throne now sneeringly proclaimed he would never be able to hold it.

But the opinion of such creatures troubled him not at all, and such matters were far from his thought just then in any case: his chief druid had come to him with a disquieting prophecy, and Laoghaire had bidden him speak it out for all the hall to hear.

Despite the dread he had of the words he had come there to give, the druid bowed and obeyed; his voice rang against the oak pillars, as harsh and fraught with omen as the cry of the War-queen's ravens above a stricken field, and the guests stopped their ears against the chaunt.

> "There shall arrive the priest Shave-head
> with his stick bent in the head
> 'neath his tent-roof with a hole in its head.
> He will chaunt impiety and blasphemy
> from a table in front of his little house.
> All his people will answer 'Be it thus,
>   be it thus.'"

The king made no sign when the prophecy was ended, but looked sidewise, first at the young woman, then at the older, and then spoke to the druid.

"And what might it mean?"

The druid spread his hands. "Nothing good, my king… But I have Seen it: a priest most strangely tonsured is coming to Tir Gaedhil, with a crómag as his sign of office, wearing an unsewn vestment that has but a hole for his head to pass through. He will speak against our ways of the Shan-vallachta from an altar that he will set before the small clochan he builds for himself; those who follow him say endlessly 'Amen Amen Selah Selah.'"

Duvessa the queen leaned forward, so that only the king and the druid and the king's mother did hear her; the silver apples at the ends of her long black braids chimed softly, but her voice was softer still, and colder far than silver.

"Then put a stop to it. To him. Before it is too late."

And Cairenn the beloved ban-charach of Niall's father Eochaid—she who had been so vilely ill-used by the queen Monuinna, her lord's chief-wife—added her word to Duvessa's. It was a word that ever carried much weight in her grandson's ear; and in this matter the two women were in agreement—as they almost always were.

But Lucet Mael, the royal druid who had with dread and trembling recited the prophecy, shook his head.

"It is already too late. It cannot be undone."

Laoghaire looked at his wife, but spoke to the hall. "My father Niall threw down Emain Macha of the Ultonians; shall it be said of me that I allowed some Tree-priestling from far elsewhere take Tara likewise?"

"Nay," said Cairenn then, in a voice so strong it was heard throughout Midhcuartaigh. "Never so. But it might be Tara that betakes itself far elsewhere."

And many remembered her words, and spoke of them after.

While he had lain suffering and prostrate in the boat that had carried him from Gwalia, Pátraic had determined that before his mission could properly begin, he must first return to Fanad, to buy himself free from Coll

with a triple ransom. The idea much pleased him, and
for more reasons than the obvious. *Triple for the holy Trinity, not for the pagans' unholy Goddess; though the law only
requires a double ransom, three times will pay for all and more.
I cannot begin my mission in this heathen land as a slave, only
as a free man freely preaching Christ's free word...*

He was no seaman—once out of the Gwentish harbor of Porthvaur, the little masted curragh bought with
Vortigern's coin had drifted more than he had sailed
it—but after a few days he had come in to land at
Inveraira on the hard stony coast of Argaill. He had
notably met with no success: the perpetually quarrelling Aulbannach and Pictoi of the district, on hearing his errand, had looked at one another, and then
without a word spoken had come together in unprece-
dented unity to throw him back into the sea like a bad
herring. Nothing daunted, Pátraic had berated them
roundly, then wringing out his sea-soaked clothing he
had cast off again, piously commending himself into
God's hands, letting the tide take the boat. *God will
bring me where he will...*

But God did not seem a much better seaman than
his advocate, for the little craft had been pulled by the
powerful currents of those parts straight toward the
giant whirlpool of Corryvreckan that stood between
two island headlands, and only by dint of much hard
paddling—*Good to trust in God, but true also that God
works best through men's acts*; hence the mighty feats of
desperate oarsmanship—had Pátraic missed being
sucked down into the roaring foam-flecked spiral.

Much history would have read very different if he
had been. Instead, he had come safely on against all
odds, praising God all the while, passing Rathlinn

Island low on his right, making land again near Ard Mhacha—latterly known as Armagh. Having climbed slowly up from the beach—not even the guardians of the shore had noted his arrival, and bitterly would they blame themselves after—he had spent a few days resting and praying in the oak-woods that clothe those hills, then had taken up his staff again and headed west and north. And dán, unseen, went with him.

Few men in all Éruinn that day can have been more surprised than Coll mac Gréine, when he saw enter his hall at the supper-hour, when the gates of all brughs stand open to all guests, one who last had stood there, many years since, as a slave.

Slave still, in the eyes of the law, Coll reminded himself. *That collar is by no means unbuckled; Brandoch's labors were honor-price to clear his* own *name, not to buy this one's freedom of me…*

But coming forward Pátraic mac Calprin bowed three times, and when he stood before the high table he thumped down triumphantly before Coll and Beirissa three leather pouches—three times his purchase price—coin saved from his scriptor's labors, augmented by the gifts he had had of the pope of Rome and the bishop of Gaul and the High Lord of Britain.

"Twice my price according to the law of purchase, lord, and once more again, as honor-price. It is more than the law requires, but it is my honor that requires it be paid."

"And my honor is required to accept it," said Coll, a bit sourly as some thought who heard. He nodded once, and his rechtair hurried up to bear away the pouches; only then did he bid Pátraic to a seat at table, as brehon law also requires. In all those lands then, guestship was sacred; indeed, hospitality must be offered to any chance comer, even if that one had the host's father's blood upon his blade.

"I seek leave to preach in Fanad," said Pátraic in answer to Beirissa's polite question, having already given brief account of how he had passed the years since his escape and before his return arrival on the eastern coast. "I had not even time to visit again my homeland in Rheged, which is yours also, lady… But I come bearing commission from the Holy Father himself, and the leave of the High Lord Vortigern of Britain the More, to bring the word of God to the folk of this island; and as it was here in Fanad that I came to know the one true God, here I shall begin, once leave is given."

"Not mine to give," said Coll thankfully, though withinwards he was appalled. "And no more the Tassans' or Vortigern's to give it you, most presumptuous of them both… Though I tell you now few will wish to hear you, and fewer still will heed— But you must ask of the lord Fergus, if you wish to speak within his maigen."

Pátraic gave a guilty start. "His heir—"

"—who freed you to do your tiresome work," murmured Beirissa, eyes demurely on her plate.

"—is returned here to dwell," said Coll more loudly, shooting his wife a quick quelling glance, "from the country of the Laighin, where he wedded a lass of his mother's people. I sent him there as enech-clann for abetting your escape. Perhaps you owe honor-price to him as well," he added thoughtfully.

More he did not offer, thinking the atonement of a lord's son to be no concern of a former slave; but Pátraic said no word more, only attended silently to his supper, and when that was done, with an unexpected show of finer feeling he declined Coll's offer—again law-dictated—of a guest-bed for the night.

"God will roof and couch me," he said simply, and bowing to his hosts he left the hall.

"Do you think Fergus will allow him to speak?" asked Beirissa, when all the hall had emptied and still Coll sat brooding in his chair beside her.

Her husband startled, as if suddenly recalled to awareness; he had been thinking darkly of Vortigern, and of others with perhaps even greater purpose, but he did not wish to discuss his misgivings just then.

"I do not know. Were it I, it would be against my resolution quite to do so, for nothing but ill can come of it. But—if he does not obtain leave, he will only preach anyway and say that Fergus feared to let him speak; if leave is given, at the least he cannot claim he was silenced. I hear the Christom have already many martyrs to their tedious cause; by gods, my Rissa, let us make them no new ones, and let us go now to our bed."

CHAPTER SEVEN

rendan watched Fionaveragh and Rohan run laughing ahead of him, and smiled with proud indulgence to see them. It was a sunny spring afternoon perhaps a fortnight after that remarkable scene at Magheramorna, and he had taken his two children, home on holiday from their fostering, for a walk in the hills. He was rightly proud: they were well grown for their age, the girl tall and strong as a lass three years her elder, the boy scarce less so, both of them fair and merry and clever as otters, with a grace and shine that came to them from their mother and grandmother.

Across the valley, he saw a crowd of folk gathered at a place called the Struell-wells, where a stream cut a fern-shaded cleft in the hillside and fell away to the glen floor—a well-known healing spring, sacred to the goddess Armída, frequented by many for its powers. He shaded his eyes with his hand, curious to see what was toward—save on feast-days, those who made pilgrimage to holy wells came usually by ones and twos, not in throngs—but he could make out little, and before he thought about it he had altered his steps in that direction, calling to the children as he went.

As he drew nearer, and saw the one who stood in their midst, upon a small flat boulder to raise him up—

the rough-cloaked man with the peculiarly shorn hair who was the center of their impassive attention, a foreigner, a Brython by his looks—Brendan felt a strangeness begin to steal over him; a feeling of pounding dread, but with more to it even than that. *This has happened already; this is a thing I know...*

He paused on the outskirts of the crowd, and he looked long, recognizing at once, with no astonishment and a slow grim smile and a sense of dán completed, the man who stood upon the rock. Without turning his head, he raised a hand to beckon the two Fian warriors who accompanied him as tail that day, and at his bidding one took the protesting children back to the dún where their mother was waiting on their return. The other, Rozen, stayed close beside him, and together they listened in silence to the stranger's preaching.

"This is assuredly that Tangavaun we have been hearing so much of," said Rozen with contemptuous recognition. "That shavepate one your father gave leave to speak in Fanad—you remember, Coll's runaway slave, the one whose freeing sent you down to the Laighin sixteen years since."

Brendan startled as the connection crashed into place and his dread found sudden focus, and he turned to stare at her.

"Tangavaun! Surely I have heard of *him*! But I did not know he was— His name was never spoken—how long has he been here, why then did my father not tell me?"

"Not long—a few days, the inside of a week; the captain of Fians at Magheramorna told me of it. He came first to Coll mac Gréine, and bought of him his free-

dom—with honor-price added, and Coll was by no
means pleased about it—then sought leave at Creavanore to speak in Fanad. I would have mentioned it
sooner," she added humbly, seeing the look upon his
face, "but I thought you surely knew. It seemed a thing
of little matter, and you were away at the dún of Aileach
with the Lady Etain, any road... Aye, well, 'Tangavaun':
the folk have taken to calling him; it seems to be the
only word in his mouth, the only word he has any
respect for. But no wonder folk did not speak of him to
you, thinking that it would bring back to mind something you might not care to be minded of."

"Anyone may speak in Fanad," said Brendan then,
who seemed to have recovered his composure—and
his sense of screaming irony with it, for a real grin
threatened to split his face beneath the beard. "Anyone at all. As to being heard when one speaks by those
who may *listen* in Fanad—that is a very different matter.
One would have to have somewhat of value to say for
that. Let us listen, then, and determine."

The others who had assembled to do that listening
seemed much of a mind with their lord's son: Pátraic,
for it was surely he, was receiving a courteous attention,
if hardly a receptive one, though it could never be said
that he was not a most eloquent speaker with all his
heart in his preaching. *For you never know when you will
be speaking your last...* But he tailored now his message
to his hearers, and subtlety was not in it.

"Now I shall tell of my escape from vile enslavement, here in this very country: on the hill Slemish one
night, where I kept sheep at my pagan master's bid-

ding, a vision came to me of the angel called Victoricus, which is Buach in your tongue, who told me that I should be safe delivered from the hands of my captors, spared to guard dearer sheep. So I fled the place where I had been held six years in harsh cruel thralldom by the enemies of God, and alone I walked east as God commanded. After many miles' hard dangerous journeying I came to the coast, and a ship was waiting there, even as God had promised. But when the captain saw my cross and staff, he refused to take me on board. So I prayed, and walked away again, and then one of the men shouted out to me to return—surely God heard my prayer, and put it into his heart to do so! And the captain's heart too was miraculously changed. 'Come, hurry,' he said, 'we will take you aboard in good faith; make friends with us whatever way you like.'"

Not quite the way I *remember it happening...* Brendan grinned again, but he said no word. Above him on the slope, Pátraic paused to accept water offered by one of his followers—the day was a hot one, and he had been speaking in Fanad now for almost a week on end. But in Rome he had acquired, among many other tricks of his new trade, a voice almost the equal in power of a trained bard's, and he had learned well how to use it; he calmly continued, still in the face of that perfect, negative silence.

"It would take more than that to make friend of *me*—I refused to suck at a pagan breast, as it were, or kiss pagan hands in liegedom, for fear of God's wrath, but I knew that the Lord Iosa Chriesta would forgive me accepting passage with such creatures, as it was all for his divine purpose. Indeed, I heartily prayed that

these mariners would come to the true faith, because
they were but heathens ignorant of the Word; and I
myself might be God's humble instrument in their
deliverance. Three days after setting sail, then, we
reached land—some islands off the west Aulban coast,
then down to Gwynedd in Gwalia, where we went
ashore. For twenty-eight days we travelled afoot through
deserted country. No food was to be found, and those
who dwell in that hard land would not give us any, for
they are hard people, and they saw that we were not of
their kindred. 'If your god is so powerful, let him feed
us,' said the boatmen, 'or else we shall find a druid to
aid us.' But I said to them, 'Do not call upon druidry,
but be truly believing with all your heart to God, and he
will send you food, for his abundance and his power
are everywhere.' And lo, no sooner had I prayed so
than a herd of fat wild pigs appeared."

Smiles all round at that—the smile a grown person
has for the swaggering boasts of a child—and a young
girl shouted out in derision and annoyance, "Magic!
No fear! But greater is the magic of Gwydion Rhên,
who, as everybody knows, once came by some pigs himself, and did not need to beg any outfreyn god for
help!"

Pátraic crossed himself at the blasphemy, though
the general laughter stung more than the gibe, and his
voice in response was sharper than he had yet allowed
it to be.

"No sorcery, my daughter, but the will of the one
true God! I tell you the pigs came, as God himself, and
no wizard prince of pagan Gwynedd, did command!
We men ate our fill; and the hounds that had been
almost dead fed well also, so that when we arrived at

Rome they were ready for the games." He paused
again, voice once more honeyed. "I dwelled then long
years in the Holy City, recovering even as did those
hounds, learning much from many, to become a
hound of God. Then I came again to Britain the More,
to my own people who besought me that I should stay;
but God put it in my mind that the folk of this land had
more need of me, and so I now am come."

But they were not impressed, and let it be well seen
that they were not, and that no matter what his god
might put into what it pleased him to call his mind,
they themselves had no need of that god, whatever; no,
nor of his priestling neither, and god and man would
have done better to have stayed in Britain the More,
which doubtless deserved them both. Despite his elo-
quence and mellifluity, he had lost them from the start:
his error had been that his audience was very well
acquent with that so-called harsh pagan master of his—
Coll mac Gréine, than whom for all his bark and gruffness a more humane lord could not have been found
in Éruinn—and would not buy the tale of evil treat-
ment. More than a few of them, also, even knew
himself from of old—knew what sort he was, and were
impressed still less. And not one of them but deeply
misliked being tagged 'pagan' and 'evil' and all the
other names that had been so lavishly and undiplomat-
ically put upon them this day by a former slave.

Long before Pátraic had finished speaking they
had begun to drift away—the young girl who had challenged him declaring snappishly to her friends that she
was no daughter of his *or* his god's, thank you never so
much. At the end only a few remained close by him—
admiring followers already acquired, who had heard of

Pátraic's arrival and had come from other parts to join
him; no one new-swayed in Fanad.

Brendan lingered awhile; then when Pátraic stood
alone, for a few moments unsurrounded by his companions, he approached him, and was pleased immod-
erately to see recognition, and no small alarm, leap
naked to the other's face before it could be mastered.

"How comes it you did not tell them that I myself
was the hand of your God who brought you here?" said
Brendan, smiling. "Ungracious! Or did you fear that
such an admission would give far too much credit to
the unholy Unensouled? You see, I remember very well
how it was, and I think that you do too—that without
my abetting your escape you would never have come to
your ministry. For my part I have always known you
would return among us, even though your own folk
back in Rheged be deprived of your presence."

"You have wedded one of those Soulless, so I have
heard," said Pátraic, ignoring the honest gratitude
that moved in him—the remembered youthful friendship, the knowledge that he had only ever had kindness and patience of this one, and owed him more
than could ever be repaid—and moving instead to
attack, though why he could not say. *How well he has
grown into his manhood; but however much an impressive
warrior lordling, still he is as pagan as I left him, aye, and
worse...* "If marriage I can call it, and got children by
her, Godless bratlings..."

Brendan's face went black as iron, and behind him
Rozen's hand drifted casually to the hilt of her leaf-
bladed sword. But he motioned her hold, and mastered Pátraic's gaze with his own, and spoke soft
enough.

"The lord Fergus has given you leave to preach in Fanad—and had I only known that you were asking, be sure that I had put a stop to *that*, and speedily too— But now hear *my* preachment, son of Calpurnius: you may have bought your freedom of mac Gréine, but no freedom is buyable on Erith to allow you to speak so. Therefore keep that White Tongue of yours off the names of my lady and my bairns, or by all gods, and by your god too, I will rip it from your head and feed it to such hounds as those you spoke of. At the very least, you and your Iosa owe me honor-price. Do not make me repent, as I am already beginning to, the pity and the deed whereby I set you free to speak your Christom word."

"I owe you my freedom indeed," said Pátraic presently. "That much is certain. But know it or not, love it or not, in this matter you are an instrument of God."

"And as that young lass said," said Brendan, more softly still, "I am no instrument of any such god as yours. Nameless you may be no more, and slave no more, and for that I take all blame and dán; but one of your rank may not offend one of mine, not without éraic to be paid for it. I paid honor-price for my hand in your escape; do not make me claim from you now a higher than you can afford."

The threat, well-aimed, lodged deep where it was sent—though Pátraic allowed Brendan to see no sign of it, but merely sketched a cross in the air and bowed and turned away. Brendan stood still a moment, then went to the Struell-wells and cooled his face in the waters of Armída's spring, feeling the need of cleansing. *Water that can heal sickness...but can it heal* this *sickness? One way or the other, I am not so sure I wish to know...*

Pátraic preached no more in that region for that time, and his followers noted that he seemed unusually subdued after his encounter with the lord of Fanad's son. But as he and his small company made their slow way over the hills—so familiar to him from his herder days—and down into east Connachta, a thought came to him, and he spoke it that night at the frugal meal they made themselves, after the holy silence was broken over meat.

"We will celebrate Easter at Tara of the Kings," said Pátraic, in a tone that was not suggestion but command. He feigned not to notice the wave of consternation that ran round the little band at his announcement. "Do not trouble yourselves, God has put this into my mind... Easter comes this year close on the spring Daynighting; the pagans' own law holds that in such season none may light a fire before a fire appears on the hill of Tara. Shall the druids and ban-draoi have their heathen way in the true God's despite? I think not!"

Those who went with him—he had won easier-swayed Gaelfolk than those of Fanad to his side, and some of his own race had come over from Britain the More—were doubtful, a few even muttering against the wisdom of such a course. For challenge it was, and no mistake: the High King, Laoghaire mac Niall himself, and all his folk, and many others, would be at Tara to celebrate the spring feast, and this action Pátraic proposed would be a gauntlet flung in their very faces.

But though his followers wavered he himself was

obdurate. They need not come, he told them loftily; if God did not give them the requisite heart or stomach for it he would go himself, alone if need be. And of course they would not have it so, or if they would they dared not admit it; and if they privately thought their master's change of plan to be small-hearted revenge for the slight he felt he had suffered at Brendan's hand, they did not admit to that either. But gathering up their gear they turned their steps southeastwards in his wake, following dutifully after, to Tara's green hill high on the windy plains of Meath.

Each year at the times of Sunstanding and Daynighting—the quarter-days, the four spokes of the rolling Year-wheel that space themselves between Bríd's feast and Lugh's, between the Goddess's Beltain and Samhain that is the God's—the hill of Tara, which is ever the center of Éruinn, becomes a place of festival and assembly, heart-home of the Gael.

At Tara now the court was already preparing to celebrate the spring Daynighting. If not so great a feast as Samhain or Beltain, when all fires in the land, extinguished for the observance, are relighted from the blaze at Tara kindled, it was a holy festival all the same, and the king himself would light the sacred fire; no other flame might be lighted before it.

It had been some time known to King Laoghaire that the former Brython slave who now called himself Pátraic had been preaching the new religion throughout all Éruinn. Known too, much to that king's further distaste, that Vortigern of Britain had presumed to give the man leave to preach so; indeed, on hearing *that*

Laoghaire had muttered venomously to Duvessa that he could just as well crown her little cat high king of the moon, since he held as much command over that distant orb as Vortigern did in Éruinn. But they had neither dreamed nor dreaded, not just yet, how deep the Christom rule already ran, and among whom it had found footing.

An hour or so before sunset, the king and queen, with their court and their warriors and their sorcerers, went out upon the faha before the feast-hall. As far as they could see to the east all was shadowed; but the west burned.

"All the fire has gone into the West," said Laoghaire, lifting his arms in ceremonious gesture. "Let us wait for the dimming, and then step forth to light the holy blaze."

As sunset flamed and died and a hush fell on even the birds, and the druids and ban-draoi stood by, in the twilight a small golden spark flared uncertainly on the hill of Slane that rose across the vale, twin to high Tara itself. Though they could not see him for the distance between, another had been watching that portentous sunset, and he had just that moment acted as he had told his followers he would: a defiant, and for all his vauntings a deeply frightened, Pátraic had lighted forbidden fire outside his own tent, before the high king could kindle the blaze on Tara. The druids and ban-draoi observing were shocked but not surprised, and headed by Lucet Mael the royal sorcerers took the news to their king.

Who could see well enough for himself what was

toward: if his priests and priestesses were calm and cool, Laoghaire was hotly furious, and stared across the valley's width as if he could put out the offending flames with the wrath of his eyes, or at the least set light to the one who had unlawfully lighted.

"He knew of the prohibition, of the geis," said Laoghaire, not turning.

"Lord, he did," said Lucet Mael.

"And he lighted the fire in its despite."

"As you see."

Laoghaire spread his hands, still gazing across the vale. "Well. It is but a small flaming, easily put out. As he may be."

Now Lucet Mael spoke gravely, and he spoke to be heard. "King, unless that fire is extinguished this very night, be assured it will never be put out. It will rise above all the fires of our ways, and he who has kindled it will set it like a darkness into the hearts of all the peoples of all the lands."

And hearing the iron note of prophecy in the druid's words, Laoghaire turned in a swirl of red cloak, and his queen and his Fians with him.

"Order the chariots," he said.

Twenty-seven war-cars, Laoghaire and Duvessa in the one leading and the king himself his own charioteer, thundered across the Tara plain; and while most of the cars circled round the hill of Slane like hounds around a campfire, the king with five chariots behind him drove straight up the easy slope, and came to a halt before Pátraic's goathide tent. Before any of the visitors could step down, Pátraic himself came out to welcome them, smiling, bowing slightly but making no bent knee. *He may be king at Tara, and she his queen—but I bend knee now to none save blessed Christ alone. Yet if I could turn them to Christ...*

That king he wished to turn had look and words for him straight and unbendable as a sword. "Put out the fire you have lighted, priest, and go from here. No harm shall befall you or yours for your work this night."

But Pátraic, smiling still, with honeyed words refused, and raising his hand he summoned up his disciples. The sorcerers that had accompanied Laoghaire dismounted from their own chariots, and coming forward immediately engaged Pátraic and his disciples in goodly, godly argument.

No one gained glory or mastery that night: the druids and ban-draoi argued most well, but so too did the Christlings, especially Pátraic himself. Indeed, so passionate were the exchanges of word and thought that one of Pátraic's own followers defected then and there to the pagan side, and a ban-draoi to the Christom; and a warrior of Laoghaire's so insulted the Christom faith that Pátraic, forgetful of where he stood and in whose name, cursed him so blackly that he died on the spot.

The king and his companions drew back, murmuring amongst themselves, and some of the Fians shifted their weapons at their sides. Pátraic, who had seen at once that he had made a bad mistake, liked not the gleam of speculation he saw in the eye of more than one who stood by. *I have let them see that which they ought not to have seen. If I do not wrest the moment from them, they will surely attack—and even with God's powers to my hand I cannot stand against them all together...*

He reached out a hand; Lucet Mael, instantly divining his intent, began a counterspell but was already too late. The ground rolled beneath them, then twitched, then heaved; the horses snorted, but their training held firm and they did not bolt.

"That is only the smallest showing of the power of the true God," said Pátraic when all was still again. "Take care you do not anger him, nor yet me, I who am but the humblest of his servants."

"What would you have, then?" said Laoghaire in a voice so hard and sharp and edged it was a weapon in itself. "You who are so humble a servant—"

Pátraic ignored tone and thrust alike. "It is said in the holy Word that while what is Caesar's by right must be rightly rendered up to Caesar, what is God's is God's. I ask of Caesar—for 'Caesar' read 'king at Tara'—mere leave to speak. To walk the land, and preach of my Master, to those who have ears to hear. No more than that."

Laoghaire stared at him for many moments, then inclined his head sharply, one curt nod, and mounted up into his chariot; following his lead, Duvessa swept her hand along her skirts, the merest flick of a reverence delivered with what was not reverence at all, and joined her lord.

As the chariots headed home, Pátraic watched them dwindle in the growing dark, and began to breathe again; it seemed he had not drawn breath since Laoghaire's arrival. *The count is two for one, king at Tara: you take with you a disciple of mine—a weak vessel, and, as we see, not fit for Iosa's service—but also you take the body of your soldier that the word of God has slain, while remains with me one of your sorceresses, to be a holy nun. We will see whose strength proves greater at the test—for test there will surely be...* Whatever else he may have been thinking he kept for once within his own breast, and those with him, cowed and shaken by the encounter, dazed at the victory, dared not ask.

Back on his own royal ground, the sacred fire having been belatedly, if anticlimactically, lighted, Laoghaire spoke to no one, but went straight to his own chambers in the palace-dún of Rath na Ríogh. Even his queen was commanded to leave him alone for a time, at least until he ordered otherwise—which with him could be a few hours or a few days, there was never any telling.

But after a surprisingly short interval, summonings came. Duvessa, joining her husband as she had been bidden, found him already deep in converse with his Fian cousin, Amris mac an Fhiach, who had lately come up to court from the Laighin, and who had risen rapidly in his royal kinsman's councils—and in his esteeming affections. She smiled and held out her hand to him, and Amris bowed his warrior's frame over it; he was one of those she wholly approved of, and in those early days of her mate's kingship Laoghaire's queen could not—and would not—say that of very many who were near him.

"Power of the true God!" Laoghaire was saying, his voice full of contempt. "You saw?"

Amris nodded. "I did; and if that was not druid-power I am Christom man forevermore."

"Which you most clearly are not," said Duvessa. "But what are we to do against it?"

"I must destroy him by whatever means I have to

hand, or can lawfully come by," said Laoghaire then. "You understand me, cousin?"

Amris looked up. "Then, lord, I suggest you summon one I know—and one he knows also…"

"This Brendan whom Amrach bids me send for," said Laoghaire later in the privacy of the bedchamber, as Duvessa kneaded the muscles of his shoulders, scowling horribly at their rigid tenseness. "He is son of that Fergus Fire on Brega who was friend to my uncle Fiacha, and to my father also. And in their youth in Fanad he himself was friend to the Tangavaun, who then was thrall to Coll mac Gréine."

"Friend to a lying meddler Christom slave— You are tighter than a swordknot, Laoch, you must untense your muscles or all this working is for naught—"

"Friend nonetheless, and by all reports the only friend the slave had." He put up a hand to hers in wincing protest, as she laid sudden exasperated arm-strength into the join of his neck and back. "Ai! Softly, asthore! It is only flesh and blood… Well. I am told too it was this same Brendan son of Fergus that was responsible for the Tangavaun's escape from mac Gréine's service. And it is because of that escape he comes now back to plague us… I have summoned him also—Pátraic—as Amris bids me, for Brendan to bespeak when he arrives." His grin split his face, all unwilling, but it rejoiced her to see it, and she softened her touch. "Perhaps it is Brendan I should be punishing, for criminal lapse of judgment— doubtless he has already paid éraic to Coll, but as king I just may require him to pay some more. What *is* the honor-price these days for abetting a slave's flight?"

But the Lady Cairenn, who had come in and now sat quietly by, shook her head.

"There is something higher being cropped out here. Let be."

And her grandson and his wife, both of whom adored her for her courage and her grace, and knew she had uncommon Sight on her when she chose to use it, or to share it, were silent.

On the hill of Slane across the valley, stealthy movement: Pátraic, ignobly fearing that the king's men should fall on him and kill him in the night, had taken action, despite Laoghaire's decree that he should stay.

In the white hour before sunrise, eight deer and a fawn went in a line away from Tara: Pátraic, and those who went with him, under magic of the fith-fath— which he had judged sin enough, but justifiable under the circumstances. Flitting like footless ghosts across the misty plain below the hill, vanishing into the concealment of the Rathard woods, they went not unnoted by the druids who were early awake, and by the Fians guarding the palace.

By the king's own command, no warrior set arrow to string or bent bow to slay; but the queen, wishing she only dared, would have commanded very different.

CHAPTER EIGHT

"He speaks against our ways and lives and faith, and yet he uses druidry for his own end. Aye, truly! We have all seen him do it; he can neither dispute nor deny, and in his everlasting traha doubtless he does not even believe he does so... Now, I know from Amrach that you and the Tangavaun were friends in your youth. I know too that you are half Danaan by grace of your mother's blood, and that you chose your wife from among that kindred. Out of your youth-friendship, then, and its memories, out of the knowledge of your mate's and mother's people, is there any word or fact, or sorcery even, that might serve us against this Tangavaun and what he brings among us? At the very least, do we know, or can we learn, how he came by the magic we all saw him employ?" Laoghaire stood up and began to pace. "Great Dagda! There were no Christom ways *there*! As king, I could command you; but as your fostern's cousin, we ourselves are kin, and so I but entreat."

So speaking, voice calm and compelling, a king's voice in a hard place, Laoghaire seated himself again, and passed a quaich of ale across the corner of the table to Brendan, who accepted it proudly from his hand and drank with gratitude. It was a fortnight after

the lighting of the fire: the son of Fergus had ridden in
from Fanad a little before sunset, and after the usual
bath he had gone straight to Rath na Ríogh as he had
been entreated—or commanded. There he had been
greeted warmly by Amris, and presented at the nightmeal to Laoghaire himself, and Duvessa and Cairenn,
and a few others close and deep in the royal confidence. But Lucet Mael the king's druid had bowed
gravely to the man of the West, for he saw the high dán
that was on him—though this he did not speak of, to
the king or to anyone, or at least not yet.

Brendan drank from the quaich refilled, and from
behind the bowl he studied the man who sat in his
high-seat across the oaken board, looked upon him
with a sudden eager shyness, a hoping wish to be his
friend: a man younger than he by perhaps a hand of
years, no more, with long well-tended gold-brown hair
and the deep-set eyes of his mother's people. No sign
of rank or kingship was on him—no ring or brooch or
crown or jewel—but all round him clung that indefin-
able remove that is the invisible garment of all royalty;
and a warmth that was his alone.

*This is the High King! Laoghaire, son of Niall, king at
Tara… That is Duvessa his queen, and over there the Lady
Cairenn who was mother to Niall Nine-Hostage…*

"I would obey all and any of the High King's commands," said Brendan presently, plainly, "and no
entreaty needed. But truly, lord, little comes to mind
that might serve. When we were herds together with
the flocks on the hill, Ferganam—Pátraic—and I, we
spoke little enough: boys' matters, hounds and hawks,
stories and histories. But what I can recall, I will share
full willing—"

For an hour's time, for his king's sake, Brendan
walked long-ago ways in memory's glass: falling silent
from time to time as his recollection came dim, speaking eagerly when the reflection was a clear one.

The queen Duvessa, now and again brushing back
strands of loosened hair into her dark braids, listened
intently as he spoke, and at last she asked, as her lord
had asked earlier, a question to which more folk than
he and she alone sought answer.

"The man prays all day and night, signs himself
with the cross a hundred times each hour, every third
step when he walks about—all of us have seen it, endlessly—yet still I have the oddest feeling that the most
of it is mere show, put on in equal parts for those who
follow him and for us who study him. I must admit, he
is honey-mouthed with words—a most glib and facile
tongue—and so folk can be easily persuaded to an easier way... But how comes it, Brandoch"—already it was
'Brandoch', such was the easiness that had sprung up
among them and the nature of her own charm—"that
the Tangavaun knows druid ways, and how to employ
them in his own cause?"

Brendan's face closed a little, but the queen's exasperation, no less than her question, needed answering,
and the others at the board were all looking at him.
Only honesty with these...

"I cannot say for sure, lady, but this much I do
know: when Pátraic was slave to Coll mac Gréine he
spent much time observing the local druids and ban-
draoi, how they did things—healed and avenged,
made blessing and bane, raised power, did worship.
The Christom priests are commanded 'Know thy
enemy'; plainly, he spied and gathered what informa-

tion he could, and in his days at Rome did build upon
that knowledge."

Laoghaire gave a short harsh laugh. "Plainly he did!
He says it is God's revealed purpose that he, Pátraic,
should use druidry to destroy itself."

"To my own face he has said it," said Lucet Mael,
nodding. "And to those of my order who have challenged him, and to the ban-draoi also."

"I am myself but an indifferent sorcerer," admitted
Brendan. "Though my mother is rather more... I do
not know what magic may be lawful here, nor can I
offer any, and I feel guilt unspeakable—if I in my
hatred of enslavement had not freed him, he would
not now be threatening our ways."

"If not he, then another," said Duvessa. "Such creatures are thick on the ground these days."

Brendan smiled, grateful for the queen's words.
"Then I will speak to the Tangavaun, and hope he will
hear me, for old times' sake." He paused a moment,
then went on. "Yet also I have been charged to deliver
this message from my mother's kin: 'Tell the king at
Tara from Donn Rígh that there are higher crops than
heathgrass, and roads easier far to the foot than the
Heroes' Way.'"

There was silence a while in the chamber; the fire
could be heard faintly crackling. Then Laoghaire:
"How came that message to you?"

"My mother gave it me before your messenger had
even arrived at Fanad. It seemed she knew I would be
summoned here; but how she knew I cannot say."

"Calatin's daughter," said Cairenn, surprising them
all; she sat against the wall under a canopy of woven
cloth, having listened all this while in silence, and now

she smiled at Brendan, her eyes flint-green in the fire-light. "Greet your grandsir well from me when next you see him, lad. Tell him we have a work to make together before the end, he and I. He will know."

"Lady?" said Brendan, puzzled, just the tiniest bit alerted and alarmed; but he bowed to her as he would have bowed to his own mother, to the queen that Cairenn had been in her lord's eyes and her son's and grandson's, if not in the eyes of the world.

"And the meaning?" asked Amris mac an Fhiach, just when it seemed that no one there would ever speak again.

But Geilis, ban-draoi to Duvessa, spoke up clear and hard. "That the event shall prove."

The next morning saw a sight portentous: in the mist before the sunrise Pátraic and Brendan together walking; on the plain below Tara like brothers they spoke.

Or at least Pátraic spoke, like a stream in spate, until dawn turned to daylight, caught up in the fervor of his faith and his words alike. *By the king's own command to speak to Fanad's heir: to set a capstone of the now upon our lives that were, when we were youths, and maybe even yet to win his soul for Christ! Now that would be a mighty capture—and it would ease my way to capturing so many, many more...*

"God works in strange ways his wonders to perform; his step is set upon the sea, he rides upon the storm... That you, a pagan licentiously mated to one of the Unensouled, should by your pity for a slave be the means of bringing this land to the one true God—surely that is miracle unquestioned."

Brendan looked evilly upon him. *More like a curse foreordained, some fell duergar's jest; at best, dán deserved. In my last life I must have been a very, very wicked person indeed, to have built myself such a fate in this one... And it is cold, and damp, and oh gods I am so hungry—and if he does not keep his tongue off my lady's name and our marriage, I swear to Malen Rhên herself I will rip it out by its dripping bleeding stump... But my king has commanded me bespeak him, and I said I would obey...* He shook himself back into the moment, forced himself to calmness, chose his words with care.

"Aye, well, let us not be so swift to judge of *that*! Gods—whosoever's gods they may be—have their own plans, and no mistaking. What happens, happens; and we may not know until long years hence just whose plan it is that has truly ripened."

For a thought had been set alight in his heart just then, kindled like the tiniest spark in darkness, and he felt the need not to speak of it but to cup his hands round it and blow it into flame, lest it flicker and die in the cold blast that was coming upon Tir Gaedhil. *A long winter till the Goddess's next green spring...*

But Pátraic was drawing breath to speak again, and with a sigh Brendan straightened his shoulders under his cloak, and turned his head again to listen.

When he came wandering back to Tara in the full of morning, Brendan found the place well abuzz. After his talk with Pátraic, he had walked alone in the hills for hours, not feeling himself fit company just yet for decent folk. But catching the mood he went straight to the king's house, and there he met Amris sitting alone

in the hall, stabbing his sgian again and again into the
blameless wood of the table before him.

"Lucet Mael has accepted a challenge from your
Tangavaun," said Amris by way of explanation. He
spoke with a certain grimness: the thing had only been
done within the hour past, against his bitter shouted
advice too, and he was still smarting from the defeat.

"Challenge! But Ferganam is no warrior—what is
the weapon?"

"Magic—what else? The power of Draoícht is to be
tried against the power of the White Christ—"

"Aye, but you saw yourself how Fer—Pátraic!—
dealt with that druid the night the fire was lighted. I
was not here, but I heard all about it, to know that he
has power, right enough—though whence it comes to
him I still cannot tell, not even after the entire morning spent with him rabbiting in my ear. I am told this
Iosa bids the Christom that when one cheek is struck
they must turn the other, but perhaps all his folk have
not yet heard this message—"

*This is so deeply not good…did I precipitate this, did it fall
out so because of our converse in the dawn?* But when Brendan took his trouble to Laoghaire the king at once
cleared that guilt from him.

"Nay, both of them have been nursing *that* chick
ever since the firelighting! That it hatches out now into
a fighting-cock is by no means fault of yours."

But Brendan was not so certain.

The contest between the Tangavaun and the King's
Druid was set for noon; their dueling-ground the plain
between the hills of Slane and Tara. At the appointed

hour, Pátraic and the druid Lucet Mael emerged from
the tents where each had spent the night alone, in
prayer and contemplation according to his own way.
Now walking forward, bareshod, they came to a flat
ground where, drawn up like opposing armies bordering a strange battlefield, Pátraic's followers faced the
nobles of Tara.

When perhaps a dozen feet separated them, the
two principals halted; they bowed to the king and
queen who stood by, and they bowed to each other, and
then, without a word spoken, the contest commenced.

Lucet Mael worked the first working. He reached
his fingers up to the cloudless spring sky; when he lowered them, frost clung to his beard, and those who
watched could see the steam of their breathing in the
suddenly steel-sharp air. And out of clear sky, snow
came whispering down over the bright grass. It dusted
the ground, drifted round the feet of those who
watched, seethed on the new leaves.

With a small brushing gesture of an unraised right
hand, Pátraic melted it, as if he had brought summer
heat up from the earth or down from the sun. Lucet
Mael, untroubled, faintly smiling, turned both hands
palms upward, and the mountains behind them, the
palace crowning the hill, the nearby wood, all vanished, as the céo-draoíchta, the druid-fog, shut down
like weeping veils. But again Pátraic, with little visible
effort, burned it off.

And so it went: for every sorcery of Lucet Mael,
Pátraic had an equally effective counterspell, though,
unlike that night on the Hill of Slane, when he had
summoned the earthshake as not-so-gentle reminder,
he did not venture any magic of his own but was care-

ful to act purely in response. For his part, Lucet Mael
politely but firmly declined trial by water, since he
knew Pátraic used that element to baptize, and could
therefore be expected to have a friendly relation with
it; while Pátraic, equally well aware that druids are
longtime servants of the Secret Fire, demurred with
equal politeness at the suggestion of a flame-contest.

But there were many other magics to their hand,
and over the course of the afternoon they played them
all, like moves on a fidchell board: a thorn-hedge from a
comb cast upon the ground, a net from a single hair,
knives in blades of grass, magic beasts and phantasms
summoned and dismissed, collars that choked, cloaks
that burned—every manner of magic they could devise.

And gradually, Lucet Mael began to structure his
workings so that his opponent must begin to act, not
merely counter. Pátraic was visibly angered, for he saw
where the druid was leading him, but he had no choice
but to respond, and thereafter the magics began to
grow in gravity and power. It was well on to sunset when
Pátraic aimed a sorcery at his opponent; not a Great
Working, by any means, but far more than a pishogue.
And, while both camps watched in the stunned unmoving silence of disbelief, instead of throwing it back
upon its source, Lucet Mael smiled, and opened his
arms to welcome it home.

Thus Lucet Mael, royal druid, died of his own
choice to prove the peril that Christery was bringing
against the Gael, to attest the danger of the Tangavaun
before the people. Though he perished, he took the
victory with him; he left his opponent dumbfound, and
more than a little afraid.

"If the pagans die for their faith even as nobly and

gladly as we do, how are we to prove we are their bet-
ters?" cried one of Pátraic's minions later, when the
throngs had dispersed in deepest silence and the body
of Lucet Mael had been conveyed in honor to the
palace. But to that bitter despairing question the apostle to the Gael—for so he had begun to style himself in
his traha, though as yet in his own heart alone—had no
answer, or at least none that he would give.

In the dolorous aftermath of the death of Lucet
Mael—though Laoghaire the king had even in his own
wrath and sorrow held all of angry Éruinn strictly to the
terms of the duel, that the victor and his folk should go
unharmed and unmolested—Pátraic grew ever more
fearful of being murdered by magic, or assassinated by
more mundane means, even, though none who followed the Shan-vallachta would have sought to do
either, not wishing to take on any part of his dán, or
even the éraic, for such a deed.

But though he continued to declare that he trusted
only in the power of the God he followed to protect
him, from then on Pátraic went privily clad beneath his
rough shirt in a lorica, the wrought-link warrior's sark
that the Sassanaich favored, and as for his followers
they now openly carried blades.

"A fine statement for those who boast of turning the
other cheek!" said Duvessa, smiling scornfully, when she
heard of it. "Well, perhaps he misheard; perhaps his
Tree-god said not 'turning' it but 'arming' it…"

But others were smiling not at all.

*   *   *

A week later, in the deep owl-time of the day he had chosen to depart Tara, Pátraic roused from his devotions as a shadow moved in the deeper shadow beyond the tent. Not fearing, but sensing who it was, and on what mission come, he did not turn but spoke into the darkness.

"Once before you came to me in the deep time of night; and that time brought only good. What would you have of me now? My life? You gave it me that night at Magheramorna; only Christ can take it now, or put it in your mind to take it for him."

Stepping into the firelight, Brendan swept back his hood and grinned at the very idea. "Tempting," he admitted, in an easy tone, "but much too simple, and no doubt it would please you far too much. I will make your White Christ no more martyrs; he has goleor, and will have others still before he is done... But now we must talk, you and I, son of Calpurnius, and by your faith and mine alike I swear that we *shall* talk, as never we have talked before."

And quite suddenly Pátraic felt something akin to relief come over him, and agreed.

They argued for hours, fencing and feinting, no nearer at the end than when they began. Pátraic had begun by charging Brendan as usual with pagan practice, to which Brendan had hotly charged him in return that the name of his faith was not to be used as a malison, that his faith was as true a faith as Pátraic's own; truer, for Pátraic was no true Christling, that in his exercise of power he was no different from a druid, and his duel with Lucet Mael had only proved it.

"Druids control the elements, can strike dead, can change themselves and others into animal shape, are adepts at cursing—you have done all those things, like any druid who ever lived. And—unlike almost every druid who ever lived—you are most vindictive with those who disagree with you. Where druids show tolerance you show only hate and bane and spiritual pride; you yourself hold this to be sin of grave weight, and I swear again, by whatever god you like, neither of us is going to our bed this night until I learn the reason."

"Then *what?*" Brendan drove the despairing question home like a dagger; dawn was beginning to light the sky, and he was bone-tired. "You have hinted and danced round the thing all night long, not only tonight but ever since I have known you, and never have you said, and I grow ever so weary of asking. *What was it?* For clearly there was something; even back on Slemish I felt it—"

Pátraic, just as weary, was silent for a long time, and as he waited for him to speak again Brendan felt the night begin to change around him, the texture of the air and silence palpably altering. *It is coming. Whatever it is, or might mean, or for whom, it is coming now at last, as surely and unstoppably as the sun is coming up to the horizon over yonder...*

"My kin were Christom, and of Rome's flock, as I have many times told you." Pátraic's voice was neutral, unstressed. "But there is more, and this that I tell you now I swear I have told to no living man save the Holy Father himself... When I was a youth in Britain the More, I was given training as a druid."

Brendan sank back against the tree-trunk, closing his eyes. *At last the truth, and it is no more than we all suspected, but still I am surprised to hear him admit to it...*

"In Bannaventa?"

"Nay, eastaways. In Brigantian lands—my mother's home lands. They—and she—held ever to the pagan way."

Brendan's eyes popped open. "You have always told me your kin was purely Roman Christom—was that a lie?"

"No lie. But I spoke only of my father's folk, and we followed Rome for, dare I say it, expediency's sake; my faith in those days was from the teeth outward. When my mother's chief chose me to learn druidry, I feigned obedience and went along, thinking to infiltrate and convert from within."

"Or that you might at the very least learn some useful tricks?"

Pátraic's face did not change. "As you say. But all, ever, only in the service of Christ."

"Indeed." Brendan's voice cut like a sgian. "How pleased with such true service the White Druid of the Tree must be! Even such an unenlightened pagan as myself has heard of how he whipped the moneychangers out of the great temple at Caersalím, so fond was he of liars and of cheats—though there must have been a bit of blood of the Gael in him, for that sounds a thing one of *my* people would have done, none of your famous cheek-turning there… Now I will have the rest of it, for well I know that there is more."

Pátraic's words came low and slow. "There was a young woman of the Iceni, sent as hostage to my mother's tribe when a child. Later her parents were slain, and her people would have had her back, but by then our sett—our small-tribe, our hearth-kindred within the great-tribe—had come to love her, had taken her to our hearts. So we kept her to live among us, sett and flett as we say, and she was well pleased to remain." He fell silent, and Brendan barely breathed. "I met her many times when I was among the Brigantes, and I took her to my heart also. And more than my heart, in the end— She became a priestess of Briginda, the tribe-goddess of the Brigantian folk; I fell in love with her, and she with me, though her guardians, and my mother, were not best pleased. Nor I, even; I had already heard Christ's call in my heart, a pagan priestess had no place there! Then, one Midsummer—in an oakgrove beside a sacred spring—"

Pátraic's voice ceased again, his face was hard and dark as carved wood in the firelight. Then Brendan, very quietly, thinking he knew what might cause such an agony of suffering and shame: "You raped her? In the God's grove, by the Goddess's spring? A most vile deed; but there are éraics for such offense—"

"*NO!*" The word came furious, swift as a flung spear. "Never *rape*—we both—she wanted me as much as I wanted her."

Mighty Macha! Then what in the name of hot horse-apples is the problem... Brendan tried again, more confused than ever.

"But that was right and good, the Goddess loves to see love! And Midsummer is Her marriage-night: as the Annir Choille, the Maiden of the Wood, the Young Queen weds the Young Lord, the Stag-Prince, and lies with Him in the fields; together They bring the summer in. She is the Summer Queen, and rules until Samhain, when She gives place to Her mate the King of Winter— You did no wrong there, only sweet and natural worship."

"I did not see it so. God does not see it so. And when I awoke in the dawn and the girl was gone from me in our shared dishonor, such shame and sin filled me that I cut down the holy wood and blocked the spring with filth…" He was silent, his face turned away; Brendan could not see his eyes. "For that deed I was cursed by the Draoícht and banished from the Brigantes," he went on at last. "It was then that I was taken by Coll's raiders, as I rode home to Bannaventa, and in my sinful disgrace I thought it best that it should be so. I did not fight against capture, did not tell the raiders my name, and so they called me 'Ferganam' and brought me here to Éruinn. The rest you know. I had only Christ left to me, and in my shame I turned utterly to him, and he received me, defiled and impure as I was, as I had in my weakness made me. I am his man now, always, and that for a reason above all other reasons…"

He plunged on like a hill-force, plainly bent now on making clean breast of all. "When I left that night from Magheramorna, I did not head straight to the coast as you did bid me. I went first to our old place in Voclut, and there, in the grove where you saw the Mother of God and I for my sinfulness did not, in penance to God for my offenses—if thy right eye offend thee pluck it out—as éraic I removed, with the sgian you yourself had given me, those parts that had offended."

Brendan did not trust himself to speak for many moments. *Ah, Ferganam, though the dishonor is yours entirely and not in the slightest degree your priestess lass's, I see plain that your god was not the one those parts did most offend…* Then, aloud: "No true and loving god would ever ask for such a sacrifice. The One who made

woman and man equal and like, and gave us union for
our joy—"

"A sinful joy, an evil that must be cut out at the
root." Pátraic's eyes were shining again, and Brendan
had learned long ago to distrust that shine; now it
seemed to him as the glitter of scales upon the side of a
dead and rotting salmon. "In time all will see the foul
shame of the body's vile desires; for Christ's sweet sake
I gave that shame away forever."

"I very much doubt your Iosa requires his followers
geld themselves in either body *or* spirit. The sin, if sin
there even was, was yours alone; even she, and She,
against whom you sinned would never have demanded
such atonement. Whatever honor-price you felt you
owed—to your lover, to the Goddess, to whomever—
you paid for your reasons, not theirs and not the law's.
You say the body is the temple of your god, but you
seem full bent to tear it down. To us who follow the Old
Ways the body and the pleasure it can give are wholesome and sacred, no sin in it."

"Then you must learn your error."

It was no good. He would not be moved. But Brendan, as he turned into the risen sun to head back to
Tara, resolved that this failed attempt should by no
means be the last. *Not even for Laoghaire but for me, for our
friendship of old; not even for that but for himself. He does not
know what Darkness he espouses in the name of Light; and I
fear—oh gods, how I fear!—that he will not be the only one to
suffer for it...*

CHAPTER NINE

"hat explains much," said Laoghaire. He ran a hand over his face, and did not look at anyone else in the room.

Brendan had just related to the king the words he had wrenched from Pátraic in the night. He had not been forbidden to speak of the grueful and startling revelation—indeed, Pátraic had seemed to take it as expected, was eager, even, that his unwilling confidant would do so, that his tremendous sacrifice might be known by all—but all the same the son of Fergus planned on sharing this particular intelligence with very few folk. *Not a thing I would gladly speak of; but the king and queen must know...*

Duvessa stirred where she sat. "Indeed, it explains almost everything! To unman himself as éraic for his offense against the Goddess and the girl—well, if nothing else, at least it shows a proper spirit of repentance. I trust the sacrifice pleased that very strange god of his." To the nervous sidelooks cast in her direction by her husband and her friend: "Oh, come! *Men*— No woman would ever do such a thing! Well, not to herself, any road—"

Brendan shook his head, laughing, almost it seemed in spite of himself. "Nay, lady, the Goddess has given Her daughters far more sense than that… Even so, however great a gift it might have been to lay upon the White Christ's altar, I fear, I think—"

"What?" asked Laoghaire, when Brendan's sudden silence had lasted the better part of a half-minute. But in that same instant Brendan spoke again.

"He will use it, or his masters will, to fasten a halter of fear and shame onto his brother priestlings, and upon folk of the Gael and other races, not even priests but mere souls who follow the Christom way in what they hold to be good faith—the evil teaching that the body is a thing of unclean shame, that only virginity can be pure and have virtue."

Duvessa made a sound of contemptuous dismissal. "A keeve may be kept unused and empty, but I would scarce describe it as virtuous when its plain purpose is to be filled and drunk from! A man may lie with a hundred women, sacredly and lovingly, in the Goddess's name, or with one only in the service of lust; which way is his shame the greater, if shame there is at all? Virginity and purity are by no means the same thing, and this the Goddess has taught us. We know it, Brandoch."

"*We* know," said Brendan after a while; it seemed that he would say more, but though again they waited, he did not.

That summer and autumn passed in uneasy quiet; though Pátraic's conversions continued, they were fewer than he liked, and harder won than he had hoped. His ministry, well established in that most of the Gael were by now aware of it, still seemed to have little effect, if indeed any, on those he most transparently sought to convince and convert: the nobles and royalty of Éruinn, the chiefs of the island and their kin.

"And we see why he hunts such high game," said Brendan darkly to his mother, "for the capture of such souls away from the Shan-vallachta would be the capture of many souls—Rome's purpose. And not forgetting Vortigern's purpose, either—that these preachings and teachings should weaken Tir Gaedhil from our ancient strengths, should turn us from the Warrior's Way, and Vortigern be able to extend his rule across the sea, at less cost to him."

Nia made him no reply, and he did not expect one. Silence was the way with her more often than not these days: since her son's return to Fanad she had been passing more time than heretofore beneath the hill in various palaces of her folk; Brendan did not know if his father ever accompanied her, though he knew that sometimes Etain did. But Nia had spent all summer with her parents Calatin and Súlsha, in the south at Rinn na gCroha, and had broken her return journey at Knockfierna itself—indeed, she was only a few days home again from a secret errand that the king Donn Midna had set her.

As to where and why she went and what she did, she had not said, and her son would not have dreamed of asking. If there was a purpose to it that he needed to know, doubtless she would tell him when time was right; if not, it made no differ if ever she told him at all. He knew her well enough to know at least that. *No question but that there is something afoot here, something high and tremendous in which she plays a strong part, and in which maybe I do also. But I have not yet been told what my role*

*might be in the masque—until I am given my part, what use
to con the lines?*

Midwinter morning at Sidheanbrugh, that ancient
place of many names—Cashel Aonghus, Achadhalla,
Ros na Ríogh, that later generations would call Newgrange. But no matter how folk might name it, it
remained what it had ever been, the Womb of Éruinn;
and would ever be so.

It was an amazing construction: a cave-chamber
delved deep into the heart of the hill Cruach Aogall, a
long corridor opening into a high wide chamber all
faced with smooth stone slabs, under a soaring cor-
belled roof; not a scrap of mortar had been used, but
so tight-fitted were the joins that not a drop of rainwater ever found its way between the stones. No living
soul knew why the long-dead builders had made it, or
even how; those builders were gone and had left no
word behind to speak for them, only that which they
had made—but the theories were many and ingenious,
and they almost equaled the strangeness and the
power that the place possessed.

For on Midwinter morning, alone of all mornings
of the year, the rays of the sun returning to Sidheanbrugh, the Palace Mound of the Sidhefolk, strike past
the great spiral-decorated lintel, of such a size as to be
a doorstep for giants, if any giants there be, through
the carefully framed roof-box above the door, below
the vaulted ceiling, to splinter like a spear of light
upon the farthest wall, the stone heart of the secret
chamber.

That was all. Light shone: no stones walked or

danced, no portals opened to the Otherland, no horn
of omen sounded. Light shone; no more. But why? To
what purpose, or whose? Who was meant to see the sun
strike deep into the inner chamber of Sidheanbrugh,
on the shortest day of the year? The dead? But none
were buried there; or none that anyone knew of. The
gods? And why had the whole enigmatic structure been
so carefully faced in pebbles of the purest white
quartz? Surely not for mere decoration's sake! Nia,
appealed to once by Brendan's friends in heated discussion, had only smiled. But the feast was one of the
great ones, and of all the many holy places in which it
was celebrated Sidheanbrugh was the heart and crown.

For the Christom too that morning was a time to worship; but though Pátraic rang his bell so hard it broke,
it availed him nothing. He gazed seemingly without
understanding at the all but empty clochan and the
emptier hillside outside, where his growing flock had
been wont to gather of a morning before the little altar
table he set for them, and his eyes were dull.

    "I know where they are," volunteered the monk Pyl-
las Nadron, and a stir ran through the little knot of
faithful. He was a new recruit to Pátraic's following, a
Gwalian with pale eyes and light red hair, come over
from Britain the More as a refugee—or so he said—out
of the sink of depravity—again, so he said—that was
pleased to call itself Vortigern's court. Pátraic had welcomed him with uncharacteristic eagerness, admitting
him almost straightway to the inmost of his councils,
and all had seen how often of late Pátraic had come to
take Pyllas's advice over that of his formerly senior fol-

lowers. If they had not been good Christom, they told one another...well!

And at first it seemed, indeed, that Pátraic had chosen to ignore the Gwalian's suggestion, for he spent many moments putting the broken bell carefully away, though none could determine from his countenance what significance he attached to the breaking, or indeed to the careful preserving. But when the bell was swaddled from further harm in spare vestments and safely stowed in the altar kist, he fetched a deep breath and stood up. He did not look at Pyllas, or at anyone else, but spoke lightly.

"Then let us go and find them."

When Brendan rode up to Sidheanbrugh, with Amris on his right and Etain on his left and the usual tail of retainers fanned out behind, it was to behold the familiar throngs come to the holy place for the Midwinter rites, and at once he felt comforted and at home. He glanced up as he dismounted, and for all his ease could not forbear a shiver of deepest awe: the gleaming white quaratz that paved the hillside like ashlar of ice, the dark keyhole opening, the tiny roof-box above the lintel through which the sun would strike. Within the darkness of the chamber, a druid and a ban-draoi waited in the silence and the cold.

But awe strikes chill to the bone here even in high summer... Sidheanbrugh was the oldest of the old, Earth-womb and Lifetomb, the Belly of the Goddess; it reached down to the deeps of earth and the secret places of being. No one knew, even, how it had come there: it had been ancient when the Danaans came from Atland, when the Beaker people, the Folk of the Keeve, had camped roundabout its foot; even the Oldest Ones could not say who had delved it deep into the side of Aogall—or would not.

Each successive wave of incomers to the island, Brendan reflected, each faith, each way, had recognized its sacredness, had honored it and kept it holy. *That is, each until now...*

When a king's rider had come with yet another impassioned letter from Laoghaire and Duvessa, beseeching Brendan return to Tara for the Midwinter feast and bring the Lady Etain with him, Nia's urging had not been necessary to persuade them. It was Etain's first visit to the High King's court: Fionaveragh and Rohan were both away in fosterage—one in Ulidia and the other in the Laighin—and she intended to make the most of it.

When the summons had arrived, she had been eager as a child to go; though, once there, mooned after on the instant by every ox-eyed young noble in the palace, she had perversely grown bored and a touch fretful—though the instant and warmly mutual friendship that had sprung up between her and Duvessa, so much alike were they, did much and more to improve her mood. So that when Laoghaire, hearing rumors, had commanded them go find out what mischief the Tangavaun might be making at Sidheanbrugh on Midwinter morning, she had ridden out ahead of them all.

"I think perhaps Laoch's caution was wide of the mark this time," observed Amris, scanning the eager crowd cloaked and hooded against the winter air. "Not a Christling to be seen here, Brandoch, much less your old Ferganam."

Brendan shook his head. "Early times; he will come, right enough." *And I am so not up for yet another go-around with him, the pestilential bannock… Goddess grant that Amris has the right of it, and we can all have a peaceful Midwinter and hail the sun returning and then go back to our lovely warm beds with our lovelier warmer ladies…*

But even as he looked round once again he saw that his pious, selfish hope was not to be.

Pátraic and his following had prudently ascended the hill from the far side, hidden from the assembly; they now stood before Sidheanbrugh's narrow stone-framed opening, and the angry muttering protest against their presence that was beginning to rise like steam from the crowd below was plainly audible on the still air.

Leaving Etain and Amris amid the throng—having seen at once what Etain was, the respectful crowd stood well away so as not to press her; the honor of their lives, it was, to be in the presence of one of the Sidhefolk on Midwinter morning—Brendan dutifully climbed the hill, pushing forward with a smile and a word when earlier arrivals did not seem disposed to let him pass, and halted a few yards away from Pátraic and his companions.

And yet another Midwinter spoiled… They picked up as if they had never left off, and all the while the light was growing in the east.

"M'chara—even now I will call you friend, the friend of my youth—you are a good man according to your lights. But you are wrong. It is only men who have writ-

ten those words you set such store by. Men. Not
women. Not gods. Not always even good men, if one
may judge by what they say of their fellow creatures and
how they treat them. Iosa of the Tree bids us love our
neighbor; well enough, that is a fine and good message. But it is only half the message. And you are
entirely the wrong messenger."

Brendan and Pátraic had been disputing many
minutes now, but still Brendan's voice was gentle. He
leaned forward, his hand on the other's arm, though
he did not know he touched him, so desperate was his
need to reach.

"This here—this today—this is a thing you *know*! It
is our way, it is in our bones— You were taught it as a
lad; even in Roman Bannaventa you knew it, for it
came to you from your mother's people."

He saw Pátraic's face close against him; the stones
of Sidheanbrugh were now more yielding and less
cold. "And it was a wrong way! By grace of Iosa who is
Christos the truth has been vouchsafed me at last."

"That does not preclude the coexisting of our two
Paths in Éruinn."

The reply came quick as a duelist's riposte. "Two
shepherds cannot share one flock."

"We did so once, even upon the same mountain,"
Brendan said softly reproving, but his heart was cold
within. *No use; he is gone. Between us now, nothing but
war...*

"Iosa is a more jealous shepherd."

Now Pátraic's voice was smug, and Brendan felt
anger returning, hot and warm and inexorable as the
sun whose return they had come that day to hallow.

"Oh aye? Has he himself said so? Or is that only

what others have put into his mouth to say, in the
Whitetongue Book, once he was well dead and could
not prevent them? Kelu in absolute wisdom has made
many roads for souls to travel; all of them lead to the
Light. As voyagers, we may journey as suits us best—
afoot or ahorse or under sail, taking the long way
round, or the prettiest path, or simply the shortest road
home. Even the hardest, if that is our need and we
please to do so. But the choice is ours and ours alone. I
doubt not your Iosa would say the same—if only you
ever let him speak for himself."

But Pátraic shouldered him aside and leaped to
stand forth before the sullen crowd, his face white and
drawn, working with anger and effort and exaltation.

"Do not listen to pagan lies!" he shouted, forgetting
in his excitement that apart from his own followers he
addressed naught *but* pagans, as he would term them.
"Here in this place on this day of Midwinter, I cast the
serpents of the Old Way out of Tir Gaedhil forevermore! The poisonous reptiles shall sting themselves to
death! By the Son of God's coming see the Serpent
Wisdom stripped of its skin!"

He bent to the grass beneath his feet, ripped something from among the winter-wiry stems still green;
when he straightened again he was holding a shamrogue in finger and thumb. But the angry buzzing mutter that had begun to build at his words died away, as
behind him the walls of Sidheanbrugh suddenly flamed.
The Midwinter sun, standing above the horizon, had
caught the quaratz pebbles and set them ablaze, piercing the long dark tunnel opening with pale gold rays;
the three-armed spirals carved on the cavern walls and
doorstep seemed to pulse and spin to greet the light.

Now the power was palpable, the ancient strength and certainty: Pátraic and his followers were swept aside unnoticed in the light-tide that rose in every other soul present. The watching folk cried out in welcome to the Sun Returning, and the priest and priestess who stood within the chamber raised their arms as it came flooding through the narrow opening, to spill light and warmth upon the cold, cold stones at the back of the tomb.

"Hail to the Sun in the South!"

Brendan had cried out with the rest, his arms shaking where he had lifted them up, and knew that Etain and Amris, somewhere below him in the throng, were caught up in the moment also, rapt in timeless unity. *No matter how often I see this, how much lore I learn, the reasons for it, still it is a joy and a wonder to behold! We worship not the sun itself—as the Christom claim, who put on us the name of idolators—but the force that lives in it, the Power that rules the sun, the stars, the moon, the planets, the waters...the One Who made it, Who made all. The sun that dances at Midsummer now begins the road back north, for we have called upon her to return—in the womb of darkness, the rebirth of Light—the Cabarfeidh brings the Sacred Fire back from the south, the living flame between His mighty horns...*

But some there were who saw in this brightest moment only blackest dark... Pátraic still stood there, his face that had been white with fervor flushed now with fury, and he held the torn shamrogue high for all to see.

"Nay, hear now the *true* lesson of this day: hear *me*, people of the Gael! The trefoils of the Trinity have come to replace the Goddess's triskells. This is no longer the Goddess's plant—behold the symbol of the One and

Threefold God!" A shudder ran over the crowd at the
stridency and blasphemy together; their high mood vio-
lated, they seemed uncertain whether to kneel or to
flee.

Not, I think, so fast... Brendan stepped forward to
face the murmuring throng, and never even knew he
did so; his voice rang out on the wintry air like the bell-
mouthed bronze trumpet that summons the clanns to
war.

"The Tangavaun speaks rightly: it is indeed the natural law of things that snakes shed their skin. And this
is a time for shedding. But those skins are shed only to
reveal a newer, finer one; beneath that skin the Serpent
is the same. So this dán I put upon you, Tangavaun:
beneath the new skin you give it, the new names you
may put on it, the ancient way will live and grow. And
that Serpent you can never drive out, for it is Wisdom
and Eternity, and it is coiled round the hearts of the
people as it is coiled round the World Sacrifice Tree.
Whether you call that tree Hethel or Yggdrasil, Creavanore or the Cross, its deep root is the same. You
cannot stop it. You cannot change it. You may mask it,
torture it, call it evil; for a time you may even seem to
win. But you cannot destroy it, and in the end you will
only lose, because though love of Iosa Crann-draoi may
be ever in your mouth, it is only love of power in your
heart. It is not Light you bring them but the Darkness.
The true King in the Light is not yet come among us."

Brendan's voice had grown in power and passion as
he spoke; now it seemed of a strength to shake the holy
hill. Pátraic stared at him, for once bereft of easy
pieties, a look of fear upon his face. Behind him, his
followers—who earlier had drawn back with mutter-

ings and ostentatious crossings of themselves when they caught sight of Etain—now crossed themselves even more vigorously and huddled together, shorn sheep shivering in the windstorm of Brendan's wrath.

But on the slopes below, as his voice fell upon them and they heard his words, the watching Gaelfolk raised a cry, the high jubilant shaking yell heard on the battlefield.

And battlefield it is... Brendan drew a deep calming breath, spoke now only to Pátraic, though he was heard by all.

"We learn through all our lives, all our turns upon the Wheel, to become gods ourselves, to do battle against the Dark on the marches of the stars, the Last Battle that shall win the world or lose it. It is what we are here for. Did you not know? Or has your god not seen fit to tell you?" Brendan turned away from Sidheanbrugh as the sunglory died, and himself bent to pull a trefoil shamrogue, but gently—the Goddess's plant from the Goddess's earth. "You are wrong," he said again, still quietly, and briefly touching the tiny green scrap to his lips he reverently laid it down at the door of the sacred cave, a Midwinter offering. "You are wrong. And you will have to learn which one of us is right."

"They are as children so ignorant they try to milk a bull; the miracle is that sometimes—just sometimes—the bull gives milk." The voice belonged to Etain: the drawling tone was reflective; amused and contemptuous both, it held in Brendan's ear more than an echo of Duvessa's. "Though whether that is a miracle of their god's making or their own is yet to be determined."

Behind them as they rode from Sidheanbrugh back to Tara, they could see the tiny form silhouetted against the stormy sky, black sickle-winged shapes swooping and wheeling and stooping above him: Pátraic on Cruach Aogall, tormented by ravens.

Thanks for that last dramatic touch were due Amris mac an Fhiach, who, exasperated and disgusted beyond all enduring, had before departing with Brendan and Etain raised his arms and summoned the great dark bird that was his fetch, and earnestly petitioned. That magical creature, landing upon his gauntleted forearm like a falcon to the fist, had listened intently, then had closed its wings with a sound like thunder and taken flight. When it returned, Ravens indeed came with it—Malen's own ravens, Lanach and Brónach—and the sacred birds of the War-red War-queen had called all mortal ravens for nine miles round, to harry the Tangavaun, for as long as might amuse them to do so.

"Tha fios fithich aige—thou hast raven's knowledge," observed Brendan mildly. "I see you are not called Son of the Raven for nothing."

Amris shook his head, and the long straight black hair flew like water. "He courts persecution, does he not? Then by all gods let him have some! He should count himself fortunate the folk did not rip him limb from limb... Is he never pleased?" he burst out after a brief silence, aggrieved anew. "How he badgers the very god he swears he fears! For my part I would never presume to speak as he speaks to any deity, whether mine or anyone else's, and I would expect to be slapped silly—and rightly so!—if I did."

Brendan laughed. "Were there an angel about, as

the Tangavaun so often vaunts, well might he warn his
earthly agent 'The Lord thy God is getting bored with
thee.' And who could blame that god for feeling so?
Not that Ferganam would take the warning, mind:
after all, angels have spoken with him before now, and
have proved to be not quite what they seemed; he is
more wary than he might have been beforetimes. But
let us leave him to it—and to his god."

Etain kept her glance straight ahead. "And pray he
leaves us to ours."

CHAPTER TEN

nd so it seemed he did, for a few years more at least. Though the lines of the great rivalry had now been drawn in earnest between Brendan and Pátraic, cut with crosier and claymore into the green breast of Tír Gaedhil, they were drawn elsewhere also, and on a scale of which these two antagonists were utterly ignorant. That Galilean carpenter's son, if he had ever existed, would not recognize what had been cobbled up in his name out of even the good preachings he had made, or the less good ones that had been put into his mouth by now five centuries conveniently silent.

But that is how it is when the mediocre, the time-servers, the weaklings, the lackeys are left as caretakers to the legacies of those great spirits who were their masters and pathfinders: the Sacred Kings and Graal Queens and Sacrificed Deities. The churchmen who so zealously, and jealously, claimed the Crann-draoi's spirit for their own were at the same time hungrily acquisitive, as their gentle teacher had never been, of worldly wealth and power (though he too had made use of such when he had need, and rightly rendered it up where it was due). Busy consolidating their political and material gains all across the known world, soon they would turn their full attention to the conquest of Éruinn. But it would not be easy, and it would be long in coming: in the end the victory would be accomplished only by treachery and seduction, not by fair persuasion and not by honest conquest—and it would never, ever, be complete.

For now, most of the Gael were content to dismiss the attempts on their ancient way of life, thinking them but aberrations surely bound to fail—and who could blame them for thinking so, who would have dreamed it would be so staggeringly otherwise? But the true measure of their contempt was a simple thing: the byname they gave the clerics who so attempted. They called such men Crómmaun, 'crooked'—and not just for the crosiers that they carried.

For a while, though, Tir Gaedhil lived under a strange, strained peace. The two warring faiths moved along in uneasy coexistence, as Brendan had hoped and suggested; across the water, Vortigern seemed content merely to watch, and in any case he was about to have very great grief and trouble of his own—not the least of which would be dealt him under the lessoning sword of that young captain out of the West Country. Though Pátraic had not wavered in his opposition to the Shan-vallachta, at the least he now knew enough to preserve diplomatic silence, to mostly avoid negative confrontations; he pursued his convert prey in a newly discreet manner, which brought him unexpected floods of success, especially among the chieftains he had so eagerly sought for their great and general influence.

And if Brendan sometimes longed to rip the new creed out by the roots, grub it up like vetchweed in a

grassy clune, still he kept to his own path and policy of
tolerance and peace, still clinging to the hope that the
two ways might survive side by side.

   But it was a matter of sands in a glass. Time was running out: one way or another, one faith or the other
must triumph—and one way or another, the champi-
ons of both knew it.

The summer weather that year had been chancy and
unpredictable: hot and dry for weeks at a time, so that
the roads turned to white dust; then full of endless cold
rain and blustering winds that stripped parched leaves
from brittle branches. Later, some would claim it was
the freakish weather that had brought the destruction
across the Eastern Sea from Britain the More, though
which may have been the guilty carrier, the sulter or
the chill, none could say for sure.

   But there was no doubt whatsoever that destruction
had come: that summer fell like a mailed fist upon Tir
Gaedhil the first blow of the buidhe-chonnaill, the yellowstalk ill, that terrible and mysterious pestilence that
had already slain a fourth of the population of all the
western lands. From Gaul right back through Rome
itself it had run, down to Grecaia and north to Rhenia;
even the Helvetic lands behind their mountain ram-
parts, safe from all other conquerors, had not been
able to defend themselves from the plague's heavy
hand. Its name well described it: those afflicted were
blotched sallow as withered cornstalks; they wasted
almost as thin, and died as swiftly. The healers of the
Gael were as helpless against it as their counterparts in
the other lands had been; in Éruinn, the yellowstalk

was preceded by famine and dearth, and its follower in many districts was leprosy.

Pátraic, preaching now in Connachta—that wild-hearted strong-willed province proving as stonily resistant to him as to the pestilence, or as to a pestilence of another sort—flatly declared the plague and its attendant afflictions to be God's incontestable judgment upon pagans, the faerie folk and their friends and kin, all those who kept the Old Ways, who had been so perverse and obstinate in their defiant refusal to accept the Tree-druid's way.

"No surprise there!" said Brendan, when word of Pátraic's claims came to his ear in Fanad, which had so far been spared the worst of the plague.

"He is blessing certain rivers and cursing others," said Fergus, shaking his head, "and has been especially diligent in appropriating holy wells and rededicating them to his god, claiming miraculous cures will soon come of it—though we have seen no evidence of that, at least not so far. But with the yellowstalk running through the land like groundfire, desperate folk will take any hope of cure they can find. If he can cure as he boasts he can, he may win many to his side over this."

Caught by an odd note in Fergus's voice, Brendan looked at his father, truly looked, and truly saw him, for the first time in perhaps many years. *He has grown older*, he thought, surprised and shocked to realize it, likewise at himself for not having seen it sooner. *Weary, too; I must take more from his shoulders, as much as I can, to ease him—if he will allow…*

"He has claimed the Struell-wells for the Crann-draoi," said Nia quietly. "And bidden folk come there to get healing of his god."

Brendan looked at her for a long moment, and she met his gaze serenely. *She sees something I do not; this is bound up with her secret purpose these last few years, though how it fits I cannot imagine. Still—*

"What will you do?" asked Fergus. "Will you speak to him?"

"Why is it all for *me* to do?" he snapped, all at once cross, but not with his father. "I *have* spoken with him, you know, and more than once too! At my king's command and out of boyhood friendship, I have argued and debated, I have squabbled and disputed, I have reasoned and considered and discussed. I have had revelations. I may even have been able to seed revelations of my own. But I have not—as you may have noticed—been able to turn the spate. He is more glib and persuasive than a púca; few seem able to resist him once he is roused to speak. Though goleor now are set against him, more are inclining toward—novelty has ever been the downfall of the Gael. What of you?" he asked, turning to Nia. "Will *you* act? Will your folk—our folk?"

"Go to the wells," said Nia after a little silence. "See how it is with those you find there. Act as you are moved to. Then we will speak again."

The scene at the Struell-wells was enough to make a stone weep: folk sick with the yellowstalk ill, some nigh to death, strewn like fallen leaves among the little dells and mossy corries bordering the sacred springs. Fevered children lay limp and still in their parents' arms, men and women drooped strengthless against the boulders: the young and strong struck down as hard as the older and weaker, the patchy color of the dreaded sickness plain upon them all.

Brendan, who had ridden over as his mother had enjoined him, to see for himself the plague's ravagements, was wrung with pity for the sufferers.

"It is like the aftermath of a battle, and they the conquered army… They have come here in hopes of some cure, any cure," he said to his friend Ríonach Sulbair—'of the pleasant speech', and her low sweet voice bore the byname out—and his young cousin Donn Aoibhell, a Fian aspirant up from Killary on a visit, both of whom who had accompanied him. "They care not whence healing comes, or from whose hand, so long as it does come, and who can blame them? It is a cruel thing, what he has wrought here. But we will see what may be done."

Even as he spoke he was looking round for the one he well knew he would find there, absently fingering all the while the ties of a leather sack that hung at his saddlebow. Etain had given it to him privily before he left Clanadon, with very clear instructions as to how he was to use its contents…

Then he saw him, Pátraic, the Tangavaun. They had not set eyes on each other for more than three years, and even from a distance Brendan could see that his adversary was greatly altered. *Older, thinner, more worn—nay,* used—*he looks as one of those wights in the old tales, who venture into a palace of the Sidhefolk to revel and dance and come out again next morning, as they think, but it is a hundred years later…* He paused, constrained by honesty. *Worn, used, aye; but stronger than ever now, like a fire-tempered blackthorn, hard as iron; his purpose has refined him. He would always break sooner than he would bend, but now he will shatter long before he will snap...*

If Brendan had been expecting to find Pátraic at the Struell-wells, just as clearly Pátraic had been expecting him to come; the spark of recognition and unsurprise had been plain to see. As his adversary piously sketched a blessing in the air, Brendan felt annoyance spark just as plain, and spoke first, calling out across the hillside that separated them.

"I had heard you were here working cures in your god's name; pity it is that I see so little result for the effort!"

Pátraic refused to be drawn, though the tone even more than the words flicked his pride on the raw.

"The One True God works in his own good time. Perhaps these are too sinful to be saved, or God has merely ordained that they should perish."

"Oh, aye, perhaps indeed—and only a god of love would say so! Well. Easy enough for gods to take their time in such matters: though they have more calls upon it than mortals may, also they have more time at their disposal. But time runs short for these suffering folk; it seems your god will not spare the time to cure them."

"If my God will not, certainly your Goddess cannot!"

So easy to bait him, for all his tempered ways! But lives are at stake here, I have neither time nor inclination for yet another bootless gibefest... Brendan smiled, and throwing his right leg over his horse's neck slid lithely to the ground; though he was by no means close by, Pátraic took a hasty step backwards, and Brendan's smile widened to see it.

"You shall judge."

Ignoring the tirade that broke from the other Christom who were present, though Pátraic himself said no word more, Brendan made his way down the slope to where most of the worst afflicted lay, out of the wind and near to the healing spring, and slung off his shoulder the leather sack that had been tied to his saddle.

Kneeling, he plunged his hands into the cold waters of the Struell-wells, sacred to the Lady time out of mind. His thought fled back to that spring high on Strivellin, and the One who had met him there, the day he left the south; and he besought Her without pride, as mighty Dâna, and as Armída also, goddess of these springs, as he had prayed her the last time he and Pátraic had met in this place. *You knew, Lady, right enough… In Your name I do this, to prove Your power; if it is not counter to their dán, then heal these poor sick folk for their sake, not for mine, nor even for Your own…*

Rising, he turned to the stricken, and spoke easily, in a voice that carried across the hillside, to reach all ears.

"This remedy the Sidhefolk have given; it comes as gift, by the command of Donn Rígh himself. Though the Goddess could wave Her hand and all Éruinn be healed in the twinkling of an eye, this is how She chooses to work, by Her own natural powers that are of Her own natural world—the world that She created. Take your cure of the Sidhe, then, and of the Goddess, and the Goddess's holy earth. Heal and be healed."

Opening the leather sack, Brendan removed small folded linen packets of powdered herbs, passing them out to those who could still cope, giving clear simple instructions as to the dosage. To the weakest he ministered directly, kneeling to help them sit up, holding

their ravaged bodies in the curve of his arm, pouring
between their cracked dry lips the infusions that Donn
Aoibhell and Ríonach Sulbair worked swiftly to make,
mixing the herbs with the water of the wells. The healers and bards and sorcerers who had come, who had
been helpless to help, now leaped to assist him, glad of
something they could do. All was forgotten now but
the task: as he went among the victims of the buidhe-
chonnaill Brendan spoke soothing words that worked
a magic of their own, so that the sick ones brightened
at his touch, and the hope that was as necessary as the
herbs for their healing leaped up like a white flame as
he passed.

"Soon now, better now, much better, aye, good, better straightaways, only drink. You shall see. Drink.
Drink. Heal—"

It did not matter what he said; the mere sound of
his voice was enough, the murmured repetition, the
soothing assurances, the air that clung to him of certainty and trust—and his plain absolute faith in the
power of the Goddess to heal them. And it was not lost
on them, that faith: they heard, and they drank the
herbal drench as he bade them; when they lay down
again, though still in weakness and weariness, it was
somehow a different weariness, as if healing had been
gently wrapped around them like a soft warm blanket.
And all the while Pátraic and his folk watched in stony
silence.

When at last all had been attended, the remaining
remedy parceled out to be brought to those too sick
even to come to the wells, and the healers and the
bards well instructed in how to make more, at last
Brendan turned to look at Pátraic, and his heart almost

failed him at what he saw in the other's face.

Can he be so selfish of his claimed prerogative, such a fox in the grain-kist, as to actually begrudge them their cure, merely because his own precious god did not accomplish it? Or is it that I accomplished it, that so inflames him? Either way, it is very evil; but does the evil lie within him or upon his Path? Which would be worse, for Éruinn or for him? He has hated me from the beginning, I see that now—though I have never been able to puzzle out just why: for who I was, or for what I am? Envy because I was Danaan, or because I was a free man? And what of the others who follow, or who will follow? The Sidhefolk may have magic or specifics to heal many ills of body and of soul— but I think there is no herb or rune or rann even among them to give the cure for such an ill as this...

"A fine day's work," said Ríonach quietly, as they rode back to Creavanore. "And not just yours but Etain's, and Donn Rígh's... But however much good you have done here and everywhere—oh, and Brandoch, it is so very much!—I think I need not tell you it has done you no good with the Christlings, whatever."

Brendan shrugged. "That was plain or ever we rode to the wells. A cure that the Sidhefolk gave to mortals— the Goddess's magic!—I should have known he would see it so. For such a one, the end can never justify the means—unless of course that end is of his own making."

"Maybe so," said Donn Aoibhell, "but can his means justify the end?"

And to that they had no answer.

Word of what had happened at the Struell-wells raced across Éruinn with greater celerity than even the yellowstalk, cure and word alike spread by healers and druids and ban-draoi who made very sure folk knew where their healing had origin, and to whom the thanks were owed; and the plague was soon ended. A miracle, many said, and blessed the name of Brendan and the Sidhe in equal measure. And they were right. But a new plague, and a worse contagion by far, would soon spring up from the yellowstalk's unhallowed grave.

"Where is the lord of Fanad, girl? Quick now! I have business with him."

It was a month or two after the last of the buidhe-chonnaill, a fair warm day of early autumn. Beneath the covin-tree at Creavanore, where she had been sitting in calm happy contemplation, young Fionaveragh looked up at the newcomer who had hailed her, having reined in his horse just beyond the great yew's shadow. One of the shavepate monks of the Crann-draoi, she supposed, unimpressed, though it was unusual for one of Pátraic's minions to be mounted, and more unusual still for any Gael to be so rude. In any case, she liked neither the stranger's manner nor his manners, or rather his lack thereof; but she had been taught the courtesy of her rank and her race—both her races—and it did not fail her now. Even so, in the one level three-second glance with which she favored him she saw no reason to bestir herself from where she sat—and that was purely manners of her own.

"Aye, well, and the greeting of the One and the Three to you too... I am Fionaveragh, daughter of Brendan and Etain; you are welcome to Creavanore."

And all this was ritual politesse, which the stranger should certainly have been the one to initiate. "If you inquire of my father," she went on coolly, "he has ridden south a week since on business of his own; if you speak of my grandsir Fergus, he is within. As are my mother and granddam," added Fionaveragh, after a moment's thoughtful pause, as if she had only just remembered, "perhaps you care to speak with *them...*"

She smiled like a cat to see the alarm flicker over the sharp-featured face—*He knows, right enough!*—and without another word the monk turned the coarse garron he inexpertly bestraddled and kicked the tired patient beast back down the track. Fionaveragh watched until he passed the forest turning, then went like the wind in bare feet up the steep hillside behind the maenor, to a secret stone-built lookpost just beyond the crest, where she could spy on the road to the south and not be seen.

Aye, there he rides; but see now, three others meet him. Plainly they were lurking about waiting on him while he rode to our house, or perhaps they have just now joined him; but either way, why did not they too come to the house? She drew back suddenly as one of the newcomers gestured in her direction; though she knew he could not see her at that angle and distance, her fingers instinctively flashed to weave a quick concealment, all the same.

Now it seemed that the monk too was gesturing and arguing, disputing with the other three; but after a good quarter-hour's discussion they seemed to come to some agreement, for as one they wheeled their horses and flung off furiously southwards, away from Creavanore.

When, straight down off the hill, she told her

mother and her grandmother of the curious incident, Fionaveragh saw them exchange a swift look. *And a swifter thought behind it…or do they think me still too much a youngling to have noted, or that I would be feared of it? I have had my moonrites, I am* not *a baby—*

"Nay," said Etain, smiling, "that is not it at all! Lass though you are, it seems you are grown enough and 'ware enough now to See; therefore you are old enough to know. It is only that there is little enough to tell… Some of the Tangavaun's minions are seeking your father—no new thing there."

"But not to hurt him? Because he cured the yellow-stalk? Did I do right to say he was from home? They would not go south after him, would they? Or come again here, now they know he is away?"

Etain put a comforting arm round her daughter. "You did nothing wrong! They would have learned all that in any case, merely by asking round Fanad; it is no secret where your father has gone, nor need for it to be so. As to the yellowstalk cure, they already know all about it. I promise you, hen, your father is perfectly safe, and so are we; your grandsir is here, and all the folk of the maenor, and Coll mac Gréine is near as ever, in the unlikely event we should need his sword." She grasped the girl's shoulders, gently, turned to face her. "Listen now, alanna, and take a lesson here… When you give knowledge, by the way you give it you can—sometimes—control the way in which it will be used. And by that giving—sometimes—you can learn more from how it is received and who receives it than the one who receives it may learn from it and you."

Fionaveragh took it in bright-eyed. Seldom had her mother spoken to her as if she had been a grown woman herself; though in recent months such occasions had become more frequent, they were no less thrilling. As a very young child, she had seen that her adored mother and worshipped grandmother were different from the other women she knew, at least the ones who dwelled on the maenor and in the country roundabouts. Later, a little older, instructed now, she was able to understand the nature of that difference; but only very recently had she come to realize that the same power she so admired in them was growing within herself. *Perhaps that is what mamaith means here...*

"Your heart misgave you for good reason," said Nia then; she had been watching the girl's face, following the play of emotions. "Glad and proud am I indeed, to know you have such instincts, ingheann, and such a gift! But it is not enough merely to See: what is Seen might not yet be, and might not ever come to pass. That is how it is with Sight. You carry more Danaan blood within you than blood of the Gael, three parts to one; because of that, you will ever be more open to such things than the great run of the Gael—though they are by no means ungifted in that capacity. But because you are Gael as well, one part in four, you will ever have more of a hold on the world around you than the great run of Danaans—and that is a different sort of gift."

"And my brother?"

"Rohan will be a man," said Etain. "His gifts will be different gifts—a man's gifts, as your gifts will be a woman's. His will be no greater than yours, no less— only different. But we speak now only of you."

"Will it make a difference?" the girl asked eagerly. "That I have both bloods?"

Etain smiled, and made some soothing small reply. But Nia did not answer at once, and her countenance remained grave; in her somber stillness she suddenly appeared to her granddaughter as a great sibyl, a sorceress, mighty queen of unknown and unknowable powers. Fionaveragh felt touched with awe, daunted—feared, even—as never she had been before in her granddam's presence, and without even knowing she did so she shrank back a little against her mother's side.

Nia's answer, when it came, did nothing to ease her. "On that difference may dán itself depend."

CHAPTER ELEVEN

is daughter had told no untruth. Brendan had ridden to the south on business indeed: he had gone to Rinn na gCroha, to properly thank the Sidhefolk healers who had compounded it for their great gift to the Gael, the specific that had put lasting paid to the yellowstalk ill. But though he did not yet know it, there was another reason as well, one he had not put into thought, much less cast in words; if Etain and Nia had seen its shadow in his eyes, or on his soul, they were keeping their own counsel on the matter, or if they confided at all, had confided only in each other. But Súlsha divined his problem as soon as she set eyes on him; and, like all grandmothers everywhere in all times, she knew well how to draw out of him that which he maybe would not have said to any save herself alone…or at least not yet.

"If you had the power to do as you pleased, against the Tangavaun?" she asked one day, with apparent carelessness, as they walked on the open side of Strivellin. "I know you see him as an enemy: but would you stop him and his word? If you could? Would you turn him, or slay him, or find another way?"

Brendan gave a short laugh. "However much it would please me to put a stop to him—and it *so*

would!—there will only be another after him with
another word, or the same word. Or a worse word." He
paused a moment, then continued, slowly, wonderingly,
as if he were shaping the thought for the first time; as
perhaps he was. "Still—I have thought, sometimes, that
I would liefer remove us from the problem than the
problem from us: that it might be easier, too, a better
solution. To take our folk out of Éruinn before the new
faith has rooted so thick that no shoot of our own way
can ever again find space to grow. Before Pátraic raises
some of the new Christom lords against us in earnest."
He gave his grandmother a sidewise glance. "And before
we forget completely that highest lore we brought with
us from Atland, and from the stars before that; we never
think of them now, dama-wyn, never speak of them or
employ them, those ways and designs—you have seen
how we forget. We came here from far stars, if that is a
true telling, and I see no reason to make me think it is
not. How if—well, if we were to go back there? To leave
Éruinn—" He broke off, amazed at his own thought and
words, not having meant to say so much, not knowing
that so much was meant.

But Súlsha said only, in a calm even voice, "A terrible thing, to leave your own land."

"A worse to remain, maybe," he returned. "If the
Tangavaun prevails, as it is beginning to seem he will,
we shall soon be strangers at home, exiles in Éruinn.
There will be no place here then for us, or any like us:
by then we might not be able to leave even if we should
wish to—might not be permitted to." Brendan gave a
dismissing flick of his fingers, made a small exasperated sound. "The purest ashling, any road—where
even among the stars could we live as we choose, with-

out fear of incomers, and how could we get there even if we found it?"

"That is beyond my knowing, amhic," said Súlsha, and she kissed her grandson unexpectedly, smiling at his surprise, then paused for the briefest instant—a complete stillness of mind and body—before she spoke again. "But if you go to Knockfierna, and ask that question of Donn Rígh, it is on me you will have your answer—or an answer."

Brendan glanced involuntarily to the north and west. The mountains that rose between barred his sightline, but he knew well enough where it lay— Knockfierna, palace of Donn Rígh. Donn was high king over all Sidhefolk in Éruinn; the tales told of him were many and wondrous. Oldest of the Old, they called him, and other names beside. *Truth! To such a lord such matters as these must be less than nothing, and any road he may not much care to aid mortals in their woes...* Then he remembered the aid Donn Rígh had given in the matter of the yellowstalk cure, and was a little less doubtful; and when he remembered his kinship and acquaintance also he was less doubtful still.

"I have only ever met Donn Rígh the once," he said aloud, "when Etain and I stood before him to be married; though we are great friends with the prince his son... If anyone would know— But I would not wish to trouble him."

"It is on me that you will trouble him more times than once before all this is done," said Súlsha presently. "Yet it is also on me, right enough, that he will think it no trouble at all..."

*　　*　　*

Three days before Brendan had planned to ride home to Fanad, a visitor came to Killary: the Gwalian monk Pyllas Nadron, as ambassador from Pátraic himself. Domhnall Avarcagh and Aoifa Fínneachta, though not best pleased when they learned who their unexpected guest was, and on whose business he had come, nevertheless offered correct hospitality, as far as the law required and not a whit more—though with a politeness so icy that it was only just short of chargeable insult.

But Pyllas, well aware of the nature of their courtesy, and the reason also, ignored them; he had come a-purpose to speak to Brendan of Fanad, and the morning after his arrival, he sought a private word…

When Brendan at last stopped laughing, he looked sidewise at the monk; chagrin sat hot and red on Pyllas's face, but the eyes fixed on Brendan were clear and cold.

"Ah me—I have not laughed like that for far too long, count upon the Tangavaun to give good mirth… Well. First, I am no sorcerer, monkling, so do not even dream about it!" Brendan informed him, still smiling. "More to the point, I was there when your master and the king's late druid, the noble Lucet Mael, had their own little contest at Tara some years back. Oh, aye, I was forgetting, you had not yet seeped over from Britain the More—well, you missed something, though I am sure you have heard all about it. And now you suggest that I should meet my former friend the former slave in yet *another* duel of druidry? I do not think so!"

"The holy Pátraic has already agreed to such a contest." Pyllas had long since decided to refrain from making public the knowledge that he himself had put

it into Pátraic's head to offer a combat of faith—
though the Tangavaun had eagerly accepted the suggestion, as he did so many of Pyllas's making these
days. "He is eager to prove once for all the power of the
new way, the true way of Iosa Chriesta, over the old
pagan practices to which so many of you benighted
souls so stubbornly cling."

Beneath Brendan's brown beard, a glint of bared
teeth, though neither he nor Pyllas seemed sure it was
a smile.

"I do not doubt that eagerness! Especially since he
has had so much more time to practice since his last—
encounter."

Pyllas sketched a small bow. "As you say. But his
offer is to meet any champion of the Old Ways at Tara;
it need not, of course, be you. Still, it seems to me that
you, lord—you who are Gael and Danaan both—standing forth for the Shan-vallachta, and my master as the
voice of Iosa in Éruinn, whom you yourself set free to
do God's work—you two are destined for this. Who has
ever heard of such a contest, or would dare dispute the
outcome as dán?"

"No one," Brendan told him flatly. "And no one
ever will hear of it, or dispute it either, because it is
never going to happen. That is dán too, if anything is."
*And if it is also true—or merely dán—that no good deed goes
unpunished, then I am well and endlessly chastened—but
must all Tir Gaedhil be chastened with me?*

For all his refusals, though, so far did Brendan
allow himself to be swayed that, rather than riding
home to Fanad, he slipped away from Killary, alone, in
the night, and galloped straight north to Tara, there to
crave speech of Laoghaire mac Niall who was his

king—and his friend. But for all his precautions, his nightride did not go unobserved.

At Tara, oddly enough, his arrival seemed a thing utterly expected; Amris mac an Fhiach fell on his neck with a great welcoming shout; and others of his close acquaintance—Conn Kittagh, a Fian commander, and his mate Shane Farrant; Corlis Typhult, a ban-draoi friend of Etain; Ríonach Sulbair; a few more—also greeted him with delight, though they gracefully put by his amused gibes as to what an incredible 'stonishing coincidence, that they should all chance to be there, at all...

That night he supped privately with Laoghaire and Duvessa and Amris; over supper, and ale after for which some of the others joined them, Laoghaire gave him terse account of the gains the Christom had made over the past year, and Brendan was struck afresh by fear at the extent of Pátraic's successes.

"I had no idea—"

"Nay, well, we scorn him still, as you know—and ever shall; but since you were last here we have found it—expedient to alter somewhat our public stance. I tell you this now, so that it does not come as a surprise to you; either way it is unpleasant, better that you hear it first from us. Truly, my sorrow to admit it, we now give him certain face and precedence: indeed, we must, for in spite of what you wrought at the Struell-wells, for which all Éruinn is forever in your debt"—Brendan waved a dismissive hand—"and what others have done in other places, many are being swayed by his words. Too many." Laoghaire scowled, and poured out more ale. "And that is the truth of it."

"And that would be because—"

Duvessa made a sound that in any other creature would have been a snarl, and began to pace like a panther. "Because they are sheep and slothels and cowards; and never did I think to say that of any Gael! Sometimes, I tell you, I am ashamed to be queen of such a people— The Shan-vallachta is a demanding way, and a rewarding one; until now, it has been the only way we knew. We were made for it, and it for us: dán, and the Wheel, the great cycles of Abred through Annwn and Gwynfyd—it requires each man, each woman, to bear responsibility for themselves, to think and choose for themselves, tried and tied by their own actions over many lives, to save their souls alive. Perfection must be fought for and striven for, and that is how it should be for a warrior race. But the Way of the Tangavaun is easier far: all folk need do is admit sin and unworthiness, and accept the Tree-druid, and then sit back and let him do all the work. And to my everlasting sorrow and disgrace, far too many of our people seem to be willing to hand themselves over."

"Nay, Duvách, hold not back, tell us how you truly feel… As I rode here I heard that he has newly won over major chiefs of high standing," said Brendan cautiously. "And that Turlough king of Cashel has just turned Christom man?"

The mood in the room altered instantly: Amris and Ríonach and the rest were already rocking helplessly; in spite of her wrath even Duvessa's delicate shoulders began to shake. Laoghaire was grinning from ear to ear, though he spoke to the others with mock rebuke.

"'Tis no laughing matter, queen at Tara, king's counselors—but had you only been there to see, Brandoch!"

"This is what I am always saying—but why so merry?"

Duvessa, her fury momentarily forgotten, was fighting back with main force the mirth that threatened to double her over. "Turlough being after all a king, the Tangavaun and his creatures decided to have the saining rite—baptism, they call it—out of doors in public on the hill of Cashel, so all could see and more of the weak-minded be perhaps swayed to follow suit. Well. Midway through the ritual, the Tangavaun dramatically drove his crómag into the turf, or so he thought. Now you have seen that thing he carries, Brandoch, its point is so sharp that it might be a spear; and you know how vague old Turlough is— Instead of going into the ground, the point went straight through Turlough's bare foot. When the rite was done, and Pátraic looked down to see the grass and his own feet all over blood like a stuck pig, and his new Christom lamb nailed fast to the sod, he asked why in God's name Turlough had not spoken up. And Turlough, Goddess bless his pointed little head, replied that he thought it was all part of the ceremony…"

For many moments the hall was ripped up crossways with laughter; at last Brendan, wiping his eyes, shook his head.

"Nay, but we should not laugh—" Which only set them all off again, sobbing and aching; and gasping apologies to the king for his precipitate exit, Brendan fled to his chamber while he still had a breath left to him. He fell bonelessly onto the soft bed, head buzzing with ale, while fresh hilarity tore him in two every time the indelible picture recrossed his brain. *'Once a shepherd knows how stupid sheep can be': if all Pátraic's sheep are*

*as stupid as Turlough, perhaps we are worrying ourselves
needlessly— All the same, it is on me that it will take more
than a spear through the foot, however public—even through
his own foot—even through his throat—to stop him...*

Two days later, with a train and pomp that would not
have disgraced the Tassans himself, Pátraic arrived at
Tara. No humble goatskin tents for the son of Calpurnius these days: he deigned to accept lordly accommo-
dation in the palace of Rath na Ríogh, as if it were his
by birthright, while his followers made noisy shift to
dispose themselves in the valley between Tara and the
scene of his first victory—as they accounted it—the hill
of Slane.

All amusement set aside—though one would be
less than honest to deny that on first sight there might
well have been a grin or two, a mirthful quiver at once
put down—Brendan grimly watched the arrival from
the edge of the crowd. *The king was right, it is no laughing matter... Name of Dâna! He behaves as if he were royalty
himself; wraps himself in the mantle of Iosa Crann-draoi and
the dubious sanction of the Tassans. Well—'Once a slave
makes the worst of masters.' Now let us see if that indeed is
truth...*

The next morning Pátraic celebrated the rite of
Christom mass—not atop Tara's hill, that would have
sat too ill with too many, but in the vale below—and
Brendan, again watching from a distance, was unpleas-
antly surprised to see how many of those who dwelled
in Tara's halls, how many chiefs of neighboring districts, were in rapt attendance. As they had warned
him, even the king and queen themselves made an

appearance—though they arrived late, left early and were deeply shamed about it after, that they had seemed to give the Tangavaun countenance before the folk.

Duvách was right: they do see it as an easier way, where they do not have to think for themselves. They can be as weak as they please, and their choices and weaknesses will not be brought to bear on them, as is the way with dán, but forgiven, over and over again, as long as they grovel suitably to the priestlings and beg forgiveness and lay all at the foot of the Tree-druid. Truly, they are sheep...

Apart from that, though, Brendan stayed well away from any chance encounter he might have with Pátraic, coming upon him face to face only once, one evening upon entering the grand banqueting-hall of Midhchuartaigh, where the practice was for all at Tara to take the nightmeal in the king's company. They inclined their heads to one another in civil greeting, but had no more interchange than that one cool moment, though as Brendan brushed past, for once passionately glad of the chieftainly rank that gave him precedence in entering and a seat far removed from the place Pátraic would have at table, he caught sight of Pyllas Nadron, smirking at him from behind his master's shoulder.

But when once more in private with the king and a few others, and the subject of the combat touched upon, Brendan unburdened himself at length, with clarity, point and no small wrath. Some of his account of his long history with Pátraic was news to some of those there, and they were frankly amazed.

"He is a pious fraud, and worse, and he will be damned by his god for it," said Laoghaire bitterly. "He claims the purity of the Christom way—certain it is he riveted *that* particular fetter onto himself beyond all breaking!—but as we have seen, he is not above using druidry to his own purpose when it suits him to do so, and blasting it when it does not. Why should we think he will not do so this time also? And Brandoch, though doubtless he has magic to him of his mother's kin"—he looked inquiringly at Brendan, who shrugged but said no word—"is no druid."

"A fraud, aye, this Tangavaun, but a clever one," said Conn Kittagh. "He uses words like weapons, twists meaning like knotwork, steals our symbols and corrupts them to his use; he confuses the folk with similarity and unreason, and they are finding it harder and harder to resist. And some of them do not wish to; they see little differ between his way and ours, and it is easier to give in than to fight."

"Then why do you push Brandoch into this duel?" demanded Ríonach Sulbair.

"Who is pushing?" protested Amris with all innocence. "Have we pushed? Has the king pushed? The challenge was issued to any who would stand forth to champion our ways; Brandoch, does your traha tell you it must be you?"

"It might!" snapped Brendan. "And if it did not, I have a feeling that yours would!"

"Ah well, as to that now—" began Amris, but the ban-draoi Corlis Typhult spoke across him, quick and suasive.

"Nay, Brandoch, it must be someone, and for those very reasons that the odious little monkling gave you—and if he is not a spy for Vortigern, then I am no priestess of the Lady!—it must be you, because you bear the

blood of Gael and Danaan together. That is why the
Tangavaun is so eager to face you: he knows that if he
defeats you, he defeats us all."

"But if you win—" said the queen Duvessa into the
sudden thoughtful silence; and though they waited,
she left the rest unsaid.

Though for all the folk knew no champion had yet
been found to accept Pátraic's challenge, the combat
was nevertheless set to take place. Laoghaire, appealed
to, had chosen the Hill of Tara as the site, the feast of
Samhain as the time. "For as we know the walls between
the worlds are thinnest then," he had said, explaining
his choice to his counselors. "And it is on me that we
shall need all the help we can get—from both sides of
the Door." To which they had all of them fervently
agreed.

So it was, a few hours before sunset on the evening
of Samhain, that all Tara assembled itself in the open
space upon the palace's western frontage, a broad
grassy faha that fell away downslope, affording a view
on three sides, by reason of the hill's height, of half the
cantreds of Éruinn. Laoghaire and Duvessa, and the
Lady Cairenn, had chairs set for them; all others stood,
or sat upon the turf.

Brendan had placed himself a little apart, where
he would not be immediately visible to Pátraic and his
minions, who were even now making their way upslope in a processional that entailed much chanting
and ringing of bells. He watched impassively as they
came over the crest and filled the space left for them
in the faha, those who could find no place merely

stopping where they stood, in rows on the hillside. Pátraic bowed slightly to Laoghaire, whose return nod was even slighter, and stood away from his followers.

He said no word of challenge or explanation, made no address to his creatures or his opponents, but dramatically flung aside the ragged cloak he usually wore, to reveal himself robed in white beneath, a knotted cord round his waist. Raising his arms, he set aside his crómag—its point by now cleansed, presumably, of King Turlough's blood—and began to chant in a high clear voice.

> "At Tara today
> I put on terrible strength
> against the powers of Darkness.
> Sun's lightness,
> snow's brightness;
> fire's splendor,
> wind's starkness;
> in deepness of sea,
> in steepness of earth—
> Invoking the Trinity,
> confessing the Son,
> with faith in the One
> I face my maker."

"Pátraic's Breastplate!" The cry went up from the Christom ranks, and fled down the side of the hill like a landslip, to echo in the vale below; but a very different cry went up from those grouped round the king.

"He steals the Faedh Fiada!" gasped Corlis Typhult, shocked into speech at the first syllables; she was robed in her rank as priestess to observe the contest, and until that moment had maintained the sacred silence.

"The Deer's Cry, Fionn's Lorica—he dares to name it his, and twists it to fit his god!"

Others who stood by, not quite so swift as she to recognize the source, were just as aghast when they did. The Deer's Cry was an ancient prayer of Gaeldom, an invocation to that one of the High Dânu known as Fionn the Young, called Friend-of-man, who had met his consort, the goddess Saighve, in form of a deer. It was for her that the prayer was named, and for the Tangavaun to change the words, and claim through that prayer the power of the very elements he despised, was blasphemy and presumption beyond what even he seemed capable of working.

But Pátraic, his brazen theft accomplished, now bent a glittering eye on his shaken opponents, and spoke in a voice harsh as stone.

"If you will not turn to the Son to worship, then let the sun you worship turn to blood! See now the power of the living God whose servant I am!"

For a few long deathly quiet moments, nothing happened; then, all but imperceptibly at first, it seemed that a red mist was settling down upon Tara, as if the very air turned to blood. When it grew redder and yet redder, sky and land one unnatural crimson, all realized that the color was not in the air but in the light itself. The sun that had been round and gold, a good three hours above the horizon, now showed redder than on a hot summer evening through the smoke of burning bracken.

Another triumphant cry went up from the Christom; but the others exchanged troubled looks, and a low fearing murmur ran through the faha. Laoghaire the king sat unmoving in his chair, his hand to his chin, and whatever he was thinking he kept to himself.

The 'miracle' wrought, Pátraic stood aside, calm without, trembling like a shiver-oak within. *Now let the pagans fear the one true God...* But though he waited, and his creatures scanned the throng for a challenge, no one came forward to face him. Then at last Brendan of Fanad stirred where he had stood, and walked forward, slowly, as if in dreams; the crowd parted for him as water parts before an oar-blade, but he did not see them, saw nothing but Pátraic, the white robe glowing red in the ghastly light.

This has happened, this is a thing I have done before— This moment was set in motion when I stole into Magher-amorna one night in owl-time and set free a slave—nay, before that, even, in some other life long since—and after, in lives to come...

The movement where no other moved had caught all eyes now; his name ran like whispered flame across the hilltop, but Brendan and Pátraic saw only each other. *He knows as I know—Ferganam—this is fíor-comlainn, the truth-of-combat. Whatever happens next, we have drawn the battle lines for all time between us and our ways...*

As his opponent had done, Brendan wasted no time with words of challenge; he raised his arms, he began to chaunt. He had not thought beforehand what his counter to the Tangavaun might be, but had trusted to the moment, to the gods; and his trust and faith were rewarded. Upon his lips now he found a rann greater even than the prayer to Fionn that the Tangavaun had reived away, and he spoke it with a will: the mighty rann called the Dord Faunya, a magic that came to him from Nia his mother, a sorcery of the Danaäns, used against the Dark. *And what is here is dark enough...*

"To my friends, to my foes, to my kindred
     and all,
To the brave, to the knave, to the free,
     to the thrall:
The power of Kelu be on thee
From the lowliest creature of Abred
To the Name that is highest of all!"

He chaunted on, in a voice that rolled up like thunder
from the ground and forked down like lightning from
the skies; then with scarce a pause to draw breath,
standing there in the red light he began the great
Litany to the Goddess that Nia herself had made in her
youth, his own mother, long before she had ever ridden out from the hill to win Fergus Fire on Brega for
her mate.

"Breastplate of the Gael—Queen of the Danaans—
Tear of the Sun—Hawk of Morning—Storm on the
Mountain—Sword of Perception—Shield of Silver—
Dancer in the Moon—Fire of Roses—Oak of Mor-
ven—Water of Vision—Wind out of Betelgeuse—Spear
of Midna—Horn of Camha—Mountain in the West of
the World—Queen of the South—Well of Stars—Rose
at the Heart of the World—"

And as Brendan chaunted, the blood that Pátraic
had put upon the face of the sun was cleansed;
moment by moment the gold light grew strong and
clear again, the crimson fading, and Brendan's voice
grew in strength and in the power of the Goddess upon
Whom he called.

"Caer of the Valiant—Caer of Magics—Caer of
Compassion—Caer of Dán—Silver-circled Caer of Des-
tination—Help of the Kinwrecked—Refuge of
Wounded—Avenger of Blood—Protectress of the

Oppressed—Queen of the Caer of Sunset—Breasts of the Moon—Mantle of Womanhood—White Rose of Desiring—Light of the Perfection of Gwynfyd, Mate of the God!"

But when the litany was done, the sun clean again, he did not stop there: raising a hand, he cried words in a tongue that was ancient even among the Danaans; he commanded, though none there could tell what command he gave, or to whom—or what. And as the moments went by, and the shadows did not change, the light did not shift, the people began to mutter fearfully, Christom and Draoícht alike. For the sun, bright once more, was no longer descending its sky-road in the west but hung there unmoving, like a round bronze shield hung upon a fortress wall.

"He makes the sun stand still!" came the awed cry, and even his own folk feared. Brendan had stopped the sun; as, long hence, a daughter of his line would make it dance. But that would be a different sun, another story...

He lifted both hands now, spoke again in the great tongue that sounded like lances and banners, like all the hosts of the Light going forth upon the marches of the universe to do battle against the Dark.

"...Nor sword shall wound,
nor brand shall burn,
nor arrow pierce,
nor seas shall drown.
Harm shall not come nigh thee
Ill shall not befall thee
Evil shall not touch thee
Wrath shall never cloud thee.
Truth shall walk beside thee

> Loyalty shall arm thee
> Light shall ever bless thee
> Love shall never leave thee."

And that was the prayer that would come to be called Brendan's Lorica, set over against Pátraic's stolen Breastplate…

When Brendan had spoken, there was silence on Tara for the space of many minutes, and then, softly, silently, the people, Christom and Draoícht alike, began to vanish away. He stood there like a great oak, unmoving, unbending, until the faha was empty; even Laoghaire had gone within, though not without much reluctance and many backward glances, and anxious inquiry of Brendan as to his weal and condition—he had been gently assured and put by.

But in the shadows across the faha Pátraic stood also, his tail impatiently dismissed, unsubtly lingering that he might have speech with Brendan alone and aside. No pretense was left between them now: they were declared implacable foes, and each knew it. Pátraic spoke first, and Brendan's head came up at his words.

"You may have won here today, right enough, by pagan tricks and evil powers, but I will win in the end, and shall I tell you why?" Not waiting for a response: "Because I will use your own ways and strengths against you; indeed, the Holy Father has already shown me how it shall be done. 'Tell the pagans of Éruinn that they will still have their Goddess,' he said to me when he gave me the charge to come here, 'only now they will call her Mary; she already has a hundred names, one more will make no differ—tell them so. The warrior god Lugh of the Light? Tell them he is now to be known as Michael Archangel, captain of the forces

against the Dark; build churches to him on the high
places where Lugh has been worshipped. The holy
springs and wells sacred to the Mother—make them
Mary's, or consecrate them to some blessed saint, as
seems good to you. Tell them that the Son is a maker-
god like unto their own pagan Gabhain Saor, the Tanist
of Heaven, while the Father is the High King over all
gods of the world; if you put it so, in such a way, they
will understand and accept. The great thing is not to
forbid their practices but to turn them. If it is done
with skill enough, by the time they realize what is being
done, it will be too late and they will be ours, nevermore to break away'… So spoke the Holy Father; and
so I will capture the Gael, for him and for Christ."

"By lies."

"If lies are what it takes to bring folk to the Truth,
aye."

Brendan shook his head. "Do you even hear yourself? I put it to you thusly: once you were a shepherd,
you call yourself a shepherd still. Shear sheep so and
what sort of flock will you have in the end? You will be
as a sheepdog who turns sheepkiller, not to feed your
sheep but to fleece them. As for your Holy Father,
there seems little either fatherly or holy about him, if
he can counsel so vile a course against fellow creatures." He looked round him, drew a deep breath of
the cooling night air. "We stand alone upon the hill of
Tara," he said. "None stand nearby, none can hear us,
none even to read our lips… Let you tell me, then; for
a secret between you and me and the gods we swear by.
You have seen me act with power, you have acted with
power yourself: do you truly believe, for yourself, in any
god at all—yours *or* mine?"

Pátraic calmly returned the gaze. "Whether I do or no," he said with equal candor, "it makes no differ." He gestured out at the land before them, invisible now in the dark. "I will make your folk believe in the God I have said I believe in."

Well, that is honest enough; and answer enough too, Goddess help us all... "And I swear by That by which my people swear," said Brendan presently, with a terrible slowness and weight to every word, "by the gods I do believe in, the gods who believe in me, that I will take the folk away before I let you do so."

But though the Tangavaun's face had paled suddenly at the unlooked-for threat, or promise, that Brendan had just now made him, he returned no answer, only spun away and descended the hill into the dark below. Brendan watched him go, stood there a moment longer, then turned at last to the bright-lighted hall behind, where the Samhain festivities and a jubilant victory feast were in full cry, and where his friends awaited.

Well, the challenge is made and delivered. Fíor-comlainn it is—but, hear me Goddess, hear me God, I would give much and more besides, that dán had ruled it other...

CHAPTER TWELVE

hen Brendan went to take his farewell of Laoghaire a fortnight later, and head home at last to Fanad, the king kissed him lovingly as a dear kinsman, and gave him great gifts as befitted his deed and rank; but gave him a warning also.

"Since the yellowstalk fell before your herb-lore, and not before their god's much-vaunted healing powers, Pátraic and his followers have not taken kindly to their loss of face, nor to the fact that conversions have fallen off—quite counter to their original intent and plan. Nor will your victory here do anything to further endear you. Before, you were merely unfriends; now you are declared enemies."

"There is more," said Duvessa, a suppressed urgency in her usually sweet voice. "Hoping to breed sympathy, the poor persecuted lambs—weasels in lamb's clothing, more like—the Christlings are now loudly claiming there is a plot afoot to kill Pátraic. Though I would not cause you alarm, m'chara, I think it most likely all this talk of 'plot' is but a mask for quite another target."

"And that would be?"

"Well, *you*, thickhead, who else! Nay, Brandoch, only listen!"—as he began to scoff and protest—"As

Laoch has said, the work you did at Samhain will win you no new friends among the Christom. You defeated not only the Tangavaun but the power of his White Christ: you made Pátraic, and all who look to him, look foolish in front of all Éruinn; forgiveness may be ever in their mouths, but I tell you, this they will never forgive. It cuts at the root of their very survival; and any animal will fight as it can for its life when it must."

"Even so—"

"Only take care," said Laoghaire. "That is my command to you. Be 'ware and be watchful. No more. But assuredly no less."

"And what of *your* carefulness?"

Laoghaire steepled his fingers and looked into the fire. "I will make a folkmeet, here at Tara," he said at last, "to discuss some way by which it might be contrived for our Ways to run side by side in what shall pass for peace. It may hold off their victory a few years more... A company shall be assembled to draft new laws for Éruinn: three kings, three brehons, and three Christom priests—in public; three druids, three bards and three ban-draoi in secret." He grinned at the look on their faces. "Nine may be a sacred number to their kind—being thrice their godly trinity—but nine is sacred among us also. And so it shall be."

And to the eternal honor and glory of Laoghaire mac Niall, so it was. That council was held, the code that those who sat there hammered out among them finding fame beyond even Éruinn, and rightly, as the Senchus Mór. But for all their worthy valorous work and care to heal the great wounded past and wounding present, and prevent the wounds to come in future—no. There they labored all in vain.

*   *   *

One of the reasons King Niall Nine-Hostage had held the iron control he did over his often fractious and sometimes outright rebellious realm was the system of the waypost—his own invention. That astute and prudent monarch had kept heavy chariots stationed at forts the length and breadth of Éruinn, to use for local shows of strength as and where they might be useful, and light ones for speeding of crucial messages and information, and, sometimes, people; knowing a fine plan when they saw it, his successors had kept up the practice. As a signal mark of favor—and also to guarantee his friend's safety as much as he might—in the aftermath of the confrontation at Tara, King Laoghaire had granted Brendan the freedom of the chariot-post to make his way home to Fanad, and with delighted gratitude Brendan had accepted.

He set out after the daymeal, two weeks after the festival of Samhain the Less: a fine clear cold morning. Though the chariots were built for maximum speed and not overmuch comfort, he found himself enjoying the ease and shortness of his journey. *I could very quickly grow 'customed to so royal a method of travel, no doubt about it! If the roads stay clear, I shall be at Creavanore in half the time it would take me to ride there on my own—and a good thing too, I have been too long away from my home this time, and from my Tamhna also...*

The changes of chariot, every three leagues or so, went smoothly at first—one team and car turned in, another taken. The Fian drivers were skilled and pleasant, glad of the company; the light-boned horses, specially bred for the purpose, were of the swiftest. But

the fifth changeover, at a remote waystation called Lissard, just beyond the border of the royal province of
Meath, was different...

Brendan always maintained afterwards that he had
had not the smallest presentiment of danger, more
fool he; not even when the charioteer who should have
taken him forward from Lissard unexpectedly begged
off, claiming sudden illness, and there was, strangely
enough, no other driver or even a riding-horse available. Of course, as the post captain pointed out—
deeply mortified at the lapse, and with the king's good
friend too—Brendan was more than welcome to stay
there and wait for someone to walk over to Granagh,
the next station west—as soon as any such someone
could be spared from other duties, they were so very
short-handed just now—and return to Lissard with
another charioteer who would then drive Brendan *back*
with him to Granagh, where he would have to find yet
another team and driver to convey him on again. But
that would be a foolish reduplication of effort, and a
delay of many hours, if not even overnight, and they
could all see that the noble lord of Fanad, the king's
close friend, was anxious to be on his way, and why
should he not be, though they would be pleased
indeed to have him as nightguest...

There was a simpler way, the afflicted driver suggested, as if by sudden inspiration: if the lord Brendan,
the king's dear friend, would deign to such labor, he
might take the fresh team and drive himself to the next
station, where a new team and charioteer would be
waiting to take him onward. Foreheads were smacked—
so logical a solution, what stupids they all were not to
have thought of it sooner!—and before Brendan knew

it, it was agreed. So, himself pleased with the solution and the need not to delay, after a pleasant respite for a meal and converse as to the state of the road ahead, Brendan stepped up into the car, took the reins and drove on westward alone.

He was by no means unskilled as a driver; after many miles as a passenger it was good to have some vigorous activity to warm him up, as the bright November day began to chill toward dusk and shadows lengthened. Under his hand the new team of horses went well and obediently, and the car itself was easy to manage. But just on sunset, at a fordplace a few miles short of Granagh, where the road ran close under wooded cliffs, the chariot gave an unexpected lurch, nearly throwing Brendan from the car, and then rocketed down the road like a partridge startled from the nest.

He hauled himself painfully upright from the spear-rest across which his middle had come down hard, and grabbed for the handrail. For no apparent reason the horses had bolted, running wild and suddenly maddened; and as the light car jounced over the stones of the ford, water splashing in all directions, he was horrified to see the carriage beginning to separate itself from the frame and the wheeltree. *The wood is not breaking up but coming apart; timbers sawn clean through, or the leather webbing unlashed— Laoch and Duvách were quite right to give me warning, and if I live through this I swear I shall not be slow to tell them...*

When the horses first bolted, the leather traces had been pulled through his fingers so swiftly they had burned and torn his skin; now the reins dragged along the ground, impossible for him to recapture. *I will have to jump from the car before it comes apart entirely—no other way of dismounting...* In another few moments he would himself be under the grinding wheels, or the flashing hoofs; but he looked at the roadbed flying past and still he hesitated to leap. Then he heard the muffled thudding sound of three or four horses galloping alongside the road, on the wide grassy verge before the deep woods began, and felt two spears whistle by in the darkening air, not a foot from his head; and that decided him.

Whether they are bandits or assassins, and whoever sent them either way, nothing for it but to leap before they throw again—if I do not break my neck in the jump I may have better luck afoot... He slung his sword across his back, thrust his dagger through his belt, then prepared to fling himself free. But he had left it just that one instant too late: the timbers and wickerwork were splintering to wreckage beneath him; the horses, screaming, went down entangled in the traces, and he felt himself falling. *If I survive the wreck those riders will certainly finish me off, they were sent after me for just such a purpose—but perhaps I may take some of them with me to Arawn as I go...*

Then, just before the ground came up to meet him, Brendan felt a tremendous pull and surge and drag, and found himself caught up, by an iron grasp and a more than mortal strength, to the back of a tall black stallion galloping more swiftly than the swiftest horse he had ever seen.

He instinctively straightened astride the horse's powerful quarters, turning round to look for his attackers, then before him at the rider who had saved him; but he saw only a red cloak that snapped like the sails of a war-galley taking a storm-wind, the stallion's streaming mane, the sparks his hoofs struck from the smoking highway.

And then there was no highway beneath them but only roads of air, and Brendan knew beyond doubting, though indeed he had known from the first, that he rode with one of the Sidhe. He peered round the red-cloaked shoulder to see that they were heading straight for the unyielding side of a towering mountain. It was upon them before he could speak, though any words he might have managed would have been torn away in the wind, for their terrific speed did not slacken. Just as it seemed they were about to shatter themselves against the rocky waste, the mountain opened before them, its secret gate swinging wide and light spilling out in a warm golden blaze; they passed within to the hidden stronghold, and the hill closed behind them. But in that brief burst of light Brendan had seen and recognized his rescuer, and he was struck silent.

Donn Rígh, king beneath the hill, had pulled him from the wreck.

Brendan never remembered the rest of that night, only bright brief flashes of image and sensation: strong gentle hands supporting him, helping his bruised and shaking body to a soft silky-pillowed bed, where calm healers came to soothe and tend him; a cool drench that had sleep and more healing in it; at least one day and night in bed, with savory and sustaining food whenever he had need of it, and all the sleep and rest he wished. But when he rose the next day after—or it might have been several days, or weeks even, given

what way time passes in the palaces of the Shining
Folk—and went with the one who had been sent as
escort, after several turnings and passages he found
himself in Knockfierna's thronehall; and he was not
alone.

The great chamber was filled with Sidhefolk: Brendan saw his grandsir Calatin, and Nia his own mother;
Donn Rígh seated in his crystal throne with Aobhinn
his queen beside him, and their tall golden-haired son
Kelver Donn Midna standing at his father's right hand;
many of their court, and some from Rinn na gCroha
and other secret strongplaces of their folk. High
Danaans all, and with more on their minds than even
the attempted murder of one who was of their own
blood and kindred.

He had time enough for only the briefest glance
round before Nia came skimming swiftly to him across
the hall, folding him into her arms as only a mother
can do, though he topped her by a head.

"Tamhna is with the children," she said at once,
allaying his instant fears. "They are safe and well at
Creavanore—she brought them from Clanadon when
first we had news of what had befallen. Coll mac Gréine
and half his folk have joined your father to guard
them; no harm will come. There are—others there
also," she added, and with deepest relief Brendan took
her meaning: that her own folk also stood secret hidden guard without.

He turned then to face Donn who had saved him,
meeting the deepness of that king's dark glance, where
assessment and amusement glinted in equal measure;
and after he had voiced proper gratitude to his royal
rescuer, Calatin's voice came from behind.

"Glad we are to see you well again, Brandoch, and your kin's thanks too to Donn Rígh"—here he bowed, and the king inclined his head to acknowledge—"but listen now… From what we have learned, the attack on you had been intended from the first. We do not believe the Tangavaun planned it himself, though he may have been aware or had suspicions, and if so he did naught to stop it. For our part we knew only that you were to be lured to Tara for the contest with the Tangavaun, and word would be spread of a plot to slay him, so as to divert attention from the attempt on you. We could not thwart it, but we could keep you under our warding: from the time you left Killary you have never once been out of our sight."

Now Nia, her green eyes hard as emeralds as she looked upon her son: "The chariot-horses were stung with elfbolts, poor beasts—we found these in their necks and flanks." She showed him six tiny darts, their bronze barbs sharp as pins—much favored of assassins. "The driver who was to have taken you from Lissard was in it from the first. When you arrived there, he feigned illness, to delay you long enough for him to tamper with the chariot, and for his confederates to get out ahead—two to lie in wait for you on the cliffs above the ford and shoot at the horses as you went by, three others to hide in the woods. But as we were watching you yourself and not the road—our mistake, it will not happen again—they went all unseen."

Nia fell suddenly silent, and after a moment, seeing she could not bring herself to say what must next be said, Calatin took up the tale. "Once the horses bolted, Brandoch, the ones who had hid in the forest came after you along the highroad; two more were on the road from Granagh, so that you could not escape by fleeing ahead, and the two from above coming down to join them. Seven to one is long odds, even if the crash had left you unhurt. Either way, you were to have died there, and the tale put about that it had been bandit reivers out of Lissard—and that your death was a wonder of divine retribution, for that you yourself had planned murder against Pátraic, from which fate his god had miraculously spared him. That you took the chariot-post home only made it easier for them to plan it."

Brendan's face showed his shock. "You do not suggest that the *king* had anything to do with—"

"Nay, nay, not he! He and his queen are as angry as we are—we sent a messenger to tell them what had befallen, and Laoghaire has already taken action." Nia smiled at last. "That is a brave lord and a good friend you have there—but this was nothing that he could have foreseen."

"It was not his fault," murmured Brendan. "He did warn me."

"Aye," said the prince Kelver Donn, speaking for the first time, and looking fondly at Brendan; they had become friends on Brendan's marriage to Etain, though they were seldom in each other's company. "He blames only himself, since it was his idea to send you home by the wayposts. But he did not know how deep the zealot Christom have penetrated into his own guard; as a man of honor, he is slow to see what those who have no honor might do in their own cause... Any road, as you suspected, Brandoch, the monk Pyllas was a spy for Vortigern all the while—though again we are inclined to give the Tangavaun the benefit of the doubt as to whether he knew. He is just stupid enough not to have had any idea—when someone professes a thing he wants to hear, that is all he hears, and cares not whether it be truth or lie."

"Well, that is it, then," said a Sidhe lord whom Brendan did not know. "If they would go so far as to kill, or try to kill—in the name of their god who forbids it—"

Others joined eagerly in the discourse, and all while they debated Donn Rígh sat unmoving in his high seat—though more than a few glances were cast his way. He looked regal and dangerous—tall, brown-haired, clad in black, fingering often a great blue stone that hung on a gold chain upon his breast; he had spoken no word, neither aloud nor in the thoughtspeech the Sidhe commonly used among themselves, though he listened attentively, and impassively, to all that was said—and to much that was not. But at last he rose up from his throne, and the hall fell suddenly silent as he spoke in a clear calm voice; his words were a command to those who heard.

"Not hard. They have struck against us; now we will take éraic where it is owed. No more. But also no less."

Brendan bowed with the others as Donn left the chamber, but as he turned again to his mother a line from an old poem about the High Danaans was running through his head. *'Good they are at manslaying'*— *and we may all yet be glad of that...*

Justice was therefore left to the Sidhefolk, who carried it out correctly; as Donn had decreed, no more and no less than what was required. As it fell out, the five who had tried to kill Brendan on the road, and the two who had been sent on from Granagh, and the driver who had professed illness so that he might meddle with the chariot, were slain simply—though with the

exquisite battle-courtesy of both Gael and Danaan they
were told the reason why before they died.

But for the traitor monk Pyllas Nadron, a fitter fate:
he was found three days later, lying before the gates of
Vortigern's own castle in Gwent, in the south of Gwalia
across the Eastern Sea. No wound of sword or sgian was
upon him, but so broken was his body, such a look of
terror upon his face, that it appeared he had been
dropped from a very great height.

After that duel at Tara, and that coward's attempt on
the road from Lissard, the battle lines were drawn in
earnest. Fierce quarrels began to break out like tiny
wildfires all over Éruinn, newly converted Christom
chiefs and lords turning with war upon their neighbors
who held to the Shan-vallachta, and who fought back,
unsurprisingly, with equal fury and fervor. The policy
Pátraic had boasted of to Brendan was well in train
now, even its enemies reluctantly admitting to its clev-
erness. "Not so much divide and conquer as replace
and rule," said Laoghaire bitterly, but he could do little
to halt it; indeed, it seemed to take on a dark life-
energy of its own.

As their pope had commanded, the Christling
priests who followed Pátraic were now beginning to
build churches, siting them near or even on ancient
holy places—not the major sacred sites, they did not
dare so much, or at least not yet. But as they grew
bolder, that too would come—and it would endure.

Though Pátraic still piously proclaimed he sought
no violence in his work of winning the Gael to Christery, violence there was in plenty—as if the new

Christlings were bound and determined that everyone should be as themselves and would beat them into submission, in the name of their god of love, if that was the only way it could be managed. And it was noted by both sides that Pátraic did not preach against it when it occurred.

Thus the infection of the trouble grew and spread, like a new yellowstalk ill—save that it was blood-red—so that in the end, a desperate and angry Laoghaire made shift to humble himself, and went to beg a truce of the Tangavaun. But the astounding terms he was instantly offered were terms the king was more loath to implement than any ever put forward in all his reign...

One spring day in Fanad Brendan was surprised beyond all measure to see come cantering up to Clanadon a brave party of riders. They were led by the High King himself; Duvessa was with him, and Amris, and many others that he knew. *All unannounced! But what joy and honor that they should visit...* He gave swift orders as to lodgings and banquets, then hurried out to welcome his unexpected guests.

After supper, Laoghaire, who though he had been cordial enough had seemed somehow distracted, as one with heavy matters on his mind, rose and spoke thanks to his hosts and their tuath, then, turning aside, asked a private moment with Brendan for himself and his queen. Once apart, in the little solar Etain sometimes used just off the main hall, the king seemed even more troubled than he had been at the board.

After a glance or two at Laoghaire, who most uncharacteristically would not meet his gaze, Brendan shrugged inwardly, and made amiable smallchat with Duvessa, wondering why in all the seven hells they had come all the long miles from Tara, and taken him privily aside, only to remain silent...

It seemed that Duvessa had heard his thought, for cutting the flow of converse short she spoke curtly to her husband. "A bootless errand, Laoch, to ride all this way and then hesitate to bring up the very reason we came. The swift clean stroke is best. Tell him."

Laoghaire flushed, but plainly he saw the wisdom of her words, though his own words came slow, and still he would not look Brendan in the eye.

"As your friend," he began, "know that I would sooner die than ask this of you, or even say this to you; as your king I must command you to it, though I tried my best to have it other wise." He paused, and Brendan waited. "For my part I will never turn Christom," continued Laoghaire at last, "not for myself, and not to abandon those of our folk who likewise will not turn. But over the past months I have come to fear that I will be the last king in Éruinn who holds publicly and completely to the Old Ways." He waved away the protest that leaped to Brendan's lips. "Nay, I have Seen it, and I think you have too. You also know that because of the Tangavaun's great success in converting the folk, my queen and I have been obliged to pay public reverence to the way of the Crann-draoi. Now it is your turn to bend."

"Gladly, if I can, to help you," said Brendan, though he was by now completely asea. "What would you have me do?"

Laoghaire glanced swiftly at Duvessa, and his words came even more slowly than before.

"The Tangavaun's sister, Darerca, has recently come over from Britain the More to join him. For sake of peace between the factions, Pátraic has offered alliance through her. You saw the lady, I think, when you were at Tara for the contest."

Brendan nodded. "I did; she was fair and gentle, biddable even, perhaps too much in her brother's shadow for her own good. But what is she to do with me?"

Duvessa laid a gentle hand on his arm. "To whom else but you, his friend from youth and his great adversary now, does he offer such alliance— Pátraic bids us to order you to wed her, to make public peace between the sides. And we have said that we would do so—well, that we would ask."

At first Brendan thought he could not have heard correctly; his mind rejected the words as surely as his heart.

"I am wed already," he said at last, fighting back a white blazing anger greater than any wrath he had ever known. *He is the king, and my friend, and Etain's, or so I thought, how can he ask this...*

To his credit, Laoghaire looked desperately uncomfortable, and almost as bitterly angry as Brendan himself. "But not in Christom marriage; and Pátraic and his folk do not hold any other form of marriage to be lawful—or even true."

"Well, if they do not, I most assuredly *do*!" said Brendan, leaping to his feet to pace the little solar; only so could he keep himself from drawing blade on his king and friend, or the one he had believed was his friend. "And, I had thought, so did we all. Name of Dâna! If he were not unmanned already— I will kill him with my bare hands, for even daring to suggest it—"

"Or kill me first for asking you?" Brendan swung round on him; but Laoghaire was not smiling. "As your friend, Brandoch, sooner would I have fallen on my sword, or run it through him, than speak of so unspeakable a thing. But as your king, and his also, I must ask, and I could command... If you wed her the Tangavaun has promised to cease attacking; if he ceases attacking, the Christom lords will cease their raiding. It could bring about that peace you have said you would do anything to attain. Surely Tir Gaedhil is worth a wedding?"

"And how if he had asked this of *you?*" Brendan, dangerously calm now, was no whit less enraged, the anger well alight just beneath the surface, ready to flare up again in blaze. "If he had demanded *you* wed his sister, insult the lady of *your* heart—would you have done so, even for Tir Gaedhil? And you!" he added, turning now on Duvessa. "As woman, not as queen— would you not feel as Etain must feel, when she comes to hear it?"

Laoghaire began to reply, but Duvessa cut across him. "Aye, Brandoch," she said. "No question. But there might yet be a way."

Brendan seated himself with a grimness, laid his arms along the chair-arms, leaned back. "Then, lady, pray you tell me. And by the Goddess Herself, pray you make it good."

CHAPTER THIRTEEN

ll the Tangavaun's care is that you should say the Christom words with his sister, not so?" said Duvessa, with care herself, and no small amount of guile. "But our own brehon law, the law of the land, in its wisdom and compassion allows for seven different sorts of marriage, and folk are permitted to wed in more forms than one at any one time."

Brendan, no less wrathful but seeing where she was going, nodded curtly that she should continue; and after a moment she did, well aware that one word wrong or ill-chosen would mean an end to a great deal more than their present converse.

To our friendship surely, with Brandoch and Tamhna both, perhaps even to my lord's kingship, or to Éruinn itself... Gods, how I curse the Tangavaun, and the black evil duergar-spawned day he set his baneful foot upon our shore—and upon our necks—and I will by no means be the last to curse him...

"Say the Christom words with this Darerca, then, as Pátraic would have it, but make clear before the brehons that she will be banaltrach, secondary wife, wedded in fourth-form marriage, the 'union of visitance'. Etain shall be your chief-wife; to you and her and the rest of Gaeldom, your only wife, in launamnas, the first-

form marriage of equals. The Christom will have their
alliance, or appearance of alliance, the king will have
peace, and your truth, and Etain's with you, will remain
untouched."

Laoghaire looked relieved as he saw Brendan's face
change. "Make the Tangavaun's sister ban-charach,
then—"

But Brendan shook his head, calmer now, though
still profoundly angry. "Nay, that name and rank are of
love—as your grandmother's grandson should know
better than anyone. 'Banaltrach' she shall be—if it
must be. You are right that our folk will understand; as
for the Christom, let them think as they please. It will
matter nothing to anyone who matters to us... But hear
me well, king at Tara: I do this at your order only—the
command of the son of great Niall. Nothing and no
one else could bring me to it."

"And Etain?" asked Laoghaire, steeling himself
anew. "Shall I speak to her—to bring her to it?"

"Nay," came Brendan's quick reply. "Kings even at
Tara mean little to one who bends the knee to Donn
Rígh alone. And such a word as this to such a wife must
come from her husband—even such a husband, who
goes now to pray devoutly to the Goddess that that wife
will not renounce him for the offense of it." He rose to
leave, abruptly, uncaring of showing discourtesy to
guests, and royal ones at that. *Discourtesy'! They have
lain enough offense upon me this night to offset anything I
might do to them short of drawing blade—and maybe not even
that...* But he paused in the doorway and turned to
them again.

"Brandoch?" said Laoghaire, very softly, when he
did not speak at once but only looked long upon them.

"I do not know," said Brendan with great precision of speech, "why even Ferganam would wish to condemn a sister he presumably loves to such a lacklove match, merely for sake of his god—or his politics." The ghost then of a bitter smile. "But I would bid you both—and him also—remember two things: that according to this same marriage law you cite me, no power on earth can make a man visit a banaltrach he has no wish to visit; and that a chief-wife is permitted three days' worth of unrestricted bloodshed, no penalties attached, upon any banaltrach her husband may covenant."

Duvessa ventured a small smile in return; though she knew now that he would obey their asking, and their friendship would even continue—if perhaps not quite the same as before, at least near enough for them all to live with—she knew also that in his deepest heart Brendan would never forgive them for forcing this upon him. *And I cannot say that I blame him—nay, I do not, will not, blame him! We do not even know for sure if it will help, if the Tangavaun is out for mere revenge, though why he would do such hurt to his own sister... Is it simply to spite Brandoch, or is it rather a demonstration of his power— to show to slackers and laggards how the servant of the Cranndraoi now can make even the king at Tara bend to his will? Either way, I do not think that the Tree-druid can be pleased to see such deeds done in his name...*

"Let us hope, then, that this Darerca can defend herself," she said aloud. "A great quantity of blood may be drawn in three days, by one who has a mind to do so."

And Brendan smiled very thinly back, and left the solar.

*   *   *

But Etain, when her husband spoke to her that night, giving her every chance to forbid the proposed action and refuse the king's command, or even to end their own marriage by reason of the insult and offense, as brehon law allows, acquiesced at once, and never even mentioned bloodshed—though whether her calm consent was because she saw the political necessity, or saw that such an espousal was no espousal at all and mattered not a whit to either Brendan or herself, or saw something else entirely, something higher and more important by far, he could not tell, and she would not say. And if bloodshed—lawful or otherwise—was a rod she held in reserve, it was a rod she never came to use; perhaps she scorned to employ it on one who after all was far from her equal and never a rival.

However it may have been, a month later Brendan and Darerca were wedded in Christom marriage, to Pátraic's gloating private elation and vaunting public triumph. For his part, Brendan refused absolutely to lodge his new banaltrach at Creavanore, or anywhere else in Fanad, but established her in a pleasant maenor not far from her brother's grand new church that he had blasphemously erected at Ard Mhacha, a place anciently sacred to the Goddess, in the oak-wooded hills some miles north of Tara. And this was all according to brehon law, which provides that a woman wedded in the fourth form of marriage may be kept and lodged well apart from the chief-wife, and visited by the husband who maintains her as and when he may, or will.

Well enough; save that though Darerca was indeed established, and her state most richly and correctly— almost insultingly so—maintained, she was not visited; and so conspicuously was she not visited that a six-month later, when Pátraic was again in Fanad to preach, he made shift to hasten along to Clanadon, and cold greetings were scarce exchanged before he was loudly and bitterly complaining…

"What did you think?" said Brendan, more coldly still, having heard him out. "She is not my wife; whatever store you in your godly delirium may set by it, the Christom bond has no hold on me. And this you knew very well, when you commanded King Laoghaire command me to wed your sister—I do not know *what* commands you gave *her*, poor lady… But being that you are her brother and her priest, she obeyed you—according to the laws of Christery. And being that Laoghaire is my king, I obeyed him—according to the laws of Tir Gaedhil. You had your way, Ferganam: you proved your power before your flock, that you can command kings and chiefs to do your will against their own wish. Be content with that."

But it seemed contentment did not enter into it, at least not where Pátraic was concerned; he continued to prowl round his grievance, as a stray cur prowls around a kitchen-midden.

"You wedded her before God, and against all God's laws you have never once lain with her! Is she not fair enough, not gentle enough? And you have not put aside your Danaan concubine, either— You are my cliamhan brother, and you shame your wife, and me, and yourself—"

"Not so," said Brendan, still calmly, though the rage that had leaped in him when Pátraic put the name of concubine on Etain was almost more than he could control; he felt it flickering like groundfire over every inch of him. "The shame is yours only. I said the words to wed her before *your* god, as *you* demanded, for *your* reasons, and also at the command of my king. I informed the brehons that it was fourth-form marriage, a union of visitance; the choice of whether I visit or no is mine—and I choose no. Anything more than that is over and above what the bond requires, and the law is on my side in this." He laughed shortly. "What of that Christom virginity you are always vaunting? By rights you should be praising me for honoring your sister's; by your words anyone would think it is *you* I have not bedded, not Darerca—though we need say no more of *that*... But I will not lie with your sister, and I am no brother of yours. And while I pity the lady for the shame you have put on her—she is indeed both gentle and fair, and well merits both a better brother and a better husband—it is not my task to mend it. She is not my wife. All Tir Gaedhil knows who is wife to Brendan of Fanad."

But, unsurprisingly, that wife had thoughts of her own on the matter, and surprisingly very different thoughts to those she might have been expected to have; and when Brendan had bidden farewell to a furious Pátraic, and, himself more furious still, told her of the bitter encounter, she voiced those thoughts to her mate.

Who—sails suddenly flapping empty of anger's winds—could do nothing else but stare dumbfound. *Goddess! Every time I think I know her, it is borne in upon me that I know her not at all...*

"*You* bid me lie with her?" he said at last. "In Dâna's own name, *why*?"

"I have Seen it." Etain's voice came serenely to his ear.

Brendan spoke through his own abhorrence of the

prospect, deeply hurt besides. "Whatever you have Seen, Tamhna, will it not trouble you, to see me go to another's bed? Do I mean so little to you, that you would throw me on her, after all that we have had between us?"

Etain cast her eyes to the ceiling, and touched the great crystal that hung as usual at her throat.

"Surely it troubles me! And aye, you mean all to me, as you very well know—I am made no differently than any woman; the thought of you with another— In any other case I would kill her with my own hands, aye, and you too if ever you sought her out for your own pleasure, banaltrach or no! But there is dán at work here, a high dán and a deep one, and all our feelings and wishes—hers, yours, mine, Ferganam's, Laoghaire's, everyone's—must go down before it." She was silent a moment, and he read in the very calmness of her words what toll this was already taking of her. "If you lie with her the once—and once is all I am prepared to allow— a daughter will come of it; and of this lass much fate will follow, and a certain degree of power over the Tangavaun as well. I would not have it said that Etain of Fanad refused to serve dán when she was called upon to do so, or that she failed at the test."

Brendan spoke bitterly, out of his own pain and anger and unalterable revulsion, and knowing too that he would do as he must. "*Is* it a test?"

Etain smiled at last. "It is *always* a test. Have you not yet learned?"

So it fell out as Etain had Seen and said, though it was beyond all doubt the most difficult thing she had ever endured, and Brendan also, and perhaps Darerca as well. The lord of Fanad and the sister of the Tangavaun had their one night, and each of them managed their part well enough, though neither ever spoke one word about it thereafter; but Christom law was fulfilled, and Pátraic was appeased.

And presumably the dán Etain spoke of was served also, for nine months later to the day, Bríd was born to Darerca—a lively pretty dark-haired child, named by her father, over her uncle's strenuous protests, for that one of the High Dânu who is mate of Gavida Forgelord, Bríghid the bright goddess of literature, magic and crafting.

But though he increased his maintaining of Darerca, and made further generous provision for Bríd as his acknowledged child by a banaltrach, by his own wish—and, once more, perhaps Darerca's as well—Brendan never saw either of them again.

And just to finish out her story, for it would have no bearing on the great fate so soon to come upon them all, Darerca went on to lead a stainless blameless life, never once censuring Brendan publicly, or seeking a divorce, even, both of which she had every right in brehon law to do, if not in Christom precept; what her private thoughts might have been on the matter were never known. When she died, she was buried with great lamentings and greater state in Pátraic's church at Ard Mhacha; what befell Bríd nic Bhrendaín—the dán that her father's true wife had Seen for her, indeed had arranged that she should be born to fulfill—will be told in due course.

Yet though his personal sacrifice had succeeded in at least temporarily pacifying the Tangavaun and his followers, who by now were many and powerful indeed, and had earned him his king's deepest gratitude, Brendan soon found that the struggle had by no means ended but had only spread inwith, invading his soul. And the more he fought, the more he realized that this was a dark combat he could never win, there was no peace he could ever find—at least, not on any battlefield of Éruinn, or of Erith…

When he was a young lad Brendan had discovered a place not many miles on horseback from Creavanore, where Fanad runs down into the sea. That coast was a high and a harsh one, and few settlements stood along it: a lone sea-shieling here and there, a handful of fisher-cotts where gaps in the line of sheer cliffs gave entry on tiny beaches and sheltered coves.

But this, his secret refuge, was never meant for folk. Not sandy enough to be called a beach—which accounted for the fact that no one else ever came there—it was as if the ocean had bitten hard into the rock of the coast, making a crescent-shaped inlet with a thin fringe of lush machair, and cliffs of red rock that looked like candle-drippings rose straight out of the water.

The great headland called Sheirnesse loomed above, like a breaking wave turned to stone. There was an ancient nemeton atop it that looked out into the west; it had seen the black sails of the Danaans as they came out of the towering seas, to make their fated landfall, long ago. But there was one place where one might walk down to the water's very edge, a shelf of sea-washed stones as flat and level as a field, where the broken water ran in, chasing the shorebirds before it.

Straight in it came, a uniform two inches deep over the stones of the beach; when it ran out again, it was as if a length of transparent white silk was pulled straight back into the sea, all of a piece it ran away.

And there it was that Brendan now went, as his long habit had been; to meditate, to think, to be alone. The sealfolk who dwelled in the waters nearby, the silkies, had become 'customed to his quiet presence, and came often to converse once they learned that he was safe; there it was that the great friendship began between the Sluagh-rón and the Gael, which was to work so long and so wonderfully on all. The merrows, shyer, soon came as well, having been assured by the silkies that the boy who walked the hidden strand was not of the sort who would do them, or any other, any harm. It was not the place most lads or lasses might choose for refuge, or even in which to pass a free afternoon. But he was not as most, and as a youth under Sheirnesse he had begun to learn that which would stand him in such stead for the future.

But now it was a man came under Sheirnesse, and called to his friends in the sea; and they came eagerly to greet him. And sitting on the rocks above the tide he confided in them as so far he had confided in no human Gael, telling them of his secret plan, the high endeavor, and at the end asking if they would wish to join him.

"We too have scented change upon the winds," said one of the younger silkies, eagerly, "and felt it in the deep places. We will come."

"But to leave our home for so far a place—" said a merrow matron, fear and wonder in her voice. "What seas would there be for us there?"

"I do not know," said Brendan simply. "But they will be clean waters, cut by no prows save our own. We shall find them. That, I promise—by Manaan Sealord and his crystal ship, and Gwenhidw his lady of the skies."

When they left him, taking their way through the running tide with great leaps and dartings, vowing to bring his words to their folk below, and the rulers thereof, and he was alone again upon the shore, Brendan stared unseeing out at the rolling ocean. He had surprised himself just now; never before had he put his thoughts and hopes into such defining words; he did not even know whence had come the huge, the tremendous idea, still less the intent.

It had crept into his awareness all unnoted, made up of bits and bobs, things others had spoken of, things he had mused on and dismissed, until now he found it riding with him in the same saddle, not to be flung off. It staggered him; the means no less than the end itself. Yet as he looked back, to trace the path over the years that had brought him to where he now stood, he saw that the road had been beneath him from the very first; and he saw too who it was had set his steps upon it— more, had given him the horse and maps and gear to make the journey...

When Brendan came into the solar at Creavanore, Nia knew at once what he had come to tell her. *His face shines with it...now,* now *it begins...*

"Mathra"—he knelt before her, looked up into her face, his hands closed round both of hers—"I have decided. The Tangavaun and his way will win out in Éruinn; our home, our ways, soon will be ours no longer—

you know this, you have Seen it, it is not news—and the
only thing we can do is to leave before that day dawns
upon us." He paused, but Nia made no sign, and after a
moment he continued, his voice calmer now. "At first I
thought to take ship across the Western Sea; there are
fair lands there, open and wide, with folk who follow a
Path not unlike to our own, to give us help and friendship—the Danaans have traded with them from the days
of Atland, they would not oppose our coming among
them. But now it is on me that even those lands will fall
in time before the White Druid of the Tree, he who does
not fight but merely conquers... We are a warrior race—
Gael and Danaan both—but this is a battle we will not
win; not the sword but the Word will triumph over us. It
is not shame but wisdom, to turn aside from such a fight,
to seek another ground. And I see none here." He drew
a deep steadying breath, his eyes searched hers again.
"So I have looked elsewhere. Before we came to Éruinn,
before we came to Atland, we came to Erith from the
stars. Now we shall return there. I will take the folk with
me, whoever of them will choose to go. But I do not
know the way."

"You know it better than you think," said Nia then,
deeply moved. "Indeed, your granddam told you
once—"

He stared at her, remembering. *This is that hidden
purpose she has carried in her heart and head these several
years now...* "She bade me go to Knockfierna," he said
then, slowly, "and ask of Donn Rígh the road."

"Go then, and ask." Nia smiled, and laid her hands
upon his head, in bidding or blessing perhaps neither
of them was sure. "And—my son—know too that Donn
Rígh gives very clear direction."

*   *   *

"You have Seen correctly," said Donn the king. "There is no place on Erith where the Tangavaun—the word, if not the man himself, or many others like him—will not by and by have rule. And, as that word is a greedy intolerant one, covetous of all, it will leave no place for any other way to live beside it. Least of all our own." He was silent a long moment. "Leave Erith," he said then, and though he spoke quietly, he and Brendan alone in the chamber, his voice rang like a trumpet-call. "Take with you as many of all peoples as you can. Not the Gael alone, but folk of Gwalia and Aulba, Manaun and Cornovia, Pictavia and both Britains; not they alone but the silkies and merrows, the sun-sharks and the piasts and the orms of the lochs."

"And the Folk beneath the hill?" asked Brendan, his heart stirred, a clear path before him at last. "You are my people and the Tangavaun's foes no less than my father's folk are…"

Donn smiled; it was as if a crown of ice had melted, as if after a long winter sudden spring had come to a glacier.

"We will find our own road; do not fear for us. We will be there before you. And we will not be the only ones there to greet you when your ship touches sand at last."

"But the way?" asked Brendan, still hesitant to ask.

"It is nearer than you have thought," said the faerie king. "And longer than you have dreamed. Though not harder than you can thole." He rose from the high-seat where he had been sitting—not his crystal throne but another chair in another, less grand chamber—

and as he passed he dropped a hand on Brendan's shoulder, a brief touch of kinship and support. "Go home again to Fanad, son of Nia. I will send the way to you."

After Donn had left, Brendan remained, with the prince Kelver Donn Midna for company, and he unpacked his heart of sorrows and doubts to the prince as he had not done to Donn or Etain or even to Nia herself. Friend to Etain in their childhood—though exactly how long ago that might have been, and where, Brendan had never dared ask either one of them— over the years Kelver Donn had become friend to her mate also, and had stood up for them both at their handfasting. He it was who at his royal father's bidding had worked the justice of Gael and Danaan on the bent monk Pyllas Nadron, Vortigern's spy, for the treachery and plot against Brendan—and the message he delivered had been by the High Lord of Britain very well understood.

They had talked for hours beneath the hill; then, feeling the need for wind and sky, they had gone out through one of the secret doors. Now, on the side of Strivellin, they walked in companionable silence. Coming upon the hillside spring in the oak-grove, where once on a long-ago May morning Brendan had met a stranger Woman who was no stranger to him, they sat down to drink of the water, first pouring out the libation from the crystal cup in reverent silence, and spoke again.

"My mother's folk—your folk—my folk!—came here from the *stars*," said Brendan at last, in a voice scarce louder than a wondering whisper. "It is fitting that we should return there; though it should have been done as a challenge, for high adventure's sake, not as mere retreat. And I can say to you, as to very few others, that I never truly believed it until now. Oh, aye, I *believed*, right enough, in that I never doubted the truth of the tale; but I never thought it *real*, if you take my meaning."

Kelver Donn smiled, with all the startling charm of his father. "Indeed I take it! But I promise you, it is real enough; as all of us shall see, and I think very soon now, sooner than you expect. And it is not retreat, either," he added, "at least not as it seems to you now."

"Is it not? What is it then?"

"A warrior's refusal—his right and correct refusal— to fence against a poisoned sword. Sometimes to refuse such a duel is a harder thing to do than to fight it."

Brendan was silent for a while. "Aye," he said at last, "but what did Donn Rígh mean—to send the way to me? I did not like to ask."

"I have found," said Kelver Donn reflectively, "that when my father speaks so, it is usually profitless to surmise aforetime. Those in need of raiment should not ask to see the cloak when it is still upon the loom, but patiently await the weaver's work."

"True son of your father!" said Brendan laughing. "But even so—" He fell abruptly silent, staring into the well, where the leaping force met the quiet of the pool. *See how the water that races in the force becomes still when the pool receives it; but energy does not die. Where then does the movement go?*

"What are you thinking, Brandoch?"

"I have three children," said Brendan after a while longer, and now his face was troubled. "Rohan and Fionagh are three parts Danaan to one part mortal

Gael, their souls are all of the Shan-vallachta; they will
find it only natural to come. But Bríd—her soul is half
Christom, half Draoícht, her blood three parts mortal
to one part Sidhe. I have not seen her since her birth,
her mother raises her, it is best that way for us all; but
still she is blood of mine, blood of ours—through me
she too has a right to the stars. What is owed to her?"

"Why, what Etain Saw for her, to be sure," said
Kelver Donn, surprised—for never before had Brendan mentioned his daughter by the Tangavaun's sister—but understanding his friend's distress. "What is
owed her is the dán she was made for in the first place;
no more, but also no less, and that dán lies here. She
will grow and thrive in the Tangavaun's despite." His
voice took on some of the far ringing note his father's
had carried. "Look now, See with me as I See it... She
will be wed and widowed, and clanned to the White
Christ at the end, and that will be the Tangavaun's victory—but she will keep the holy fire of the Goddess
alive in Tir Gaedhil, and the blood of the Danaan alive
in the Gaelfolk; and that victory will be yours. Do not
fear for her, Brandoch, or sorrow to leave her behind."

While Kelver Donn was speaking Brendan had
been quite silent, turning over and over between his
fingers a loose stone he had found in the pool coping
beneath his hand. Now, still giving no sign that he had
heard—or, if hearing, had accepted—he tossed the
stone into the pool, and rising to his feet he took up
the crystal cup, the cup of the Goddess. Leaning pre-
cariously far over the coping, he filled it again: but this
time, as only One had ever done before him, he filled
it not from the captured quiet water of the pool but
straight from the white spouting torrent, that fell and

foamed fiercely over his hand as he held the cup in the cold clean stream.

Then, standing still and tall, drawn up as if in priestly presiding at a solemn rite—and Kelver Donn who had risen with him did so also—Brendan poured out one last libation.

But this time, as no one had ever done before him, he poured it out in threes. One third splashed onto the emerald turf, the second third fell sparkling back again into the pool. And the last third he flung up into the air with a strong sweep of his arm, their heads turning and lifting to follow the arc and curve of it, where the wind and light caught it and broke it into a scattering of diamond droplets, and made those droplets to flash like the very stars.

BOOK II

KELTIA

CHAPTER FOURTEEN

hen Brendan, who had ridden with Kelver
Donn and no other companion straight from
Knockfierna to Tara, confided the incredible
plan to Laoghaire and Duvessa, they first wept, then
called down blessings on him and it alike, then cursed
the Tangavaun fluently, and his pedigree for a hundred generations fore and aft in volleys of blistering
inventive invective, and only then gave in shamelessly
to bitter wild envy, lamenting that they might not go
themselves.

"That is what it is to be king, and the wife of a king,"
said Cairenn, not without sympathy. "To abide when
others fare forth, to lead the vaward when others dare
not. But even the onetime mate of a onetime king has
her part in this. Time draws near for that work which
Calatin of Rinn na gCroha and I must do together."

"He knows, lady," said Brendan, who had more
than an inkling now of what that work might be, and
made a respectful bow to the mother of Niall Nine-
Hostage.

"The Tangavaun will surely try to stop you, when he
learns your plan," suggested Amris, from where he
lounged on a fur-piled couch. He was not so envious as
the others: indeed, he was more than a little compla-

cent, and a great deal more thrilled with himself than he could quite bear, for Brendan had already told him he was to go on the great journey, if he so chose; and the asking had not yet been done with before Amris had been accepting. "You know how many chiefs and lords he has to his side now," he added. "There will be war."

"Whyever would they wish to prevent Brandoch's departure?" asked Duvessa. "They hate him, as you well know—more than they hate anyone else who stands publicly against them—because of his influence and honor, because they know he will never be turned, because he holds the center in the battle line against them. Surely they will be only too glad to see the back of him and all those other fortunate who shall go with him—and smuggery does not become you, Amrach, so do not salt our wounds. We are envious enough as it is."

Amris laughed and sat up. "Devil-magic. That is how he will put it, that sort of thing is ever in his mouth these days. Folk going to the stars? Tch! Too much usqua! The sun's force holds the worlds to their roads round heaven? How can *that* be, when the priestlings know incontrovertibly that God created Erith the center of all things? Nay, nay, here are blackest dark workings, must be stopped, and a stop put also to those who work them! People must not be allowed to flee beyond the writ of the Tassans, any more than they can be permitted to follow the Old Ways alongside of it. It is Pátraic's way or no way in Éruinn now: he is drunk with his own power, and he will bring that way to war before the end, you shall see."

Kelver Donn Midna, who like most of his folk was restless withindoors if it was not one of their own places, liss or rath or dún, spoke from where he stood by the hearthplace.

"Amris son of the Raven speaks truly," he said, and all heads turned to him, caught by the beauty of his aspect as well as the music of his voice. "They have not scrupled to use the strong hand uppermost to persuade folk to their side; why should they stay that hand from punishing, when punishing is all they still may do? I have no more an-da-shalla than any other of my folk, but it is on me that we need very little Sight to see this coming."

"Are you *quite* sure I cannot come?" asked Laoghaire, breaking the sober little silence that had fallen on them all like a sudden blanket of snow, and the hopefulness in his voice was only half in jest. "I have seven brothers, you know, Brandoch, all of them royal sons of my royal father, each of whom would be happier than the next to take over as king…"

And they laughed, as he had meant them to, and the tension faded for that time. But they did not forget the words Amris and Kelver Donn had spoken.

Two hundred years before great Niall sat to reign at Tara, the equally great Cormac son of Art, he who had first caused the huge stone brughs to be built upon that royal hill, had founded another mighty strongplace, a fortress upon a bluff rising up out of a broad plain in the midsouth; Cashel, he had called it, which name at once became the general term for all such places. There it was that Brendan next rode, to speak with his old friend Conn Kittagh, who was by now a renowned captain in the service of old King Tur-

lough—known now as Piercefoot by reason of his
unusual baptism, though that was not quite the holy
saint's name Pátraic had envisaged gracing his royal
convert—who reigned there, and the others he had
summoned to meet him there as well.

"So you see," he said to those who listened, chins
cupped in hands, their upturned faces bearing the rapt
dreamy look of children being told the most wonderful
tale of all their lives. "And so I intend to do. I have
asked you to hear this; now I ask you to join me in the
venture. If you do, that is well; if not, that is well too.
But I ask your pledge of secrecy—your hands to the
gods—either way."

He let them talk a while amongst themselves, not
watching, busying himself retying the lashings of his
scabbard, which had come loose on his journey southward. At length the gradual quieting and shifting
told him they had sorted matters out, and he looked
up expectantly. They had been sitting scattered any-
how throughout the chamber; now they had drawn
together, and they had a common look of purpose and
unity stamped upon them that had been utterly absent
before. *Indeed, it seems to crackle from them like skyfire.
And—a good omen—they decided with speed; though not, I
trust, in haste...*

"Since Turlough turned Christom it has been thin
times here for those who keep the Old Ways," said
Conn Kittagh, rising to speak, as was the Fian custom to
a superior officer—a compliment to Brendan, no Fian
he, as well as an indicator for the future. Conn glanced
at his mate Shane Farrant, received a single vigorous
nod in return. "Dangerous, even, to have met here
tonight. And—in especial for such as we—it will only

grow worse. It is a wondrous choice you bring us, such as there never was to choose before. Therefore we will go with you, and seek what we shall find." He placed his open hand above his heart. "And we are sworn already."

One by one, the others there, all of them friends of Brendan and of each other—and therefore he had chosen them, knowing that little suspicion could accrue to a meeting of old comrades, even in Turlough's newly Christom, and deeply distrustful, court—rose to say much as Conn had said, and to swear likewise.

"It is well begun," said Brendan, when all had sworn and spoken. "And I have well chosen," he added smiling. "You are all folk of name and standing among the clanns—chiefs, bards, Fians, ban-draoi, druids. You can be trusted to carry the message correctly to those who need to hear, and to seek out those who are of like heart and mind, and above all else to keep silent when silence is the order. More even than that, you are Draoícht and you are fighters, every one of you—and you are friends. What footing could be better found, upon which to found ourselves a world?"

When Brendan returned to Creavanore from his journeyings, Nia was there beneath the covin-tree to greet him, turning her cheek to his filial kiss and walking with him to the stablesheds. She watched while he unsaddled Liath, his horse, and began to methodically curry the beast's damp coat with a straw wisp.

"I have been speaking to friends," he said at last.

"And friends have been speaking of you."

He smiled, but kept his eyes on the patch of gray

hide under his hand. "Aye, I was forgetting you would know—" He broke off, said no more until Liath, dry and shining, was contentedly munching hay, and, for special treat, a hoarded few of last year's apples, shriveled but still sweet.

"I never thought to say it," he muttered then; he gave the thick curving neck one last scrummage, and the big gray nodded vigorously and blew down his muzzle. "But it is going to happen. I am still not sure of *how*, but we are setting sail for exile, into banishment. And far more than nine waves' distance from our homes."

Nia slipped her arm through her son's as they went back toward the house. "Nine waves—in brehon law, that is the traditional distance of exile. But have you never wondered why nine?"

"Well, now that you mention it, I have not. But there are nine elements; ninefold are the ways of the Goddess; nine Worthies of the ancient world; nine Heroes of the Fianna…"

"And nine planets in the Fields of Súl."

"Nay, seven, count again," he said unthinking; then checked, looked sharply at her. "Is it so?"

"You shall judge." She smiled as they entered the house, and Fergus came to greet them. "That way Donn Rígh promised to send to you—it is here. And it awaits you."

When Etain and Brendan first were wed, they had lived almost five years at Rinn na gCroha with her parents, then had come north to Creavanore, to dwell with his. Most new-wed couples do so, dwelling with parents or mateparents or fosterparents until a new home can be raised for them or, not to put too fine a point on it, the elders die and leave the maenor vacant. As tinnscra, Fergus and Coll had joined together to give the young couple lands carved out from their own vast holdings, building for them the brugh of Clanadon, and Nia herself had hallowed it.

But there was another place that they had claimed as home, and not they alone... When Nia rode out from the hill that day in high summer long ago, it had been from the dún of Aileach beneath the Fanad mountains, not far from Creavanore. Long had she been there on a visit to her mother's kin, who had sway in that airt, where Síoda ruled as queen of the liss and Kian was lord; and once Nia met Fergus she never returned to dwell in her old home again.

So that when Brendan and Etain came to Fanad, it was to Aileach as much as to any place else; and it was to Aileach that Brendan now rode, early on a washed blue bird-loud morning of middle spring, the new leaves a green mist upon boughs, streams foaming white over the fords. He did not fear the liss for itself; he was kin there, he had dwelled there, he approached both by right and by command. But the hill of Tallaght, beneath which lay the dún of Aileach, had ever had a haunted look to it, a watchful grimness that even the spring glories could not cloak; and there were ancient reasons that it should be so.

He drew rein and dismounted, leaving Liath to graze the lower slopes. The secret gates of Aileach swung wide for him; he entered unchallenged, he saw no one in the soft-lit halls or stone-paved corridors—and that was as he had come to expect. Then, turning a corner, he came to a door, ajar, and looking inside—

"Books," he breathed reverently. "Not scrolls but *books*—" Well might he marvel: in all the world at that time, scrolls were the usual medium upon which to write; bound books were a very new thing, prized above jewels, above furs, above hawk and hound and horse— even above edged weapons, with whom the true Gael would sooner sleep than with a lover. His folk did not much hold with scrivening in any case: the druids had long contended that writing things down would only be the ruin of memory, and they were doubtless correct, for their feats of pure remembrancing were prodigious indeed. But books were different, books were holy...

"Aye, books! Real books too. We learned the art in Atland, you know, printing and binding, nothing like a good solid chunk of leather and inked paper in your hand. Well—crystals for our permanent recording, to be sure. Not time now to teach you about crystals— later. When we build the ship. For now, books."

Brendan startled violently, at the apparently disembodied voice no less than at the words. Then a flicker of movement in his sidesight, little small snorting noises like an otter talking to itself... He peered round an archway into another, smaller chamber. A man was seated behind a heavy oak table piled high with books and scrolls and papers, as old a man as ever he had seen among the Sidhe, who did not by any means age to mortal measure. *And that being so, this lord must be of vast an age indeed...*

The stranger had long silver hair bound back with a cord of silver leather, and his clothing was of such surpassing randomness that it appeared to have been thrown at him as he stood revolving in the middle of a darkened room. But when the head came up from the book he had been perusing and berating—it was the flicker of turning pages that had caught Brendan's eye, and the rumbled running commentary his ear—and their gazes met, the blaze of intelligence and the ancientness of wisdom that stood in those dark depths caused the younger man to flinch, and garb was suddenly unimportant.

The voice when it came again was mild, and only slightly mocking. "I am Barinthus, called Barrind by your folk—well, your father's folk. And I may have something that can help you. —Oh, aye, aye, I know why you are here! That young pighead Donn has told me—never can tell him anything, will not be told, always he knows it all, always, always. Sometimes he even does. Well—he must know something, he sent *me* here... To meet you, you know. Come forward, come, come, come."

Brendan came, and bowed respectfully, but did not sit, as he had not yet been invited—though he was secretly charmed to hear the stern awesome Donn Rígh so described.

"Indeed, lord, my mother has said that the way I sought had come. I had not expected it to be—well, you."

Barinthus gave a half-smothered snort of laughter. "A fine lass, but she has ever been one for understatement—she has been preparing that way for you many years now, you know, she and I and Donn and others... Well. Not to waste any more time; we shall have little enough as it is." He reached out to the thing Brendan had noted but which his mind had refused to take in—a clear crystal set in a wooden stand, that flung warm

brilliant yellow light upon the table—and though
Brendan could not see how it was done, he drew a finger over the crystal so that the light brightened and
spread to illuminate them both. "There, now."

But when he drew himself up in his seat, and
looked Brendan straight in the eye, all his haphazard
aspect fell away; the old man in rumpled clothing was
gone, and in his place was a stern lord and venerable
captain, one who by his mien had seen very much and
had done vastly more.

"I am the last of the highest Danaans," came the
incredible words. "I have all the lost designs preserved
from the sinking of Atland, carried before that from
our dead home Núminôrë and the star that killed it,
when first we came to Erith in flight for our lives."

Brendan heard the words and did not hear them;
they seemed to be so much what he wished and hoped
to hear that they could not be real. Then:

"But—Atland was destroyed, in the wars between
the Danaans and the Telchines. All our folk know that
our great foes the Telchines escaped back to the stars,
and the Danaans came here to Éruinn; I learned that
when I studied at Rinn na gCroha, after I was wed."

"Aye, we came here, where our high ways were
thought to be magic and sorcery; therefore we kept it
to ourselves, and ended by forgetting most of it."
Barinthus paused, smiling. "But not all. What remains,
I offer to you. It might prove useful in your quest. As
might I," he added diffidently. "I have been out there,
and I have not forgotten."

Brendan's mouth, well agape for the last minute,
shut with a sudden snap as he surged forward, ablaze
with eagerness.

"You? You yourself? *You have been among the stars?*"

His legs failed him, and reaching out blindly he sat down, bidden or not, on the nearest chair.

"I am the last starfarer left on Erith," said Barinthus quietly. "Oh, my poor lost people! I fled with them here, to Éruinn, when Atland died, and now I will flee with them hence. The circle will be complete. Perhaps that is why I have been spared all these centuries— either that, or else the gods have forgotten me. Even among my race none has ever lived so long as I. But perhaps the Alterator has a purpose in it. Maybe I will even get to learn that purpose at last. We can hope."

"You were there," said Brendan again, trying by repetition to make it real to himself. "And you have been here all this time—"

Barinthus nodded, somber now. "I was only young then—but I was a captain in the fleet, the black ships that brought us eastwards, over those terrible seas. Donn Rígh is called Oldest, but by compare to me he has never been born."

Brendan was trying to keep it where he could still understand. "And you know a way—"

"To go back. Aye again. Well, not *back*, just so, not to the same place; our star and its worlds are long gone, even *I* am not old enough to ever have seen it in its life. But there is a region, very large, uninhabited, where we might find a home. If dán allows. If we are lucky. I have maps. And books." Divining the younger man's thought: "They did not go there when first Núminôrë came to die because Erith seemed the better choice; who knew?"

"But that was long ages since; there may be folk dwelling there by now, who would not take kindly to our arrival."

"Possible. Not likely, though. You will see. No certainty that we will even find it, even with my maps."

Brendan laughed shortly and bitterly. "That may well be! But there is absolute certainty in the fate we face if we remain. I have told them, the ones I spoke to, and they will pass it on. They know that the choice is once for aye; that there will be no chance of return. And even though what lies ahead may well be only death in the stars, I will take with me all those who wish to go. I have promised." He leaned forward. "*Can* we go? Can we take them?"

Barinthus was sketching rapidly on a piece of strange parchment, smooth and tough and shiny; though he craned to see, Brendan could make nothing of the straight and spiralled and intersecting lines.

"What? —Oh aye, not hard, not hard. The ships I have in mind to build will be big enough and to spare."

"Ships? More than one? How many?"

"One big, six smaller... You did not think we would walk there, did you? Nay, ships it is—though we have not time nor materials to build one of the very big ones, so— Well. Perhaps fifteen thousand in the one, then, twice that again in the smaller ones combined. Say fifty thousand all told. More, maybe. And beasts, and stores. Not so bad. A fair start."

Brendan blinked, caught back a gasp. "*Fifty thousand folk?* Seven ships? All in the one faring?"

"One faring at a time. There will be more. We cannot carry at one go all those who will wish to join us."

"And you say those are not big ships!"

Barinthus laughed and sat back, his eyes seeing something not in the room. "Maybe we will even have one or two of those, one day, if we have the luck. Oh,

but they were mighty! The royal flagship, Aoroth Kalerri'aren, a great golden thing like a star-dragon, three
leagues long—it could carry fifty thousand together
and still not be full-laden, yet a child could sail it alone
if need demanded... Well. Our own transport will be
rather humbler. The voyage will take longer, too—we
have not the makings for speed, and I would not build
for it even if we did. Not yet. We will do very well. You
shall see. Everyone shall see." He drew a chair to his
side, patted the seat for Brendan to take it. "Now. We
begin. First, the properties necessary for travel in space
are these—"

Emerging into the soft blue evening air outside
Aileach—the same day, though for all he knew it could
have been years later—Brendan mounted Liath, let
the reins fall loose on the beast's neck; the horse would
find his own way home to Creavanore. He was still too
staggered at what had been offered him, in too much
of a daze to pay heed how he went, his head still spinning with the wonders he had been shown, the new
knowledge he had just barely begun to learn.

   *To have come from Atland, and before—ten thousand
years old! Or even more, maybe... I would not be in his boots
for any sake—nay, not even to have had what he has had,
seen what he has seen... But he knows the way out, the way
back—the way home!—and perhaps he has the right of it, perhaps the Goddess has granted him such vast length of days for
just such a reason... Well, the choice is made now, and cannot
be unmade; we are caught into the swordknot. But to leave the
planet! And to be able to! Great Kelu!*

   And so thinking, he rode home; or rather, Liath,

eager for his stable, carried him there. Not far from the
road fork that led to Clanadon on the one side and
Creavanore on the other, out of the corner of his eye
Brendan caught something moving that had not been
there a moment before, and though his head did not
turn his gaze flicked upward.

Upon a crag of Darinlaur, that rose behind Creavanore like a blue-shale whaleback six hundred feet
high, a shape was silhouetted against the sunset; he
assessed it instinctively, as he had done when a youthful
shepherder on those very hills. *Wolf…nay, too large.
What then?* Then the shape moved. *Wolf! The biggest wolf
there ever was…*

More than twice the size of any he had seen or
heard of, with a brindled black-silver coat and an
immaculate white ruff, the wolf began to pick its way
delicately through the shaled outcrops, downslope to
him. He knew enough to rein in and stand, watching
the creature's leisurely progress. *Run! It could catch me
in three bounds even at the gallop, if it were so minded—
though it is very strange that Liath does not seem troubled…*
Indeed, the gray horse was almost dozing as he stood,
his head drooping as if he were already safe in his own
stable, and Brendan had a growing suspicion that, fan-
tastic as it sounded, the approaching wolf himself was
responsible for Liath's sudden drowse.

The wolf was less than its own length from him now,
watching him steadily out of eyes like green lamps; he
had the distinct feeling it was smiling. And then he
knew he must be mad entirely, for he heard it speak,
or at least heard its words in his mind, and in a daze
he dismounted as the words bade him. *After today, nothing will ever be strange again…*

"I am the Faol-mór," came the voice of the wolf—a deep furry voice, as if it came out of the earth itself. "You are mine, and I am yours. I will go with you when you go, go where you go. I will stay with you, and with those of your Name and blood and body. I will stay until the end."

In one bound it closed the remaining distance between them. Brendan felt its thick mane under his fingers, the cold-nosed muzzle in his palm, the rasp of the tongue upon his hand. Then it was gone; and he was alone upon the darkling hill.

But not alone... He remounted Liath, and the horse seemed to wake up again, seemingly no worse for his nap and still unaware of what, or who, had been and gone. Brendan gave him more than a touch of leg and collected him hard to hasten him along, suddenly no longer inclined to idle on the road but wishful of reaching lights and folk, walls and doors, as soon as might be. *But not alone. Mighty Dâna, not alone! And never once alone again...*

CHAPTER FIFTEEN

s word began to spread where Brendan had laid his lures and sent out his first messengers, leaders of the various tribes and nations began to come in secret to Clanadon, or Creavanore, or Aileach, or Knockfierna, or Tara, or wherever he might be found, to speak urgently and secretly to him, and to Nia and Barinthus and the others who were deepest in their counsels. As more and more made their hopeful covert way to him, Brendan rejoiced to see he had not trailed his cloak in vain: of those who came to bespeak him, not one went away lacking a promised place for their folk in the great endeavor, and promising secrecy to Brendan in return; not one would betray the trust.

Among those later to be among his chief captains were Scathach of Lochaber, she who led a clann alliance of the western Aulbannach folk; Kunera, a princess of the Boarholms, leader of the Crúithin, the Pictfolk in those isles and the northern mainland regions, with Dúnomaglos her mate; Galon Braz C'haloned, from Less Britain across the Narrow Seas, who brought with him many gifted folk to speed the work, among them the master-builder Gradlon of Ys, whom Brendan had met at Laoghaire's court, turning a hand to shipcraft now and with even greater things to build later on; Elved ap Dynevor, leader of the Gwyneddan Kymry; Dai Rogan Alibando, speaker for the Manxfolk; dark-bearded Kynmarra, from Templarian in the wild far southwest of Cornovia; and more beside.

Even the Sidhefolk sent emissaries from their hidden strongholds, not those of Tir Gaedhil only but of every nation who had part in the faring. Though repeatedly offered honored place in any ship they chose, or even a new ship to be built to carry themselves alone, they smilingly refused, turning aside even the politest inquiry as to just what their travel arrangements might be—though some few would choose to sail with the immram fleet, when it came to sailing. But Brendan remembered the words of Donn Rígh, given him at Knockfierna before this venture had even been dreamed on: "We will find our own road; do not fear for us. We will be there before you. And we will not be the only ones there to greet you when your ship touches sand at last." And in those words, which he kept to himself, not even Nia to share them, he found reassurance.

And one night, under cover of darkness and storm and muffling hoods, came even some of the Christom themselves to Brendan and Nia; came in shyness for fear of Brendan's lack of welcome, came in secret for fear of Pátraic's wrath—but came nonetheless, and brought unexpected purpose with them in that coming.

"We of the Celi Dé are not slow or shy of declaring to any who will hear," said Dorren nic Cána, unhooding in the solar at Creavanore to reveal the bright red-gold

hair that is particular to the northern Aulbannach; a
small-statured woman, sturdy and round like a candle,
with a wicked wit to match her calm faith. "But Pátraic
will not even listen."

"What he preaches these days has little to do with the
words of Iosa of the Tree," said Malise mac Guaire, her
companion on the errand to Brendan, "and the Lord
Iosa himself would no doubt say so. For this, and for
other things we do that are contrary to his preachings—
though not contrary to our Lord's teachings—Pátraic
has threatened us with public excommunication, brand-
ing us heretic and anathema."

They had come to petition Brendan for a place for
their folk in the Immram Mhór; when he, naturally curious if not outright suspicious, wondered aloud how they
had heard of his intentions, and asked them to explain
themselves further, they answered frankly and at once.
Nia, who had happened by—it seemed through purest
chance, though with her, Brendan privately reflected,
chance was never, ever, what it seemed—studied them
with compassion and a searching measuring gaze, and
they returned her look with open honest plainness and
respect.

"Your Tangavaun would never look so upon me or
my folk," she said at length, very pleased by what she
saw in them.

"And that is why we wish to join you," said Malise
simply. "The Celi Dé we call ourselves, the Friends of
God; we have a maenor on the little isle Ionagh, where
we worship and work—which for us is much the same
thing—and we were here in this island before Pátraic
showed his face and opened his mouth. You have said,
lord of Fanad, that freedom before the gods, freedom

to worship the Highest as one's soul requires, in whatever guise one needs, is the greatest good, and if we are not free to do so, we are all slaves alike. Well, we are Celi Dé, friends of that same Highest, and any friend of the Highest is a friend of ours. So we seek to come with you, to free ourselves from slavery to Pátraic's will and way. But we are not spies, nor is your secret betrayed, for I see that thought in your eyes: it was Scathach of Lochaber who spoke to us of it, and she said that you would not oppose our coming."

I might not, at that... "No doubt Pátraic would have rather more than somewhat to say about it?"

Dorren's amused glance matched his. "No doubt he would, if only he knew. But, lord, we are here and he is not. Hear now what *we* would say—"

She spoke long and earnestly, and Malise also. Brendan listened more than he spoke, though when he did speak he laid out for them with clarity and firmness the many uncertainties, the disadvantages, the dangers, just as he had done for any of the other prospective voyagers. But they were as firm in their asking, and their own clear will would not be swayed; and he was deeply moved. *These are no sheep but brave and loyal hounds, only in the wrong pack, and trained to follow the horn of the wrong master; they should be free to hunt their own line of country—even as we are. I could lift such a pack from the scent they follow—*

"What Pátraic preaches now is his law, not God's," said Dorren. "His hatred of Draoícht and Danaan, his black intolerance of any way but his... It is blasphemy to put limits on God: you have said it yourself, lord, and I have even heard you—many roads have been fashioned, and all of them lead to the Light. It is up to each soul to choose the path best suited for it to travel, and none may order otherwise. And all those roads run side by side, forever, to the same destination."

"As for the Danaans," offered Malise, "they are but the higher octave of mortals, our elder cousins. A parallel creation—not better, not worse; merely different. If God has seen fit to create so, who shall dare gainsay?"

Brendan glanced at his mother, but Nia made no sign, one way or another. "I can see where my old friend Ferganam well has named you heretic," he said presently, but now he was smiling. "And for my part, that is more than recommendation enough. Be welcome among us."

When they had thanked him over and over, vowing prayers and whatever other earthlier help they might give, and had vanished again into the sheltering storm, Brendan's promise safe with them and theirs with him, their new captain sat staring into the fire before him; then looking up he saw his mother watching him. Her face was serene, lighted from within as if she smiled; but she was not smiling.

"Traitors?" he asked presently.

She shook her head slowly, face still alight. "Not to us."

He laughed aloud at her careful distinction. "Not to us," he repeated. "And not, I think, to their Iosa either... It was the only choice," he said after a long comfortable silence.

"It was well done," said Nia after a silence of her own. "In the long run it will prove even better done than you know—or will know."

"Ah. Sight again?"

"Sight always."

*   *   *

Now for Brendan and Barinthus came the long patient careful time, the years of the Making. They had planned and studied, debated and considered, the least little particular, the tiniest detail, the most seemingly insignificant scrap of magic or science that could have bearing on their tremendous work. Brendan had proved a brilliant student, and for his part Barinthus had found deep fulfillment in using, and passing along, the knowledge he had so long held.

But even that time came soon enough to completion; now they delayed no longer but began to build, with folk to help them that were bound by the fearfullest oaths to the deepest secrecy. As Barinthus cheerfully pointed out, it had been a very long time since he had fashioned such toys as these, so their first proud constructions were testing ones only. But astonishing for all that: midget curraghs made of strange new metals and alloys, that could move in air with none to guide them save the thought of those who directed from the ground. Incredibly maneuverable, they could be seen at all hours darting through the passes of the Fanad hills—gleaming hawks of preposterous size, making their overhead transits in unexpectedly eerie silence.

As the novice makers swiftly mastered ancient skills newly learned, their uncertainties grew less and fewer and the midgets grew larger and sleeker, of ever stranger design—wheels, spheroids, flying stars—going farther, higher, longer, faster, so that they could no longer be tracked by even the keenest-sighted among the Sidhefolk but instruments must now be devised to follow their trail in the heavens. One unexpected boon of the artificing, most welcome to them, was that no more need they rely on horses and ships and chariots for transport: they had cars of the air to carry them now, even over the waters to Albaun and Gwalia and Cornovia. So that instead of sails of many days in chancy galleys, dependent on wind and wave, or jouncing passage over the safety of ill-maintained drove-roads, Brendan could now take air as easily as once he had taken horse or taken water, to be in the Boarholms with Kunera in the forenoon and consult with Kynmarra in Templarian at the daymeal, to draw plans over supper with Gradlon at Ys and sleep in Laoghaire's palace at Tara that same night.

But at last there came the day when Barinthus and Brendan adjudged the best-built of the test-craft safe enough and strong enough to carry human cargo; and to take that cargo farther and higher than mere fast dashes over the local seas. They were ready for the first ship-trial in space itself; and though many offered and pleaded, begged and bribed, whined and wheedled, to have share in the honor and the heart-pounding excitement, the builders would permit none to take the risk but themselves alone.

From his seat beside Barinthus, Brendan looked gingerly out and down. And gasped: they were already several thousand feet up and rising more swiftly than he could draw breath to speak of it. The ship that carried them was the second largest of the vessels so far adjudged spaceworthy: a lovely crescent-shaped craft, its hull made of dark-green metal, one of the new alloys. They were seated in a small cabin at the center of the outer curve, with two chair-couches contoured to support them in what seemed to Brendan to be unlikely positions indeed.

Then under Barinthus's hand the little ship, still climbing, turned lazily on its right, a movement like a sun-shark rolling over in a warm blue bay. They found themselves looking up at land streaming above them where a moment since there had been sky, and Brendan understood why the seats were built as they were. *Now the sky is* beneath *us... It is* very *confusing, and yet it seems most right, and somehow familiar, too...*

"Are you well?" came Barinthus's voice, hollow in the rush of sound that filled the tiny cabin. Brendan realized the other was delicately inquiring after the well-being of his inner balance; he had been warned that sometimes the unfamiliar motion could outrage the senses, with disastrous, and untidy, effect.

"My breakfast stays where I put it, if that is what you are wondering."

Barinthus laughed. "A star-sailor born! I knew it as soon as ever I saw you..." He patted the helmboard affectionately, as if it were Brendan's head, or the gleaming neck of a horse. "These craft are fine flying hawks, not like the little cleggan ones—though those too have their uses. These handle differently, and they put different stresses on those who sail them. And the dromonds, the greatships, the ones that sail the stars, are different yet again." He gestured down and ahead, proudly, a host inviting a guest into a house of particular splendor. "Look below."

Brendan did, and caught his breath. *And the monklings dare to teach the world is flat, and the crown of cre-*

ation! But then they have never sailed these seas, nor seen these skies... They were so high now that he could see the very curve of the planet beneath them. The ocean looked like a dull silver shield, and what land he saw was not Éruinn but a vast green continent, with red smudges in the north and south that must be desert places; clouds white and tufted as marsh-cotton crawled by far, far below, the distance of their remove shown by the imperceptible slowness of their motion.

"Strange that a world with so much water is called Earth. Its proper name should be Ocean."

"Land or water, we are the first to see it from this vantage for many centuries." Barinthus touched a silver stud, and the planet streamed below them now south to north. To their left, they were moving up the coast of an unknown landmass, like an hourglass heavy at the bottom and top and waisted in the middle; to the right was more ocean.

"The Western Wastes," he said in answer to Brendan's looked question. "Before Atland fell, we made some settlements there, and befriended the folk who dwell in those lands, a noble race, bronze of skin and great of heart, with whom our own people and your father's alike have much in common; but none shall come across the seas to it or them for many lifetimes."

Oh aye? Or has done?... "I mind me of a tale Laoghaire told me, of how mighty Cormac, grandson of Conn the Hundred-Fighter, Laoghaire's own great-grandsir to the fourth, once went missing many months," said Brendan then, in a voice shamelessly calculated to coax confession. "And how when Cormac returned, he said—I say, he *said*—that he had been to magic isles beyond the worlds..."

But Barinthus only smiled, and would not be drawn. Giving up, and looking up as the ship turned sharply east again, Brendan saw the sky dense and black and deep, set a thousandfold thicker with stars than ever he had seen it on even the most moonless night. *We came from out there! That is 'space'— This is our birthright, and now we take it back again, that which should always have been ours...* Or so, at least, he had always been told. Some believed, some not; for himself he could not doubt, and never had. *For if I doubt that, then what else may come to be doubted in turn? Good it is to question; but better it is to know—and to know more surely—when one has been answered in truth...* And still the ship climbed.

Brendan, presently, remembering he had a companion in the cabin: "Amris and Ríonach and many others berated us for claiming this for our task and no one else's; they said we were selfish greedy piglings who only wanted to have all the fun for ourselves."

"And your point would be—?"

Brendan grinned, spread eloquent hands over the spectacular sight without. "I will not call them liars." He fell silent, staring. "I confess I was a little—well, more than a little—feared. To go into the heavens... into space." He tried the word on his tongue, finding the sound as strange as the idea or the reality. "Most will find this as splendid as we do, or so I hope. But do you think—do you think they might instead have terror of such a sight?"

Barinthus shook his head. "Nay, for they love you and trust you. They will be like horses in a stable-fire; feared, skittish, but so long as you are there to grab their manes and fling a cloth across their eyes, they know you will lead them out of the doomed stable to safety." He gestured left with a jerk of his chin. "Over there—that is the Hollow Crown, the opening at the Pole of the energy wall that surrounds Erith like a veil; you can just see it, where the Crown of the North divides and parts. That is how we first came here, through that portal."

"And will we leave so?"

"Even so."

"And is that how *you* came here?"

The old man smiled, but did not look at him. "So proud we were, so many of us had been saved; and yet not so many, not when Atland died. We thought we had found a home forever—and now we are once again put to the road."

"You did not answer my question," said Brendan, when his teacher seemed to have finished speaking.

Barinthus laughed, and touched a certain crystal, and the little ship banked like a stooping falcon that spies a careless hare.

"You would only question my answer. It is all one. Attend now to our rate of descent, amhic, if you do not wish to see us smeared like butter over those great white peaks below."

They eluded a flaming end on the flanks of the mountains that would one day be called Himalaya, and fleeing westward again made planetfall on the terminator— more new words that had sprung up to fill the need folk had of them, so many new things needed naming—that arc dividing night and day which sliced the planet as cleanly as an apple between light and dark; its blade cleaved across Éruinn like the shadow of some monstrous sword.

As they glided in to land, Brendan saw with satisfaction that nothing of their work was visible from the air. *And if not to be seen from* this *vantage, then not from neighboring hilltops or high ground either...* Nia had taken it upon her to screen their comings and goings, and the work itself, from eyes that saw for Pátraic—his spies were everywhere—and these days she was not slow to draw upon the magic she had heretofore so seldom used. "All that is changing too," she had said to her son, laughing, when he taxed her with it.

But caution was ever the word now, so that no hint of the plan should leak out untimely soon: aircars left under cover of night or cloud, hugging the ground contours or threading glens, and went long distances out to sea, low above the waves, before their pilots dared acquire height and speed; the great works where the various ships were being assembled lay deep within woods and under mountains—thanks were due the Sidhefolk for that—and all the rest of the crafting was easily disguisable. The mining for metals was the least concealable of their activities, and they had despaired of how to hide it until, again, Nia took a hand. Brendan had shaken his head in wonder. *No mines at all: the needed metal comes out of the hills when she calls it, as once she called needed water from the rock...*

They landed safely, unable to resist a few intemperate aerobatic flourishes—but only a few—and gave brief report of all particulars to those who clustered round; and that night there assembled by prearrangement at Clanadon all the chief captains of the Immram to hear for themselves.

"As you know, we leave soon, and we will leave in secret," said Brendan, having given a fully detailed account of the day's test-sail and answered the questions that flew at him from all sides. "Therefore for the protection of the ships and lands alike I have chosen places in the remote far north and west. Only the site at Ys in Less Britain is closer to folk than I might wish; but it cannot be helped."

"Protection of the lands?" asked Kunera. "Protection from what?"

Barinthus stood up, began to pace. "We did not have the time or the skill to build the ships in space, where it is best and easiest to do so, you understand, though we have managed very well. But this was a fence we could not leap… Remoteness to hide what we do, understood, well enough. But we lack the makings to shield the full power of the engines when the ships rise at last, and we would do as little harm to the land as we must. So—we choose out-of-the-way places, and resign ourselves to their obliteration."

"We have used ship-engines already," Conn Kittagh pointed out. "Many of us have even been aloft by their grace, if not perhaps so high as you two today. The land took no great harm of it."

"Those engines are to the ones we now have building as a rush-dip is to the sun," said Gradlon of Ys, who had seen some of the small-scale tests and knew whereof he spoke. "These are the motivers and amplifiers that will drive our ships among the stars; and even they are not yet the mightiest that could be made— though quite mighty enough for the purpose. Listen now: when our ships rise from earth, so great will be the force unleashed that the ground beneath, the very rock and soil itself, will melt and turn to glass. And where that by merest chance does not occur, the lands will sink beneath the sea."

There was a sudden silence, and talk languished— no real answer could be made to that, and none had heart to ask for more details—and presently Brendan turned the talk to what the guests could tell him. They had little of good to report: though the great secret undertaking remained secret still, Pátraic and his priestlings were spreading their hold and tightening their grasp, and newly Christom chiefs were raiding with increased fervor and ferocity against their dree-folk neighbors.

"Surely, just what a god of peace most loves to see," remarked Kynmarra, his voice dripping irony. "Only think of the slaughter that might have been done had he been inclined to war! What kind of bargain did they buy into—not wanting to think for themselves, they sought one to think for them; and before they knew the slave-collar was locked around their throats they were bought and sold for all time. Well is it said that onetime slaves make the harshest masters…"

"It is not so much Pátraic, nor even his white godling of the tree," said Ríonach Sulbair. "—Nay, I do not excuse him, hear me out! At first, 'tis true, he did encourage it; but now it is far beyond him. Those who have gone over—they but fight as the Gael have always fought; their Christery is mere excuse. They have turned against our ancient beliefs of many lives, throwing in with a god who alleges love but apparently thinks nothing of damning souls to eternal torment after one wrong step. They wish us all to be as sheeplike as themselves, and are angered because we refuse to do it."

"They will be angrier still when we leave," remarked Scathach of Lochaber, "because we escaped and they did not—because we avoided the trap that the rest of them fell into."

"Even that is not the whole reason." Corlis Typhult spoke quietly, as befitted a priestess. "Have you never wondered, Brandoch, just why it is that the Tangavaun hates you even above the rest of us?"

Brendan started, surprised by her tone no less than by the words she spoke in it. "Surely I have; but I have ever put it down to history—envy, what we shared as lads, what we know each of the other—" He broke off; only Etain, Nia and Fergus, Duvessa and Laoghaire knew of the story Pátraic had told him, of what had taken place long since, in a sacred wood in Brigantian lands of Britain the More, and in another on the side of Slemish. *That is not my tale to tell...*

Corlis said no word but taking a polished bronze charger from the table she held it up as mirror; from where he sat across from her, Brendan saw his own face dimly reflected in the gold-colored gleam—the pleasant even features, not strictly handsome but alive with intelligence and wit, the dark eyes, the beard and hair still untouched by silver, all familiar as ever.

He shook his head, smiling. "M'chara, I know the man well enough—what is it I must look for?"

"You already see it, though you think you do not," she said. "Your mother's gift to you." When he still looked bewildered, plainly not taking her meaning: "The blood of the Sidhe."

CHAPTER SIXTEEN

"And his fear and jealousy and envy of that blood," said Etain later that night, when the guests had been lighted to their beds and she and Brendan had gone to their own. "What else? Corlis put her finger square on the bruise, and with her mirror showed you where it lies." She drew a finger over his cheek, along the line of his bearded jaw. "You may never have thought so or felt so or even seen so, my Brandoch—you spend very little time looking into mirrors, at least not so as I have noticed—but believe me when I tell you that though your looks have deepened, boy to man, you have aged scarce one year in the past ten. It will be so all the rest of your days, and not for you alone. Through us, and others who have wed and borne as we have, Danaan blood will pass into the generations of the Gael, to bring magic, Sight, length of days—things pure mortals, having no share in, will indeed envy and fear—and hate. And—mortals being what they are—seemingly endless youth and strength and beauty will be prime among those hating reasons. As they have ever been 'twixt you and Pátraic—"

He drew back a little and looked at her in his arms. In the glow of the grieshoch she seemed to glow with a light of her own—pure-blooded of the People of the

Star. The thought was unspoken between them: she would age even less swiftly than he, and would survive him by not centuries but perhaps millennia. *That was the choice we made…the choice my parents made…*

"And Gael blood passed into the generations of the Danaans?" he asked presently. "How does that work on *your* folk? Do they fear and hate and envy in their turn?"

"It brings us to feel, not to fear," said Etain quietly. "To joy and grief, love and hate, and all other feelings; that tremendous gift of the Highest, which mortals take for granted, owning and yet not treasuring… Also children come easier to a union of Gael and Danaan than to a pairing of two of my folk, or even two of yours—children with the high gifts of both their parents. Perhaps that is what the Tangavaun dreads more than anything else—a race of such as Fionagh and Rohan, a blend that is bred from the best in both our kindreds, a race that does not fear him, that thinks for itself. A race that he and his kind cannot command— or control."

"He is the worst thing that ever happened to this land," said Brendan after a while, and in his voice was a judgment as well as a vow. "And I will take the best of it away from him."

After a few more flights, tests both more disastrous and less so—though by the grace of all gods no life was lost nor limb was maimed, there were bruises and broken bones and concussed heads aplenty, the upshot of ungentle landings or ill-timed maneuvers—Brendan and Barinthus agreed that the star-mastery that had been within their reach was now at last firm within their grasp, and delaying no more they began in secret and in earnest to build in Fanad.

So Fergus Aoibhell sealed the borders of his maigen, so that none were allowed in, and of those who were already in, laboring on the great new work, not one wished to be allowed out. Laoghaire, quietly petitioned, posted soldiers as picket-guards on the roads and rivers and passes that led into Fanad, though he gave no reason why he did so—a king's prerogative, not to make excuses—and let them think as they pleased, if they thought at all. But for all intents, and Brendan's purposes, Fanad now was cut off from the rest of Éruinn, and what work went on there, in such deadly secret, only its own folk knew.

And that work was more tremendous than the most extravagant bard could imagine: the building of a dromond, a ship to carry fifteen thousand souls to the stars. When completed it would have not only engines of unimaginable power, fueled no one save Nia and Barinthus and Gradlon entirely understood how, but also vast silver sails to let it run before the stellar winds—such a ship as had never been seen in the skies of Erith since the Telchines deserted Atland and left the Danaans to their fate.

Its keel and vast rib-structure had been laid down beneath the hill, in the hidden caverns hollowed for them by the Sidhefolk; its masts were not tree-trunks but long spars of poured and tempered metal. Lost crafts newly relearned built it day by day, and living magic kept it hidden; all of Fanad would leave in it on the day it rose from earth, and many others beside.

The day its gleaming silver skin went on was the day

it got its name. Brendan stood on a low green hillock, surrounded by kin and friends and commanders and all those who had worked on the ship, many hundreds of eager folk; Yellan vale that day was full of proud watchers. And not mortals only: from every dún in Éru-inn—not Aileach alone but Knockfierna and Carrig-navar and Rinn na gCroha and Knocknarea, and not from Éruinn alone but from Cartlane Crags in Aulba and Lostwithiel in Cornovia, from Caerseion in Gwyneddan Gwalia and Carn Brea in Manaun's isle, and all the other halls of their people—had come Sidhefolk to witness. They did not hold themselves apart but stood close among their mortal counterparts; no great task to pick them out—they blazed like torches, like pillars of silver and gold.

The vantage point had been chosen because from here the whole of the Yellan valley lay open to view. Only a year before, it had been a deep-mouthed green trough like many another in those lands, dug out by passing glaciers long ago in their advancings and retreats, its contours smoothed and rounded by aeons of water and wind, empty of habitation. Empty now no longer: where once a lord's son and a Brython slave-youth had kept their flocks and shared their friend-ship, though the friendship had turned to fear and hatred, now the flock to be guarded was the future itself. The great ship, drawn out of the hill—or more accurately, the hill drawn away from it—now filled Yel-lan vale as neatly as a sword in its own sheath, as com-pletely as the white tongues of ice had done; it was as dangerous as the one, as majestic as the other.

Brendan could not take his eyes off it; none of them could. *We have made this—we, alone, ourselves... We have fashioned it out of the past, to alter the present and claim the future: it took us so long, since Danaans came to Éruinn, so long; and all this time we could have been free of the stars...* But he had called his folk to Yellan that day for a purpose indeed. The last of the ship's structure had been completed and ground-tested, and before it could be trial-flown it only remained for it to be clad in the skin that would enable it to withstand the cold and stress of space. Now those who had part in the great endeavor of making were here to watch—a fitting reward for all their work and hope.

But to the surprise of many it was not Brendan but Nia who now stepped forward. Brendan smiled at his mother, nodded once, raised an arm for silence; then, standing a little apart, Nia the Golden lifted her arms, palms outward, and for the first time put forth for all to see the real power that was in her.

For the space of three breaths nothing seemed to happen—or rather her labor and effort were not visible to the eye, for she looked unchanged and so did everything else; in all that waiting valley nothing stirred, not a breath was drawn. The giant craft itself was all patchworked metal strips and welded squares, a curragh of the giants in a slipway beyond mortal measure; though it was as tight-clad as the artificers could make it, for spaceworthiness it might have been a wicker sieve. Then the metal that had been joined to make the hull plating began to move. It heard what Nia had commanded, and it obeyed: it shivered and shimmered, it flowed like wind-ruffled water or the muscles of a horse; and when it ceased to flow and move the skin of the ship was seamless and shining, reflecting the sunlight so fiercely that the metal looked white-hot, so smooth and sealed and perfect that not a stray solitary atom could penetrate the hull.

The ship seemed to quiver from bow to stern, shook once all along its tremendous graceful stretch and span. And then it was as it was: a league in length, higher than the hill of Slemish and broader than the Sinan in flood, it stood in Fanad like nothing else that ever had been or would be. Now that it was clad, many who had not thought how it might look startled back, for its aspect was that of a sweep-winged swan. But many more thought it had another look—a great silver dragon, a drake of the stars, or the Salmon of Wisdom himself, glittering in the Pool at the Heart of the World.

"It is all of a piece," said Barinthus, looking upon the gleaming craft with the rest of them, from the prudent distance upon which Brendan had insisted. But the distance in his eyes was more than yards: star-miles away he was, and centuries...

"Name of Dâna, *now* it is!" said Amris mac an Fhiach, as staggered as the rest of them.

The old man smiled, half-turned his head, looked back at the vessel. "Nay, amhic, I did not mean the ship. The lore that built it, the force that will drive it, the Way that we follow—it is not the same, but it *is* all one. The Tangavaun is wrong: he seeks to unpick the fabric when he should rather be adding threads to the weave. Much sorrow and grief will be wrought of his unravelling, before this island once again comes to the pattern that was made for it from the first."

There was silence for long moments, as eyes stared and hearts filled and brains tried to encompass what had been wrought. Then:

"Have you found its name, Brandoch?" asked Laoghaire quietly, who had travelled there with Duvessa in deepest secret to witness the great day; and who, king or no king, found himself possessed just now of the most furious desperate envy of his life. *I would sell my brothers into slavery and my queen into a bawdhouse without a second thought, give up twenty kingdoms and all the riches thereof without a backward glance, if only I might have the smallest, meanest place in this faring, a hard comfortless corner to sleep in aboard this star-drake...* "It should carry a fine and high one."

Brendan stirred, drawn back from his own ashlings, and bowed to Barinthus. "I had thought to give that honor to the one who made it."

That ancient starfarer shook his head, though he was deeply moved. "And honor it is, my dearest son... But I have done now with doing and with making. From here, I am passenger and guide. No more. Past time for it. And any road, the making was not mine."

"Then, mamaith, you—?" Brendan turned to her where she stood, and in the same movement Nia swung round to him, tall and vibrant, more alive, more *there*, than anyone or anything else in the valley that day save the ship; the aftermath of her magic swirled about her like a cloak, so that those watching almost visibly wilted under the force of it.

"Nay, lord," she said to her son in the High Gaeloch, her face brighter than the silver ship itself with the pride and love she had in him. "Thine the vision; the honor of naming is to thee. Only thou hast heard its truename."

"I have heard its name," said Brendan then, almost whispering; then reaching out his right hand, palm out and down, fingers wide in blessing and salute, he spoke in a voice that carried across the valley. "Be sained and named of me, then. Be named among us. This is the Hui Corra."

But that was by no means the end of their labors. Newly named, the Hui Corra needed as much care as any newborn: it must be armed with weapons to insure its survival, systems of guidance and shielding must be constructed, the mechanisms perfected that were to supply air and water and food once in flight—and the means found to power all these things.

And here again the magic that was Nia's came into its own; if they had relied on mere science they would never have left the ground. Even in these later, lesser times, magic and science, though not the same, in some mystic way are one—as heads and tails are both the coin, as the hand is the hand whether it is palm or fist—but in those days it was truer still. On many, many occasions Barinthus and Gradlon and Nia and even Etain attempted to explain such matters to the others, but always they failed.

"How and why does not concern us," said Ríonach Sulbair firmly, and she spoke for just about everyone. "It only makes steam come out of our ears when you try to tell us, so do not trouble yourselves. Tell us what will happen if we do such and such a thing, and what will happen if we do not, and no more. That is all we ask. As long as you know it will work, that is enough. We do not need to know, and we do not want to. Believe it." And so it was.

But the Hui Corra, though the largest, was not the

only ship of the Immram that would be. While they were building in Fanad, six other starcraft were likewise taking shape—in the Boarholms, in Ys, in Sulyonessa, in Gwalia, in Aulba, in the Out Isles off the west coast of Éruinn; in all the remote places that Brendan had chosen to his purpose.

And all this time of fevered doing, they heard not the smallest word of Pátraic, or of his own doing.

"Which is well enough," said Amris, aggrieved as usual every time he thought of the Christom leader. "Though it is on me he is most dangerous when he is least visible—I like to keep my enemies where I can see them."

But he was not to have his wish; or at least not yet a while.

Though the Tangavaun had not been forgotten, other matters now pressed more sharply: at last it had come time to sail the Hui Corra, to lift her off from earth. It would be a trial sail, but a true one, into deep space out past the orbit of the moon, and perhaps even farther. Brendan, Nia, Kelver Donn Midna and Barinthus made up all the crew; they would ask no others yet to risk the danger, though there had been no shortage of volunteers. "The dangers to come will more than suffice you," said Kelver Donn, to silence the supplicant clamor, and with that the unchosen had to be content.

So in part for fear of those who longed to come and in part to ward off harm from those who longed to watch, the four who would take the Hui Corra on her first sail had told no one the day or hour they had set for the trial. They had chosen a dawn of low fog and dense cloud after a wild chill night of wind and rain; none would be early abroad on such a day, and the clouds would veil the rising ship as soon as it began to move.

An hour before dawn Brendan approached the Hui Corra, the others close behind him; no one else was astir. As he set his hand to the ship's flank, the silver metal drew aside, to form a door where an instant before there had been only solid hull. *Never shall I get used to that...* They entered then, the hull sealing itself behind them as seamlessly and silently as it had opened, and went to the command deck. The ship had been designed by Barinthus to be sailed by one person, if ever such dire circumstances should demand; so by that count their crew of four was pure luxury. But though each of them had spent aboard the ship thousands of workdays and every scrap of leisure time for more years than they liked to think, this time was different. *This time is real...*

By unspoken agreement Barinthus took the helm: the last starfarer alive on Erith now captained the first starship to take to the heavens for centuries uncounted— and centuries to come. His guiding movements as he prepared for planetrise were barely visible; like all the ships of his people's making, the Hui Corra was not sailed so much as thought-with. There was no jar at starting; beneath them they felt the upsurging motion of the ship through air, smooth, steady, immensely powerful.

"Not the true engines at work, no," Barinthus had said, when anxious folk had reminded him of the perils he himself so often enumerated. "Those will be fired only on the actual day, to clear the pull of the planet, to boost into star-flight; when we are in that mode we will feel no movement at all. But for this little jaunt, the lesser engines will suffice; and the starsails too must be tested and tried."

Now Barinthus placed his palm on the helm—a single solid crystal of clearest quaratz, man-length and arm-wide, mined in the Aulban mountains—and thought his will, and the ship responded. Their speed of ascent could only be determined from the way the stars spun beyond the viewports, the pace of shrinking of the blue-green orb that was Erith; they felt not even that sense of hollowness as may be felt by landsmen stepping aboard a ship, that feeling of nothing beneath them straight down to the seafloor, the thinness of keel and hull and the empty water that supports them. Here there was none of that: they felt safe and enclosed and protected, in a great thick-walled dún of the air, a fortress that had somehow learned to move among the stars.

They were closing upon the moon almost before they knew it. Brendan stared entranced as the rough lunar surface rushed at him; it looked mere yards off, though he knew it was still thousands of miles beneath them. *Pull back*, came Barinthus' calm quiet voice in thoughtspeech, and Brendan touched the panel to his right. The ship's nose lifted smoothly as a horse taking a stone wall, and aimed itself at the stars. Beneath them, the moon glowed and dwindled again as the Hui Corra swung round its farther side.

"Be first of all folk, since my own last journey here, to see that face turned ever from Erith," said Barinthus; his own face had that upon it which none there, not even Nia, could long regard.

Brendan had risen from his seat and now was plastered against the viewport like a wet leaf against a stone in an autumn gale. "It is like a shield slashed and dinted in battle; the inner face, the one we know, is pocked and cratered, but smooth as ice on a pond by compare to this."

"The targe of Erith," said Kelver Donn, for all of him as awed as his friend. "It is the planet's buckler against stones flung from heaven—see at what cost to itself."

"Have any ever dwelled here?" murmured Brendan after a while, still gazing raptly at the waterless plains below, soft with the dust of aeons and of worlds.

Barinthus had been lost in some memory of his own. "What? —Nay, nay, not so much, not dwelled. But there were folk here once." More than that he would not say, and Brendan did not press him. Still—

"You know, you never have told me if you came to Erith on the great journey," he reminded his teacher.

"Now have I not!" said Barinthus laughing, his mood turned as Brendan had intended. "But even *you* should be able to do those mathematicals... Nay—we are long-living folk, right enough, but not *that* long. That journey is more than twenty thousand years in the past now; we have seen ice and fire and flood cover this planet, change aplenty, since we came... But true it is that I was among the last to see our old home. Before Atland fell, I went on the final voyage back to Núminôrë, to see if anything remained. All the others who went with me are long gone, and so was the planet; I am the last Núminôrian, and there is nothing left of my homeworld but dust of the stars. Now—by grace of the fate of Gael and Danaan—I will return, to scatter my dust with its own."

"Raise sail," said Nia, speaking into—but not breaking—the long respectful silence that fell then, and Kelver Donn Midna moved his hand on the helmboard. Outside the cithóg viewport, a flash and ripple: all eyes went to it. A sail of silver, barely of the thickness of a leinna, was slowly unfurling itself, falling like mist from a slender mast; the screens showed the same scene to deosil, above and below. As the Hui Corra crossed in front of the sun, and threw its shadow clear and black against the moon, Brendan gasped.

The ship and sails—they form the suncross! Four sails to make the four equal arms, the solar rigging for the circle, the ship itself the central boss—how fitting that that holiest of shapes and symbols should be the way we sail the heavens... The sails belled out as they caught the lightwind, and Brendan glanced at his mother. "I had not realized it would look so."

Barinthus snorted. "Where do you think the pattern came from in the first place? It is the sign of our faith, but it is also the reality of our power."

"There were other signs," said Kelver Donn quietly. "And other powers."

"And of them we must always be 'ware and watchful," answered Barinthus after a long pause. "Once was enough, and too much."

Of the brief dazzling moments they spent in star-flight, even Brendan could afterwards find no adequate words to put on them. But it was what they had come to make trial of, and so they did. They had gone what Barinthus deemed a safe distance beyond the moon's orbit; then Kelver Donn aimed the Hui Corra's prow at the red planet Malen, and hands and minds alike engaged the star-drive—or perhaps it was that the drive engaged them.

Whichever was the way of it, the starfields beyond the viewports became a fretwork of light, and everywhere a blue glow haloed round, like the seafire dripping from the oars of a galley in a stormy ocean. But this ocean was calm as a pond; though Brendan and the others knew from Barinthus that such placidity was not the rule.

"This is a backwater, an eddy," he reminded them when they marvelled at the ease of the passage. "It is always like that in close, within a star's or planet's maigen. We will get out among the swift fierce currents soon enough; today, a quiet sail, just to get a feel of the helm."

So they had flashed through Malen's tiny moons, then turned back, cutting across Erith's orbit, streaking toward Gwener behind her cloudy veils on the far side of the sun. Brendan immediately sensed the alteration in the ship's handling, and looking at Barinthus for confirmation he saw that his mentor was very pleased that he did. *Outbound and inbound, the sails configure differently, because of the wind off the sun—just as running before the wind differs from tacking, or jibing to come about, on a ship that sails on water. I had not imagined what it must feel like, but—I can feel it!*

After that, they did not linger, but looped around the moon one last time and turned for home. They had learned what they needed to know; learned too the temptation, how easy it would be to lose themselves in those new seas, to steer toward the sun, or toward one of the many glowing spirals they could see—galaxies, Barinthus told them, each of those bright smudges made up of as many stars, or more, as were in their own heavens, as many distant suns as there were sands on a beach. *Who, seeing this, could doubt the power of the Goddess and the God? Her hand sowed the stars in form of Her sacred spirals, and His did kindle them alight—*

The descent was smooth and swift and easy. Without a groan of earth or air the Hui Corra kissed the land again, settling down to fill the Yellan vale as if it had never left. If none had seen it depart, many were now awake to watch it return, and when the door slid aside in the hull—the metal once again closing after them seamless as water—they ran forward to demand all details and particulars.

Brendan told them as much as he could—most of it was in any case unrelatable, and they would be seeing it for themselves soon enough—and they were perforce content with his account. But the impatience was real and growing. *They are ready; after all our labors and teaching and hoping, they are so very ready. Not resigned and reluctant to abandon home, driven forth like beggars and nomads, but eager to adventure to new lands for high cause—true heirs of the starfarers they sprang from. And that is a very great difference…*

So now he commanded that folk be more widely and openly sought to join the journey, sending out those he had already recruited to enlist others; there was no lack. Indeed, over the thousand years that the Immrama, the Voyages, were to last, a full third of the Celtic peoples of Erith—Gael, Aulbannach, Prytani, Cornovian, Gwalian, Manx—would choose to make the journey. Others too: the ancient folk, the Crúithin, called by some the Pictoi; Brythons of various tribes, who had no wish to live among the incomer Sassanaich; the nonhuman races, the merrows and the silkies, the sun-sharks and the orms; even simple patient beasts. The Sidhe themselves went gladly, taking the Low Road as they had said they would, and arriving before all others—and so magic began to die upon Erith, leaving only crumbs and dregs and lees for the generations who came after.

But these thousands were first and bravest, not knowing into what they sailed, but trusting in those who led. They were the best of Erith and of Keltia in Erith, those who left: the ones who were strong enough to hold fast to their ancient way, that way that was by no means an easy one. They went with matchless courage, though not without matching fear—for courage is not mindless unfearingness but rather the mind's steadfast refusal to let fear rule—and the realm they would find and found would be built from their bones and their blood, the folk who would come to call it home would be bred of the strongest and the best.

But all that came later. For this first sailing, later to be known as Immram Mhór, the Great Voyage, the Hui Corra and her six sisters formed all the fleet, and now at last the day of departure was upon them.

CHAPTER SEVENTEEN

ho calls? Brendan, waking in the night, startled and sleepy. For an instant it seemed to him as it had been for Pátraic, that fateful night at Magheramorna. *Who called my name?* But though no angel or Sidhe lord, nor even shepherd boy out of the past, appeared at hand, the call hung in the air, like faint smoke-scent from an autumn bonfire; he could not settle down again. So leaving Etain deep asleep he rose and clad himself, and went out from Clanadon; smilingly declining the offer of company made him by the Fians who guarded the Hui Corra, he set off into the hills, alone, with the long springy stride of his youth.

He had no fear of coming to harm, or even losing himself. He knew these lands far too well for that, he could fare them blindfold in a blizzard in the dark; nor had he in his mind any particular plan of going, but walked where his steps would take him. So that before long he found himself on the familiar path that wound up the side of Slemish, to the wood of Voclut that held such deep and differing memories, for him and for another. And then, bounding ahead of him on the trail through the trees, though it was dark of the moon and difficult to discern shapes from shadows, he saw,

unmistakable now, the lithe, tremendous form of a
running wolf.

So, then… Voclut was restless as an inland sea, new
leaves rustling in the cool breeze; but deep in its
springtime heart a light moved beneath the old oaks.
Knowing now Who had called him from his sleep, Who
awaited him there, and fearing not at all, Brendan
went with joy into the heart of the wood.

As he emerged from the trees into the clearing by the
spring, he saw the wolf—his wolf, the fetch, the Faol-
mór that had claimed him not long since on a hill not
far hence—sitting on its powerful haunches, joyful and
alert as any hound in its master's presence; it did not
speak, not this time, though it lolled its tongue and
grinned at him and thumped its tail as he drew near.
But he was not the one to whom the wolf paid such
attentive heed…

She was as She had been, ever different yet always
the same, and Brendan hoped that this time he would
be able to keep Her face in his mind. She smiled on
him as he stood there; he bowed his head, but remembering their last encounter he kept his feet, and knew
by the quality of the smile, the air around Her, that She
remembered also.

"You have wrought well in Fanad," said the Goddess. "And elsewhere, as I have seen. Now your journey
begins."

"If I had wrought better," answered Brendan after a
moment, "perhaps we would not be needing to make
that journey at all."

"That was not one of the choices," came the calm

swift response. "And what shall befall after you have gone is one of the choices still less. Do not fear."

Brendan gave a short incredulous laugh. "'Not fear'! Not fear what is ahead for us, not fear what the Tangavaun will work in Éruinn after we are gone? Lady, You are Who You are, and I do not question Your wisdom, but I fear those things more than I can say."

The Goddess smiled again, and now it seemed that light flooded all the wood, until those far below, looking up to the hillside, must surely see Voclut a flaming portent in the dark.

"You think that you have feared, but you have never done so; not in all your days. Fear is not merely the occasional flagging of courage or a now-and-then failing of heart, any more than peace is simply the absence of war; there is far more to it than that. Fear is active and real, a power that takes its strength from unstrength. Fear is the father of all evil: fear of loving and being loved or not loved, fear of knowing or not knowing, of having or not having. And as fear is the sire of evil, so envy is its dam: the bitter mother who bears the grudging child, the child who will not give but only takes and takes. Such a soul is as one who sits in a corner with a food-bowl, and hoards and hides and mumbles the stale dry crusts, when all the time there is a feast set for kings at the table, if only he will quit the corner and sit down freely and openly at the board. But you are no hoarder or hider; you have not been so for lifetimes beyond counting, and you will never be so again."

"But evil?"

"The mating of fear and envy is altogether the work of the Unlightness: its get is evil undoubted, no matter the name of holiness or piety that clothes it. No rule lasts forever save the rule of Love alone: two thousand years of fear may just be fear enough and time enough to learn."

"It has not been so long as that—"

"No. But it will be."

Brendan accepted this with only a widening of his eyes. "It is not that he is wrong, but that he damns *us* as wrong," he said then. "But I have thought, there is right on both sides."

"And so there is. He is right for himself, and for those who choose freely to hold with him: though he carves out the stoniest, coldest, most joyless path there is, that is their choice. It will grow colder and stonier still before the end, and all the while there is no need. The Christom call it faith, but it is an abdication of their own sovereignty: they choose to give up their power of choosing, laying it at the feet of their god in exchange for forgiveness. Therefore they remain children forever, never growing to the measure they were made for—not the blank slate of absolution but the wisdom that comes from accepting the result of personal choice. It is by no means their god's fault: like any good and loving parent, he meant only to teach them to fend and feed themselves. But they cling to him as weanlings who fear to give up the breast, and so he ends up doing for them forever what they should be doing for themselves."

"But we chose otherwise," said Brendan.

"Indeed you did—you chose to follow the Heroes' Way, and that is why they hate you as they do, and why you must leave. But it is also why the world you will find and found will be both strong and loving—because it will be built on choice and the willingness to accept the consequences of choosing. And only in such places, and as result of such choices, can joy and wisdom, and the truth of the One, be truly found."

"But why would they choose to follow Pátraic at all?"

"Oh, many reasons: novelty, a glib persuader who knows how to subsume all symbols and usurp our holy things to his own ends, the lure of an easier way than the Shan-vallachta—which, you must admit, asks a great deal of those who follow it, though its rewards are greater still. Correctly practiced, the Christom way is every bit as difficult and demanding as our own, with rewards every bit as great; but it has never yet been practiced correctly. Because they think one god easier to deal with than many. Because they see that god as High King, and Iosa as Tanist, and that is a thing they can understand. Even fear and resentment of the power of women comes into it—and of goddesses too, though Mhúir is as good a name as any I have had, I daresay I will answer to it as well as to any other." She laughed, and shook Her head. "You said it yourself, m'vhic, long since: it is the right message—the Word that is now carried by the soul now called Pátraic mac Calprin—but he is the wrong messenger. Even so, even he cannot prevail against the truth that is the Highest's: and that great truth is that all souls are right for themselves, and all souls are free to choose for themselves. There was never a promise that it should be easy, and it should not be: a free unforced choice between two good things is the second hardest choice there is."

Brendan laughed shortly, mirthlessly. "And the hardest?"

But the Goddess did not smile. "An unfree forced choice between two bad things…as you have learned by now. But what the Tangavaun has forced upon both those who are his and those who are not is neither good nor free—though they think it easier, it is not; though they beg the Crann-draoi to forgive, only they themselves can forgive themselves, not by dismissing their errors but by embracing them—nor in the end is it even a choice."

"You know that we are on point of leaving Erith," he said after a while. *Well, surely She knows, bonehead, She is the* Goddess…

If the Lady shared his opinion of himself She did not show or say. "On Beltain's morrow. Aye. I will be with you on your road. And there. And here also." She reached out to him then, and he knelt, to feel Her hands upon his head in blessing—the hands of Macha, of Banbha, of Fodhla, the hands of threefold Eriu in all Her love and might and splendor—like being touched by Light itself, the joy that coursed through him. "But—My promise to you—and to all who follow Me— that freedom—you shall find it."

Next day, while the folk were busy readying the Beltain fires—the last they would ever light in the lands that had borne their race—Brendan making his final rounds went in haste to Sulyonessa in the southwest, where Kynmarra commanded, and to Gradlon in Ys, and far north again to the Boarholms, where Kunera and Dúnomaglos would lead, to Scathach in Aulba and Ríonach Sulbair in Inishglora of the Out Isles and Elved ap Dynevor in Gwynedd. All the grounds from

which the ships of the Immram were soon to rise in fire
he visited that day, and his captains assured him that no
readiness was lacking, all was in order. But still he took
time for a readiness of his own, a private farewell
moment...

So it was that Brendan and Etain greeted the dawn
of May, alone at the great circle called Turusachan,
'Place of Gathering', on its bleak island off the Aulban
coast, not far from where one of the ships would be rising on the morrow. They renewed there their marriage
vows, and passed their hands through the holy Ring-
stone, and sought the blessing of Goddess and God on
the voyage and the people. It seemed to them the
proper place to set seal on past and future both, on
Beltain morning, when Something, or Someone,
comes down the great avenue of stones to the holy
heart of Turusachan, bringing the summer with It, and
the cuachs call. *And this too we take with us...*

Standing with Etain in the circle between the four
lines of stones, the formation that had so strange and
so fitting a resemblance to the Hui Corra, Brendan
recounted to his wife what the Goddess had said to him
at Voclut, and then laid a reverent hand on the giant
dolmen that marked the western airt.

"Power places for those who know or guess the
meaning—places such as this, sacred stones and holy
caves, tracks and circles and alignments—all of them
directions, markers, means by which the power may be
raised. All these long years, we never knew what they
were, what they meant, what they could be set to do; it
took the knowledge of Barinthus to unlock those
secrets. But they were made for this, and will be so forever—maps, for those to read who can."

Etain laid her hand over his on the stone. "And to follow us, if they will—or if they dare."

They stood there awhile in silence, arms around, her head upon his breast, peaceful and joyful, gentle and sad, storing up memories in their hearts as supplies had been stored aboard the Hui Corra; and then they returned to Fanad—flying openly, it mattered not who saw them now—for their last day in Éruinn and on Erith. Their leavetakings were done with, all their spirit turned to leaving.

But of his 'wife' Darerca, and their daughter Bríd, Brendan spoke no word, not then, not ever after; though he left them all his land-wealth to fend themselves—in a settlement sealed and signed before Laoghaire the king, as lawful as ever could be—he left them no message with it; not one syllable did he leave them of farewell.

That Beltain night was joy and sorrow, festival and sending: a death and a birth, each to be marked and celebrated and given full due. At the various ship-sites, Brendan knew, all was in perfect order for the journey—as he himself had seen; those who had gathered there would be spending this night much as they were doing here in Fanad. But here with a certain difference: Laoghaire and Duvessa themselves had come to bid the voyagers farewell and gods'-speed, as king and queen, but also as Laoch and Duvách; and they were not the only high ones who had come there...

From where he sat with his wife and his friends and his kin in the dimness just beyond the light of the Beltain flames—heart-full, silent for the most part, too

happy and too sorrowing to speak—Brendan looked
up suddenly, though there had been no sound nor
even flicker of movement. But where none had been
only a moment since, Donn Rígh now stood, with
Kelver Donn his son, and Etain's father Gwastor with
her mother Liriagh, and Calatin and Súlsha the parents of Nia, and a tall lord with graysilver hair and
beard whom Brendan had never seen before.

"We who remain have come to gift you upon your
leaving," said Donn smiling. "Now my first and greatest
offering to your journey is my own son, who shall go
with you, and he is not alone in the going; but these
other things too shall make immram. They shall find
safety with you, and bring safety to you; each in their
time ordained."

Gwastor came forth first, in his hands something
solid, blue-gray, shot with gold sparks and crystal veins.
It was a rough, unpolished stone the size and shape of
a loaf of bread, heavy and dense with more than mere
stoneness, as if it were a live, aware, thinking thing. He
held it out, and Etain reached her hands to accept it
from her father.

"This is the Cremave," said Gwastor, "the magical
clearing-stone which has been for untold centuries a
treasure of the Danaan people. It has the power to tell
truth from lies; it cannot be deceived. Whoso lays hand
to it must speak the truth or suffer the justice of the
stone. Take it, and use it when there shall be need. And
there will be."

Etain bowed to the stone, and to her father, and
taking it from him she swathed it carefully in white silk,
then in red silk, then in black silk; hugging it reverently
to her breast, she went aside with her parents to make

their parting. Brendan looked after them, and a stab of sorrow pierced him. *I will give them time, then join them, to make my own farewells; I know it will not be forever, but still it is so hard…I must bid farewell to my own father presently, and how that will be for us both, for all three of us, I cannot bear to think on. Must* all *be dán? I only wonder…*

Then the tall stranger lord stepped forward, and Brendan saw that a long coffer of age-black deep-carved oak stood beside him. It had at each end dull gold handles worn smooth with use, a latch but no lock; it was knee-high to a tall man, and of the length of a taller man still—or of a spear.

"I am Melidren, of the Gwalian Sidhefolk," the stranger said then, his gray gaze holding Brendan's own. "I will be of those who go before. You will see me again; and though I may seem to depart for a time thereafter you shall see me once more before the end. But these I give you now; you will have need of them." He gestured at the chest. "The Thirteen Treasures, the ancient holy things saved from the four cities of Atland lost—from Falias, Findias, Murias, Gorias. They too will play their part, will come and go across the ages, serving dán of their own; but the stories left behind will say that Merlynn Llywd took them to the Green Islands of the Flood, or to the stars in a ship of glass, and neither they nor he were ever seen again. I will not say they will be wrong to say so."

"No lie," said Súlsha, who stood beside her daughter and smiled at that daughter's son. "'Ship of Glass'—that is Corach Gwydrin in the Vallican tongue. In our own, Hui Corra… As to those green islands, who can say in what flood they will be found?" And with Calatin, who would have business of his own next morning, she too drew aside with her child to make farewell.

Then last of all Donn Rígh stood out again, and now he addressed Brendan, only and directly. "Some of us ride before; others remain behind. My last gift to you is a threefold gift of knowing; these other gifts shall help to keep that knowledge safe. First, know that because of the Danaan inblooding among the Gael that you yourself have part in, the lifespan of your folk in the new lands will be thrice that of mortals of Erith; they will see the double century and more, in full possession of all strengths and senses. My second gift: the worldsoul of our people, whose dán it is in Erith to withdraw. I give it now to join with that of yours, whose dán in Erith is to be driven as you once drove others before you. Know that these together shall become the worldsoul of the race you will found in the new home you will find; it is in your keeping now. And my last gift to you is a name: know that the name of that new home is Keltia. Know that you shall be known as Kelts."

The visitors were gone then, vanished away as softly and suddenly as they had arrived. Brendan ran a hand over his face. *Did that truly just now happen? Were those gifts truly given us?* But the great chest remained for proof of it, and the silk-wrapped stone Etain still bore in her arms, held as she would hold a child—and the name that sang within them all like the horn of Fionn himself.

Keltia… Keltia! And we—we are the Kelts that shall be—

Beltain's morrow; and morrow of greater things beside. Brendan and the others were awake betimes— if indeed they had ever slept. After the revelry, most of the folk of the voyage had gone aboard the Hui Corra the night before; the thinking being that an early settling in, at their leisure, and a sleep aboard the starship would save time and heartwrenchings alike when it came to the actual departure in the morning.

And so it was that there were only a few hundred caught outside the ship's protection, when the Fanad maigen was broken by Christom reivers, an hour before dawn.

They swept into the Yellan valley ahorse and afoot and in wicker war-chariots, slashing at any who stood in their path, even trying to attack the Hui Corra itself when they could come close enough—though somehow, strangely, however close they came or hard they struck, their blades could never fall within a yard of the hull, still less land upon it. The folk not yet aboard strove now to get safe within, and the attackers tried with equal desperation to prevent them.

It was forces commanded by the Christom lords under Pátraic's sway, lords who had somehow gotten wind of the planned exodus and thought to thwart it in their god's name, and if they could slay and punish unbelievers at the same time, well, so much more to the greater glory of Iosa of the Tree. They had marched many days in secrecy to reach Fanad—perhaps under enchantment as well, to preserve the element of surprise. Their master was known not to scruple to use his enemy's weapons, when his need—if not perhaps his god's—required it.

So intent had the voyagers been on their departure that none had been 'ware of the armies moving to stop it; if the Sidhe had known, as they knew most things that passed, they had kept it to themselves, for reasons

of their own. Pátraic would later claim—or at least his
monkish chroniclers would claim for him—that he had
no part in the surprise attack, not by wish nor by will
nor by design, that he had only joined in to prevent
greater slaughter, and in time to come would loudly
boast, further, that not one drop of blood (well, saving
the blood of King Turlough Piercefoot) had been spilt
in all his conquest of Éruinn.

But chroniclers have been known to set down
untruth for their own purposes; and Pátraic had reckoned without the truth that was the Gael's...

CHAPTER EIGHTEEN

n recent years, Fergus Aoibhell had happily contented himself with a position of near-retirement, proudly watching his son gather the reins of the province into his own hands, seeing his grandchildren grow and thrive, simply being with his lady. But when Brendan and Nia and Barinthus turned all their energies to departure, Fergus took up chieftainly rule once more; without his guarding and guidance the Hui Corra could never have been built—though he had known all the while that those he best loved would sail, and he would stay behind.

It had seemed more than passing strange to more than passing strangers, that Fergus took this parting with such seeming calm: knowing that he would die apart from his lady, watching his son and grandchildren go where he could not follow, that he would never see any of them again. But Coll mac Gréine, who since the death of his own wife Beirissa had come to live at Creavanore, knew better, and now, as they sat their horses before their war-band upon the hillside Darinlaur, he looked at Fergus; looked, and said no word.

His friend, feeling the glance, smiled, though he did not take his eyes from the gap where the Christom forces, if they came to bar the Hui Corra's leaving, must show themselves. *I am content it should be so; I have made my farewells—last night, and all nights and days of my life, and lives; never have I not been with them, and never shall we be apart…*

"It is the dán I once spoke of to you, son of Morna," he said. "You remember."

"I remember well, old friend. Even so— They may not come, you know. We have no word that they are coming."

Fergus looked down at the ship below them, last-minute stragglers still filing aboard; then sidewise at the armed and patient kethern and horsemen waiting on his order, and shook his head.

"Nay, he will come, the Tangavaun, be sure of it. He does not love to see souls slip through his nets to freedom, and he will use what means he thinks is right to catch them. But after today, my dearest ones and these others of our folk will be forever beyond the reach of those who have sought to harm them. Theirs is to go, ours is to guard. That is what we do here, you and I: it is to be the kethern-a-varna, to hold the pass so that others may escape to safety. I would do far more than hold the gap, or die in it, to buy that safety for them. But you and I, shield to shield again—that is not so bad an end for two old Fians."

Coll shook his head, dashing tears from his eyes. "Indeed it is not! Laoghaire and Duvessa are well away," he said after a moment. "They made their farewells, and now must act their part as king and queen, and pretend to know nothing about any of this, for all the rest of their lives. A harder task, I am thinking, even than ours."

Fergus's grin scythed across his face. "I would say

so, since we end here and they must go on long years
uncounted… Any road, we have only to die to protect
what we love; that is easy. They must live to protect it,
and that is harder."

"Well," said Coll, with a grin that well matched his
friend's, pointing with his unsheathed sword to the valley entrance, "see where the Tree-priest does come
down to battle after all! My sorrow that ever I doubted
you— Let us go down from here; I have a sudden wish
to take some heads from this army that preaches love-
your-neighbor and peace-on-earth all at the point of
the sword."

"We are Gaels," said Fergus Fire on Brega to Coll
Son of the Sun, as their horses began to gather speed
downhill in the charge; he had to fling the words across
to his comrade at the gallop. "Heads at our saddlebows,
heads on the field—all one! It is—you know—it is what
we do!"

Thus began the Battle of Fanad, a great holding action
that carpeted the ground with dead, and that would
surely have been counted among the epic battles of
Éruinn, had any true bard been by to make song of it
after—or if any true bard who had *not* been by, even,
had known of it to sing of; or, if he knew, had been permitted to so sing. But the priest Pátraic fervently
wished no word of that day to come out, and the king
Laoghaire equally fervently forbade all account of it;
each had his very excellent reasons, and each had different reasons, and both of them were obeyed.

But Fergus and Coll with their war-band behind
them came down now off Darinlaur, where once Bren-

dan had looked up to see a giant wolf that was more than wolf, and they went through the Christom lines like a blade through summer butter, protecting those who were still streaming, in haste but not in panic, into the Hui Corra. The Sidhefolk who yet remained in attendance by no means held themselves apart, but fought with blade and spear and all the terror of their presence; and where they went with war but few were left to tell of it after. And all the while the ship continued to take on her freight of souls.

One part there was of the high endeavor that so far Brendan and Nia and Laoghaire and a few others had kept to themselves. It had to do a little with the spirit of the undertaking, and more than a little with the powering of the ships, and for both those reasons the particularities of it had not been much noised abroad by those who knew. But now it was time: and clear on the other side of Éruinn, at the enigmatic hill of Sidheanbrugh, Calatin father of Nia and Cairenn mother of Niall, Danaan prince and lady of the Gael, stood ready to begin their part of the great labor—the task they were meant to do, the fate that had been foreordained they should share.

These unlikely partners had arrived at the sacred hill from different airts and by as different means as possible: Cairenn had come by curtained horsedrawn litter from Tara, travelling all night to get there, while Calatin had merely stepped into the air at Yellan vale, where he had parted from his daughter and her mate and son and grandchildren, and out of it again upon the slopes of Aogall. But they came to the same purpose, and they arrived at nearly the same moment: Calatin now stood atop the hill, before the great carved lintel stone; a few dozen yards below, emerging from her litter, Cairenn dismissed her outriders. Who were more than willing to obey their mistress's command: unhitching their horses and setting heel to flank they fled thankfully and at once, only glad to get away from so eldritch a vicinity.

For Sidheanbrugh on that May morning was a fey strange place indeed. The very grasses that clothed the hillside seemed alive and whispering: though no wind breathed, a ring and ripple of moving air seemed to lap like tiny wavelets at the foot of the hill; within that ring all was deadly calm. Though only the previous day the hill had hosted Beltain throngs, today it seemed as if none had set foot on the slopes of Sidheanbrugh since the dawn of the world. The hill brooded whitely in the sun, dreaming in timeless solitude—but it was a watchful solitude, and an expectant brooding, caught now out of timelessness into time for a long-awaited purpose.

It seemed the new arrivals were much and well 'ware of that purpose, and their own. Though no movement or sound gave her the clue, Cairenn turned her face unerringly to the ancient doorway where Calatin stood half-hidden in the dimness; and though one watching might have thought he would in courtesy descend to help her climb, ancient lady that she was, it seemed he knew better and best, for her stride up the few steep hillside yards was the stride of a young girl over the summer bracken, and her walk was the walk of a queen.

She came to Calatin and held out her hand, and he

bowed over it. "Long and long," he said smiling, "since we met on holy ground."

She smiled herself, well pleased to see him. "On any ground! I came by night," she added, as Calatin gave her his hand over the lintel-stone, "so that my idiot grandson might not follow. He knows what must be done, and that you and I must do it, and why it must be so—I told him myself, the tiresome little bonnive, oh, ages since. But king though he is, he never did make up his mind to it, and even now I daresay he would stop me if he could—his poor ancient granddam! So my women will all swear themselves barefaced that I have taken to my bed and cannot be disturbed, and by the time Laoghaire learns the truth our work will be accomplished."

"King indeed, but no idiot, and I know you do not truly think him one... Niall's son will face necessity as Niall's mother faced it—and Niall himself." The mobile face of the Sidhe lord shifted. "He was my friend, your son, and I miss him greatly. But do not fear for Laoghaire; he will do better than he knows."

Cairenn laughed. "And if not he, then his queen! Much as I love my grandson, sometimes I think Duvessa is twice the king he is—and I love her for it even more. But he will be the last in Tir Gaedhil, my Laoch," she said briskly, without a trace of self-pity. "After him it will all be Christom kings—I am glad I shall not live to see the Tangavaun in triumph. That is no Éruinn I would care to dwell in. Nor you, I think—"

Calatin shook his head, somber again. "I stayed only for this, for my daughter and her child and his children, as you for sake of your son's son. Donn Rígh, Maeve in Connachta, Fionnbarr and Aunya in the southwest—all they will have precedence in Éruinn henceforth, kings and queens over such of our race as remain, so that magic does not altogether die. We never ruled here, you know, or if we did we were ruled as well: we were the land's as much as the land was ours. Mortals will forget that—well, not entirely, not all of them: not the poets and the singers and the bards, not those who will be born of our blood come among the Gael. But of our own choice we will dwindle—not in Éruinn alone but in Gwalia and Aulba and all the other lands where we have dwelled—and withdraw to our dúns, and live within ourselves, and turn not again to the world."

"But not forever? It would be a cold drear world without Sidhe magic, and a grim harsh one without the gods—"

Calatin was looking at some future only he could see. "Not forever. But not until the children of Dâna and Dôn return to the Shan-vallachta, setting aside the Tangavaun and all his works and brethren and minions as if they had never been. Then we may return to what was ours, and it to us; and Éruinn be what she was ever meant to be."

"That may take long," said Cairenn quietly.

"As long is counted."

But though she waited, he said no more, and presently they turned to the work that was at hand.

It was a fact well known throughout all lands roundabout that every Midwinter the sun's shaft would pierce the chamber that was the heart of Sidheanbrugh. But what was not known to more than the tiniest few was that the white stones set so carefully and deliberately to form a facing to the hill, paving it as solidly with quaratz as Nia's chamber walls at Rinn na gCroha had been paved with pearls—the very stones that many had wondered at, that Brendan himself had remarked upon—hid a high and purposeful secret, and one linked indivisibly to that light—and to the Light.

And that secret was this: Midwinter to Midwinter, the force and power of the light returning is caught and held in the stones of Sidheanbrugh; held and stored simply, for simple use, as grain or ale or hides may be kept in any storehouse of any maenor in Éru-inn, and can be drawn upon, as any rechtair might draw at need upon more usual domestic stores—though the steward who would tap these particular reserves must be master of more than household skills.

And by no means these stones only, but nemetons and dolmens and stone circles all over those islands, from Stonehanger on the Great South Plain to cold Turusachan far in the Western Isles to the bluestone armies that march to the sea in Less Britain: all are as giant engines to take in the earth energies and retain them; and if unlocked by one who held the key, those treasuries will yield up their hoards for magic's use.

Of those few in possession of this knowledge, fewer still knew why it should be, or how, or who had made it so. And fewer than that again knew that such power could be raised for purposes with which none now living, save one alone, was acquent. This knowledge Barinthus—for he was of course that one—had long since imparted to Brendan and the others; and they had made full use of it in their plans, incorporating the knowledge and the principle alike into the ships of the immram: magic and logic, the powers that would move those ships among the stars.

"For you must know and never once forget, Brandoch," the ancient star-mariner had said—and more times than once, too, though with Brendan mac Nia a single telling was ever all that was needed—"that this power can be used for ill as well as good, and so Atland was destroyed. But by that same power we came to Erith from the stars; and by it we now return there. There is symmetry in that, and great correctness."

And now there was correctness and symmetry indeed: a prince of a dying race and the mate of a dead king stood upon Sidheanbrugh—Achadhalla, Cashel Aengus, Ros na Ríogh—to call that power into being; for this magic needed man and woman, Gael and Danaan, to work it, and dán had chosen these two for it, once, long ago, in spring.

"Swiftly," said Cairenn in an anxious voice, turning her face to the sky and scanning the blank blue depths, as if she could see Brendan's need, or sense the urgency. "They fight now—"

"We fight also. Be easy, lass."

She laughed, but took calmness from his calm. "True enough! But this trifle of witchery that we work, this little small pishogue, will not be done again in Éruinn any time soon, I think."

Now it was Calatin's turn to laugh. "Not likely! Not until the Old Ways come again—as come they will." He had been carving a sigil or two in the soft turf, and now he stepped back to survey his effort. "Little to do beforehand; but now begins the real work." He glanced at Cairenn. "Glad I am that the Lords of Dán gave this task to you, to be my partner in the work. No surprise; you raised a king, and a great one."

"Nay, that was his doing alone; he chose correctly, his brothers did not."

"Even so, it was you who put into him that by which such choice could be made."

Cairenn smiled with the memory, and her voice took on softness, a story-telling tone. "And now that choice is legend: how Niall son of Eochaid went hunting in the hills with his six half-brothers who disdained him; and on a dark cold stormy night, with the wind like knives and the rain like stones, a huge and most uncomely hagling came to the door of their hunting lodge, begging each prince in turn to feast her with meat and ale and bread—and then to take off his clothes and sleep with her, she who had not lain in a warm soft bed with a handsome youth for many a long winter. And each in turn refused in horror, giving her foul abuse only and railing speech, and they were the queen's sons, who should have shown better training. But out of his honor and courtesy and compassion, Niall—scorned son of Cairenn Chasdubh, the king's ban-charach that the queen despised—pitied the frightsome creature, and bespoke her gently, and gave her all that she had asked."

"And when he wakened," said Calatin, taking up the tale in the same voice, "it was no grisly hag but the goddess Dâna herself, in all her beauty and splendor, who lay between him and the wall. And for his great worthiness at the test she bestowed upon Niall the crown of Éruinn for his own, and the sovereignty of Éruinn that was herself in her own matchless person,

vowing that as he had lain with her as hag and goddess
both, he should have a royal bride and fame imperish-
able, and be the mightiest king ever to set foot in Éruinn to the Lia Fail."

"He did, and he was... And when Dâna Rhên
brought Niall's bride to Tara as she had promised, she
brought our dán as well."

"She is the mother of your race and mine," said
Calatin. "She had purpose bespeaking us as she did,
commanding us to this task; though we would never
have refused her. But despite all that she showed us,
still we did not realize how high and hard the task
would be."

"And if we had, still we would have accepted."
Cairenn sighed and straightened. "And if we are to
complete it before my bones stiffen entirely, m'chara,
let us begin. I would not die with the task ill-done, simply because I was too weary to work. When I meet my
lord and my son this day in Moymell, I would stand
before them both with no cause for their reproaching."

"There is no cause, nor ever was. But let us begin."

For all that, they did very little; little needed to be
done. Though mighty, the working was simple; yet
not so simple that it could have been done by one
untrained or unintentioned. Purpose was all; and of
that they had enough and to spare, and also they had
the word and the will of Dâna who had besought this
of them—for even a goddess has her reasons. Gael and
Danaan, these two went out together to their work, so
that Gael and Danaan might go out together to the
stars.

*   *   *

Calatin stood back, and Cairenn with him, and for long moments of screaming silence it seemed that nothing happened. No such summoning had been made on Sidheanbrugh for many centuries; perhaps the stones had first to recognize the call, and then consider their own response. But it seemed that they too remembered, for deep in the crystalline structure and substructure of the quaratz the atoms now began to stir from their long strange sleep, to come together or to fly apart, to move faster and faster as the liberated energy awakened.

Cairenn and Calatin, holding the rising torrent of power like a hound in leash, bound with their strength and will alone, heard a low hum that came in on a spiral from a direction they could not understand. Then the spirals carved in the stones at the entrance to the chamber of Sidheanbrugh began to twirl like spinwheels—as other spirals were doing in that same instant on similar stones from the Laighin to Belerion in Aulba, from Penwith in Cornovia to Kerrec on the edge of the sea in Britain the Less; the sky seemed to throb above them with unseen lightnings, like heatflash in summer, their sight pulsing in rhythm with their own beating hearts.

And then the hill flamed up in white-gold glory halfway to the sky. Calatin stood like a beacon tower, gathering the light to him and also somehow feeding it, deepening it and flourishing it, coaxing it to strength, inciting it to intensity. Knowing the precise moment to do so, Cairenn stepped into the light to stand beside him upon the sigil he had carved, to add her strength to his; the splendor fell and fed upon her too, the low hum became a howl—and the last part of

the great working found its place. They looked at one
another then, a look of dán completed, a look too deep
for words or smiles or tears, joined hands—and
launched the ancient lightnings.

With a soundless shudder and concussion Sidheanbrugh gave up its secret hoard. Light shot from the cavern that had drawn it in and the quaratz that had held
it; directed by Calatin and Cairenn, from Cruach
Aogall it went where it was needed, gathering other
light from other sources as a rolling river picks up
smaller streams along its road to the sea. Light called to
light all across those northern isles: and standing in
Fanad on the bridge of the Hui Corra, Nia, daughter of
Calatin, received it, her power kindling the answering
power within the seven ships of the immram, bringing
them to life.

And still Sidheanbrugh flamed like all the fires of
Beltain and torches of Samhain there ever were; and
still Calatin, prince of the Sidhe, and Cairenn Chasdubh, lady of Éruinn, let pass that lightning through
their own selves and souls. None in Éruinn, ever after,
would remember what they did, their names and deeds
and kindreds; but it mattered not in the least, that was
not why they did it.

And that too was as they would have it.

CHAPTER NINETEEN

n Yellan vale they knew nothing of this, not yet. The Christom forces had been flung back by Fergus and Coll and those who rode with them, though the losses on both sides were many. But Brendan stood like a rock in the sea, unmoving on a hillock above the press and scuffle, until all his folk were safe within the ship; and even then he continued to stand, as if he waited on something. As the battle below swirled and eddied, he caught sight of Fergus his father, fighting back to back with Coll mac Gréine.

Fergus fought with a shortsword in either hand, and Coll swung his far-famed war-axe as if it had been a feather; death was in that plume, death dwelled upon the points of those twinned swords, the Heroes' Light glowed round them both as the dust rose. There was no time or chance for anything more, and they had made their farewells the night before in any case; but father and son now exchanged looks that carried more than farewell, looks that went beyond time and place and space. They reached out one to another and received blessing back, though Brendan never moved and Fergus never ceased to fight. Then the dust of battle rose again between them, the press closed in, and Fergus Fire on Brega was seen in Fanad no more.

Etain came up, in swiftness though not in haste, laid a hand on her lord's arm. "All are safe aboard now. It has begun at Achadhalla. Your mother has given the alert to the ships. We alone are waited for."

"Go you," said Brendan without turning, but he covered her hand with his. "As for me, I have some words that I have a longing to deliver before I leave. The ship must wait on me a moment more. There is time," he added reassuringly, sensing her hesitation. "I will come presently. Tell my mother I will come."

She fled in silence, at once, not fearing; he was aware of her departure, though he did not look after her. His gaze was all for Pátraic mac Calprin coming toward him through the smoke and blowing dust; as the Hui Corra began to throb and hum, gathering in her power, he smiled to see the Tangavaun flinch. *For all his prayings and crossings and sprinklings with water, his beshrewings and malisons, he did not truly believe in the power of Draoícht; but now he knows for sure...* He called out, his voice riding over the noise of battle and the low purr of the engines, and moved then, leaping down the hill, easily, lithely, closer to the ship.

"The first time we met, Ferganam, you saved my sheep not far from here."

Pátraic halted a few wary yards away. "And the last time we meet here, I cannot save yourself, who might have been one of my Master's best sheep." He pointed to the Hui Corra. "Nor save from certain doom the flock that follows you over a deadlier cliff than Slemish."

Brendan shook his head, more in anger now than sadness. *The time for soft words is through; he came here today to try to stop us, and failing that, to slay us, that we might not escape—he shall hear the truth at last about what he does, if I die for it, if he dies for it, if the ship must leave without me...*

"Folk are not blind stupid sheeplings to be led, whether it is shepherd or sheepdog that leads them, and any road a wether self-made is hardly the ram for the job. But the Gael are not sheep; rather we are wolves, creatures who hunt and think for themselves, who teach our cubs in loving freedom and who fawn at no master's heel. We will not be shepherded, and we will not be shorn, and so we are leaving."

Pátraic, ignoring the petty gibe—most uncharacteristic of Brendan, who indeed had repented it almost before it left his lips—was still staring at the giant starship. As well he might: the ship was as she was, the Hui Corra, huge, gleaming, her sunsails furled on masts bent back like wings, close to her silver sides; not until she took the starstreams would she shake them loose, as a maiden shakes loose her long unbraided hair. But the averting sign Pátraic made as he looked upon the ship, a gesture half-hidden in his robe, was by no means one the Tassans would have approved.

"A lymphad of the skies—truly it is the Devil's work—"

But Brendan, quick as ever, had seen the furtive warding sign, and laughed aloud.

"Still the hypocrite, even in such an hour and such a place... You put the name of evil on us, as you are so swift to put it on all things you do not love or understand, or that might threaten your hold on your flock. But there is no evil here, only knowledge and purpose—two things you seem to think your Tree-druid despises. How if you are wrong, and it turns out he values them after all? He could think and act for himself well enough, aye, and work magic too when it suited his purpose—though he did choose himself doubters and disavowers for companions, so perhaps his judgment was not all it should have been, especially for a god... But hear now what name I put on evil— You came here uninvited. Uncontent to make your way side by side in peace with those who believe elsewise, you required that all other ways go down before your own. And when others did not obediently turn up their bellies at your bidding, you worked against them lies, and hatred, and murder, and even the very magic you claimed to be sent to destroy. You even prinked and puffed yourself with Vortigern against Tir Gaedhil's interests, before his own traha destroyed him. At the order of your Roman masters, you made sacrilege and desecration against the faith of souls on which you had no call or claim—for which you will answer before not only your own god but the Lords of Dán. If all this is not what you yourself call sin, I do not know what is. Because of what you have done—and all the others who will come after you and do as much, and worse, here and elsewhere—the Way you seek to force on others has called its doom down upon itself. Nay, do not speak but hear me! And fear me... A high road that began in Light will go down into the Dark. It will become a way of shalt-nots, a way that rules by fear and hatred, control and contempt—of women, of free unfettered thought, of the body, of love, of life, of knowing, of nature, even of itself. And in the end, bloated and stinking and rudderless as a drowned pig in a flood, it will explode and sink. And it may be that only then will it find the clean clear way it was meant to go from the first."

As Brendan's voice went on and on, calm, measured, each word a whip, each whip tipped with thorns, each thorn dipped in brine, Pátraic's face had turned gray, then red, then white altogether, though whether with fear or fury those watching could not tell. And still Brendan spoke, his voice ringing with prophecy; to those who watched and heard, it seemed that a mighty Figure stood behind him—cloaked and hooded, faceless, hedged round about with power—the Third One, the Alterator, God immutable, incontestable, absolute, Who declares to the Two in the worlds what the Highest decrees in Gwynfyd.

"As for you, Ferganam, better you had remained nameless, such dán is upon you. Your name will be writ with Vortigern's for treason, for you have let into Éruinn a worse invader than ever the Sassanaich will prove. Oh aye, they will come to Tir Gaedhil, right enough, those Sassanaich, as even the Roman armies could not; but the Christom armies will have invaded long before, and will sell Éruinn to them in the end. You will have your slave's vengeance on those who enslaved you: but there are worse slaveries than that of the body, and those you will teach the folk of this island—a slavery of the spirit, until they cannot lift their heads among the nations for the ancient weight and shame of it. You rage at the thought of Gaels leaving Erith to spread their ways among the stars—but are you not sick with envy because you cannot do likewise, to spread your own ways, would you not slay us out of sheer spite to keep us from it? Whatever, you dared come here at the head of an army to forbid our leaving— Well, none so commands the Gael; we come and go at our will and pleasure, or we die in the doing. It is our way, Fer-

ganam—and so I call you for the last time. You have
never understood it, and you never shall. And now we
take it."

Pátraic, who had only a moment since been all asea,
beside himself with fear and fury and frustration, now
gripped his new cruciform crómag with both shaking
hands, and gathered up all his strength as he held it
out before him. Though the black cross-shadow, its
upright longer than its other arms, fell long and far
upon the green hillside, not the merest besmirching
smudge of its darkness touched Brendan or the Hui
Corra, as the Tangavaun, face working, voice as a hissing adder's, pronounced Christom valediction against
the Gael—or it may have been malediction after all.

"Then take it! Go! Go to the deaths you deserve,
and may you come to them soon! Go to the hell you
have assuredly earned for yourselves, and to which the
Living God the Father for all eternity condemns you!
Go hence accursed, as snakes and serpents, whom the
power of the one true God, *my* God, has driven from
the lands! In his name—*my* name—*GO!*"

The ground had begun to tremble now. *Indeed, it is
time we went—but, by the Loving Goddess, not as he does bid
us...* Brendan, whose head had come up like a hound's
at the huntsman's whistle, looked once to the east,
then looked his last on Fanad. *'Sé do bheatha—life to
thee...*

"You cannot touch us," he said briefly, almost
abstractedly, as one who heeds not the rainshower mist-
ing his cloak because the cam-anfa that is coming howling down the road commands his larger attention.
"One last word to thee, Tangavaun. Seek the high
ground, as soon and as high as you can; else, when the

ship rises, not even your god will be able to save you from saltwater drowning."

"But—the sea is three miles distant—" Now fear alone stood plain on Pátraic's face.

"Even so."

Brendan lifted his hand in farewell—to Pátraic, to the fallen, to Éruinn and to Erith—and as the hillbrow behind him began to blaze and glaze and melt, light rising and spilling over it like water over the edge of a cliff, he ran for the door in the side of the ship.

And now all things converged. On the hill overlooking Yellan vale, where not very long ago Brendan had stood and given the Hui Corra her name, many were still dying to protect the ship's escape, Danaan and Gael alike. They took many of the Christom with them to the halls of Arawn Rhên, where no doubt they were surprised indeed to find themselves—and doubtless the Lord of Annwn, in his perfect justice, dealt with them in suitable fashion.

On Sidheanbrugh, clear on the other side of Éruinn, Cairenn was dying with Calatin as they had long ago Seen—if 'dying' was the word for such a living glorious change—becoming one with the Light, giving their last strength and their very spirits to the other light that they themselves had summoned; at the end, her lord and her son came to fetch her away, smiling at her, proud indeed. And at seven sites scattered like jewels round the seaward fringes of the lands, the ships took in that light as dry earth takes in water, and transmuted it into power.

In Fanad, the light that lanced from Sidheanbrugh

came over the hill in a curving tide—though how light
might be able to bend, no one in that astonishing
moment troubled to wonder—and as the crest of it
broke and fell upon the Hui Corra like a white wave
upon a silver shore, Nia nodded once, and Brendan
gave command. And in that same moment his word was
relayed to Kynmarra in Sulyonessa and Kunera in the
Boarholms, to Scathach in Aulba and Corlis Typhult in
the Out Isles, to Elved in Gwynedd and Gradlon in Ys.
And it was with them as it was with Brendan in Fanad:
seasoned they all were by now in the ways of space, and
their crews with them; and though none had been
much beyond the orbit of the moon, they knew how
they must go, the road to take, and they took it.

And then the ships of the Great Immram began to
rise. If a watcher had been standing on a high enough
place, he would have seen seven rays of dazzling glory
emanating from one point near the eastern coast of a
green island, and then a lattice of light leaping into
being, as if it answered—blinding lines of brightness
rising from stone circles and chambered tombs and
lone dolmens, all the holy power places of those isles,
linking island to island, realm to realm, more and
more every instant, until it seemed that the lands were
stitched one to the other by this blazing broidery.

And if he had been puzzled enough to keep on
watching, very soon he would have become aware of
seven tiny silver splinters rising out of that radiant lattice like shuttles from the weft, leagues away across seas
and hills and forests; would have felt the ground
beneath him shake in faint resonance with their distant
passage, the air vibrate against his face; and however
great his wonder and puzzlement, perhaps he would

never have known any more about it than that.

But for the Hui Corra herself, greater than all others she rose from Fanad, like a mighty swan laboring into the sky from a standing start, and the land, groaning, sank from the strain. Wherever the ships were launched, their power broke the earth: the ground sank and shattered, so that what had once been dry land now let in the wild waters—becoming land with sea between, or sea with land between. Southwest of Cornovia, the great island-realm of Sulyonessa split in three before it drowned, to make the Sullia Isles, only the peaks of the highest hills now standing above the tides, giving witness that once a fair country had stood there; souther still, the coast of Less Britain fell away, and so was Ys destroyed. As the Hui Corra lifted, Fanad itself trembled and went beneath the waves: what had been a sizable district was now a remnant peninsula, its hilly spine and shelflands alone remaining. Many warriors of both sides went with it, and the swirling seas came inland even so far as Brendan had warned, wetting Pátraic's feet and draggling the hem of his robes; a strange baptism.

Indeed, he and his minions were fortunate that they did not receive baptisms of earth and fire and blood along with it: so powerful were the motiving forces, as Barinthus had foretold, that even where the ground did not break and drown it turned to molten glass beneath the rising ships, fused by the power of the engines; and many centuries later, those places are still to be seen, the glass castles, the mysterious 'vitrified forts' of the Boarholms, of the Out Isles, of Gwynedd, of Belerion Aulba beyond the Mounth, for which no logical acceptable explanation has been found by folk in latter times.

But Pátraic mac Calprin, clinging to the piece of drowned and broken Fanad rock that bore him up as a spar in a shipwreck—it may be that he was spared, and it may be not. The one that bears his name in Erith history, and is honored as apostle and saint, may be that same very one whom Brendan freed from slavery and defeated at Tara and denounced in Fanad; or it may be another, one who took the name of Pátraic—or who perhaps was ordered by the Tassans at Rome to take it—the better to build upon the start that Ferganam-Pátraic had made. Indeed, it was to be much the same story with Brendan himself; but to tell that now would be to get ahead of the hunt...

And from the bridge of the Hui Corra as she climbed to the clouds, surely the highest place there was just now in all of Erith, Brendan looked out the giant port to behold those six sparkling spearpoints rising into the blue like distant lances, and felt the heart of his people, the soul that Donn Rígh had entrusted to him, the soul of the greater Keltdom that would be, rising with them. *We are going home—home at last...*

As he had done on Slemish side at the first, and in Yellan vale at the last, Brendan raised a hand in salute—in blessing, in farewell, in greeting—to what had been, and what was, to then and to now, and spoke aloud a rann that came to him; from where, he did not know.

"Like the snow off the mountain,
    like the wind in the heather,
    like the foam on the fountain,
    we are gone, and forever..."

And turned his eyes ahead, to what would be.

CHAPTER TWENTY

hen standing off from earth the Hui Corra unfurled her four sails, above, below, to one side and the other. The wind from the sun caught them, filling them out, curve-bellied like a woman in whelp; their devices of wolf and dragon, raven and stag, stood clear against the stars. If any had looked up from beneath as she raised the moon, they would have seen a silver suncross, a dromond moving slow and stately through the blackness of space; six smaller ones surrounded it, sun-sharks proudly escorting a great whale of the deeps.

Since they rose from Fanad, Brendan had not moved from his place by the huge viewport. Kelver Donn and Barinthus and others worked to keep the station the ship now held, hove to on the moon's far side, while the sister ships of the little fleet came up and into formation: the Hui Corra's charts and readings must be checked, and compared with those the other captains were transmitting; the motivers must prepare themselves for the first of their powering shifts—much there was that needed doing. But none would trouble their commander's vigil or mood: he had done enough to get them there; now it was their turn to spare him what tasks they could, for as long as they could.

"Pestilence does not make its way farther than nine waves. His plague will not pursue us as we go. We have left. Now you must leave too."

Nia had come to stand beside her son. He did not look at her, or even give sign that he had heard her, but stared through the port at the planet behind them. It glowed green-blue as a huge round opal, its cloudswirls like the fire-flecked veils such stones have at their fragile hearts, burning against the dark. From this height he could barely make out Éruinn itself; Fanad not at all. *Gods, how greatly we have wrought! But she is right to bid me leave—I am still there, and some part of us all will ever remain here, ever be far behind us however far we may go. But even though we have left, how can we leave...*

"It is not the first time of leaving. And it will not be the last."

At that he did turn. His mother's gaze on him was serene, starlight reflecting in her clear eyes; but his were haunted.

"And were you one of those who left, that time that was not the first? Or the time before that, or the time after? That is my home behind us—if it has not died, it is as good as dead to me now... I have never asked to what you yourself did bid farewell: did you see Atland whelmed in the waves? Were you watching from a black-sailed lymphad on mountainous seas? Not you, but what forebear of mine looked back on Núminôrĕ to see it vanish in rolling sunfire? And—however many homes shall die behind you—what can you know of real farewell, you who will live forever?" His voice that had begun soft had sharpened to bitterness by the end of his speech; but his mother knew whence his pain had origin, and that the anger was not meant for her.

"Not forever. And who knows more or better of farewell than one who lives so long—one who must take it, and make it, so often down the years? And any road, your home—our home—has not died." She took his arm, and though he trembled he did not throw off the touch. "Look." She gently turned him round to face a different quarter of the heavens, where already the stars hung in new configurations that never they had appeared in from beneath. "There. That is our home. We have only to go."

Brendan stared until his sight blurred. That part of space was thick with stars and cloudy with drifting galaxies—those unimaginably distant shoals of suns, far beyond the reach of even their most powerful enginery—but by now he knew its patterns as well as he knew the lines upon his own palms. He closed his eyes then, shutting in as much as he shut out.

"Will others of the Folk come with us?"

Nia put her hand upon the crystal of the window, as if she touched the planet in farewell caress.

"They ride before," she said then. "They are already there." She paused, did not look at him. "Your father is aboard, and Coll."

Brendan started violently, that terrible, heartbreaking, altogether most deeply human battle of hope renewed against grief accepted fighting itself out upon his face for all to see. "But I thought—"

"Nay—we caught them up from the press; sore wounded, but living still. Though not much longer…" She linked her arm through his. "Come. Let us say farewell to those two we love, and bid their journeys thrive."

*   *   *

In a chamber below, Fergus Aoibhell lay on a low couch in an alcove near a viewport; Coll mac Gréine had been placed on another within arm's reach. One look told Brendan past all doubt and hope alike that nothing could be done for either man; another look, that neither of them wished it any different. Nearby, Fionaveragh was leaning against her brother Rohan; both of them were weeping softly.

"They called him Fergus Fire on Brega," said Nia then, softly, lovingly, looking upon the man who lay there, who had lain beside her all these years, "for an exploit in his youth. His kindred had old battle-enmity against some other rival clann, I forget which, and when still a very young man—oh, years before we met, he and I—in one of the endless skirmishes between the tuaths he rode in broad daylight straight up the hill of Brega, a stronghold of the adversary tribe, and personally set torch to the bruidean there. When, later, they asked him what possible grudge he could have against a blameless guesthouse, he explained, deeply aggrieved, that he had only burned it down because he had thought the enemy chieftain was inside."

Brendan laughed full and unforced, and shook his head, though his tears flew. "I remember very well, and I have ever thought it sounded such a thing as only my father would have done…" *I remember, too, the tale my father would tell me of how he met my mother— It is not often that a man gets to see his parents as they were, golden youth and silver maiden—perhaps it would be better for all if he did…*

"They were taken from the fight, and brought aboard, so that they might see Erith from space as the last thing," said Barinthus quietly, from where he stood near the chamber door.

"And so they did—a mighty sight, they would have done far more than die to get to see it—and they will be laid to rest upon the moon itself, they who could not sleep in peace beneath it in a land no longer theirs."

The voice from the low couch was Fergus's: if the tone was less strong than its wont, the words and will expressed were no less clear. He bade farewell then to his grandchildren and to Etain, kissed and blessed them, gave his sword to Fionaveragh and his torc to Rohan; then spoke long and gravely with his son, whom he had given to Etain long since. Brendan knelt by the bedside and raised his father's hand to his forehead; not even Nia heard their last words to one another in this life.

Coll mac Gréine too was kissed and blessed and comforted; he had been as matebrother to Nia, uncle to Brendan, another grandfather to Rohan and Fionagh. Then Fergus reached across to Coll, and Coll reached back; they had no need of words, but only looked, and smiled, their fingertips barely touching, their hands still rust-gauntleted with their own blood. That was all their last farewell and converse—between those two friends all had been said long since.

And last, in the dimness of the chamber, lit by the twin radiances beyond the port that were earthlight and moonlight together, Fergus Fire on Brega and Nia the Golden looked long at one another; then she seated herself upon the couch, and took his head in her lap, and bent her head to his, her arms around him, her long hair veiling their faces. Together they looked across the widening distance at the planet that had been their home—knowing that an incalculably greater distance was about to be put between them, knowing also that such distances are as nothing to the soul that loves. Brendan, watching their farewell, himself tear-blinded and rocked with pain, was for all his anguish touched by prescience, and that calm certainty of faith which smiles past even grief. *I am given to see this for more reasons than that these are my parents. It may well be just so for me, in my own time, with my own lady—and after...*

But another's 'after' now was here: Fergus's voice came clear and strong; he took Nia's hand and kissed it, sighed and smiled.

"I leave you in another age—yet I am with you still."

So died Fergus Fire on Brega, his head in his lady's lap as long ago he had told Coll he would wish it at the end. Coll himself, friend and swordbrother, went out with him in the same moment, and they were seen no more on Erith. By Brendan's order they were given an epic sending, a farewell that was as one with the practice of the valorous Northings, who are 'customed to lay their battle dead in curraghs with swords and other arms to hand, and then to launch the tiny craft out upon the tide, setting it ablaze with flaming arrows as it sails—as it bears the earth that was once a warrior home at last, by fire and water and wind, to the endless Halls of Heroes.

There was no curragh to sail these oceans, no water on the moon to float it, in the windless void between the stars no fire would burn; but Fergus and Coll were laid side by side in a cleggan—one of the tiny scout-ships—with their swords unsheathed upon their breasts. Nia herself sent the craft like a silver arrow down into the deep soft dust of the moon, kindling its wake to trails of fire, and the moon received her honored guests.

Brendan watched the sparkling arc until it was lost in moonshadow and winked out. *The ground that is the Goddess's own body takes us back into it when we die, or the sea that is the God covers us with its blue cloak; but the moon too is Hers, Her own Self, of Her making and changing, to draw up tides in women and in seas, and the sky is yet the God's—all at Kelu's will. They will sleep there forever, and sleep in peace, these two lords of the Gael—it is fitting that they lie side by side now, as they stood back to back and shield to shield all their lives...*

They made the Last Prayers then, not for Coll and Fergus only but for all who fell at Yellan vale, aye, for Draoícht and Christom alike; and nor were Cairenn and Calatin forgotten, who had stood to their dán at Sidheanbrugh, and who went now before. Words were spoken of the fallen by those who had loved them—indeed, the only ones who can speak truly of the dead in such moments are those who have known them, for they alone have known the living, loving soul and not the mere image. But it was Barinthus who offered the last word, and, for all its freight of grief, strangely, the word of most comfort to those who wept and smiled and listened.

"Of old heroes were entombed standing upright and armed in sacred hills, their heads turned to enemy lands, so that their keen eyes might keep good watch to guard and warn—here let it be not eyes alone but hands and hearts as well. From the Breasts of the Moon—Arianvron, the high silver heart of the Goddess Herself—they shall keep watch over Erith, so that no enemy can come upon the world unseen. They will be as eyes to see, and hands to wield blade, and hearts to keep faith with us and with our Way. Each time we pass the moon on immram, we shall think of them where they are—and they of us."

Brendan murmured with the rest the closing blessings—which in the loving liturgy of the Shan-vallachta are as much for those left behind as for those who have gone on—and remained awhile with Etain and the children and a few close friends. But Nia had stood there unmoving, her back to them, as close against the port as she could get, her hand resting on the cold crystal pane, until there was no more to be seen. Then she had gone without a word to her own chamber, whence, they well knew, she would send her spirit out to ride escort to her lord, upon the Low Road to Caer Coronach, or Annwn itself, as far as she might, as long as she could, all as her love commanded.

"It matters not where that road begins or ends for each," said Etain softly, quietly weeping, watching her mate's mother, whom she loved as her own, retreat straight-backed down the ship's corridor. "All roads run to Argetros, all ways meet there at the last; perhaps, from here, the way may be a little shorter. For her sake I pray that it is so."

But they stood there a while longer, the four of them together, until the curve of Arianvron, slowly turning, carried Fergus and Coll with it beyond their sight.

Thus began Immram Mhór, the Great Voyage, the first sailing. It was to last nearly two years; of those fifty thousand or more who set out with Brendan in seven ships, all were to come safe to journey's end, save perhaps two hundred only who perished on the way. Though Brendan grieved to lose any soul who went with him in trustance of safe passage, that so few were lost was great tribute to his leading, and he had main praise of it from those who came after, and from many of other nations that also sailed the stars. But he had always been a careful shepherd with any flock of which he had the tending.

Perhaps surprisingly, there had been little discussion among the captains and commanders of their ultimate destination; all their efforts and energies had been geared to mastering the enginery and building the ships and making an escape without letting half the world know about it, either then or later. Everything else they had left to Brendan and Nia and Barinthus, in utter confidence that these three who had brought them safe away would bring them safe to land again; where and what that land might be did not matter nearly so much as they had thought.

So, following the directions Barinthus and others before him had preserved as a sacred legacy from starfarers twenty thousand years dead, Brendan swung the Hui Corra away from the sun, and pointed her out along the Stepping Stones route that, long ago, the Danaans had followed in.

"Stepping Stones for that we cannot take the one big step to our new worlds, but smaller ones only," he explained that first night to his gathered captains. "We lack the ability to move fast enough—to shift high enough—nay, I cannot explain, it makes my ears bleed! Barrind, you?"

Barinthus considered a brief moment—how best to convey complex information to the eager ignorant, whose upturned faces were so nakedly hopeful of enlightenment—then began.

"When our people came away from our first home, they had science not only to enable them to sail among the stars, but to move faster than light itself." He met a roomful of stares as famously blank as King Cormac's shield, and laughed. "You look like baby birds, mouths wide to be fed! I see I must start from *before* the beginning, then... I cannot explain the deep theory to you— well, at least not without making *your* ears bleed—but just to give you something to go on with: you know that nothing in creation moves more swiftly than light." Happy vigorous nods all round—now this they could grasp!—and he smiled. "I *know* you know this, it has been told you many times. But that is not strictly correct—or rather, it is correct in an incorrect way."

Smiles froze, eyes glazed over—hastily Barinthus recast his explanation. "Well then, consider this: if starfarers had to travel at such a limping footpace as lightspeed, they would all be dead long before they reached their destinations and no one would ever get to go anywhere. Now the Núminôrians—and many other races too—were not best pleased to be so constrained, and soon developed a way of surpassing such snailish limitations, so that the distance it takes light to go in a year, their fastest ships could go in an hour. Not by going faster than light, but by going around it, by bending light through magic, if you can call it that; and by sailing not through the normal everyday space we see but through the ard-na-spéire, the overheaven, though even that can be traversed at differing rates of speed. By such means they travelled among many stars, and when their world died, they were able to leave to find another home."

There was a short, sharp silence, though whether it

was the silence of those who were deeply impressed or those who were deeply terrified or merely of those who deeply still did not comprehend, Brendan could not tell.

Then Kunera of the Boarholms, laughing: "It is no use, Barrind, you might as well tell the cat as tell me— But a very stupid question in very little simple words: tell us how is it, if these high secrets were lost, that we are where we now are?"

Her lightness of mood cut the tension—everyone else had felt every bit as stupid, only they were much too vain to say—and Barinthus threw her a fond glance.

"The only stupid question is the question that never is asked for fear of seeming stupid; and any road that question is by no means so stupid as you think... Hear now: though those drives of course are the swiftest and best, there are in fact other ways of moving in space without them—if not perhaps so quickly, not particularly slowly either. We could not build such stardrive motivers in the time we had, with the materials we had, in such conditions as we were forced to build in; therefore we built next as good as we could. And our sails, combined with the motivers we *were* able to construct, will take us to our journey's end—not in the hours we might have liked, but at more than a snail's gallop. Still—we must count our time aboard ship not by months but years."

"Years!" There was a general dismayed murmur, and some of the captains of the smaller vessels exchanged troubled glances.

"However shall we live until we get where we are going, if it will take these years to get there?" asked Scathach, voicing the single fear.

"Not *many* years," said Brendan reassuringly. "Two, perhaps three at most—and the voyage will by no means be unbroken. We shall, and must, stop periodically—to refuel, to reprovision—for our minds' sake as well as our bodies'. Nay, do not fret, it has all been planned from the first."

"Therefore the Stepping Stones," said Nia. "The original farers to Erith mapped a path, not the most direct but the safest and surest, with sources of supply and settled worlds marked along it."

"Settled worlds?" asked Shane Farrant. "Other peoples?"

The mood in the room shifted again, this time even more uncomfortably; even for these high-hearted voyagers, who had learned and built and dared beyond belief, the thought of strange folk on stranger worlds was still a daunting one.

"Indeed," said Nia composedly; she had caught the underfeeling, but chose not to take note, or at least not to let it be known that she did. "We are by no means the only folk in Kelu's creation; and I never for a heartbeat thought you thought so. Most of those others are like to prove friendly—to those who come as friends."

"But not all," guessed Kynmarra.

"Not all." Kelver Donn Midna spoke, and all heads turned to him. He stood silhouetted against the stars beyond the viewport, as lordly in bearing as his father Donn Rígh. "This too I tell you again: there are folk among the stars whom the Danaans know of old. We parted ways, we survived, we even prospered; but no thanks are due or love lost, and the old enmity has not improved with the ages."

"And they are out there still," said Brendan. "Now,

we may encounter them, and we may not; even if we do, it may not be straightwway—perhaps not for many years to come. But we must be prepared for battle all the same. They will not love to see us once again among them, or settle new worlds to become their rival."

"Or their master," muttered Amris. But there they left it.

"What is *that*? It looks like a road of cinders."

Barinthus nodded vigorously in the direction of Brendan's pointing finger. "It is. Well, of a sort. That is Knavogue—the asteroid belt that lies between Malen and Dagda. You remember; you saw it on the charts."

The Hui Corra was under way in earnest now, the other ships with her, running before the solar wind. They were not long out past the War-red War-queen's own red planet, and already they had come upon the first new peril of the journey…

Brendan stared at the image on the quaratz-crystal screens, and then at the reality beyond the viewport, deeply uneasy, troubled by something he did not understand. *It feels like a memory, almost. Though how that could be…* He was looking at a vast band of clinkered slag, chunks of iron solid and shining, moving like a wide weary river between the two great islands that were ruddy Malen and mighty Dagda—Mars and Jupiter to classical astronomers—with Arawn brooding behind his shining rings, a startlingly undistant way away.

"How did such rubble come to be here among the planets?"

"It was once a planet itself."

"Truth! What killed it?"

"No one knows," admitted Barinthus. "It perished long before we came this way. Someone so minded could have smashed it, right enough—there are nations out here that have the means to slaughter the stars, such a planet would be as a mere pebble their foot spurns aside in the road. But it might have exploded on its own: some weakness that would not let it stand the strain, a crack reaching deep into bedrock that a firemount could have set off, an earthshake even."

"A whole world shaken to death—"

"It has happened. But as I say, we do not know. Our records tell us only that this once-world was called Gavida by our folk, and ancients of Erith called it Hephaistos. It was named long after it was dead; but none can say who named it first, or when it died."

"Strange that two races should have named the same dead world for the Forgelord," mused Brendan, fascinated still by the slow majestic motion of Knavogue. "Perhaps it was a firemount after all; under any name the Gabhain Saor is lord of such."

"But dangerous?" asked Donn Aoibhell, who had duty that day on the bridge for the first time, and was listening with all his might. "These cinders?"

Barinthus shook his head. "Not a bit of it." And though Donn was heard to mutter comparisons of the Hui Corra to an unsprung chariot on a road of riverstones as she passed through Knavogue—not favorable comparisons either, and he was not alone in making them—it was as Barinthus had said. But then it almost always was.

*   *   *

Past Dagda then—whom others call Balor or Othinn or Iau Rígh—with his great red single eye; past Arawn and Midir, and mystic Dahût of the waters, and stormy Síon rolling alone in darkness at the rim. A month after their departure—though such measurings were now formalities only, ship-time for the records' sake—the Hui Corra came to a boundary indeed.

Brendan, summoned, stared out at the strangeness. "Is it—"

"The edge of the Fields of Súl. We have come to the end of the fields we know. Beyond"—Nia pointed ahead, past the dustclouds, the ring of comets like a misty hedge, a maigen round the maenor of the sun— "is the space between the stars."

Even as she spoke the Hui Corra crossed the boundary, plunging into a strange pulsing phospho-rescence that mantled the ship like a cloak, a heartbeat of living brilliance. *It is like being within the Dancers, those polar lightveils...* There was a strange electrifying sensa-tion all through the ship, like sparks in long hair or a cat's fur in cold dry weather, and looking out at the starsails Brendan could see red and blue ghostfires flickering along the hulls and masts and spars of the fleet. *Like the Solas Sidhe itself...*

"This is the highroad," said Kelver Donn. "Now, once clear of the edge, we can put on full sail at last; from here outwards we will be moving much more swiftly. Is it not a better road we take, m'chara?"

"A road easier far to the foot than the Heroes' Way," said Brendan. *This is the real beginning of the adven-ture—soon we will be beneath the light of another sun, another star will be closer to us than the one under which we lived so long—I had not felt it, not until now. Now we are truly gone...*

He felt a stab of piercing sorrow and loss. *All our world and life lies behind us; I had thought our leaving over, but now I see that it has scarce begun...* A sudden memory leapt, a word of long ago, those words about the Heroes' Way—someone had charged him with that message, he could not recall from whom to whom, in what hour it had been delivered, and in his surmise he spoke aloud. "And the crop that is higher than heath-grass?"

"Has yet to be harvested. But it has been sown." Barinthus was silent a moment. "So that here, at the edge of the Fields of Súl, I give over command to you. Nay, no protests, m'vhic, though they do you much credit!"

Brendan ignoring him with great completeness protested both fluently and strenuously, and in the end, sorry to say, very swartly indeed. But Barinthus was adamant; in that moment his speech took on the high idiom and ancient locution of his own people, and the short humorous gruffness that had served him through the years of the work vanished away. He was once more what he had been; but now he set that too aside.

"If you recall," said Barinthus with force and clarity, after Brendan's protestations had fallen long enough upon his ears, "I said that I would give you the secrets of the shipmaking, and guide the sailing out from Erith; these things I have done. I am, I have been, as a harbor-pilot who takes the ship out to the mole, to the last beacon-light; the in-home port-waters are the only waters that he knows, though he knows every shoal and bar and current. But beyond the arms of the breakwater lies the true Ocean; there the harbor-pilot must yield.

And there the ship's true captain sets hand to helm and calls the rowers from their oars and the sailors to the masts, for the open seas are his domain and on those waters he alone is commander. This is thy ocean, son of Nia," he said, in the High Gaeloch, and the sudden sound of his matronymic startled Brendan yet again. "Upon it thou art captain. Take thou the helm."

"But I know no more than anyone else on board!" cried Brendan despairingly. "I will do it, because if I do not we all drift rudderless to our deaths; but I have no knowledge! You are the one who has been out here before—I can only sail to the currents as I find them."

Barinthus was unmoved; at least outwardly. "That is all any sailor can do. We have no wise-iron to point us true north in these new seas, but we have that which is a better lodestone far: our own judgment—and now, your judgment." He smiled suddenly. "Oh, never fear, lad, I am still your sailing-master! I shall be advising you, doubtless to such meddling tiresome extent as will make you ask why ever I bothered to give up command at all, and you will be right to ask so—but from now, you alone direct our path."

He watched as Brendan walked away, defeated, squaring his shoulders and lifting his head, in triumph all unknowing, as he went. *He has taken the burden on him—but he did so long since...* And then he spoke aloud, he who was the last of Núminôrë, though Brendan was too far away to hear, and of those on the bridge of the Hui Corra Kelver Donn Midna alone did note the star-mariner's words.

"Brendan the Astrogator. In time to come, they will call him saint."

CHAPTER TWENTY-ONE

hey were deep into space now. The luminary that had been their sun, the only sun they had ever known, was now merely a star among many others—an undistinguished one, not the brightest, even—and sometimes Brendan himself found it difficult to pick out, which sometimes troubled him. But there was little leisure for backward glances: in the starfinders and spacescopes, on the quaratz-screens, through the viewports, their world lay all ahead.

Once the Immram was well launched, the voyagers had quickly lost their very natural fear of the utter strangeness of their situation; and as folk do everywhere to impose order and feel what small control they might in a state of essential powerlessness, they contentedly settled down into pattern and habit. *As if they had been living in a campment,* Brendan often thought, *or on a well-run maenor, where everyone has a task assigned, and each is glad to perform it, knowing it is not only for the good of all but for their own particular good as well...* There were those who sailed the ship and those who gave it the power to sail, those who tended the needs of folk and beasts, those who made and mended, those who taught and diverted; and each job was as important to the Hui Corra as the next, or the last.

But the ship too had habitude and pattern: sometimes when he waked late or woke suddenly, in a watch
that was not his own, Brendan could sense the ship sailing itself, moving with purpose all around him. *It knows
that purpose better than we do; knows for what it was made, the
home it was born for. And it is going there as swiftly and deliberately as it may, a bell-yowe of the stars leading its flockmates
with it. It will take us too, because we have asked to come, but
there are times when I wonder if it has need of us at all. We are
merely roadfriends, fellow travellers chance-encountered on the
way. But the ship is a creature of these seas, and it is on a quest
for home…* He was not certain if that heartened him or if
it made him more afraid than ever. *Truly, I think a case
could be made for both…*

Barinthus had kept his word; apart from advising, he
left Brendan to sail the ship and earn the byname he
was already becoming known by, if not yet to his face—
that byname which Barinthus, indeed, had been first
to bestow. But in the empty watches of those long
uneventful nights Brendan became reacquent with his
almost-forgotten bent and love for poetry, that he had
first discovered beneath the hill at Rinn na gCroha, in
his earliest wedded days with Etain. As he chanted to
himself for company, quietly, idly, just for comfort of
the sound, others who also waked and worked would
gather as they might on the bridge to listen. They
seemed to find the same comfort that he did in the
familiar words of song and saga, and engrossment in
the new poems Brendan composed to suit his need;
and they shared tales and songs of their own remem-

bering or making—in some strange way chaunting to
the ship as much to their fellows.

His cousin Donn Aoibhell, who had been rather
shyly and sweetly courting Fionaveragh, was one who
customarily came; and Etain herself, who oftentimes
would wake to bear her husband company on watch
rather than sleep alone; and Dorren nic Cána of the
Celi Dé, who on occasion could be prevailed upon for
a song or a poem, in praise of her own god or simply in
praise of ale, or love, or war, and they were always well
pleased to hear it whichever it was; and Fiaren of Clannrannoch who had been showing signs of smittenness
around Rohan mac Brendan; even Conn Kittagh and
Shane Farrant, who also planned to wed once journey's
end had been reached—though such unions were
already fully lawful by Brendan's own decree, as they
had been damned by the Tangavaun's.

Sometimes Brendan looking round at these and
others would find his heart more full than he could
bear. *All these—these who will build and love and hold and
make and fight—I have chosen them well to be founders of
worlds. And they chose to be chosen—chose me and my purpose, chose to trust, chose to take this staggering leap into the
unknown. If the saw is true that one gets the friends one
deserves, then I am so very grateful and humble to have gotten
these; and so very proud to know that I deserve them...*

Although the Hui Corra and the other ships of the fleet
had been built with the science of Barinthus and now
were powered by the magic of Nia, they were pre-
eminently workaday ships; nothing aboard them was for
show but fashioned all to the purpose, and often to

more purposes than one—a kind of sacred redundancy. But though time had pressed them sore and luxury was not a priority, the deep inborn love of the Celt for art and beauty could not be denied, and indeed had not been—things could be functional and beautiful at the same time, and it was best for use and spirit alike if they were. So it was no surprise that control panels were set off with elaborate knotwork just as swords and scabbards were, or walls inlaid with fair images and hung with tapestries: even handrails had been twined and twisted into shapes of the beasts the Pictfolk did love to carve cavorting on their standing stones—sun-sharks, piasts, orms, nameless grinning droop-nosed creatures with globed headtufts and curving bodies. Many found the beasts' enigmatic smiles more than a little unnerving— especially when unexpectedly encountered after a long tiring stint on duty—but the children were enchanted, and so the images stayed.

As the weeks became months, the Hui Corra became not so much a monolithic starship as a loose- knit confederation of small spacegoing villages. Though there was no least trace of enmity or tension, still it seemed most comfortable and natural that folk should hive off for familiarity's sake along the ancient, man- ageable alignments of clann and tribe and tuath, and Brendan made no attempt to force another pattern on them. *Whatever makes them feel safest and happiest, however they can make themselves most comfortable and most at home...* But that was the way of it in the Hui Corra only, because of its diversity and sheer size: in the other, smaller crafts the shipboard populations had been sorted from the first along more or less national lines—Cornovian folk had gone in the ship from Suly-

onessa, Gwalians in the one that lifted off from
Gwynedd, and so on—and there seemed no need of
further boundaries.

Too, in keeping of the promise made by Brendan at
Sheirnesse, there had been special accommodations
set aside on several ships for the careful conveying of
those folk—those Kelts, as the voyagers were already
beginning to call themselves—who though indisputably faunt were not human in either their form or
their physical needs: the merrows and the sealfolk and
the sun-sharks, all of them every bit as thrilled as their
fellow starfarers with the high adventure.

But in every ship of the Immram, one rule held
paramount: nothing was neglected that would give the
voyagers the feel of normal life—families and kindreds lived together, pairings were encouraged, crafts
were practiced, children were born. And every hour of
every day in every ship, grown and young alike were
being taught by bards and ban-draoi and druids the
knowledge they would need, both in the new worlds
and while they were still shipbound. Brendan would
often make excuse to walk the corridors through the
Hui Corra's schoolroom precinct: it was a joy of which
he never tired, to hear voices raised in discussion and
debate, to hear the children being taught the old
familiar tales and songs and lore—they reassured him,
their voices affirming the future as they echoed the
past.

*These will grow up free of all taint, these and the ones who
will come after... I have done the right thing. We were so very
right to go; but it was not right, never right forever, that we
were forced to. And we must never forget just why it was that
we did, and were...*

*   *   *

The wave came out of nowhere, as rogue waves will even when they are made of seawater; that is why they are called rogue. There was no warning: one moment the Hui Corra had been sailing plain, the next she had simply rolled over onto her port side and kept on rolling. Caught off guard like everyone else aboard, Brendan, who was just then at the helm, wisely did not fight to right her when she reached the toppling angle, but let her carry herself completely over and up again, righting herself, as a curragh will do when swamped in home waters, if the boatman in his panic can allow. The sails, losing the starstream, billowed and flapped as they were emptied of ion-winds; there were some stress fractures to the hull plating, and one spar had been snapped clean through, but otherwise the great ship was undamaged.

"What in all the seven hells was *that?*"

Barinthus was busy taking soundings, and did not answer at once. "A wave off the Black Ice," he said at last, and Brendan understood. The Black Ice was a vast and dangerous belt of ice planetoids in a region of space they were soon set to cross—spacebergs the size of small moons. For the most part the huge field was untroubled, but sometimes a gravity tremor or collision among the bergs, or a comet passing through, would cause a surge in the starstream that could overset nearby ships—much as happens in an earthly icepack, when glaciers calve and drop chunks of ice the size of small mountains into the polar oceans, the wave thus generated running up to ravage unsuspecting coasts many miles away. And so it had befallen now.

"The other ships?" asked Brendan then, and waited, breath held, for the answer.

"Nay," said Rohan at once, from his seat at the side helm that tracked the fleet. "Being smaller and lighter, they rode up and over it like cork-ducks. Nothing but a little broken crockery."

"And ourselves? I know that in space there is no up or down, but we *capsized*—are there injuries reported?"

Ríonach Sulbair, who had been checking just such matters, looked up with deep relief on her face. "Bruises, a few broken bones—the rest is also broken crockery only, thank the Goddess."

"Oh, I do, I do… It will have to be crossed straight, this Black Ice," said Brendan then. "Over or under would take too long, and so far away from any sun we cannot tack; at least not until we pick up a stronger wind."

Proud amusement flickered on Barinthus's face. "I see you are becoming more used to thinking in three dimensions, not a paltry two."

Brendan grinned. "Well, there is a harbor-pilot I know, he once taught me a few things… And though I say so myself, I learn swift enough when learn I must." He swung the ship's head round, his grin gone now. "When the spar is mended and my mother has healed the hull breaches, tell everyone to go to their chambers and lash themselves to their chairs and couches. We are sailing through."

But for all Brendan's wariness and warnings, the Black Ice was crossed without further incident, and now they entered a region of space more thickly strewn with habitable planets than any through which they had so far passed. Habitable—but not inhabited; and

Brendan had been struck, not for the first time nor yet by far the last, with a renewed sense of the sheer vastness of space.

"I know I sound like an idiot," he confided to Etain, who did not appear disposed to contradict him, "but for all Barinthus's books and lore and crystals and maps, I did not truly have a sense of the hugeness of all this." He waved out the port at the stars. "Maybe if I had, we would not now be here. What are First Causes, any road?"

But Etain had had no doubts on the matter. "Ask that of the Tangavaun. You may get a very different answer."

When duties were being allocated, back before the Hui Corra had even seen keel laid, the vast task of life-support was claimed by Nia for herself. Some had tried gently to dissuade her, saying that her sorcery was already well taxed with the powering of the ships—and indeed once the Immram was under way few would see her about, and fewer still have words of her, so great was the toll the working took. But she had said that matters of life were the Goddess's care and concern, and she, together with the priests and priestesses, would order it, herself choosing the sorcerers to assist her. How it was managed Brendan did not know and did not ask. It was real food, real water, real air; how it was produced, or obtained, was no concern of his. He was merely grateful that by means of his mother's magic—or whatever—the food stayed wholesome, the water clean, the air fresh, the supplies of all plentiful, not for the Hui Corra alone but all the ships of the Immram.

Still, there were many thousands who had this
unceasing need to eat and drink and breathe. Even Nia
could not make something from nothing, there had to
be at least a small somewhat for her to work upon—
and even Danaan magic might not be forever equal to
the task. So they replenished the onboard stores whenever they could: brief foragings on uninhabited planets, the occasional expedition to trading worlds to
barter for such things as they needed and could not
supply or find for themselves, periodic venting of air
tanks and swooping runs through suitable atmo-
spheres to refill them. They would neither starve nor
thirst nor choke in foul air, though their destination
was still many months ahead.

Nor were theirs the only mouths to feed or be fed.
There were beasts aboard every ship, many of them in
the sleep of induced hibernation which Barinthus had
determined to be both the safest and most practical
manner of transport—his star pupil was only regretful
that the process could not yet be made to work on
humans. Though a good portion of the beasts were
indeed along as consumable ship's stores, most were
destined for a higher fate than the cookplace. As the
settlers could not be sure what creatures they might
find in the new homeworlds, they had brought with
them breeding stock of familiar animals of many kinds:
mares and stallions, cows and bulls, yowes and rams,
boars and sows, barnfowl and cats and hounds; not
tame creatures only but wild as well—wolves, deer,
eagles, owls, hawks, salmon, foxes.

And all of them that were not in coldsleep—even
those destined to be eaten themselves—had to eat...
In Barinthus's seemingly inexhaustible lorebooks and

data crystals were detailed maps of planets where, though no folk dwelled, beasts and plants were plentiful. Though the information was many hundreds, even thousands, of years out of date, it proved surprisingly more correct than they had hoped, and whenever they passed such a world they went down to hunt or glean what they could find. But Brendan and others felt uneasy about it, though none could put a finger on any reason.

"Perhaps it is that it merely feels wrong to hunt another's herds or leaze another's fields, no leave asked or given," speculated Donn Aoibhell, one night when he and Brendan sat up late over the fidchell board, discussing between moves why they should have such qualms.

"They are no one's herds or fields at all," remarked Conn Kittagh, from where he sat contentedly idle, occasionally saving a piece from disaster by impartially whispering advice to one player or the other. "What harm do we do, and to whom?"

"Who can say?" said Donn. "In the sense that no one planted the fields or slipped the fruit-trees or bred the herds, perhaps no harm at all; perhaps they *are* no one's. But do not the fields and the trees and the herds belong to themselves?"

"We give proper thanks when we go foraging," said Brendan, a touch defensively, for he had thought much the same himself. "Whatever field-gods and herd-goddesses may have rule in those places, they will not be offended. We take only what we need—food-beasts, swamp-grains, fruit—never more than we can use or in such quantity as would harm the natural cycle. If we did not, it would merely rot or die unused.

No creature will starve for what we take; and we might starve if we did not take it. That is only natural law, and the Goddess's gift."

But Etain, who had been talking with her daughter and some friends across the room, suddenly looked up, as if she had heard a note in her husband's voice, or caught a thought, to cause her alarm or concern.

"It is not the same," she said, gently but firmly. "Brandoch. It is not the same thing at all." Though she did not say what same thing it was not, Brendan took her meaning, and said no more just then. But later...

"Not the same? It is *exactly* the same: to pluck ourselves a world we do not own, as for the past months we have been blithely plucking fruit from trees we do not own! How can you know, to say otherwise? For I tell you, sometimes I have doubted!"

Brendan and Etain were in the small apartments that they shared, not far from the bridge for ease of access. Their lodging was no larger or grander than any other couple's allotted quarters on the Hui Corra: Brendan claimed no special privilege for himself or his family; no one would have grudged him if he had, but that was never his way. They were continuing the discussion that had troubled the common room—or at least had troubled Brendan—save that now it was a discussion that showed every sign of flaming into discord.

Etain and Brendan did not quarrel often, though when they did the walls of Clanadon or Creavanore or Rinn na gCroha had been known to tremble. Since the immram had first been put in train, their equal and powerful wills had been utterly subsumed in the work, along with everyone else's: there was no room for doubt or dramatics where survival was the stake. But however strong the hand upon the bit, emotion cannot be reined back forever, and now reaction was at last at hand: and of the strength of Brendan's prior control, his present distress was the measure.

But he did not think of it so, caught up as he was in what was manifesting. "Only consider: we are on our way to seize an entire planet—and almost surely more than one, by the time we have finished—because we *need* it, in just the same way as we take what we need from these worlds we pass. How is it different? Who gave us leave to go and do so, without even a by-your-leave? Or, come to that, who gave the Danaans leave, when we came to Erith as we did? Nay, we invited ourselves then as we do now! By our own traha we help ourselves to the bounty of worlds upon which we have no claim whatsoever—and to a world itself."

Etain closed her eyes briefly, and besought for patience any god who could give it her—and that swiftly. *This is nothing new: we have been down this road so often before, and the landscape never changes...* Then, as she looked again upon her husband, her impatience flared and died as she saw what was in his own eyes, and she spoke more gently than she had intended to only a moment since. *Nay, nothing new; but for some reason it seems now to weigh more harshly upon him—and who can blame him...* And if patience did not come to her as she had prayed it might, something else did.

"Well then," she said, and her voice was now entirely the voice of her people, the literally enchanting tones that can charm the beasts and calm the seas and call the winds, "think of the places where we find

food and water as—as bruideans among the stars. If
folk *were* there, doubtless they would press such hospitality upon us; in their absence, we give proper thanks
and help ourselves only to what we are in need of, from
an overladen table. It is no more than the law of the
coire ainsec, after all—on a rather grander scale. And
the same with the world we go to find. We cannot steal
what has already been offered."

Brendan halted in mid-pace, caught, however
unwillingly, by her inspired logic, or it might be called
guile; and deeply, suspiciously wary, though he was
honest enough, as ever, to admit it.

"Aye, that makes a certain sense, right enough,
when you put it so—well, perhaps it is as you say. Well,
nay—truth!—it is." But having conceded one front to
superior strategy, he rallied now on another. "Even so,
Tamhna, suppose that it is not right thinking and correct information and true dán after all, but my traha
only that has put us where we now are, to lead them all
into exile and maybe death for sheer pride's sake—"

*Goddess, he is duergar-ridden tonight! He seems deter-
mined to doubt; nothing I say is going to move him from his
resolve to wretchedness...* Etain rolled her eyes and men-
tally retired from the field; but first she took his face
between her hands and turned it, so that he must meet
her gaze, and she smiled.

"Carán, if the dubhachas is on you, well enough;
wallow in it to your heart's content, until you are bored
sick, and then get over it. No one will blame you, and if
truth be known we are all only awed and amazed that
you have not done so sooner. For the strain you have
been under, the deeds you have accomplished, more
leeway is allowed you than anyone else on this sail. Let

down a little, then. But in the service of that, or indeed for any other reason, do not ever again let me hear you doubting your choice, or confusing traha with dán. It is not so, it was not so, it never will be so. And not even you are allowed to try to make it so."

It was perhaps the only thing, just then, that could have been said to him with effect. And Brendan, who had indeed been on the verge of something not very far off momentary derangement, took the hand she held out to him, and drew back from that brink, and slowly returned to his old calm self. But with a difference: there would be times when he would feel so again—unbalanced, unsure of his choices, even guilty for having made them—he was half-human, humans feel such things. Yet never again would he feel them with the same desperation, and that was Etain's doing entirely; and though they never spoke of it after, neither was it ever forgotten.

They had been sailing almost a year now. For much of that time they had been passing inhabited star systems, and it had proved as Nia had predicted: the folk who dwelled there were eager to trade and more eager to talk, as curious about the newcomers as those passagers were about the native inhabitants. They had had a handful of such encounters, and were puffing themselves on now being fine seasoned hands at star voyaging, when one day they came to a very different place indeed, and it was brought home to them yet again that they were not in Fanad anymore...

The world they raised was a planet of surpassing fairness: deep green with forests, blue of sea, gold-brown with open plains; young high sharp-cut mountains, low gravity, few cities—Galathay, home of the Eagle-people, the Hail. They made planetfall by permission of the usual authorities, settling into high orbit, and arrangements were made for reprovisioning. The Hail had little to do with offworlders—or rather, offworlders had littler still to do with them: chance visitors invariably found a planet of beings who had the power of flight to be more than a touch disconcerting, and as a rule they chose not to land—and most of those who sailed in the Hui Corra, or with her, were no exception.

But Brendan and a few eager companions sought and obtained permission to descend to Galathay's surface, where they were warmly welcomed by one Zillzaric, a guide who seemed not unaccustomed to offworld visitors and their astonishment.

What a handsome people... Brendan looked round him with interest at the native populace, who bowed and nodded courteously as they went by. Immensely tall, attenuated, staggeringly graceful whether their wings were folded neatly to their backs in repose or extended in flight, the Hail were the most long-lived of all galactic races yet known—saving the Sidhe themselves—with lifespans commonly well in excess of a thousand years. Their impossibly elegant bodies were covered with short feathers, usually white or silvery-gray, though all colors were represented; their ancient wise eyes, slit-irised and rimmed with fire, held knowledge and amusement—which go hand in hand more often than one might think. And then of course there were those wings... It was hard not to stare.

"Never in my life have I been so light on my feet," remarked Fiaren, who with her new-wedded Rohan had accompanied Brendan and the others. She tried a few long buoyant steps, more delighted with her colt-like springiness in the low gravity than curious about her hosts.

Zillzaric could not smile, but his face somehow conveyed the impression of amusement. "Khûsun Fiaren"—giving her the Hailian honorific due an offworld princess, though his own people had no such distinctions among them—"seems pleased enough to walk; but would she care to fly?"

The dazzled look on Fiaren's face was answer enough; and then none of the rest of them could bear being left out, so they all went, lifted aloft by obliging porters whose business it seemed to be to ferry any creature who could not get itself off the ground. By Brendan's standards the brief flight, across the city and back again, was only too brief; but it seemed greedy and uncivil to ask for a repeat of the favor, and he began to understand, a little, how a flying race might differ in its philosophy a million ways both great and small from leadfoot earthbound races.

They dined that night with Zillzaric at the home of Sajamana, a Kiraan or chief of the city, and her mate Delko, in a palatial abode which, though set like a roost atop a towering cliff, was obviously designed to soothe and comfort offworld guests: the access was not by air but by a broad and reassuringly earthbound road, and the house itself, though it boasted a spectacular view, was safely walled from the edge of the terrifying drop. Though, as Amris remarked, one would not think that space travellers, even such neophyte ones as they were, would still be quite so very skittish of heights...

The dinner was an excellent one, and led by the

Kiraan, the talk was general and genial. In those days when whole planetary populations were on the move, a small fleet of refugees with great resources and a clear destination was not likely to pose either a threat or a problem to any settled world. The galaxy was largely unexplored; many areas were only just opening up to many races, and the elder star-faring nations—or at least most of them, and they discussed that too—were still more than generous about welcoming new recruits to their ranks.

When Brendan and his party—Nia, Etain, Amris, Kunera, Ríonach Sulbair, Rohan and Fiaren, a few others—returned replete to the ships, it was with generous promises of provision of all that was necessary: food and air and water, chiefly, gifting the Hail in return with certain information that they had come by along the way, and help with some small tasks that Nia's magic could accomplish with ease, and without taking great toll of its owner.

But when Brendan tried to thank Sajamana—speaking to her in the galactic trading-tongue in which most of the voyagers, linguistically gifted as were all their race, had already grown fluent—the Hail chief gently redirected the gratitude back on its would-be bestower.

"Adanya Birenda"—so 'Lord Brendan' was turned in the tongue of the Eagle-folk—"where you are now, we once were, and not so very long ago either. Where we now are, soon you will be, and more quickly than you think. Best to meet next time as equals."

"And to come to that equalness as swiftly as we may," said Brendan, bowing gravely; and his hosts gracefully agreed.

*   *   *

"Look!"

They were a month or two out from Galathay. Far in the distance to cithóg, a bright streaming smudge was flung out against the blackness; though it seemed to hang there motionless, it was only by reason of the extreme distances of space that it appeared to stand still. In actuality, it was moving with celerity, and the track that lay ahead of it seemed to lie straight along the long hard road the travellers had already come.

"Tailstar," said Donn Aoibhell, interested but not much concerned. "And a big handsome one, too. That must be the comet the Hail starwardens mentioned. No danger to us."

"On Erith we used to look up at such prodigies and fear them," said Fiaren, standing with Rohan by the port, "for heralding the death of kings, or the coming of red war. We of the Immram know them now for what they are: simple spheres of frozen water and gases, roaming deep space on fixed roads."

"That is merely what they do, and what they are made of," said Nia quietly; she had come to the bridge with Brendan, and all were glad indeed, for she had not been seen by more than a handful of folk for a full fortnight. "That is not what they are."

By now Conn Kittagh had worked out the long, long path. "Indeed, it is headed for Erith—though not a very near encounter; it will pass by well and safely distant." He looked awed, as well he might. "But it will not reach there for fifteen hundred years or near—so far have we already come…"

Brendan had made some mental calculations of his

own, and was no less awed. *Not until close on the dawn of the third millennium will they see it...*

"Then—High Danaans aside"—he bowed gallantly to his mother, who only laughed—"the last Erith folk who saw it were the ones who built the Pyramids, those other ones who raised Stonehanger—and Sidhean-brugh. What must they have thought when it came blazing all unannounced into their night skies?"

"If they were last," said Dorren nic Cána, after a while, "who will be next? Whose homes will it pass? When it goes by Erith, what manner of folk will be there to see it—and where shall we be by then?"

But they were struck into silence by the weight of centuries; and far across space the bright comet fell burning through the dark. To those who stood there, watching, thinking, it seemed that it took some part of them with it as it went; and there was not a one of them who did not give the gleaming traveller a word to bring, a wish to take—and love to send again to their old home.

CHAPTER TWENTY-TWO

ow all their journey thus far had been perfectly in accordance with Barinthus's logs and
journals: if he had travelled the way an hour
previously, he could not have cried his trail with greater
precision. All the spacemarks he had predicted, they
had come to just as he had said they would: the planets,
the people or the absence thereof, the trading way-
stations, the natural features of space itself. By now
they had met with stranger races than the Hail, had
mastered more fearful perils than rogue waves and
clinker-roads among the stars.

But if the travellers were more together than they
had been at first—from disparate tribes and tuaths
they had been forged into a people, into the Kelts—
they were also less resilient, had fewer inner reserves
upon which to draw; the strain of the voyage had
begun to take its toll. Indeed, Brendan felt it in his own
reactions—he who had ever been the most easy-going
of men had snapped for no cause more often in the
past three months than in all his life before; aware of it
in himself, he noted it in many others, and seeing it he
prayed for a swift completion to their journey, before it
could grow worse.

But there were three more signposts of note to be

encountered before they would reach their promised haven, which by now, so long on their road as they were, had taken on for all of them a yearning mystic quality. The Green Islands of the Flood, the Sidhe lord Melidren had poetically called the lands they sought; and who knew where he himself might be this very moment, it might be on an immram of his own…

Each of the voyagers, therefore, kept a certain particular picture in mind and heart of what the new world would look like, what it would hold for them, and it was different for each: would it be plenteous, would it be fair, would it be like home, would it *be* home… The warriors wondered how it might be made defensible against all comers with least risk to the folk, the merchants conjectured whether it would hold wealth enough to make a trading force to be reckoned with, the sorcerers considered what magics might be particular and permissible to it—for magic, and war and wealth also, will differ on different worlds, even as the worlds themselves are different.

But for Brendan, called Astrogator, the thing was simplest of all: a place in which his people—all his people, human, Sidhe, merrow, silkie, sun-shark—could be safe alike forever. *And we* will *be,* he told himself fiercely, for comfort, many times on that voyage. *It shall happen—but what we have been doing for nigh on two years now has not been purposeless, either. We have not been merely sailing but accomplishing something very different, something I never thought about until now. In all our encounters with all the various folk along our route, we have been making ourselves known among the stars, making friends for the Kelts of the future. These whom we have met will ally with us, and we with them; we will be bound by treaties and friend-*

*ship alike, and all will be set into motion by what we have so
far done…*

"True enough," said Nia when he spoke his thought
to her. "But it is more even than that. We are preparing
not only others but ourselves. As the druids and ban-
draoi make themselves ready before a ritual, and as
each ritual requires a different preparation—so we
make ourselves ready for the new worlds, and out
there, where they are, those worlds make themselves
ready for us. Our home is making itself into Keltia, and
while it does so we are making ourselves into the Kelts."

There was, of course, a further corollary—that the
Kelts were making themselves known not only to themselves and to new friends but to new enemies also. But
however many might have thought it, no one spoke it.

As clouds tower above islands in the sea, to be seen and
marked by sailors far away, so that they know land is
near, so too do planets, islands in the star-seas, have
signs of their own that mark them out to astrogators—
or to exiles.

"What world is that?"

Brendan nodded at the rose-gold glow that filled
the deosil ports; he had noted it some time since, but
had been too enthralled, or too superstitious, to mention it until someone else spoke first.

"It is called Kholco," he said then, in answer to
Amris's question. "The Forgeworld, the Island of
Smiths—or of the Smith-god."

"A world of firemounts," said Barinthus, who spent
much unobtrusive time on the bridge, yet held ever to
his word that he should not again take the helm—save

to spell others under their captain's commands, as did they all. "The glow it throws out into space can be seen for many star-miles, it is unmistakable. And so it is the first of our last three spacemarks; it will not be long now, and this is the proof of it. Here the Salamandri dwell, the Firefolk, the lizard people; they can live in the very earthfires."

"I have wanted to meet them ever since first you told me of them," confided Brendan. "I do not know how, but I have a feeling that their fate is bound up with our own; that they and their world are more to us, or will be, than mere signposts on our journey. But what fate, or what more, I do not know, and cannot say."

Barinthus nodded. "You are right to feel so: their destiny is indeed linked with ours. But they will take a different road in the end."

Destiny or no, they put in at Kholco—the planet was now beneath them, bigger than Erith, rust-red, no blue of sea or sky, no green of field or forest, a world of heat and dust—and as ever he did Brendan accepted the invitation to go down to the surface, where he and his few companions were met by the usual guides.

The Salamandri were a tall, impressive people, with little technology and no weaponry, and yet no fear of strangers; a lacertine race, as Barinthus had said, with fine-textured scaled skin of varying colors. The two groups exchanged the customary courtesies and gifts, and the visitors received lavish hospitality; but after a brief tour of the local capital, an astonishing cliff-dwelling that took up the entire inside of a sizable mountain—an eminently sensible architectural arrangement, for protection against foes as well as weather, that Brendan and others made note of for the future use of Kelts—their hosts surprised them.

"To go up to the Hui Corra?" repeated Brendan. "Well, surely, why not?" *Aye, when my jaw clears my knees; though there is no reason why they should be denied...* "We have visited down here; we are well pleased to offer return hospitality of our own."

Rohan was more direct than his father. "Why would you wish to go to our ship?"

"Why, to pay respects to the Stone; what else?" said Esok, the leader of the host delegation, mildly surprised to be asked. Brendan stared even more dumbfound than before—*How could they know?*—first at the Salamandri chief, who returned the gaze impassively, then at his own son, who only shrugged; but recovering himself, with a courtier's gesture he bowed and with his arm indicated the way to the shuttle, and the Salamandri gathering their robes about them bowed back with equal formality.

"Come then, and welcome."

On a lower deck of the Hui Corra, Esok and his three companions peered at the great stone slab they had sought to see. A plain pillar of gray-blue granite, it was perhaps twelve feet long and half that in width, waist-high to a tall man; it lay in a small high-ceilinged chamber of its own, giving a certain air of consecration to the little room, as a shipboard nemeton, or tumulus like to Sidheanbrugh. People often went there to pray to Idris, Marshal of the Stars, for help in the crossing, or to any other deity they might be moved to beseech, or simply to meditate in the stone's calming presence. Brendan as captain, chief-of-chiefs of the migrant clanns, or Nia as queen-witch, or other of the various lords or druids or ban-draoi, had all performed rituals there, many times—sainings, handfastings, the few sendings that had been sadly necessary—and the Stone had been their witness as it had been witness to such rites for centuries, before being uprooted from Éruinn and sent on its own immram into space.

"Stone is best for ballast," said Esok approvingly, respect in his triple-lidded eyes; but he made no attempt to touch. "There is life in the stones. And Life in this Stone."

"The Lia Fail, brought from Tara to Tara," said Brendan, though he had not intended to say the Stone's name in foreign company—nor indeed the name he had chosen for their new home planet, in any company outside his own heart. *But these folk are not as other outfreyn—or will not be—and so it is well said; and any road I think they knew it already...*

The Lia Fail, the ancient Stone of Destiny, had been King Laoghaire's parting gift to the Immram, brought from the hill of Tara and given into Brendan's keeping: a stupendously generous gifting, but as usual the king had had his own very good reasons. "Take the Stone, Brandoch," he had said. "Save it from capture and dishonor, from destruction and misuse; at the least, save it from what is coming upon its old home, and find it a better." And Brendan, seeing the an-da-shalla that was in that moment upon his king and friend, had obeyed.

Now, though he was not sure why, Brendan stepped

forward, and laid a hand on the Lia Fail. As Esok had said, the Stone had life indeed, that was manifestly plain; it had not been shapen by iron tools or even bronze, but, like the Cremave, had been chipped out by bluestone adzes in the hands of a patient people, long before ever a Danaan foot was set in Éruinn. No carving was upon it, no interlace or incised creature or mystic sigil: only, at the center, a slight shallow depression, of the rough size and shape of a bare human foot.

"It is a kingstone," said Esok then, with an odd satisfaction in his voice that Brendan did not understand. "Upon it will stand at their makings all the rulers of your race; and if they are kings and queens by right, the Stone will cry out to confirm them."

Brendan forgot to be wary. "How can you know all this? And how in all the seven hells did you even know it was here?"

"The Stone told me—as it is telling me now," answered the Salamandri simply. "You yourself have thought that our destinies are linked, and you are right to think it. But why it might be so—there I know no more than you do. One day, we may both know. But not today."

"A dark cloud hiding the goal of a search—an ancient device amongst bards," said Fionaveragh one day; she sat with her father on the bridge, both of them staring out the viewports at the spangled glory all round.

Brendan smiled distractedly, and ran a hand through his hair in his usual gesture. They were some weeks out from Kholco—having left that world with the warm promise of future covenant between the Sala-

mandri and the Kelts and their worlds, once the Kelts
had in fact actually found a world of their own—and
anticipation was running high on all the ships. "Not
long now": that was the word Barinthus had spoken,
and it had fled like the Solas Sidhe through the fleet—
the joy and the hope of it. *It has been a long enough road;
who can blame us for wishing the journey's end would hasten
itself?*

"Very true, alanna," he said aloud, "and here more
so than ever, though we have more than bards to cast
such clouds aside." He turned his head to look at her,
reminded, and curious also. "How is it with you and
Donn?"

His daughter blushed. "That was what I came to tell
you, athra," she explained candidly. "We have decided
we will wed in the new land, if you and mamaith
approve."

Brendan thought about his cousin Donn. *Not that
many years older than Fionagh, yet he seems sometimes of an
age with me— But they suit very well; distant enough kin to
pose no problem in breeding, close enough to keep it all in the
tuath. And of course they are madly in love with one another.
Still, both my bairns wedded now...*

"Rohan and Fiaren did not wish to wait," he said
aloud, reflectively, and Fionaveragh shrugged.

"Half a year, a year; it makes no odds, and any road
for them there is the child now coming... But to wed in
our new home, on our own land—Keltic land—
Donough and I can wait for that."

Brendan nodded approvingly, and put a hand over
hers, but said no word more, and they sat on in companionable silence. Presently: "See there, Fionagh—
there are your dark hiding mists." He pointed; she

looked, and slowly nodded, as the thing they had come there to see, had been waiting to see, came at last into view. They rose to their feet, unthinkingly, as by instinct, to do honor to an approaching friend—or enemy. *And truly I think it will prove both—to us, and to others...*

What lay before them was something no human eye had ever seen. Even the Núminôrians had given it wide respectful berth: this vast black gulf in space, a window into empty nothingness. Yet a void that was far from empty...

"That is the Merizalda," said Barinthus who sat by them, and suddenly he looked very old and very weary indeed. "Or so my people called it. It is the Dead Sea of space—known to other starfaring nations as the Marusha-sharru and the Morasaluran and the Masu Sar. Many the ships have been lost in it. It is the next last of the spacemarks: the worlds we seek, our worlds to be, are hidden behind. Few dare to venture around it. None have ever dared to venture through."

"None until now," said Brendan, and before anyone could think about it, much less protest the action or fear the result, he took the Hui Corra and the rest of the fleet into the writhing fire-shot darkness.

It was an astral derangement. Seen from above, it resembled nothing so much as an earthly thunderstorm, full of energies and concussions and ripples, clouds of heaving shuddering light all going in a huge slow blundering cohesive many-armed spiral. But it was deadlier than the worst landlash ever spawned: laced with fireflaws and choked with spacedust, it had been

born as a monstrous misalignment of the incalculable
tides that move the very galaxies—a voided vortex
twenty lightyears wide. Its smallest eddies and corners
could snap up stars as easily as hungry salmon gulp
mayfly; sullen and inexorable, it was the womb, and
tomb, of suns. On beholding it, one of the bards
aboard the Gwydd Gwyndalcen, the ship of the Kymry,
named it Morimaruse, which is to say 'dead sea', and so
it was known forever after.

Brendan watched as the Hui Corra began to nose
her way into the roiling clouds, the six smaller ships
close beside, in her shield-shadow. *A strangely stately
place—see how the spirals curve, like the Lady's holy triskell...*
For all its frightsomeness, though, there were safe
paths that wound through the heart of the killing
labyrinth; and Barinthus knew them all, so that apart
from a gentle buffeting, as though the ship strove
against a cross-current with the tide running counter
and a gale behind, the transit of a week's duration was
supremely uneventful.

Barinthus had spoken more truly than he was ever
to know. In the centuries to come, the Morimaruse
would be chief armor and defense of the Keltia that
would be, and Nia the first to see how it could be fashioned into an impenetrable shield. She would teach
the Kelts to use those pathways of stellar flux, the leys,
as protective concealment, an invincible net of protection to which they and no others now held the map and
key, their ships alone capable of safe navigation
through its turnings and shiftings.

With her sorcery and science to show the way, in
time they would even learn to shift those paths at will—
as easily as closing or opening hedge-gates to reconfig-

ure a garden maze—so that any foreign ship thinking to cross into Keltia uninvited would soon find itself clear on the other side of the Morimaruse from that upon which it had commenced its sail. The would-be visitors were not destroyed—ambush was never the Keltic way, not on Erith, not among the stars—but after a few unsettling encounters with the Morimaruse the outfreyn nations soon learned to let the Kelts seek them, and did not go seeking the Kelts. For some, it was a harder lesson than others, and many repetitions were required; but in time all did come to learn.

"And that is the second last of the spacemarks behind us," said Barinthus, watching the black expanse of the Morimaruse dwindle in the sternward distance. "And well behind— But now we sail straight."

"And then?" Brendan knew the answer, but he wished to hear it yet again.

"Journey's ending; harbor at the end."

And not a moment before its time... Brendan knew very well that, cloak it as bravely as they all did, after a sail of nearly two years they were very close upon the end of themselves; and he knew it so well because he had felt it in himself. *Not to the end of their courage—they will fight until they drop—nor of their will nor even of their spirit; but of their hope. It has gone on almost too long, and more than long enough. We have begun to crack; if we do not come there very soon now I fear that they—we, I—will begin to break...*

His fears were real enough, but in the end vain. A week out of the Morimaruse, the Hui Corra and the other ships found themselves caught up in an interstel-

lar current that pushed them along more swiftly than
they had been moving for some time. Outside the powerful starstream, that area of space was calm and quiet;
nothing to trouble the smoothness of the sail. Then,
with no warning, out of that calm came strange beasts
curiously nosing up to the Hui Corra and the other
ships: star-whales, huge placid creatures that lived in
the emptiness, coming to visit the Hui Corra because it
was like them, quiet in the sea between the stars.

There was not a viewport or cabin window in all the
fleet that had not its full complement of watchers
pressed against it gazing at the star-whales, with wonder
and not a little awe. From his own vantage point on the
bridge, Brendan marked the tiny forms and faces
framed in every port of every ship he could see.

Barinthus had already declared there was no harm
in the behemoths, nothing to fear from them; that they
were merely as inquisitive about the strange new sleek
creatures that had appeared in their tranquil oceans as
those in the ships were about them.

"They sense life like themselves—as they see it,
many intelligent creatures swimming in a school; they
have come to find out what we are, and what we are up
to in their home space. No one has perhaps ever come
this way before, and they are curious."

"If we were as intelligent as they seem to think, we
might be able to speak to them," said Rohan, though
his face bore the same stamp of rapture as any child's
in the fleet, to see the immense stately creatures glid-
ing fearlessly alongside, following every tack as closely
as sun-sharks follow earthly galleys.

"But we can," replied Nia. "Foolish that I did not
think of it sooner…" She placed her hand on the glass

of the port, fingers spread wide, and presently her face lighted. "What joy—they sing to one another—and to us."

And it seemed that the star-whales heard her, for they began to cluster round the Hui Corra, near to where Nia stood, as if they wished to be as close to her as they could contrive. Brendan, watching with delight, hearing the whalesong now melodiously conveyed to all the voyagers on all the ships, was suddenly reminded of his flocks back on Slemish, and how whenever his mother was about the sheep would come and gather round her, simply to stare at her, to be near her. *For such is the way of the Sidhefolk with all beasts—they are able to speak to any creature in its own tongue and thought, and the beasts do love them for it…*

But for all their own presumed wonderment—and the very certain wonder they gave—the star-whales soon wearied of these boresome creatures, so few of whom could speak to them and none of whom, so rudely, would sing back. At an unseen signal they shoaled off as one, vanishing into the star-dark as suddenly as they had come. But still they sang as they went.

In the absence of their strange convoy, the voyagers felt lonelier than ever before. But one day of days, and very soon thereafter, their isolation came to its prophesied end.

There was no warning, no ceremonious announcement. Even aboard the Hui Corra no spoken statement had been made. Only, they had turned a little from their previous course, now entering an altogether unexceptional system with a strong steady yellow star and five planets, the middle three of which the scientists declared habitable by humans.

Barinthus, although he had until that moment scrupulously held to his word to Brendan and refrained from active command, now quietly ordered all sail lowered and angled, using the solar wind off the new star before them to brake their speed as they drove across; this was the customary approach to any new system, nothing strange there. No an-da-shalla had come to warn of what was toward, Barinthus had given no hint or sign that this was different from any other approach they had made to new planets in a new system; yet somehow, as day by day, hour by hour, he watched that star become a sun, Brendan knew that all the rest of their days, and ages yet to be, would be lived out beneath its warm yellow light. *The harbor-pilot has stood to the helm again; the quay is not far distant...* But though he knew everyone else in the fleet shared his feeling, he said no word, merely ordered the helm onward, and ignored the fraught pleading glances shot his way. *In good time— but in* my *time...*

On the seventeenth day of their inward sail they crossed the orbit of the fourth planet; a promising world, but still Brendan held his silence and his inbound course alike. And then they came up on the third planet out from that sun, and took station just starwards of its orbit, waiting for it to approach: a beautiful blue-green world, with seas and clouds and three large landmasses. And now it was coming toward them out of the starfields, rotating as it sailed along its assigned path through the heavens, light and dark flickering across its moving hide, as majestic in its motion as a snowslip down a mountain or a wave rising to the strand. As it drew swiftly, hugely, nearer on the cithóg side, all saw, with a sudden sharp intake of breath caught and held, what Brendan had known for some time, what Barinthus had known longer far, the third and last of the final spacemarks: the approaching planet had two moons; and like planes of silver, or the lunula collars worn by those of rank, two broad shining rainbow rings circled it round.

Even then none dared to presume or admit, or even to hope—for fear, for doubt, for deepest hunger and lonely wishing and desperate craving. They had wanted it so much that now, in the very moment of its being given, they feared to take the gift: for it is harder to get what one has desired than to continue to desire it in vain, or even to desire it at all—the longer one yearns, the more the yearning becomes the longed-for thing, and the less the thing itself is longed for. But the prayer in every heart on every ship in that emigrant fleet was prayed with violence and passion and a desperate sobbing hope, and it was prayed the same by all: *Lady, Lord, let it be so…*

As the planet spun ever nearer on its path, growing larger every second, Brendan lifted his head to stare through stinging tears, feeling the weight of every heart and soul and mind on every ship, and in his own heart and soul and mind the same prayer; then, in a voice so hushed it could scarce be heard and yet was heard by all, Brendan the Astrogator gave the order that was also the statement of unalterable fact attained and the declaration of a mighty will accomplished.

"Come about. Set to follow. Anchor in orbit." A brief pause. "We are home."

*   *   *

A few hours later, the Hui Corra went in, over the shining rings, past the two moons—the outer one larger and
dull crimson, the inner one smaller and silver-white—
and moored in standing orbit just above atmosphere,
while the other ships held station in the protective lee of
the inner moon. Then, as in a drill long-practiced—
which, now that it was real at last, seemed suddenly like
the veriest dream—in nine smallships, one from each
ship of the fleet and three from the Hui Corra, the first
party of explorers went down to the planet.

They came in over the northern pole, that gateway
in the magnetic field which, as Barinthus had taught,
on almost every world gives safest and easiest entry.
Brendan, standing motionless and rather splendid at
the helm of the lead smallship, was seeing not the new
and promised home, the achieved world below that
had a name as yet only in his own heart, but the familiar bluewhite of Erith, and the incoming ships were not
those of his Keltic fleet but the escapes of Núminôrë. *It
is not the same; and yet it is all one, all one...*

Coming down through atmosphere just on the day
side, they were suddenly flying through clouds that in
their contours did much resemble the hidden lands
beneath them. There were great mounded tullochs
that might have been the green breasts of hills, had
they not been white as bone, and in the small declivi-
ties between were cloud-valleys full of mist like to that
which gathers in riverland bottoms of an autumn
night, spawned by colding air moving over ground still
warm with summer.

It was a sea of cloud they sailed, ribbed like the roof

of one's mouth, with tremendous towers reaching to the border of space, and those were the thunderhelves, the cam-anfa's nursery, cradle of the winds. Far to the west that was still in sunlight, a huge hand of storm-cloud was reaching out over the land below, its fingers stretching across the clear air and under the cloud-blanket many miles on, a hand of air slipping up a great gray sleeve of sky.

And now the clouds ran in rills and runnocks, some in the blue distances puffling upward like hills on the edge of sight, and now they were islands of snow heaped in steaming tropical seas; and as night came on arush, its great shadowing arm flung up like a dark cloak, Brendan saw beyond the planet's curving rim the stars that had been since before this new Keltia was—the stars that from now would be the stars of home.

With Amris mac an Fhiach at the controls, the leading smallship tore southward from the pole, over ice expanses of glittering barrenness, and then a towering white-fanged mountain range, crossing just above the peaks. Those snowy giants faced another, lower range of rough hills some forty miles farther on to the south, with a broad green plain, the valley of a mighty river, in between. And when he saw that, Brendan, as a man who walks in dreams—*This is something I have done before, so often, in waking dream and sleeping alike; I have seen this, I have dreamed this, so many times, and now I do it in life, the only time that counts*—gave almost inaudible order that the ships should set down. But he was heard.

And there it fell out that their journey should find end and haven; there it was, in the wide, empty, beautiful valley that would come to be called Strath Mór, that the Hui Corra beached her boats.

CHAPTER TWENTY-THREE

he scoutships had touched down smoothly, with not even the smallest of joltings, on a level place not far from a stream that ran into the great river some miles off. No one stirred for a long instant; the profound silence was longer still. Even the Hui Corra, far above, had no word for them in that moment. Then Brendan looked round at those with him, his dear friends, his near kin, his loyal captains—*Their hearts are all in their eyes; well, mine is too, I have no doubt*—and collecting them with a glance, he drew himself up before the sealed hatch. With a slow deliberate solemnity that did not ill befit the occasion, he took a deep ragged breath, and laid his shaking hand upon the touchplate.

The door opened like a lens, and first of all Kelts Brendan Aoibhell drew first breath of the air of the first of the new worlds. Cool freshness flowed through the hatchway, around him, behind him into the ship: air clean as water and sharp as wine, overlaid with the hay-scent of green grasslands and a salt tang that bespoke a not too far distant sea. *Eminently breathable—no surprise there, we knew it would be so or ever we left Erith...*

He stooped suddenly, and though his pause was

only brief those who clustered so close behind him could not see what he did. Then he stepped out of the ship, and set his foot upon the springy green turf; and they saw that he had pulled off his boots, so that he went bareshod, as if on holy ground. *For so it is—and was, and will be...*

He stood unmoving for long moments under the light of a new sun, saying no word but only hearing the pulse of the planet, the song of winds and leaves and grasses, the silence of a world that had waited long to welcome its children who now were home at last. He knelt, he bowed, he kissed the ground, he said somewhat to it that only that earth and he would ever know. He rose, and raised his arms; he began to speak.

What Brendan the Astrogator said in that moment—the first words of the first Kelt first setting foot on Keltia—was simple enough. He gave thanks to the Goddess and the God and the Alterator, to all gods of his people; gave praise to Kelu, the One Who is above all gods forever; gave honor to the folk who had come with him from Erith, and to those ones who had come first from stars not too far distant, whose desperate journey, long ago, had allowed them to make their successful, scarcely less desperate own.

And he gave praise and thanks and honor to the planet itself, and greeting to the nation that would be, naming the nation Keltia as Donn Rígh had said it would be named; but the planet that now they stood upon, the beautiful double-ringed double-mooned world, to that Brendan gave the name of Tara. He did not take seizin of the land, did not assert anyone's dominion over anything; but rather entered into a partnership, an alliance contracted between planet

and people, the mystic union that has ever been
between land and king.

And lastly he blessed: stars and planets, sun and
moons, earth and water, plants and stones, beasts and
peoples—Saighvildanach! Saighvildanach! he blessed
all...

The others who had come out behind him, and out
of the other tiny craft, had emerged slowly, warily as little forest creatures, but with a desperate hungering
eagerness—as one will who enters a great dún of the
Sidhefolk, knowing that he is there by right, that he is
safe, that he is welcome and long looked-for, but a little
fearful all the same in a strange and awesome place.
They gazed round about them, marvelling, scarce
daring to believe—even as Brendan had done; and
then, also as he had done, they offered salutation and
gratitude and prayer.

And it was there, on the knees of the mountains, in
the lap of the valley, beyond the great river, beneath
the faint daylight smudge of the glorious rings, that the
Kelts came to their home; and it to them.

"Well," said Brendan at last, hot, dusty, exhausted but
happy beyond all measure, as he surveyed the day's
work with calm satisfaction, "glad I am to see we can
still manage the old skills as featly as we can the new! It
may prove useful in ways we cannot even think—"

They had been busy all afternoon, cutting bracken
and branches and soft green turf to make 'Fian bedding' in the ancient manner, bringing clochan tents
and sleeping-furs and provisions down from the Hui
Corra. Not one of the landing party had the smallest

wish to sleep anywhere that night but under their new heavens; it would doubtless have been easier to make a camp using their technologies, or even to sleep in the smallships. But for this their first night on their new world they had wanted to do things in the old manner—correctly, as they saw it—and they had come prepared; so that now a campment that would not have looked strange to any Gael in Éruinn rose in a sheltered hollow beside the stream, looking as if it had stood there for years.

Every now and again for the past few moments Amris mac an Fhiach, a small troubled frown upon his brow, had been casting round restively, like a hunting dog quartering for game, and now he glanced at Brendan, to intercept a smiling silent query.

"It is the knowing that we are the only folk on all this world," he said with a certain sheepishness for his own fretting. "The beasts and birds and plants, this is nothing; but us, now, here—no one else—"

"It was waiting for us, m'vhic," said Nia smiling, understanding Amris's unsettled confusion, the loneliness and strangeness of it all. "That is why those of Núminôrë never came here; they knew it was not for them. It waited for us and no others; we were meant to complete it—we the Kelts."

But even such a day of fame and splendor must find a quiet end: after a sunset of impossible grandeur, the high sky stained red and gold for miles above their heads, and a rather subdued nightmeal at the quaratz-hearths, there was no more that needed doing or saying. Though they felt that there should be, indeed were reluctant to admit that there might not be, like children wishful of staying up past their lawful sleep-time they lingered, and made excuse, and tarried; but at last even the most reluctant and stubbornly wakeful gave in to sheer exhaustion of body and spirit and mind, and went off to their Fian-style beds. It was deep night now: the ships above had long since been informed and reassured, the camp secured and warded by Nia herself. A small guard had even been posted— against what no one was quite sure; even such unknown beasts as might dwell on this world would not invade any maigen that one of the Sidhefolk had set out.

Having made one more round of the tents, offering a word and embrace and comfort to everyone, making sure those in his charge were all snugly installed if not already asleep, too weary by now to even worry, Brendan made his way to his own tent, where Etain sleepily made room for him on the bed of springy bracken. Pitching himself down beside her warmth, his last coherent thought flickering possessively across his brain—*We are home, our home, ours and no one else's*—he pulled the furs up around them both and was out before his head touched the pillow.

But in the clear dawnlight he was the first awake, as only a few hours before he had been the last asleep. *But who could stay abed* here? *I can nap anytime— We are here, we are HOME! Our first full day on the new world, and I want to see it all, see how it happens—I would not miss a moment of it...*

Dressing in haste and silence, so as not to disturb Etain, Brendan slipped out and tied the tent flap behind him, giving quiet greeting to the Fian still on guard. Just behind the campment rose a rocky knoll perhaps two hundred feet high, and he set himself to climb; reaching the top, drawing a double lungful of the diamond air, he looked to all quarters. The wind was out of the northeast, as clean as it had been the day before, smelling of the snows that still glittered atop the high peaks; though the ship air had been kept beautifully fresh, and was often replenished and replaced, Brendan realized that he had been starved for the touch of natural air on his face and in his blood, for the simple realities of damp wind and clear sky, warm sun and racing cloudshadows. *We have set foot on many worlds since we left Erith behind us, but the air felt never right on any of them; it never tasted of home. But this— This air is* ours *now, and that makes it different...*

For as far as he could see, the lovely rolling country was utterly empty; there was no stain upon the land, no sign of any human presence save their own, and he began to understand a little better Amris's unsettlement of the night before. *Strange it is, to know ourselves all alone on this entire planet...* But he was filled with a slow overspreading joy as the reality of it began to dawn, just as the day now was dawning, miles away to the east. The sky was washed clean, as blue as that which had arched over Fanad, the plains were just as green as Éruinn's own; trees that looked remarkably like pines and oaks and maples and birches comprised the thick hill-mantling forests.

He raised a shading hand, squinted upward against the growing light. *To judge by the position of the sun and the newness of the greening, I make it a morning of early spring— Beltain, even, maybe; that would be more than fitting. But we will soon determine all that, mark out the Wheel of the Year for this new world. Oh, this is a fair land! Thanks to the Goddess that it is empty, spacious and habitable, in look and richness of resources very like to the lands we left. Barinthus—*

"He was right," said Etain, coming up behind him and slipping her arm through his, hearing his thought as easily as ever she did. "Our harbor-pilot—he brought us here as he said he would."

"I cannot wait to get him down here—" Then, at a sudden tensing change in her, a shuttered expression that slid over her mobile face like a shadow over the sun, he felt his blood wash icy cold from head to foot. "What—?"

She did not speak for a moment or two. Then: "Rohan has sent word. He is gone, Brandoch."

Even then his mind would not accept or admit, though something else in him knew better, felt deeper, for tears had already begun to sting his eyes even as he denied her meaning.

"Barrind? Gone? Where would he go?" As his wife's very stillness forced him to the truth he struggled to deny, he half-turned away from her in distress and helpless angry grief. "Ah, not so, it cannot be! How could he leave us—not now, not so close? We have only just—he never—"

"In the Tangavaun Book," said Etain presently into the silence on the hilltop, "there is a tale of one Mósach, who led the clanns of his people forty years wandering in the wilderlands, until they found their home. But though he came in sight of the kingdom they had been promised, Mósach came there never with them: looking upon it from a distant high place, he watched his people enter, and he died, well content."

Brendan did not trust himself to speak for long moments, then shook his head, smiling, weeping.

"Two years in the stars, could the wretched bodach not wait one day more, could he not even set foot—"

"It was what he had foreseen from the first; he was not meant to come here. To guide us here, to see us safe, aye; but not for himself. He told you, even, though I doubt you listened—or, if you did, never would admit you heard. It is dán. And he will leave his dust among the stars, as he did wish." She laid her head upon his shoulder. "Rohan says they found him in his chamber, lying upon the couch he had set against the viewport; he had fallen peacefully asleep. The light of the rings was shining on his face; he was smiling."

"We will barrow him on the red moon," said Brendan after another taut silence. "As my father and Coll mac Gréine sleep on Arianvron, so Barinthus will sleep here, looking not to the stars he lost but to the planet he found—the safe home harbor he never made. And when we look up from beneath in years and centuries to come, we shall think of him, keeping guard over us, and what he gave us."

And so it was done as Brendan had commanded. He himself read the sending prayers for Barinthus, as he had done for his father and Coll; the devastated folk of the Immram, the sails of their ships half-furled in token of mourning, made sorrowful farewell to their pilot who had died in sight of the land long sought for, the land to which he had led them. And yet, however unfair it seemed, it also seemed—somehow—perfectly correct.

After that, Brendan made no further delay in landing all the rest of the voyagers on the planet's surface,

ferrying them down, settling them in camps widely
spaced down the vast valley for convenience's sake. Ten
camps of five thousand folk each are more manageable
than one of fifty thousand: they are easier organized
and defended and supplied, they make less demand on
local resources and leave a lighter mark upon the
land—and if danger strikes unexpectedly less will be
lost. The Hui Corra remained in orbit with a war-crew
aboard, but the other dromonds were emptied completely and berthed on the inner moon—now named
Argialla, as the red one was Bellendain—well hidden
and sheltered against future use or need. But they kept
back the smallest of the ships, the Manx vessel Partan,
with a barebones crew of a hundred, to use in their
early explorations and for immediate defense if such
were needed. Or so at least they had planned...

The first Brendan learned of it was when he saw
Conn Kittagh coming purposefully toward him, face
set as stone. *Ah, not again! Mighty Mother, not more
death—*

"The Partan," said Conn, briefly and heavily, and all
those who stood by knew from the mere sound of the
two words what had befallen. "It has crashed in the
northeast, and all aboard were killed."

But when pressed for details he could tell them no
more just then than bare fact; Brendan, appalled and
grief-guilted, gave immediate order that under no circumstances whatever was even the tiniest cleggan craft
to take air over Tara, not until they learned what had
befallen the Partan and its crew, and why. No clue was
found in the twisted wreckage; none of the motivers or
thoughtspeakers who had been in absent contact with
craft or crew had felt a whisper of anything wrong. It

was left for Kelver Donn Midna, who at the news of the crash had vanished without a word, in the sudden, silent manner of his folk, and who had now returned with equal suddenness, to give them the reasons why the ship had crashed. But even when he had told them they still wondered.

"You are saying," said Brendan carefully, as one who strove to master an utterance in a complex foreign tongue he did not speak, "that the magnetic power in these northeastern mountains will allow no ships at all to fly in air on this entire planet, save small aircars under motivers, or craft that are powered by earth-currents or gravity plummet-wells."

Kelver Donn nodded. "Anything larger, or fueled by the usual combination of means we have come to rely upon, falls under the influence of the metal ore-mass which underlies these mountains like a shield. Lachna: we knew it of old—we the Danaans—there is no way round its power." He smiled wryly, with a touch of sadness for the loss. "Well, no way that we yet know. It seems that the old means are preferred by the planet itself. So, at least until we find a source of power that the lachna does not bar, it will be horses and chariots and sailships for us on this world—and only the very smallest of aircraft—for a long time to come. And maybe that is no bad thing."

"Maybe not, but I could wish that a hundred more of us had not had to die to show us the way of it." Brendan brooded a little. "If we had let the Hui Corra and the other dromonds come down into air, not just the Partan alone—"

"All of us would have perished," said Nia, simply and somberly.

"Barrind was right as usual," said Brendan laughing, and brushing away tears as he did so. "He said there would be a use for the tiny swift fliers—the cleggans, he called them—and he was more right than ever he knew."

"As for those mountains," said Kelver Donn Midna into the long thoughtful silence, "my people will dwell among them forever; for safety's sake no other Kelt shall come near. The metal has no claim on us—it comes under the bargain we have made with cold iron—and if we may by our presence prevent, not one Kelt more shall die for it." And he and his people kept that word he gave: for more than thirty centuries, not one more Kelt did...

Perhaps surprisingly, there had been no prior discussion of territories being allocated to clanns or kindreds or nations; but that may have been because no one had known what sort of territory there might be available. The silkies and merrows and sun-sharks had already been given the freedom of the waters, and glad they were to take it, but the lands had yet to be divided, and Kelver Donn Midna's simple statement that some of the Sidhefolk would live in what had already been named the Hollow Mountains was historically the first claim made on any part of Tara. Brendan was more than pleased to allow it, but the claim and grant only pointed up all the more the vital importance of a land search. Maps could be made from the observations of the Hui Corra's long-range scanners, and many were made so; but since the use of any craft in air, even the smallest, had been forbidden until they learned more about the planet's ways, a study done at footpace and ground level was both necessary and enjoyable—and just now every bit as useful as aerial or even orbital mapping.

So a small scouting party left the campments behind—no one would come to harm or grief there, and the vote among the settlers had been unanimous, to be on the ground in rain or storm or howling blizzard rather than spend one more hour in the ships—and went slowly, always heading south and west, as if drawn there, angling toward the southern line of rough blue hills, where they plunged their last western bastion into a vast bay. Above their heads, just visible, the silver splinter that was the Hui Corra held its high lonely station, and Brendan often looked up as he walked, taking comfort and reassurance in the sight. *The other ships are too small to be seen; only the eyes of the Sidhefolk could discern them, and they are hidden now on Argialla, any road. But good it is to have sight of the craft that was our home from Erith to Tara, our bridge from one world to another...*

The scouting party had been walking many days now; Brendan had chosen some friends, some kin, some strangers—representatives of each of the nations and all the arts and trades. They found it no hardship to be afoot on their new homeworld, and were deeply thrilled with everything they saw under their new sun, called now Grian. The towering snow-mountains to the north, newly named the Stair; the forty-mile width of the rolling river valley—the Avon Dia, they called the mighty stream that had carved it, River of the Gods; the beautiful crinklecrag outlines of the Loom, that rough hill range closing off the valley's southern perimeter toward which they were heading: it was all new, all fair in their dazzled eyes.

They were proceeding along a line of low hills just north of the great river, whose speed and breadth and deepness had barred their crossing for miles downstream, looking for a place to ford, when—

"Brandoch." Donn Aoibhell—whose handfasting with Fionaveragh had been celebrated on the third day after landing—touched his new matefather's shoulder, nodding silently upslope. "I thought there were no folk here save ourselves alone…"

Brendan looked, and started. A young man clad all in black, his yellow hair loose and long upon his shoulders, was coming swiftly down the steep green scarp. Though he had a look about him that was somehow familiar, he was most definitely not one of the voyagers, and an air of high purpose clung round him like a cloak. He leaped over rocks with the grace of an otter at play, trod the hill like a stag in spring—and he was heading straight for them where they stood.

They rose to their feet, not alarmed but in instinct of respect, or in greeting for a guest. As Brendan watched him come, it seemed that he knew this stranger, though how that could be… It seemed too that he had come to welcome them, as if he had been there long before them, had been only waiting on their arrival to make everything perfect and complete.

With another jolt, Brendan, blinking to clear his strangely clouded vision, was back in himself. The stranger was standing before him now, plain to all sight, perfectly at ease, a faint smile upon a face of impossible fairness. *He looks like a spear in rest—his beauty is greater even than the beauty of my mother's people…* Brendan hastily returned the offered bow, spreading his hands in gesture of peace and welcome, but in his

abrupt weariness and bewilderment wanting to weep,
his fears and griefs suddenly overwhelming, all at once
it had become too much. *Perhaps it always was…*

"We cannot cross this river, and we do not know
how big this land is." His words sounded as a lost child's
even in his own ears, peevish and sad, and he hoped
the knot of folk who stood behind him did not know
how very near to tears he was.

But the young man smiled in perfect sympathy, as if
he knew indeed and it did not matter in the slightest;
and looking round at the company he greeted each of
them by name, with a particular low bow of surpassing
dignity to Nia, who bowed back with matching grace,
and then addressed Brendan.

"Blessed are all who shall come to dwell in this
house you have built for them."

Fionaveragh, who had been thrilled over both
moons to accompany her parents and her new lord on
this venture, brushed back her hair and began a question in bubbling wonder.

"But who—"

Nia laid a gentle hand on her granddaughter's arm,
and Fionaveragh fell abashedly silent.

The man in black continued serenely—one corner
of his mouth quirking in amusement at her break but
otherwise taking no note—and though he spoke
straight to Brendan, and looked upon no one else, his
eyes, blue as sapphires in seawater, held them all
entranced.

"From generations they will praise you. Now
behold this land which you sought so long and hard
and truly. You could not find it straightway, because the
gods wanted to show you the secrets in the starry

oceans. You wondered even if your taking of it were right and lawful, or merely a reiver's claiming, as unsanctioned and illicit as the Tangavaun's own against your homeland." Here Brendan started violently, at the naming of his secretest hidden doubt, which he had thought only Etain had twigged, back in the Hui Corra; and the stranger smiled. "No fear! It is the thing that was meant for your people since before these worlds were made. But the days of your wandering are over now; here you will rest and sleep."

"Die?" That was Shane Farrant, who stood to the rear of the spellbound party.

The god, if god he was, laughed, but not in mockery. "Aye, when it is the time for it! But not yet. And not now. For look you how this great river divides the land, as night divides the day. Just so will the land itself be divided from the Dark. For its life is the life of gods and folk together. And after many ages have passed, this land will become known to your successors that you have left behind, and they will come to join you in amity and peace." His voice, that had been ringing and clear as a war-horn, now took on a warmer tone, and raising his black-clad arm he pointed to the west. "There is an easy ford three miles on. Cross there, at the white stones, and go on southward. We will meet again, and often."

He turned then, and began to move upslope again as lightly and easily as he had descended. Brendan stirred out of his bemusement, and called after him, suddenly desolate, desperate—for what, for whom, he did not know.

"But how? We do not know where we may find you, we do not even know what your name is, who you are—"

The young man turned back to them for a moment, and his movement was a marvel of grace. "Do you not?" he asked, and though he was not smiling yet his face in its grave beauty held all the warmth of a smile. And though it could not be said that they saw with eyes, it seemed to those watching that another aspect somehow overshadowed him, or blazed through him, or lay trembling upon him like a reflection upon water—for they saw dark hair now, not golden, and above that long dark tousled hair the noble scything antlers of a royal stag.

"Do you not?" he repeated, and now he was smiling again. "Then call me Fionn."

CHAPTER TWENTY-FOUR

"**I**t cannot be"—"He *said* he was"—"Nay, well, folk can *say* anything—"

So the discussion went on, in low fierce whispers, though Brendan himself had gone very quiet and took no part, seeming to be lost in thought. Fionn! they all whispered and wondered. Could it be? Well, why not, countered others. Fionn Rhên was one of the High Dânu, not for nothing was he called Friend-of-man. His powerful interest and involvement in the affairs of mortals figured in all the tales and histories from of old: how folk in straits and peril had many times appealed to Fionn as last resort, and without fail he had come to aid them—though how he could be *here*, how he could have found them across all the miles of space…

"He is a *god*," said Amris mac an Fhiach at last, in a tone that if it decided nothing at least put paid to any further discussion. "Let be."

In any event, they pitched camp on the slope where Fionn—or whoever—had found them; now that they knew a ford was within easy reach, their minds were much relieved, and this seemed as good a place as any. They passed a dreamless peaceful night, and in the morning Brendan woke to a camp already well astir.

"We found these," said Shane Farrant in a hushed awed tone. "There was a guard posted all night long, and no one saw or heard anything, but when the sun came up these lay beside the fire, neatly stacked as little logs."

Brendan, whose only real thought so far had been casually tending toward the huge and savory breakfast Amris and others were already cooking over the quaratz-hearths—bacon, grilled gammon, hot flat-cakes with butter and sweet sirop, fried porrans from the seemingly inexhaustible shipboard stores—went very still, and forgot all thought of food, as he saw what Shane held out to him.

"Maps—"

Ysella Vyghtern, one of Kynmarra's Cornovians, nodded eagerly. "Maps indeed! They show all this country we now are in, from east to west, a huge land-mass, and a southern one near as vast, and round the other side of the planet another one midmost between south and north. Much, much land, very kind land it looks too, and all unpeopled save for us."

Brendan had taken the armful of beautifully wrought and filigreed leather cases Shane proffered, and slipping the largest of the scrolls from its polished cylinder he now spread it out before him on the ground. Whoever the maker had been, the thing was superbly done: in firm black lines on a tough smooth material they now knew to be plant-plastic, the planet's secrets were laid out before him clear and plain, and forgetting their own hungry inclinations the others clustered round to peer eagerly over his shoulder.

Look how splendid is our new home! Of course we have seen it all from space, can make all the maps we want, but this is so very different, this is real... His finger reverently traced their track from the landing site. There were the giant mountains that made a white wall to the north, upon whose southern outwash plain their first camp had been established; here was the broad river upon whose banks they now unprofitably loitered, or so it had seemed until only yesterday. Away northeast, too distant to see from this low level, other mountains rose up, those dim blue haunted hills that had killed the Partan and her crew; while due east from where Brendan now stood towered a two-horned giant, twice as tall as any other peak on the planet, by reason of its enormous height just barely tip-visible over the horizon if one climbed to the top of the bank. Along the western and eastern ends of this huge landmass upon which they found themselves, there were strings of islands like green jade beads, and another cluster in the southwest, at the end of a long peninsula with a high stony spine—and mountains everywhere, linking the continent like silver chains.

"You must have all been snoring like drunken hogs that got into the still-midden," said Brendan teasingly, sitting back at last and looking up. "How else could someone get past the guard to leave these, and you knowing nothing of it?"

But they were fierce and loud in defense of their wakefulness; not even Brendan should slander their perfect undrowsing vigilance. And though it was not spoken aloud, the memory of Fionn stood plain in all their minds. *Well, perhaps they did not doze after all; a god can do as he pleases. But never shall Kelts forget, in all the years that Keltia may be, that Fionn the Young came to greet us when our ship touched sand at last...*

*   *   *

Though, as Barinthus had long ago promised, this new world was home to no other folk, from their first day of arrival the settlers had seen plentiful animal life, and Brendan had at once forbidden hunting, with which ban everyone fervently concurred.

"We have never hunted for mere bloodsport, and never will while we are yet Kelts," he had said. "Neither will we slay promiscuously the beasts that share this world with us and precede us in residence: only at need to feed and clothe us—and even that only if and when we must. We have plenty of food and raiment in the ships, and the means to make more of both; I would not begin our lives here by killing when there is no need. Also we have to learn which creatures may be intelligent and which are but mere common beasts—only think how we should feel, if out of our ignorance we should slaughter a being like a silkie or a merrow or a sun-shark." According to their own law, such a slaying was equivalent to the murder of a human; and the horror of the idea was such that he did not need to argue his point any further.

But those mere beasts were many and marvellous indeed, and not so common either; Brendan need not have enjoined his folk so strictly as he had—wonder alone was enough to keep bow unbent and spear unslung. Vast herds of huge shaggy white bison drifted over the valley, placidly cropping the rich grass: against the vivid green they looked like clouds come down to earth, Gwenhidw's sheep; they lifted their startling blue eyes to regard the newcomers with mild curiosity before lowering massive heads to graze again, unconcerned,

secure in size and numbers. Giant hill-deer, both stags
and does carrying antler-racks twelve feet across, shared
the high uplands in peace with furry red catbears,
round playful creatures the size of a six-years'-child and
ten times the weight, who spent their time munching
vast quantities of the leaves and stalks of a bushy blue-
leafed shrub. Otter-like sleeklings with bright gold fur
chattered at them volubly from stony streambanks as
they passed, and elegantly patterned snakes disposed
themselves on warm stones in the sun; once in the distance Rohan saw a beast's form running that might have
been a kind of lion or panther—some great hunter
intent on prey. In the skies were birds like eagles, only
with twice the wingspan, and down along the wooded
riverlands tiny songbirds flickered like flying jewels
among the stands of trees. No creature large or small
showed the slightest fear of the strange newcomers.

"It is as Éruinn must have been or ever the Firstfolk
came out of the North—before the Nemedi, before the
Partholonai, long before the Danaans came." Fionaveragh held out her hand, enchanted, and a minute
bird boasting improbably vivid green plumage flashed
down at once to seize the crumb she offered, and to
stay a moment more and look at her with a bright
knowing eye before darting away again.

"Yet now the Danaans are here," said Donn, to tease
her.

But the gaze Fionaveragh bent upon her mate was
Nia's own, out of Brendan's eyes. "Not so," she said in
correction, with a slow smiling shake of her glowing
ruddy head. "Now the Kelts are here."

*   *   *

Brendan lay out upon the hillside, as so long ago he had done on Slemish, his face inches from the turf, watching a small, startlingly orange beetle climb with indomitable purpose from one grassblade to another. Below him and a little way to his right, in the angle where the line of the hills bent round and a waterfall came down spectacularly striated colored cliffs to fill a spill pool, running out its stream to the plain, folk were laboring in the warm spring sun to set up an extensive campment.

The scouting expeditions were done with, at least for the moment; when Brendan and the others had at last arrived at this place, they had seen at once that this was where they should begin to build. To that end they had sent for reinforcements, who had come from the landing sites only a few days since to begin work on the shelters they would need against the winter; and once Gradlon of Ys had sited the likeliest place, digging had commenced.

Brendan was by no means the lazy shirker he looked to be. Until a half-hour past he had been right down there among them, clad only in a laborer's leather kilt, digging and sweating and breaking stones with the rest, men and women alike; even the tiniest children helped, carrying away rocks and roots and such small buckets of earth as they could manage. It could all have been done at once and with ease by Nia's magic, Brendan reflected; but his mother and the other sorcerers had smilingly declined, could only be prevailed upon to help with boulders bigger than a horse, or a house—anything smaller than that the builders must shift for themselves.

Doubtless there is a good reason for it—with her there

*always is—most likely it is something as simple as how much
more we will appreciate the shelter if we sweated the sweat that
went into its building...* Well, I say I have earned my little
*rest; but they are working so hard—I will go down again
presently...* But the sun was warm, and the grassy turf
deliciously soft, and despite his guilty words he showed
no inclination to rise and go back to the job. After a
while he rolled onto his back, careful not to inconve-
nience the transiting insect, and stared up into a deep
sky as blue as the tiny beetle was orange. *There, over there
a handspan or two, there lies Erith...*

He put up his hand to cover the patch of cloudless-
ness, as if to touch his birthworld, and a wave of home-
sick longing smote him like a spear, pinning him to the
earth. But apart from such moments—which he was
wise enough to know would recur for all the rest of his
life, and which he was also wise enough to know were
transient, to be endured merely, not fought against—
he had very little cause for unhappiness; and that too
he was wise enough to know. He was reclining on the
knees of the rough hills they had seen so many days ago
from the north, on their first arrival. They had crossed
the great river, at the ford of white stones which Fionn
had shown them, and made their leisurely way to this
sea-lapped upland quarter, to which they had all been
strangely drawn from the first. *And why not, it is a fine
strategic place to plant a city, snug and defended, well-
watered, good to look upon and to look out from—the sea on
our shield-arm, miles of mountains at our back and sword-
hand, the whole wide river-plain before...*

It had not all been struggle and work, of course.
Ever since first landing—at the site known now as
Taghnavalla—the little band of explorers had been

indulging in the time-honored perquisite of all pathfinders: naming their discoveries—though perhaps not all that many other explorers had had fifty thousand editors in orbit two hundred miles straight up, and now that all of them had been brought to land they were even less shy about exercising power of veto, anxious that Brendan and the others should not hog all the fun for themselves.

We have named well, though! That is the Avon Dia, he reminded himself, squinting through the haze at the broad river, twenty miles away and clearly visible from this elevation, *and this range above my head is the Loom; this double-headed peak we have named Eryri, Mount Eagle...* They had assigned the newest of the names only the day before, sitting in their camp on the highest part of the naturally terraced slope, hushed and reverent beneath yet another of the region's tremendous all-silencing sunsets, crimson and crocus and violet-purple, the cloudbanks to the west towering and smoking half-way to the moons, and the wondrous rings, the newly named Criosanna, shining like midnight rainbows; and the nomenclature had seemed most admirable to their consultants.

Brendan had not been a shepherd in Fanad all those years to learn nothing from it, and even though he was at this moment relaxed and lazing, that guarding instinct was active and alive; so that when he felt the weight of a purposeful gaze on him, and no human gaze, he did not turn at once, but made a few desultory shifts and stretches and settled down again as if to doze—the herder's ploy. *Beast, and a large, powerful one too...*

When next he opened his eyes it was straight into

the direction from which he felt the gaze; and as he saw
who was watching him, he came to sharp still attention.

Lying on the hillside not a dozen yards away, the
giant wolf regarded him steadily out of green-gold
eyes. Its nose was on its enormous padded paws, its
plumed tail was curled round its haunches and it did
not blink even in the bright afternoon sunlight. He
had seen it before, for it was the same wolf that first he
had met on the slope of Darinlaur in Fanad—the wolf
that had spoken to him, as it would speak to kin of his
for all the centuries of Keltia's being.

And now it spoke to him again. "Here is thy city,"
came the wild deep voice, in his mind and ears and
heart together. "Here let its walls rise."

"But how?" Brendan had just told his mother the tale
of the wolf on the hill. "How could it come here?"

Nia seemed unsurprised, or if surprised at all, surprised only by the depth of her son's distraughtness.
"How not? Any road, you know already. If Fionn could
come among us, why not your fetch?" She dropped a
kiss on his hair. "M'vhic, be glad of it! That wolf will be
a friend to our blood for all the years that Keltia shall
stand."

"'Keltia'," he said, as if he tasted the word for the
first time. "You know that Donn Rígh himself did
name it…"

"And he named it correctly," she said, gently now.
"As you named this planet."

"It was Tara from the first," he said, and took care
that she should not see his eyes when he spoke the
name: the image of Laoghaire and Duvessa must surely

be standing there, his tears glassing it over.

But Nia, if she saw, chose not to remark on it. "Well, we have been commanded," she said in a light voice. "But not yet is it time to build."

That night Etain danced on the hillside by the waterfall, beneath the new stars; the beat of her bare feet on the earth called up answering rhythms from Tara's ground. The other women joined her; the men danced too, and then all circled round together, to the sound of drums and pipes, their arms upflung like flames among the swordpoints. The fires threw their glow against hills and black sky, and the valley seemed to strain its ears to listen to what it had never heard before in all its long empty days.

And in the morning Brendan brought reverently down from the Hui Corra that which he had cherished and cosseted and cared for like a delicate infant, ever since the leaving of Fanad—a tiny yew seedling, off-shoot of the covin-tree that had stood before lost Crea-vanore—and he planted it on the rocky crag that was the northwestmost point of the terrace just below the mountain slope, the prow of the plateau that they had named Turusachan. *Here let it grow, for as long as its parent tree did grow in Fanad, and longer still—for as long as one Kelt remains in Keltia...*

And so it did.

That first year was not so difficult as might be thought, or as another folk might have found it: they were a hardy race, well used to living out of doors, to nomadic movement, shifting campments with the seasons. They had lost remarkably few of their number in the crossing, and more children had been born than folk had died, so they had arrived on Tara with more souls than had left Erith. As the first steps to a permanent settlement, they had thrown up those early earthworks on the rising ground below the Loom, as Gradlon had directed; the great pounded-earth banks helped keep their clustered clochans warm and sheltered through that first winter—a warm one, thankfully, with less snow than that region was wont to have. But now it was spring again, and soon they would begin to build in stone—to build to last.

One full year round from the landing, the first Beltain fire in Keltia was set alight on the hillside above Turusachan, 'Place of Gathering'. Standing on the broad granite ledge, near the young and flourishing covin-tree, Brendan looked out east and north over the lower ground where it rolled away, tumbling down in wooded terraces and bare ridges to the plain. *So perfect a place for our City that is to be—it does not take Sight to see great walls rising where the hill-shoulders meet glen and sea, and all the space within filled with grand brughs and stately mansions. And a people dwelling here, and on other worlds beside, that none can conquer—not with the sword, not with the word. That is worth everything we have endured, surely, or will endure...*

His gaze fell on the as yet unlighted belfire a few yards away, and his thought flew back through years unerringly as an arrow: Pátraic, on the hill of Slane, lighting a fire in the Flame's despite; Laoghaire, his anger deep and terrible—and what came of it... He shook off the memory, then turning to his mother he bowed slightly, and an anticipatory murmur ran through the watching throng.

Standing a little apart, Nia raised her hand; white fire lanced from white fingers to the tall brushwood stack, and the blaze that leaped up then could be seen thirty miles away, a tower of light, a spark in the seamless dark. And across the width of the Great Glen and down along the valley of the Avon Dia, where other Kelts in other small settlements watched the lap of Eagle for the holy sign, other fires on other hills blinked on like red stars to bear it company.

"Once more the Sacred Fire is lighted on a hill of Tara, and all the land is set aglow," said Brendan then, and he spoke to more than those who stood nearby to hear him. "Eirias—no false fire shall be lighted before it, and no other flame shall challenge."

So summer came, and throughout the little campments the folk were glad. At Midsummer, another, greater link was soldered in the chain that was being slowly, carefully forged to bind Kelts to Keltia, new settlers to newly settled world. A few days before the feast, two representatives of each race that was in Keltia—Shane Farrant and Corlis Typhult for humankind, Etain and Kelver Donn Midna for the Sidhefolk, two merrows and two silkies to complete the count—all with great pride and solemnity went up to the Hui Corra. Though the tragedy of the Partan was ever unforgotten, they had found that the little cleggan craft, the aircars, could safely manage the dashes up to the orbiting flagship, where a crew was always posted, and had made use of them as need required, to fetch tools and technology and supplies.

But their mission now was a graver and grander one, setting a seal on their life and claim on Tara and Keltia together: they had gone to bring the Lia Fail

down at last from its high home, the Stone of Destiny
that Laoghaire Ard-rígh had given into their care
before they left Erith—with Nia's magic to float it, and
Fians and ban-draoi and druids and bards as a guard
about it. With ceremony and state it was brought to
Tara, and installed on a level raise in Calon Eryri, Heart
of Eagle, the hanging valley high behind Turusachan,
on the flat-topped rise that they had named Ni-maen,
'daughter of the Stone'. Until this moment, no stone
but those that had grown there had graced the secret
valley since the planet was made. But all that was about
to change forever...

On Midsummer Morning, a little before local
dawn, a joyful procession came up the winding path
from the settlement below; emerging from the blind
cliff-cutting into Calon Eryri, those in the van stopped
short, and gasped at the sight before them.

The Lia Fail lay where they had bedded it the day
before, gray and enigmatic upon green turf in the
growing light. But now around the crown of the raise
Ni-maen a ring of tall trilithons stood sentinel; at the
northern gateway rose two high carved pillars, and, set
a little apart from the other stones, the Helestone, a
rough, unshapen dolmen to mark the place of greatest
power, where the Tântad, the Dragon Path, the land-
tide, would meet the rising Midsummer sun as it
showed itself at a notch in the valley skyline.

*They look as if they have been here from the first—but I
think I know whose fine Danaan hand raised them up from
the ground...* Brendan, marvelling with the rest, came
up to stand before his mother as the rest of the procession disposed itself, ten and twenty deep, round the
new-raised ring of stones.

"I see *you* have had a busy night," he muttered, though he did not look at her, and sensed rather than saw her flash of amusement, and admission. *But it is so well done: it gives us power, it justifies us here according to the Goddess's purposes; it makes us real...*

Yet even on so joyful a morning, festivity was not the chief order: before the Stone of Destiny stood now not Brendan's mother but Nia the Golden, princess of the Danaans, sorceress of the Kelts, Calatin's daughter robed in white, with Kelver Donn Midna tall and silent on her right hand, and, on her left, a lord with dark hair, less tall though no less imposing, whom Brendan did not know; and it looked as if they had high purpose on their mind.

Nia had lifted her hands in blessing as the procession spilled out of the defile and filled the little valley, and when all were assembled and standing expectant she said no word, but making a solemn bow to Brendan, and to the throngs below, she turned to the dark-haired lord beside her.

Who gave Brendan the same regal acknowledgment, which Brendan returned with great correctness, if with equally great puzzlement. "I am Neith son of Llyr," said the stranger then. "Donn Rígh did speak to you of us—we who took the Low Road." He smiled at Brendan's start of surprised attention. "We were here before you; in the secret places of this world and others we have waited upon your coming. And today I give this into your hand: the Sceptre of Llyr, your heritage from the Gael. It betokens your right to reign as High King not over Kelts alone, but over all kings of the Sidhe that are in Keltia."

Brendan looked at what Neith held out to him, but

made no move to take it: a plain rod of polished find-ruinna, unadorned, with bands of rosegold knotwork at either end, but no stone or gem or other adornment. *It will be far heavier in the hand than it looks to the eye, though how I know that, I am sure I cannot say! But 'High King'? Now that I do not think!*

On Nia's right, Kelver Donn Midna lifted something in his hands that flashed as it caught the pre-dawn light: a curiously fashioned crown of spiral-embossed plaques and a high conical centerpiece; it was made of beaten copper, solid and heavy and bright. He raised the glorious thing up for all to see, for the stones to sain, and spoke to Brendan as Neith had done.

"And this is your heritage from the Folk of Dâna... The Copper Crown, made for your House and line by Gavannaun himself, Gavida Burn-the-wind, Smith of the Gods, in his forge of Cartha Galvorn that lies beneath Pen Gannion in the world between the worlds. Old it was in lost Atland before my people fled the Wave; before that, it came from Lirias, in Núminôrě that is gone; before that we do not know. Wear it now as symbol of the covenant between Keltia and all folk who are Kelts, not humans only; likewise for the covenant that is between Keltia and all realms outwith your kingdom that will be."

"I do not covet kingship," said Brendan into the eager yearning breathless hush; he spoke quietly enough, but behind his dark eyes was a glow not unlike to that which lay upon the crown. "I have never wished a crown, and I have never sought one. And I did not come here this morning expecting to be made a king, or have the kingship forced upon me against my will and knowledge." He tried to control it, but his voice had taken on a sharp glassy edge. *I know they all wish it—But how dare they ambush me so—my own mother!—when they very well know how I feel…*

"Truly, you have not," said Neith ap Llyr gravely. "And we know you have not. Nor do you welcome it, now or ever; and that too we know. But that is just why it must be you and no other to take it. This task is yours and no one else's. If you were made for the task—and you were—so also was the task made for you."

Kelver Donn Midna took up the theme as Neith fell silent; and though he and Brendan had long time been dear friends he spoke now as if they had never met—ceremonious, with a gravity beyond words and worlds.

"Barinthus Saw it for you before ever he set eyes on you, at Aileach under Tallaght's hill. Your mother Saw it for you when she rode out from that same hill to meet your father, and he Saw it too…" He smiled then, though not as Neith had smiled, but friend to friend; his voice warmed and deepened, but Brendan's face remained as unmoving as the stones his mother had raised. "Our races are alike in that, Brandoch: we are best and most ourselves when one is set to rule us. Queen or king, it makes no differ. But that one—the one who freely chooses to take on the most sacred dán of all—is wedded to the land, standing for the folk before the gods, and for the gods before the folk, to give life so that the people and the land may live. The charge is laid upon him or her, as monarch and as war-leader and as priest—and as royal sacrifice when the time comes, to offer death instead of life, so that the land and the people may not die. And you are the one upon whom it is now laid to stand so, and serve so. It is as much your dán and duty as was the Immram itself, and as you could not turn that fate aside or step away from it, no more can you turn or step away from this. It is all one, and all yours, and no other's."

While the two Sidhe lords were speaking, Brendan never took his eyes from his mother's; but when they had done, still Nia the Golden had no word for her son—or at least none that she chose to have others hear her say. *If I do not do this?* he heard himself asking, and had his answer swift as a swordsman's riposte, though if that answer came from himself or from Nia or from some unknown Other he would never know. *Then it will not be done. Some other thing, aye, but never this...* The choice was his, and he knew it; knew also that now it was time to choose, and little time was left in which to do so.

"Well then," said Brendan aloud, conceding in his tone, as if he did indeed bow to a knowledge imparted to him or to a given command, as if he beheld the futility of argument and the inutility of resistance, and bent to both. *As well plow the sea or plant the sand or bay the moon; let be what must! I could forgive; but I will never forget how they have worked this on me. Betrayal is the one sin my people—both my peoples—do* not *forgive... Nay, nor shall I ever let* them *forget it, either...*" He drew a deep breath, let it out in a swift sigh. "Be it so." And Nia smiled.

So Brendan—having exchanged a long look with Etain who stood by—removed his cloak, and unshod himself, and knelt; and taking the Copper Crown from Kelver Donn, Nia set it upon Brendan's bowed head, and Neith ap Llyr put the Silver Branch into his hand.

In that moment the Midsummer sun mounted to the rim of the valley; a spear of fire shot from Grian's heart to the Helestone, and the Helestone flung it back again. White flame went round the circle east to east,

enkindling every stone that stood, as Brendan Aoibhell, first of that Name and House in Keltia, the
bright crown circling his brow and the scepter gleaming in his hand, leaped atop the Stone of Destiny on
the circle's western edge, and in the sight of Kelts and
Keltia set his bare right foot to the foot-shaped hollow
at the Stone's heart. And as he did so, as Laoghaire
king at Tara had known it would, as Esok of the Salamandri had foretold, a note like the wind through a
great horn began to grow in the valley; it sounded
through Calon Eryri, until it seemed that the little glen
itself was the horn, so resonant and sweet and clear the
sustaining note against its steep stone walls.

And the note did not die and fade but only grew:
even below in the campment they heard it; it rang far
out across the plain to all the little steadings where
Kelts now dwelled, filling the upland vales, rolling
across Strath Mór to break like sea-waves on the walls of
the Stair, moving out over the wild waters where merrows and silkies danced for joy of it in the heart of
ocean. On the far reaches of the Litherlands the white
bison ceased to graze, hill-stags lifted heavy-antlered
heads in the thickets of the Dragon's Spine; in Drum
Wood catbears stilled their tumble-play and little dark-
furred foxes crept out of their hollow-tree lairs. Far to
the south, from out the warm waters of the Bight of
Dúma sun-sharks leaped, dazzling in the flying spray of
light; on the thermal currents above the slopes of the
Cobbler sea-eagles hung motionless, riding the air.

East and south and west and north, all creatures on
Tara, beast and faunt alike, turned wondering eyes to
Eagle; all the planet rang with the sound like a great
struck bell, when the first King of Kelts set his foot to

the Stone of Destiny, and that Stone roared out to confirm his rightful accession. And above on Yr Hela, westermost of the peaks that overlooked Eryri's heart, a great shaggy shape stood dark against the dawnlight, and riding over the cry of Lia Fail there rose the high lonely howl of a wolf.

So it was that Brendan the Astrogator was crowned in Keltia.

CHAPTER TWENTY-FIVE

ut still he would not call himself king—not High King, not King of Kelts, not King of any degree whatsoever but Taoiseach only, 'Chieftain', and he held to that all the years of his reign. But to everyone else in Keltia, and all realms outwith, it was Brendan Ard-rígh forevermore whether he loved it or no, and Etain was queen beside him.

The following summer the master-builder Gradlon of Ys came at Brendan's asking to the little settlement that thrived happily behind its earthworks; he had been engaged in building more of the temporary campments as need required, but that was well in hand, and could be carried on now by others. The task that Brendan now had for him no one else could manage.

Over a week's time they held long and deep discussions: the counsel of Nia and others had been sought, studies had been made and soundings taken; and now they stood atop one of the massive sinuous earthworks, looking out over the landscape with a professional eye. After many pacings and measurings and hand-framings of angles and areas, much tramping up and down the vale with theodolites and chain-rods and laser com-

passes and the many other arcane implements of sur-
veyors everywhere and in all times, and endless probing
of the soil and plotting of the rocky outcrops, Gradlon
turned at last to his companion, and smiled broadly.

"Now that we have a king"—Brendan looked
uncomfortable, and Gradlon's smile only widened—
"time it is that we have a capital and crown-city from
which he can rule."

"'Rule' would not be the word," said Brendan then,
with calm precision, and Gradlon laughed.

"Oh aye, I forget to whom I speak... Well, a city,
then, any road. And a city here. Look—"

His arm traced the seven-mile sweep: from Llwynogue, 'Young Lion', the great eastern hill so called for
its distinctive crouching profile, past the glowing
Painted Rocks where the Falls of Yarin descend, along
the lap of Tioram, across the rock terraces that rise in
huge uneven steps, of which Highfold and Turusachan
are most notable, finally to the westermost spur, where
Eagle shoulders out over the waters of the bay, ending
in the anvil-top cliffs below the peak Yr Hela, two thousand feet straight down to the waves.

Gradlon sighed with admiration, and his face took
on the look of a maker itchingly impatient to begin a
new work of his own matchless craft.

"It is a fine site, Brandoch, that your fetch chose for
us; I could not have picked a better myself—or
designed a better, even. The sea, the river, the mountains behind—beautiful to look at, but beautifully
defensible: water in unending supply, even hot thermal
water for hypocausts and energy to supplement the
crystals; back in the hills, little clunes to serve in time of
siege, for herds or crops or both." He steepled his

palms, spread his fingers and tapped them twice, eyes gleaming, beholding not the bare hillside but the splendid city-fortress that already stood in his mind, all alive and shining. "I will make this a place that armies will break their hearts against, as little coracles tear themselves to pieces on a great rock in the ocean. It will be greater than Cashel or Dúneidyn, fairer than Tara or Ys. Our enemies shall look upon it and weep with envy even as they despair, and never shall it be taken by war from without."

Brendan laughed, and agreed, and still afire with devising and design they went down the hill together to the little steading-huts. Gradlon had spoken truer than either of them would ever know—and the need was nearer at hand than either of them just then knew.

Since their arrival in the new world, it seemed to the Kelts that Nia daughter of Calatin no longer saw need or necessity to hold back her magic; and as the settlers began to disperse on Tara, she began to take place and power before even her son—who was by no means loath to see her do so. She had done workings enough in Fanad, but perhaps because of Fergus, a mortal, she had for the most part kept her hand close within her cloak: whatever she had wrought on his behalf, it had been wrought quietly and without fussery, not to call attention to the means.

This had not changed on the immram: though it was largely by her magic that the Kelts were now free of the stars, and for that she would be blessed forever, even aboard the Hui Corra Nia had chosen to remain in the background, stepping forward only when need required, turning aside credit and praise alike with a soft word or smile or upraised hand and headshake, retiring immediately thereafter to do her work in privacy as she preferred.

And not for worlds would Brendan or Etain or Kelver Donn Midna or any other of those who loved her have urged her otherwise: whatever way felt right and good to her, that way would they have her be. But now, on Tara, she seemed to have rooted her power at last, and set it abloom as never before, and with joy Brendan watched both it and her blossom alike. *Ever with us it is triads—this, the triad of the Three Tasks Among the Stars: Barrind's to prepare the ground on Erith, mine to sow and grow in space, and now to harvest in Keltia it falls upon Nia the Golden...*

So it was that one cool cloudless morning of high summer, all the folk well drawn back to watch in safety from beyond the Bannochburn, Nia, standing down in the plain where the ground began to climb to the hills, spread her arms and spoke words: words that had been spoken in Atland, for good and for ill; words that had been old when Núminôrë was young.

Standing beside her, watching and hearing, breath caught back as one, Brendan and Gradlon and a small knot of their close counselors and captains and friends knew what was about to happen—the rest of the folk had not been told the full of the plan, only that magic would be done, that all was well, that they were not to fear—but the knowing took nothing from their expectancy and impatience, or indeed from their awe.

Though Nia had invoked in such a voice as might

have summoned stars or gods, that which she had called took time to come to her. As when the Hui Corra shed its first aspect and clad itself in silver skin, or when at Sidheanbrugh light had been conjured out of stone, for long moments nothing seemed to happen; then everything happened at once…

Standing in the plain, Brendan and the rest felt the earth beneath their feet begin to jar and quiver: faintly at first, as when a leaf drops upon the dark still surface of a pool; then more strongly, as when a giant ruddenwood is struck by a fireflaw and so topples, crashing through the underbrush to measure its length upon the forest floor; then tremendously more strongly still, so that the onlookers swayed and staggered to keep themselves upright, as if they stood upon the deck of a ship in storm.

Something was happening far below, something called from the depths of the planet's heart was rushing to the surface to obey the summons. And now, along the curving line that Gradlon's pointing hand had traced out, seven miles from hill to sea, the grassy cover of the plain was billowing and bulging upward, like coverlets on a bed when a child is playing beneath. Then, with a deafening roar, the green ground split like the skin of a peach, peeling back, and a great basaltic sill thrust itself upward, one single solid piece forged aeons since in the volcanic fires that had formed this northern continent. Rearing itself up between plain and hill-flank, it shut off the settlement behind it—at that low angle, even Highfold and Turusachan disappeared from sight behind their new defending rampart. It drove a mighty headland into the sea on the west, so that none could scale the cliffs to invest the city by water; on the east it rammed itself against the mountain bulwark so close and hard that not even a blade of grass could have slipped through the angle between.

And still it rose and beat and roared and climbed and shook the ground, until it towered three hundred feet high and near twice that in thickness, seamless and unbroken, looking as if it had been there since the dawn of time.

As indeed it has been, but far, far below... Brendan, who had thought himself well prepared, was in the event just as staggered as everyone else who watched and witnessed. *At her summoning the earth parted and the walls of the city rose—the great reaping that Nia the Golden made on Tara...*

Then Gradlon of Ys, master-builder, nodded unsmiling approval, and pointing to a particular area of the new wall that still smoked and steamed with the birth-struggle of its passage, he nodded again, as if to say, There. Nia raised a hand; and though none of those who watched—their eyes on sticks, as the saying goes, and their jaws by now agape to their knees—could say they had seen it happen, where no opening had been a great gap now yawned, the only breach in the vast massive sill, an entryway to the space now sheltered safe behind the wall. And turning to her son Nia smiled a smile of the morning of the world.

"The gate to the City is open."

Strange as it may seem to say, that was the easiest part. Now, under Gradlon's direction, the real building began, every Kelt on the planet turning a hand to the work as never before. They had labored mightily to build the Hui Corra and the other ships of the fleet, they had greatly toiled to raise the campments and settlements and earthworked steadings, but now they were building their own city, their lasting home and the home of the future that would be, and none among them would have it be said by that future that they had given it any less than their uttermost best, or had wrought imperfectly where perfection was the charge.

So that sooner even than impatient hopes or unreasoned fears could have had it, high above even the highest level of the new wall, on the ledge of Turusachan where Brendan himself had planted the young yew, a mighty Keep began to rise even as that sapling had begun to gladly grow: a great tower, foursquare and solid, its back set firm against Eagle, its face turned outward and watchful over the line of the glen. Beautiful brughs were planned also, to crown Turusachan in majesty—future halls for each of the great orders, the druids and the ban-draoi, the Fians and the brehons and the bards; and more and more, the Kelts began to realize what they owed to Brendan's foresight, and his Sight—and to his mother's magic.

Farther east and lower down, in a sheltered hollow of ground not very distant from where the first earthworks had been raised, a spell of change seemed to be transforming the little steadings. As if by glamourie or fith-fath, the humble cotts were being translated into stone, becoming a covey of spacious solid-built housen, each one different from the next, all delightful to look upon or dwell in, growing themselves into an enchanting tangle of closes and wynds and yards that at once was named the Stonerows. Built to last a thousand years, they were, with thick stone walls and slate-flag floors for warmth in winter and coolness in summer, and leaded windows set in deep frames under carved pediments; and roofs of many-colored tiles, steep-pitched and gable-ended to shed the deep snows those lands enjoyed through the long cold winters, capped all. The many streams leaping down from the summit crestline were captured in leats for water, and as Gradlon had noted, the superheated springs beneath the mountains' roots, remnant of ancient volcanism, amply supplied the baths and sweat-rooms and heating hypocausts.

The original city walls, that had been laid out like bent bows in overlapping arcs to shield the first small settlement, were remade in huge granite blocks and left where they stood, as second-line defense in the unlikely event of the outer Wall ever being breached. In the single gap in those defenses, the great Wolf Gate—named by Brendan for the fetch he had met on those very slopes, who had given him the word to build—slowly began to take shape, its massive flanking drum-towers not made but formed in the framing of the wall-dike itself, two huge paired outcrops of solid close-grained stone, harder and tougher than jade, and a connecting battlement-arch to bridge the space between.

And last of all Gradlon delved the tunnel of the Nantosvelta beneath the peaks to the south, a secret escape that led from the Keep under the roots of the Loom, emerging at a hidden exit in one of the high Dales behind. Understand that all this took many years, and required the labors of founder Kelts as well as those newly arrived on later immrama; but those

years made a strong impressive city in the end—
though for all its splendor it was little more than a
street-town by compare to what it would later become.

Yet still that city had no name: despite the harpings
and importunings of its inhabitants, who wearied of
calling it 'the City' merely—though as it was as yet the
only city, there seemed very little chance of confusion—
Brendan had kept his counsel on the matter, politely
accepting the many suggestions however improbable
or uninspired, not saying aye or nay to any, giving no
clue as to what might be his own preference or
thought.

But at last the work was done—or enough of it so that a
real city stood there behind real walls, with paven
streets laid out, and green commons and parklands
and tree-edged squares, not merely a ragtag huddle of
half-built housen rising out of bare muddy flats or
wooded swales; and Brendan decreed that a day be set
aside to mark the City's formal consecration—and at
long last its naming.

So on the day appointed the entire populace woke
early, dressed in their best, and went down in tearing
high spirits to the plain below the walls, while above
them Brendan stood alone in the Wolf Gate, the city
empty behind him and all his Kelts before. The huge
gate-doors of bronze and silver and findruinna, forged
by the Sidhefolk in the Hollow Mountains under the
eye of Gavida Burn-the-wind himself, had been but
newly installed, and now were flung wide. Even the Hui
Corra shared in the moment: though for obvious reasons the ship could not be brought close in, it had

taken up a standing orbit low enough for folk to be able to make out, if they had good sight on them, the devices on the four great sails—wolf and raven, dragon and stag—as the ship hung in the heavens above the Loom, like a shield before a hero's tent on eve of battle.

Brendan was not long alone: he was joined by representatives of all Keltia's races, and by members of each of the orders—druids, ban-draoi, brehons, Fians, bards. He spoke briefly; they gave blessing; then he dipped his fingers into a brimming silver bowl—water of the Avon Dia mixed with the last of the sacred water brought from the Struell-wells in Fanad that was gone. He asperged the City and the towers and the people and the Gate, then made the sign of the suncross in the air before him, and placed his right hand upon the gold-white stone of the western gate-tower.

"The city was built to magic," he said, in a voice that carried out over the watching delirious throngs in the plain, and to the merrows and silkies and sun-sharks who clustered in the waters of the vast bay below the cliffs. "Therefore never built at all, and therefore built forever... I name this city Caerdroia," he said then, "which means Spiral Castle. And it is the heart and crown of the realm that shall be."

That same afternoon, all ceremony done with, Nia and Brendan stood on a high turret of the newly completed Keep, and gazed out in comfortable silence over the little city—*Caerdroia!*—below. Gradlon had planned well for future need and expansion: already Brendan could see the brughs and townhalls of his dreams beginning to rise in the rolling empty space behind the walls, and in an open valley twelve miles away, a starport was even now being built among the hills of the Loom. *Good that we have built so well so swiftly... I would not let the others know, but of late I have had a feeling, Sight even, that a great need for strong stout defenses will soon be upon us. We have been warned—everyone from Sajamana of the Hail to Kelver Donn Midna has said be 'ware and watchful—and I hope and pray both I and they have Seen in error; but, may Malen shield us all, I have the dark and dreading feeling that we have not...*

Premonitions or precautions aside, Brendan and Nia had gone up there for a private moment between a mother and her son, between a queen-sorceress however reticent and a king however unwilling; given the demands on both of them, such times had been of late increasingly rare. But Nia had had another purpose.

"I have something for you," she said presently, and laughed at the instant delight that flashed across his face.

"I *like* presents," said Brendan, a little chagrined but unapologetic.

"Well, and who does not! But it was not for that, that I did laugh." Unfolding the soft leather wrappings of the object she had carried in her arms—which he had noted long since but was far too polite to ask about—she brought it out into the slanting sunlight.

Brendan stared. It was a heavy silver fillet—a browband or coronet—its deep-cut knotwork panels inlaid with black enamel, set all round with gems as clear as water. Indeed, it was the same very one that he and others had seen her wear many times in Fanad, and had thought but a becoming trinket, an ornament to her beauty. *This for me?*, and was chagrined again to realize he had spoken aloud.

"For none else," said his mother, smiling. "And nor is it by any means a simple mere ornament— It is more like protection; a weapon also, when there is need. And there may be need sooner than we might like—but you do not need me to tell you that—you who have Seen as no other ever Saw before."

Brendan took it from her hands as she held it out to him, his eye—and then more than his eye—caught by the center stone, which was larger than the rest, cut in an antique fashion, squared with rounded corners, where the other stones were cabochons. *It has a feel to it, a kinship with that great crystal ice-tear of Tamhna's...* He had chosen to let pass her warning words; but now, with an effort, he shook himself from the ashling that the stone had called forth: images of terrible destruction but of beauty just as great, men and women of power, mighty cities under strange stars, the mighty Wave coming over the land. Images that his heart bled to see: Caerdroia, so newly named, under attack by ships that looked like black falcons; the new Gate blown off its pillars, a bloody handprint on the stone where so recently he had set his own in sacred water...

Is this to come for me? Or for some other long hence? Has it already been? And how are we to know?

"That one is older than the rest," said Nia then. "Though I see you know that now yourself... The others are from Atland, ancient enough—but this comes from Núminôrë." She touched the stone; but what the stone gave her to see in it she did not say. Presently, gently: "This cathbarr was given me by Donn Rígh on the day I wed your father, as tinnscra from my people;

great Maeve herself wore it, and now it comes to you. For it is on me that today—more than the day we came here, more even than your crowning-day at Ni-maen—is the observable-day of your union with Keltia. The sacred wedding between the kingdom and the king—it seemed right that you should have this in token."

Deeply moved, Brendan went to one knee before his mother, and kissed her hand, as liege to a mighty empress; then rising he embraced her, as son to mother, and gave her thanks—not for this gift alone, but for all gifts she had given, to him and to Kelts alike—and they wept, and laughed, and together examined the glorious thing.

"The same hand that made the Copper Crown made this," said Brendan wonderingly, brushing the massive silver knotwork panels with reverent fingertips, but careful not to touch the great centerstone again. *One glimpse of what it holds locked away within it is more than enough for now...* "The workmanship alone bespeaks its provenance—no hand in earth or heaven is equal to the Gabhain Saor's when he sets it to his craft. The magic that is in it, the power that is on it... But it will not fit me, surely!"

"It fits all heads it wants to fit," said Nia. "All heads that it judges fit to wear it—and it is a most demanding judge." Reaching up, she brushed back his hair and set the coronet upon him, and Brendan drew in his breath with surprise. It was as if the thing had been made for him, the exact comfortable measure of his brow: he felt the weight of it, heavy but not burdensome. It seemed in some way to give him vitality and force, and strangest of all it seemed as if his sight had suddenly improved, grown clearer and sharper. "The Copper Crown affirms the sovereignty of the Kelts," she said then, "but this holds the Danaan soul. Wear it well."

So it was that the cathbarr of Nia the Golden began its life in Keltia: Nia giving it to her son, who wore it often, and he handing it on to his son, and that son to his daughter. Soon it would go as it had come, passing as bridegift back into the keeping of the Sidhe; and down the centuries it would come and go between the two races, as their dán and its own demanded. True to its maker's promise, it fit whomever it deemed fit to wear it, and it would be witness to Keltia's brightest moments and darkest times alike—and even as Brendan stood on the turret walk and looked into the cathbarr's stone, some of both were already on the way.

A spring storm was blundering its way down Strath Mór, a flat spreading cloud like a gray-black anvil, with torn skirts dragging in the yellow stormlight, and that was the rain. Brendan, standing at a high window of the new Keep, watched it come, with a feeling of satisfaction that had nothing to do with the refreshing and much-needed imminent showers. Below him, Caerdroia was hurrying to secure itself against the sudden turn in the weather: the craftsmen in the new-built artisans' quarter folded down their shutters and canopies; from the Stonerows parents' voices called reluctant children indoors, and on the green open commons, older lads and lasses chivvied the sheep and cattle under sheds.

We have done so very well for so very few years... The City firmly founded, a few more settlements on Tara; some soon to begin on new worlds, even, if Conn and Shane and the rest

have their way—and I am so very sure they will! By all gods,
I had not thought to see that in my lifetime... After I am gone,
they will all of course do as they please. But we will need many
such settlements founded, if the immrama continue at the pace
we have set. Already we have grown our numbers in Keltia
fivefold—on Erith they must surely be wondering by now at the
strange disappearances of so many thousands of folk! Still, the
new planets will need souls to dwell in them by and by—and
Tara itself is yet to be full settled; we will need swords as well as
souls, and that, I think, all too soon...

After only ten years, and as many more immrama,
the Kelts had already begun to venture out from Tara
to explore neighboring star systems. As Rohan smilingly put it, good neighbors were of course a fine thing
to have, but wide secure maigens were a finer thing
still, and Brendan had no intention of letting nearby
worlds become home to any folk but Kelts. *I have
learned at least* that *much from Vortigern...* That region of
space was not over-blessed with habitable systems; but
through some quirk of long-ago astrophysics, a cluster
of stars of the right sort to grow planets of the right sort
had been created, a pocket of life on the far side of the
Morimaruse. Only the terror of the dead sea of space
had kept those worlds empty and undiscovered, until
the coming of the only folk brave enough to sail
through to them.

At first the Kelts, going gingerly, claimed no more
than three new systems in all that vast stellar territory,
and pre-emptively settled, if sparsely, one new planet in
each, rather wistfully naming the new worlds for their
own old homes—Erinna, Gwynedd, Caledon. But as
their power and population increased, as trade began
to be established, and as with all these things such con-

fidence grew as befitted those who belonged by right among the stars, that maigen would expand, until at last it would encompass twelve suns, and all the planets that looked to them.

But long before that time the Kelts had attracted a notice that would in ages to come give cause for grief and joy alike—as indeed it had in the past. When one lifts one's head above the crowd, true it is that one can see farther away. But the farther away one sees, the farther also one is then seen; and the higher the head is raised, the more there are who would gladly see it brought low—or off altogether.

CHAPTER TWENTY-SIX

f they had come five years sooner, even three years sooner, than they did, the Kelts could not have stopped them. They would have stormed like jackals out of the stars, a relentless and merciless pack of predators falling upon a half-defended flock, and Keltia would have ended before it had barely begun. It did not fall out so, and that was dán at work; but they came all too soon as it was...

Ever since the boats of the Hui Corra had set down on Tara, plans had been drawn up and set in place against possible attack. Though the Kelts were alone in the sector of space they had so boldly and completely claimed for theirs, and though they knew that the Morimaruse would keep away all but the most determined brigands and that attack was on balance unlikely, still there were more than a few races in the settled galaxy who would not be eager to see strangers newly settled on promising planets of which they themselves might make better use. And neither would they be so pleased to make new friends as the Salamandri had been, or show such generous courtesy—indeed, almost Keltic!—to transient wayfarers as had the Hail.

For that reason Brendan—ever the shepherd—
kept the Hui Corra constantly patrolling, with a war-
crew on board at all times, just beyond the Criosanna,
to defend Tara if raiders came; only the smaller ships—
the five that yet survived, all of which were well able to
protect themselves—went forth and back now on the
constant immrama to Erith or on trading expeditions
with friendly nations; and of them, only two or three at
any one time. Not all Kelts thought this a good thing,
however cautiously managed: that the ships and their
crews and the precious freight they continued to reive
away from Erith should make these shuttlings—especially without the Hui Corra to guard the flocks on
such long droves through dangerous country. They
had had such good fortune and great luck with the
Immram that they feared now to press that luck and
fortune further, and they now wondered why the ships
must come and go at all...

"Because we need more bodies, that is why," said
Brendan wearily, when taxed on the matter yet again,
one drear day in council. "We have been round this
particular barn *so* many times before... Listen. Hear. I
do not love risking ourselves and our ships any more
than any of you do, but we have no choice. We are
doing our best, truly, to increase the population, but
we cannot breed new Kelts as fast as they are needed;
and also—"

"Aye?" prompted Kelver Donn Midna, when his
friend fell silent.

Brendan did not reply at once, but stared out the
window of the Keep. Under Gradlon's eye and hand,
building had recently been completed on the great
brughs in Turusachan itself, halls which would eventu-

ally be home to the various orders. And now, on the flat ground atop the ocean bastions, the footprint of a true palace was laid out, that would join on to the Keep, rising among the stands of ironoak and blue ferrens near the cliffs. *Turusachan, 'Place of Gathering'— Is it we who do that gathering, or are we the ones who have been gathered, whether we will or nill?*

"—also there are left very many of our kin on Erith, mortal and Sidhe alike," he continued at last, not taking his glance from the view, "those who think and feel as we do. You know this, I know this. And I will never abandon them. That you know also."

He spoke as one who is both lawful and correct— which are not nearly so often the same thing as folk like to think—spoke as one who knows that not only *must* he be obeyed, he *should* be obeyed; and he *will* be obeyed. He had good cause to speak so, and know so: no matter his initial reluctance to take the crown, once he was king—or Taoiseach, as he yet maintained the fiction none but he had ever embraced—Brendan mac Nia had thrown himself heart and soul into the task of rule, and had never once looked back. *A trick I learned from watching Laoghaire—when you question dán you generally get no answers but only more questions. And a king must both answer and ask, for his people and for himself—so better it is to do, and leave asking for times when doing is done with...*

But though doing had profited them all, dán had given him answers, if not always those answers he sought, or might have hoped for; had answered his folk as well. The Great Immram had been a success, and so now had ten more—the pace had increased because they knew the way now, could sail and return more swiftly. Caerdroia was the heart and center of the new realm, as he and Gradlon had planned. Folk had moved gladly on with lives that had been interrupted, or lives that on Erith had not had chance to properly begin: weddings, birthings, fosterings. Even Brendan's own house was well increased: Rohan and Fiaren, who had wedded on the voyage, had now a lovely ten-year-old daughter, dark-eyed Morna, of an age with Keltia itself; and Fionaveragh and Donn had Sithney and Tiaquin, a daughter and a son.

Brendan, listening to his council debate, went away for a little in his own mind. *It is easier than I thought it would be. Not easy. But easier; and perhaps easier still is yet to come…*

And it did; but first the raiders came.

As Amris mac an Fhiach was later to observe, it had only been a matter of time. In every town of size there are housebreakers who make their living going furtively round, pushing on likely doors to see if they be open, and if they find them so, scurrying within to steal whatever may be found; it is no different in space.

Nor was it as if there had been no warning: Brendan and many others had sensed the urgency of getting defenses built and running, and perhaps they were being unduly fatalistic, but forebodings of a more ancient kind had been thick on the ground as well, and were growing progressively grimmer. War-horns had been heard ringing on the plain below the city; the Faol-mór, the great fetch-wolf, had appeared on the slopes of Eryri; the fire-eyed Ghost Mare, the ghastly Mari Llwyd made all of bones, had come down to the Avon Dia to drink. Even the Washer at the Ford, Ban-

Nighe, had been seen, scrubbing her bloody war-shirts
in the Bannochburn where it flowed out of the Falls of
Yarin, crooning to herself a tune to freeze the heart.

And once, in the dark still owl-time hours, Brendan
himself, late awake over his papers, had heard in the
cobbled street below Turusachan the sound of wheels
and galloping hoofs on stone. Looking out in surprise—there were few chariots as yet in Keltia, and the
ones that existed certainly did not drive gaily around
Caerdroia in the middle of the night—he had seen a
red-painted war-car drawn by a team of headless black
horses, and had ducked aside in terror as a basin of
blood was flung at his face. Or so at least it had seemed:
Fians responding to his shout found no blood, no chariot, no horses; but then he had not expected them to.

Trembling all over, he had gone to his bed, where
Etain roused muzzily to comfort him and listen to his
tale; but despite her soothing words and warmth he
had lain sleepless beside her until dawn. *The coach-a-
bower—one of the worst portents there ever could be. It has
found us here, so far from Éruinn—but truly I am not surprised. Everyone from Fionn Rhên to my wolf has managed to
track us down—but in the name of great Dâna herself, what
else has tracked us down, that all these dire warnings are in
aid of?*

He did not much wish an answer; but answer came.

The Oyarzûn and Firvolgi were first, two races who, historically, when they scented easy prey would often
unite for a few surprise raids, to destroy what they
could and take what they might, preferring uneasy
opportunistic alliance, however temporary, to a stab in

the back from the other—which was never long in coming even so, taking turn and turn about as stabber and stabbed. After the first of these joint incursions, the Kelts, minded of the not unlike tactics of certain Erith enemies long ago, dubbed the paired marauders Fomori and Fir Bolc—and not in flattery, or irony even—and dealt with them in a not unlike manner, so that many reigns would pass in Keltia before they did return, though when they did… But that is another story.

Other, lesser enemies—the Lukka, the Kren, the Voritians, the Thelenite Kazwini—made their own attempts: as Conn Kittagh remarked, where one mouse finds a few crumbs, it will not be very long before every hungry rodent in the village shows up under the table. Though these contested fiercely with the Kelts for ownership rights to the claimed sector, testing will and sword-arm alike, they were not the worst of those who came. And though they learned not so swiftly as they might have, still they were well instructed, every time, as to how very not wise a thought it was, to go against Keltia; and after a while the lesson sank in, and held.

When the raids at last ceased—or at least seemed to—the Kelts settled down in what passed for peace, to live as they had so hoped to live, keeping alive the old ways while moving into a mighty future, such as the Tangavaun could never have dreamed. They made alliances of various sorts with like-minded outfreyn; among them their old acquaintances the Salamandri and the Hail; but also the Numantissans, the lion-folk, who dwelled at Dal Benzaguen on their homeworld Harilak, and the Dakdak, and the Kutherans, even the ancient Udara on the jewel planet Yjenar, and more beside.

But long before those alliances could be put to the test, before they were even made, an enemy came, a greater than any that had come before. And yet not so, for this particular enemy had indeed come before, and now was come again...

No overt portents this time: the first the Kelts knew of it was a sudden unexplainable distress among the Sidhefolk, and the merrows and silkies also reported uneasiness below the waves, some new dark current of foreboding. From his palace of Knockfierna Kelver Donn Midna sent cryptic messages, unsettling and unsettled; in the Hollow Mountains that he had taken for realm of his own, Neith son of Llyr was likewise disquieted; as for Nia, she prowled round Caerdroia like a leopard who scents danger to her cubs but knows not what the peril might be, nor whence it comes—only that it will come.

And come it did.

"We do not know when," said Brendan. "Only that they are sure to, soon or late. They know that we are here, and they know that we are—who we are."

"They know we are Danaans," said Nia, correcting him gently if firmly, "or at least that some among us are. And that is enough for them."

Dúnomaglos, mate of Kunera, who with her had ruled the Boarholm isles and now was set to pioneer the new world of Caledon, stirred in his seat.

"We have heard somewhat of the tale before—but explain again, Taoiseach, why it is that these folk hold such long and bitter hatred against the Danaan kind?"

A look passed among the few Sidhefolk present

that day in the council chamber; Brendan ran a hand
through his hair and touched the pendant jewel that
hung upon his chest, for luck, or strength, or reassurance, before he spoke.

"The Fomori and Fir Bolc we merely named for old
Erith enemies; the Coranians *are* old Erith enemies. Our
friends the Salamandri and the Hail inform us that the
Coranians have tracked us through the stars; they have
learned where we have been and where we have settled,
and they plan to attack us, at their leisure—which I daresay they will do as they have done before." He ceased,
and glanced uncertainly at his mother. *It is her tale to tell,
as much or as little as she pleases—I would not say more than I
should, or not enough...*

"You have heard some of this tale before," said Nia
presently. "But never have you heard it told as I shall
tell it. Hear now the rest... When the Núminôrian people fled to Erith, among the tribes who made that terrible crossing were two that had long time been at
odds, the Telchines and the Danaans." A sudden stillness fell in the room, and she nodded grimly. "Aye so,
and the enmity did not cease on the voyage, nor even
when Atland and the other city-realms of Erith were
settled and rose to greatness. Indeed, that quarrel was
one of the chief causes of Atland's destruction, and the
reason for the loss of the ancient knowledge we had
brought with us—and have rediscovered at such cost."

"But the Telchines?" asked one quietly.

"Blamed us, as we blamed them—as ever, the truth
doubtless lay somewhere between, and now it lies
drowned deep, with Atland. But one thing they did
which more than anything before or since has kept the
long hatred alive: as Atland sank behind them, they

fled in starships, leaving the other clans to a terrible fate. We—the Danaans, or at least more than a few of us—managed to cross the seas to Éruinn and other lands, and survive, but too many others did not. Only the Telchines; and they escaped to the stars. We hated them for doing so, and they hated us for knowing them for what they proved they are."

Brendan looked at his mother, his eyes haunted with the race-memory he shared through her. *Never before has she spoken of it so openly, to such extent, to so many who have no share in it as we have. Yet so often I dream of it, see the green dark wall of water, foam-flowered, mountain-high—higher than mountains—rolling over the lands, unstoppable...*

"They may have escaped to the stars, right enough, but so now have we," he said, to remind them.

"And so we have," agreed Kelver Donn Midna. "And the Telchines are root-race of these Coranians, as the Danaans are root-race of the Kelts. And now they know we have regained the knowledge they thought their singular possession, and have followed them out of Erith."

Nia spoke into the thoughtful silence. "And now they also know where they can find us."

They found them soon enough, descending without warning, as raiders generally do; more than that, they came in a sort of white blankness. It was not merely a matter of simple cloaking, to pass undetected the various scryers and sensors and spy-devices that looked unsleeping out upon the stars; it was a much greater and stealthier attack. Even though they were on guard against their coming, no Kelt sensed them, no Kelt saw them, not until they were all but upon them; and by then it was all but too late.

When the Coranians came, they came not in waves but as a tide, steady, flooding, all but inexorable. The Hui Corra, chief defender, did terrible destruction among them, and had the help of four of the other immram-ships, and the hundred or so powerful destroyer-craft that the Kelts had been able to build in the shipyards on Argialla. But however swift and well armed, even the Hui Corra could not be everywhere at once, so that the Coranians, who had had surprise on their side as well as more ships at their disposal, were little hindered in the ruin they rained down upon the planet below.

So the Kelts resorted to whatever other force they could raise in their own defense. It was by no means inconsiderable: Nia alone—a woman defending her loved ones and her home, than which there has never been anything deadlier—unleashed such hitherto unimagined powers and ferocity as astounded even her son, and won her the champion-mantle of sorcery that would later be challenged by only two others; lesser sorcerers and Sidhefolk—Etain and Kelver Donn Midna and Neith ap Llyr included—did little less. But after a week of ceaseless pounding from the Coranian ships in strike-and-run parabolic orbit, even such warriors as those were exhausted and spent; as for the great run of Kelts, they were bloodied, bone-weary, short of hope but fiercely resolved that it should not end for them like this, before it had scarce begun...

And in need of weapons and warriors as never before; but when the subject was broached, that the

Sidhefolk should not fight apart but join their force to that of other Kelts, and fight as other Kelts fought, those of that race who sat on Brendan's war council soberly but firmly demurred, saying that there were many ways of fighting and they were better left to choose their own. Most mortal Kelts understood; or if they did not, their honor would have taken it on trust, and never have demanded explanation for the refusal. But others there were who would not, or could not, let the denial go unchallenged; and of those Dúnomaglos, clearly uneasy, addressed himself to Kelver Donn Midna.

"I do not mean to accuse, or presume, but— Your folk do not make use of iron, but I would have thought, in such straits—"

"No more did we make use of it on Erith," said that lord calmly. "Gold and silver, bronze and copper, aye; findruinna too, and more than happy to wield it. But never cold iron."

"Yet we all saw that you yourself, and others of your kind, sailed with us on the Immram," observed Ríonach Sulbair, "and there was goleor of iron in those ships, right enough."

Kelver Donn smiled. "And all well alloyed, I assure you, else we had not been able to pass the very hatches! Even so, only some of us could tolerate its presence, as doubtless you also noted; the most of my folk took— another way here."

"Half my blood is blood of yours," said Brendan then, intervening; but in his voice was only half a question. "Iron is neither ban nor mystery to *me*—"

"No slight, amhic, but half is not all… It is not a simple thing, nor is it easy for us to speak of." The Sidhe

prince—king now himself, at Knockfierna on Erinna—
was silent for a while; and however daring they had just
now been, none thought it wise or good tó press him
further. "A part of our power over matter—a very con-
siderable part—comes from our covenant with iron," he
said at last. "It was so in Núminôrĕ that died in fire, and
in Atland that perished by water. That did not change in
Éruinn that perished to us it might be said through air,
nor shall it change now that we are again among the
stars... Earth is the one power left, and this power my
people have given over to iron. We have an ancient
quarrel and truce with cold iron, and it with us; and it
will be so forever. We cannot, and we will not, seek to
alter. I do not mean to sound harsh, but do not ask this
of us again. We do what we can, where we can; there is
no more that we can do."

"Well, however cold the iron, it makes little differ...
There is but one way to stop the onetime Telchines,"
said Brendan, his voice colder than that iron he spoke
of; and he spoke with the air of one who has taken a
great decision much against his own inclination, knowing all the time that it was his only recourse, and loving
it not at all. "Send for the lord Melidren, in Knockfierna, or the Hollow Mountains, or wherever he might
be found; there is a thing I would ask him."

Kynmarra—captain on Immram Mhór, now lord of
Cantire in the Taran southlands—was already rising
from the table, refastening his armor as he went.

"And the message?"

Brendan looked straight at him. "Tell him the Eye
of Balor must open."

*   *   *

The tall silver-bearded lord of the Sidhe who stood next day before the council was one whom Brendan had seen but once only, though that once was never to be forgotten. *Melidren, Melzier, Merlynn: the names may differ in different tongues but the person, and the power, is unchanged...* Brendan looked into the considering rain-gray eyes that he had last beheld in Fanad, that long-ago Beltain night; then, leaning forward with both palms flat on the table—and having in that moment, though he did not know it, completely and entirely the look of Fergus Fire on Brega setting light to the bruidean—he drew a deep breath to speak.

"I will waste no time, as we have none to waste... In Éruinn, before the Hui Corra lifted off from Fanad, you came to us and gave certain Treasures into our possession. Did you mean us to use them, or was it a matter of transport only?"

Melidren smiled; a rare thing with him, though Brendan would not have been comforted if he knew just how rare it was.

"Nay, to be used, by all means; else what is the point? The Treasures may be hallows, Taoiseach, but before that they are tools. And a tool is consecrated by use—and by its user."

"I am glad to hear you say so... It is on me now," said Brendan clearly and slowly, so that none there could afterwards claim ignorance of what he meant to do, "to consecrate the Eye of Balor by using it against the Coranians."

"A grave employing," said Melidren, and fell silent a little space; Brendan's intent appeared to come as no surprise to him whatsoever. "It will stop them," he said at last. "Of that have no fear... But fear this: though they flee from it, they will be angrier than any wrath you can imagine, to learn that the Danaans came away from the ruin of Atland with the Stone of Falias, and other things beside. They will never forget you used it against them, and they will never forgive you for so using it; but it will keep them shy of Keltia for a very long time to come. You are the one who must judge if the stake is worth the wager. As for the Eye itself, it will go an immram of its own, and endure long exile in a hidden land. But it will come home again: serving an outfreyn king it will open its gaze on treason, and served by a Keltic queen it will close against the Dark."

Brendan felt ice touch the back of his neck, and saw that he was not alone in so feeling. *Prophecy... It chills my bones and soul alike—but anything that can make bones of the Coranians I say is well worth a little chill...*

"I will raise that stake, and take the wager."

"My people call this the Stone of Falias, yours name it the Eye of Balor; from it the Lia Fail takes its power, and so too the Throne of Scone which now has come amongst us," said Melidren then with a little nod, looking round at each face in turn; none save Nia and Kelver Donn and Brendan himself could hold his gaze. "This is the power that destroyed Atland. And also it is the power that will save Keltia."

He unwrapped the object that had lain before him on the table—their glances had been carefully avoiding it all this time, though their thought was filled with nothing else—and disclosed something round and smooth, large as a human head but vastly heavier; his wrists bent and braced under the weight as he lifted it. It was shrouded in a fitted leather covering, and beneath that was a solid bronze casing that shuttered it as closely as an eggshell its golden yolk.

Brendan, who had ordered it brought here from its place in the ancient oak chest that rested in the strong-place of the Keep, could not drag his gaze away from it; and he was not alone.

"Not to behold," said Melidren, seeing their desperate curiosity, and well understanding. "That would be death for all within the walls of this city—a fate I think you wish to reserve for the Coranians." He paused a moment. "I gave this into your keeping in Fanad; now one word more before I give it into your use. Be judicious. It is power illimitable, but also it is limitless temptation; and it will exact a price of you every time it is employed."

And Brendan nodded, thinking he well understood; but—as Melidren forbore to tell him—he did not...

Still, they did not delay in the employment, not while Kelts in their scores and hundreds were dying under Coranian lasras. But Brendan and Kynmarra and Scathach of Lochaber took a tiny aircar by round-about ways out of Caerdroia, and meeting the Hui Corra behind the white moon, they made hurried shift to install that which Melidren had said was theirs to use by right.

When they were done, Brendan gave commands, and the Hui Corra opened a new and terrible Eye; and then it turned that blazing gaze upon the Coranian fleet.

"But they have gone," said Amris for perhaps the tenth time, still unable to understand why Brendan, seemingly alone of all Kelts, did not exult at least somewhat in the victory over the Coranians. *True enough, as a man he has great cause not to rejoice; still, as a king, he must be— somewhere—glad of the victory...* "Driven off—the Eye looked upon them, and they died or fled; we saw their ships crack and explode like stones in a belfire. We have beaten them—at great cost, aye, of which I need not remind you of all folk—but we *have* beaten them, m'chara, and they are gone."

"And they will return. Not now, not soon; but they will return."

Brendan, gaunter than he had been a fortnight since, had the look of a man who saw not what is before him—the autumn lands round Caerdroia—but something a very long way away, in time as well as in space; and he shook his head, and shuttered his eyes lest Amris Son of the Raven see more than Brendan Rígh was just then prepared to show. *What the Eye of Balor saw, before it closed again; and more beside...*

After a while he spoke again. "As to that, I am glad they are gone, who would not be? But they will never forget that we are here. And we must never forget that they will be back."

CHAPTER TWENTY-SEVEN

A sea-camp far in the Summer Isles, north beyond the northmost of the western islands. None dwelled there, and therefore had the tiny holm been chosen as refuge by its current, lone inhabitant: naught but barren gray peaks rising up from the waves, so remote a speck amid the waters that it goes nameless even to this day. The cold that had begun ten days ago was by now epic: the sea looked like milk, its everlasting huish now only a faint far boom of waves moving under a thickening skin of ice. The harder it froze, the rockier the sound; the foam at surf's edge was cream-white froth, water and sand whipped up together by the wind.

'Summer' Isles! It would make a cat laugh... A great sibilance, like a giant whispering or a million angry snakes, was niggling at the edges of Brendan's awareness; it seemed to have been going on for some time. He pulled his fur cloak closer around him and went to look. Outside the stone clochan the night dark was fathoms deep, save for the red moon's glow on snow and stone and the Criosanna arching their silvered span above—a sight that no Kelt would ever tire of seeing—and utterly quiet save for that endless seething sound.

He turned in the sound's direction, and saw the cause. It was the sea itself freezing over, sheets of salt-ice, layer upon layer, as the little waves slid in, hissing as they glazed and froze immobile, each overtopping the one before it now iced solid—floods of water transformed as if by cold-runes into sharp thin splintered skins of glass. He watched and listened for a while, awed, more than a little humbled by the visible working of the earth-powers.

A sound from the beginning of the world, a cold so deep as to freeze the sea... This is naught to do with us; it does what it does. Like an earthshake or the huracán, it does not even know we are here, or would care if it knew... Perhaps we need to be minded of that more often—or I need...

He had gone to the frozen isle alone for a reason; not even Etain had accompanied him, and many wondered greatly that she had not. Though for all Kelts there had been terrible sorrow and loss in the wake of the various outfreyn attacks, sorrow both general and particular, for Brendan and Etain and Nia, and indeed all Kelts, there was much more: Rohan his son had been slain in the fighting with the Coranians, and Fiaren Rohan's wife had died defending him. They left behind their little daughter, Morna; Brendan and Etain would raise her as their own, and Fionaveragh and Donn would foster her, as both law and love required; and that was as it was.

But the folk, already reeling from the Coranian assault so close on the heels of several other lesser ones, had been plunged into blackest sorrow at the news of Rohan's death, not knowing they had cared as much as they did, longing to console and be consoled in turn; and more than anything they longed to do something, anything, for the one who had done so very much for them.

But at the moment Brendan wanted no one to do anything for him at all save to leave him in what passed for peace with him just now, to console no one but himself, and mourn the death of his son in his own way. *I know it is selfish and hurtful not to let them sorrow with me, and a million times more so to turn from Tamhna; but I need to camp alone with my grief awhile, and though she knows it not, so too does she. Some things at some times you cannot share even with the mate of your heart; then there are times where such things* must *be so shared—we will mourn together when I return, as we have already done, as we will do forever. Like love, loss does not need to be requited; but it is at its best when it is shared. Yet just now I need to be alone...*

On being told of the deaths, in his first grief and shock Brendan had been guiltstruck, slammed to the ground with agonized reproach and self-blame. At once the words of the lord Melidren—that the Stone would exact a price of its user for each time of use—had leaped upon him like lions to his throat. He had been convinced beyond all consoling or reason that Rohan and Fiaren had been that price; then he had been angry; then tearful; and at last exhausted, weary beyond speech or movement or thought. Now he was remembering, as if it had been writ upon his heart in ink of fire by a diamond pen, the last converse he had had with his son. It had been the day before Rohan— well, it had been the day before. They had been discussing the strategy against the Coranians, the two of them alone, and then the talk had taken a higher, and strangely prescient, turn.

"You can be too much the warrior," Brendan had

admitted, himself a little surprised by the thought. "I would never have said so, or even considered so, beforetimes—it would not have gotten us where we now are, for one thing—but now I know for sure. Too long a sacrifice makes the most loving heart a stone; too long a combat and even the bravest heart can do nothing but fight. When you take it upon you to battle monsters, care must be taken that you do not become one also in the process. But it needs no outside adversary: when you fight alone the worst foe is not the one you face but the one whose face you cannot see—yourself."

Rohan had smiled the warm slow smile that lighted all his countenance, the smile that had come to him from Fergus Fire on Brega. "And where then does peace fit in, Ro-sai?"

Ro-sai, 'Great Teacher'—he calls me that not entirely in jest, I know; but I have learned more than ever I have taught; and learning is not yet done with... Brendan grinned back at his son, so that the resemblance that was not there when both their faces were in repose leaped into startling likeness and life.

"As I was once very well instructed, peace is a great deal more than mere absence of strife. It is a choice—an active principle, not a passive one; it creates its own weather, to rule deeds and lives and hearts. And each of those choices closes off forever all other choices, and all the choices that proceed from them, or that would have proceeded. Nor is war always a breaking of peace; there are times when it can even be a striving to find it."

Rohan's smile now had raised brows added to it, the faintest touch of amused puzzlement and doubt.

"A conundrum, surely—like destroying a thing in order to save it?"

"Sometimes destruction is the only salvation." But Rohan had only laughed outright at that, and turned the topic.

As very well he should have... Brendan smiled, remembering, though the pain was like closing his hand to a fist upon razor-shards of glass, feeling them slice through fingers and sinews, stirring to new agony every time he moved, the blood dripping down. *To lose a child is to lose a certain kind of immortality; it is like losing yourself, dying yourself, only you are still alive to bear the grief of it. To lose someone who was part you and part your beloved mate, someone you and she had made together yet someone uniquely and utterly himself—a time and an hour, a union and creation that will never come again, though the soul most assuredly will—never to come again, not though the work of dán be ripped up by the Alterator and a new weave laid down by the Goddess and the God Themselves...*

So Brendan, alone with his pain; and the white cold days slid by. At the end of the month Kelver Donn Midna, in the sudden way of his folk, appeared on the island; Brendan was not in the least surprised to see him.

"Come," said the Sidhe lord simply. "You have fought alone long enough."

And Brendan had no argument left but left with him, to return to Caerdroia and the world.

So it was, on that nameless island in the northern seas, that the story of Brendan of Fanad ended at last, and that of the first king of Keltia began. Of that reign and

in it many things were sung and done: tales of the epic
contest of Brendan and the Great Orm, and how Brendan got the victory by word-sleight, granting the gift of
human speech to the Orm and his folk, but winning
the Orm's promise to leave the salt oceans free for merrows and silkies and to dwell forever with his kind in
inland seas; how Amris mac an Fhiach was first of all
Kelts to tame and ride the great winged steeds, the
falair, the windhorses that were native to the newly settled planet Erinna; how when Morna the daughter of
Rohan and Fiaren was grown at last to woman's state,
tall and willowy, with her mother's brown-silk hair and
her grandmother's gold-and-amber-dew gaze, Kelver
Donn Midna, king beneath the hill at new Knockfierna, rode to Caerdroia and offered her his hand in
marriage, to make her his queen, and from that union
did great dán proceed.

Many deeds more were done and lost, only the
rumor of them remaining, throwing a spangled cloak
of legend over all that time, so that aftercomers, those
who gazed upon those deeds and doers from afar, saw
it for all its very real perils as a simpler, happier time;
viewed it through a golden haze of legend and grieved
to have missed it, though those who had been there for
it saw it very different: trouble every day, as bards did
sing it. Not easy. Not simple. Not golden, even; or at
least not all that often. But very much a legend; none
were not glad they had been there.

As king, Brendan did not content himself with having provided safety and happiness for his Kelts, though
that was ever to be his prime consideration and concern. He had other joys and protections in mind, as he
never tired of telling anyone who cared to listen. "So

that what happened in Éruinn will happen never again, and nothing may be lost."

And over the years of his reign, that too he brought about. He set bards to codify the various languages into one established Keltic tongue of the realm, the Gael-och, while preserving them as vernaculars for each of the Six Nations that eventually would be. Mindful of Laoghaire and the success he had made with the Senchus Mór, Brendan appointed brehons and bards, druids and ban-draoi, to order and devise a law system such as would fit Keltia's needs, not Éruinn's. Taking a leaf from a long-dead warrior king's book, he established the Fianna as professional soldiery, to defend the Kelts' new home against those who had already tried to drive them from it, and any other who might seek to come against them in war—aye, and those others did come...

Though no druid himself, he established the Druid Order in Keltia, and Nia founded what Pátraic and his male priesthood had so abominated, a powerful company of priestesses under the auspices and consecration of the Goddess Herself, uniting the solitary enchantresses and hedge-witches and village sorceresses to form the order of the Ban-draoi, and Fionaveragh his daughter was its first Mathr'achtaran.

In his own lifetime he was called openly Brendan the Astrogator and secretly Saint Brendan; Keltia prospered, the immrama continued, the population grew and thrived. Brendan and Etain ruled well, but they ruled *with* their folk, not over them—which would ever be the secret of monarchy in Keltia—using all their knowledge and lore and love, and the gifts they were given at the leaving of Éruinn: the Cremave to give

them wisdom and just judging, and the Treasures to
bring them peace in the heart of war.

But however immortal they may appear, not even to
the Sidhefolk is it given to live forever, and only half of
Brendan's heritage derived from that high race. So it
was that in the fullness of time—though because of the
infusion of Danaan blood that now began to course
among them, that allotment of years was soon to
lengthen for all Kelts—Brendan son of Fergus came to
die.

He died alone, as he had wished it, at one hundred
and twenty years of age, in a comfortable bed; he
looked no more than forty when he closed his eyes to
sleep, and even younger afterwards. No one was near:
not even Etain was with him at the end, which he had
chosen to meet in that same remote isle where he had
gone to grieve his son's death so long before. The Copper Crown had been left behind at Caerdroia, to await
the next head chosen to wear it; he would have no part
in that choosing, no control over it, and he was unsurprised to find he did not fear the choice. *It is no longer
any concern of mine; they will elect the one best fitted to lead
them in Keltia, as I was most fated to lead them* to *Keltia...*

So before he went out from the City he so greatly
loved, knowing his death close upon him and wishing
to meet it alone, upon ground of his own choosing, he
had set the crown upon the leather cushion of the
Throne of Scone, the great granite chair of state that
had been brought out of Aulba in the third immram;
the Sceptre of Llyr, the Silver Branch, lay beside it.

They had parted as friends, he and the crown and

throne and sceptre, though they had not begun so; but even now he wished again, vainly, fleetingly, that he had not had to die a king, as he had not been born one, though he was more than content to be the king that he had been. But the silver fillet that had been Nia's bridegift, her gift to him upon the day he sained Caerdroia, lay now on the pillow beside his head; he reached out a steady hand to touch the center stone he had been ever shy of touching, the jewel that had come from Atland. He had worn the coronet often down the years before passing it on to Rohan, who had worn it so sadly briefly; it would go now to Morna daughter of Rohan, who had worn it on the day she wedded Kelver Donn Midna at the stones and became a queen herself. Always it had sat kinder and lighter upon Brendan's brow than the Copper Crown, and now he thought to See in the jewel what might befall Keltia after him, if it was allowed him to see so.

Not for me—oh, very well, a little *for me, just to ease my mind and give me heart in going—but in the end, for Keltia only, ever and always...*

As if it had heard him, and assented—or as if the permission of some Higher had been given it to do so—the stone clouded briefly, then shone out in unearthly brightness, and a tapestry seemed to unfold itself within the clear-cut facets of the light: a long, an endless roll of small vivid visions. Many sights did he see, though of most he did not know the meaning: he saw his Etain wedding a prince of her own folk, centuries hence, and later still again a queen, and he rejoiced to see her happy; then came many kings and queens of Keltia in a long line, that somehow he knew was *his* line, *his* House, and he knew all their lives as he looked upon each. Some of those might be his own future lives, even, and he smiled at the thought; but whoever they were or would be, they came all of his blood and descent, and those lives had been unstoppably set into motion by what he had done with his own.

Or what Pátraic mac Calprin made me to do... Ferganam, my old friend and enemy—strange how one can be the Goddess's instrument and never even know it! Though that could be said of many—even of me, come to that... But if Pátraic had not been so hating and hateful against us, would I ever have even dreamed of leaving Erith? Would I have been but a sky farmer, never daring to do and scarcely managing to be? And how would the folk have suffered? If Barinthus had not held for so long the knowledge he did, would we ever have been able to leave as we did, to find Keltia as we have? Was it my dán, or Pátraic's, or Barrind's, or the people's, that has been played out here? And does it matter whose, or even what, or what comes after...

At the last the Goddess came to him for the third time in that life, and answered all those questions, and many others beside. And Brendan smiled to hear the answers She gave him—*How very simple it all is, after all!*—and taking from his neck the jewel he had worn since the very first days of Keltia and his kingship—a silverset clear rock crystal carved with the figure of a running wolf, guardian of his house and Name—smiling he closed his hand over it, and laid that hand upon his heart, and smiling he rose up and went with Her.

In that same moment, far away at Caerdroia, that selfsame guardian raised the triple howl from the slopes of Eagle: the lament of the Faol-mór for a ruler of the house of Aoibhell, cried for the first time by no means the last. And not very long at all thereafter, sailing into the Mouths of the Avon Dia and up to the landing-place that had been built there, not many miles from where the Wolf Gate of Caerdroia stood always open, came the crystal ship of Manaan Sealord running before a faerie wind, and weeping folk thronged down to the quay to meet it.

Aye, over the wild waters silver-masted Wavesweeper came, with the merrows and silkies who had escorted it down from the north as proud guards about it—and Brendan mac Nia borne amidships, lying on a bier of state upon its ice-colored deck, his hand still closed over the carven jewel. And though the king's face was perfect in death's repose, also it bore, in its beauty and stillness and high calm, the faintest, warmest shading of a smile.

The day Brendan was to be buried at Ni-maen dawned in cold wind and thunder—streaming clouds and sun and shadow, no rain. Though folk looked round Caerdroia, Nia could not be found, and neither could Etain, nor any of the dead king's kin and friends. Inquiries at the Keep produced only the brief unadorned answer that the plan had been changed, and in their sorrow the people went away wondering and hurt. But the plan had been changed indeed...

Five hundred leagues from Caerdroia, Mount Keltia rises out of the plain, a gauntleted fist that the planet shakes against the sky; a pinnacle that the great earth forces had thrust to heaven, that even the glaciers could not break but had been forced around, as a stream will divide round a jutting rock. Halfway up, the mountain spreads to cradle an upland valley, and then

leaps in two sharp snowsilvered horns to the towering
peaks called the Gates of the Sun. The road up its western face is by no means difficult of ascent; it swings
forth and back in great sweeping turns, then where the
mountain splits the road runs through a cut of gray
granite, forever wet with seeping groundwater, as if the
stone itself does weep.

There at road's end a broad plateau opens out, a
short-grassed hanging valley, edged by cliffs and
unsheltered from the blasts, on any other day as empty
as the day it was made. It was not empty this day: in twos
and threes, the friends and kindred of Brendan Ard-
rígh—the title fastened inescapably upon him in death
that he had resolutely denied in life—stood huddled
and shivering in the snow-showers and knifing wind,
their grief no whit less sharp than the cold that bit at
them, their gazes fixed on the one who stood alone a
few hundred feet away.

Nia it was who had summoned them; and there in
their awed presence on that anguished morning she
made that empty upland valley forever less empty and
alone. Long years ago, Brendan and those closest to
him had come privily to this highest place, to hallow it
and give thanks for the deliverance of the people, for
the Kelts' safe coming to their destined home; the
tallest peak on Tara, closest to their new skies, had
seemed the fittest place to do so. Then, he had asked
his mother to raise a circle there, and she had replied
that she would surely do so, one day, but not until the
time was as befitting as the place.

And now Brendan himself had made both place
and time full fit forever… With the Goddess guiding
her hand, Nia stood forth, and called up out of the

earth the stones of Caer-na-gael, as she had raised the walls of Caerdroia up from the plain, and Ni-maen in Calon Eryri and Vellyndruchia on Erinna and Starcross on the planet Caledon yet to be tamed. But of those workings Caer-na-gael was holiest—the greatest and the mightiest of them all.

Before the mourners' eyes, her love and power coaxed the stones up from the mountain's heart, as the springtime sun summons the green shoots to rise out of the grave of winter; her magic caused the dolmens to be marked with mystic sigils, such as were carven on the Throne of Scone, incised into the walls of Sidhean-brugh, tattooed upon the sails of the Hui Corra. Thus came to stand Caer-na-gael in the valley of Calon Cel-tiath, the Fortress of the Gael in the Heart of Keltia: an outer ring of mighty bluestone trilithons, with Yr Allawr Goch, the Red Altar that is neither an altar nor red, set at the circle's heart, and upon the eastern edge of the inner sarsen ring a huge stone chair, built to more than mortal measure. Though many in times to come would opine that surely it must have been the Goddess who had raised these sacred stones, for it seemed that none less than the Mother Herself could have accomplished such a task, the work here had been Nia's, and the asking had been her son's.

And now Brendan would forever rest among them, held safe within his mother's work as once her arms had held him as an infant. "I will set such a marker above his grave that none shall forget for ten thousand years where he may lie," Nia had promised the folk of Keltia, inconsolable in their grief for their beloved king and friend, and so the thing was done.

Then into Caer-na-gael Nia the Golden and Etain

the Queen, and his blood-kin and soul-kin also, sorrowfully and smilingly conveyed what was mortal of Brendan the Astrogator to rest forever beneath the Red Altar. The earth gaped for him, and his stone bed received him; the sign of the suncross blessed him, and Yr Allawr Goch settled down upon him as gently as a blanket on a sleeping child.

"Though he rest here in the peace he has won and well deserves," said Nia then, "he that guards Keltia shall neither slumber nor sleep. Neither shall he watch alone, but that my people shall bear him company. Aye, long years hence, one as great shall join him here; and, later still, a greater still."

After Brendan was laid to rest at Caer-na-gael Etain his wife and queen was not seen again in Caerdroia. She went back to her own people, joining Kelver Donn Midna and Morna her granddaughter, who reigned at Knockfierna beneath the hill and rejoiced to receive her. But never was her beloved lord forgotten among his Danaan kin: as Nia had foretold, the Sidhefolk met often thereafter at Caer-na-gael where he did lie. On nights of storm or starry clearness, when lights are seen to shift and move upon the mountaintop, and music is heard of more than mortal beauty, those looking up in wonder from below know that the Shining Folk hold conclave near the grave of their great kinsman, and perhaps he himself does on occasion join them. And he is never alone.

For her own part Etain forgot Brendan not at all, but by her own choosing she had little more to do with mortals after. Of that first queenship of hers little is remembered; of her second, rather more: but through her and Brendan together the blood of the High Danaans came down to many Keltic kindreds, and blood of the Gael began to flow among the Danaan race. Nor was that all that was passed down along the years: the great crystal that Etain had borne as Gwastor's daughter or ever she had been Brendan's mate and Keltia's queen, that sparkling stone of many names—Icefire to those of Núminôrë, Tear of the Stars to the Kelts—was making its way, slowly, surely, down to the one whose dán had ever been to use it...

As her son's mate would not, or could not, and indeed did not, Nia the Golden remained among the folk for many years, teaching and advising. She was deeply beloved by all Kelts, who thought of her as the mother of Keltia, and their own mother, even, not Brendan's alone: in her own lifetime—if that is the word for such an existence as hers—the name of saint was given her; but when the need and wish came upon her to change that life she too departed, and came never again among mortal Kelts. When she was seen for the last time, by her great-granddaughter Morna, on the heather-clad slopes of Llwynogue, her face was turned to the Hollow Mountains, and the pace of her gold-maned white mare was thither tending. She was singing as she rode; around her head three birds did fly, and they sang with her as Morna watched her out of sight.

And far away behind, in Éruinn, on Erith, in a monk's cell attached to a great stone church built blasphemously upon Ard Mhacha, the High Place of the God-

dess Macha, a man not old had died long since, and
that not well. He had lived but ten years after his
enemy, by sorcery and devilry as it sometimes seemed
to him, had ascended into the heavens. He had lived
tortured by the doubts he infused in himself and the
reining scruples instilled by his masters—upon which
bit they were never slow or shy to lean—had lived in
years of impotent rage and feverish conversions, pow-
erless to prevent further immrama draining away souls
and wealth that those masters might have controlled,
and even while he did so, fiercely denying those voyages were happening at all; had lived striving to make
up in years and numbers for that one soul he had failed
to win, that wealth of spirit he never could, or would,
have won or even matched, much less surpassed. And
for that failure millions would pay the honor-price his
dishonor would lay upon them...

But having so lived, having known ever in his heart
that his enemy flourished in freedom far beyond his
reach and Rome's alike, so too had Patricius Calpurnius died, in the year 462 of the Common Reckoning.
No peaceful death his, but a terrible ending that it ill
behove a Christom priest to make: he died in the
spring, round about the time of Beltain, before those
fires that so galled him could be lighted yet again in his
despite—as they would always be. He died calling
equally upon the name of his god and the name of
Brendan, and which of those names he cursed and
which he blessed, by the fervor and fury with which he
screamed each of them, none of those who stood
uneasily beside his final tormented bed could tell.

And it might be that another monk took his name
to continue his work and maintain the power of his

hold upon the still-recalcitrant Gael, and the two
Pátraics were by time and cunning dissimulation conflated; or it might not.

But however it was, or may have been, Christom
commentators in later times would still most boastfully
proclaim that not a single drop of blood was shed nor
wound was dealt in the turning of Tir Gaedhil to the
White Druid of the Tree; that no soul was harmed in
the battle for Éruinn that Rome waged so hard for so
long against so many.

So they say; and perhaps even believe. But they lie
most damnably who say so.

AFTERTALE

he Keltia Brendan left behind him was small but strong, and very well founded. He had learned some things from the Romans, if not from Rome, and he well understood the concept and need of a strong central government, as Kelts on Erith never would—or, if they did, never managed to stop squabbling long enough to achieve. But he had disliked the idea of a hereditary monarchy based on primogeniture, preferring the ancient Keltic way that chose by election the best candidate from among the rígh-domhna, the 'royal material'—those of a particular kindred, or kindreds, eligible to rule. And so upon his death the leadership was thrown open, according to his wishes, to any claimant strong enough to hold it—deemed so in the sight and by the vote of the folk.

On Erith this would have presented little difficulty. But in Keltia there were not so many rígh-domhna from whom to choose: Fionaveragh; her four children (their own children were yet too young); Morna, daughter of Rohan and Fiaren who had died in battle; a score of cousins of varying distant degree. It was a powerful tribute to Brendan and his achievements that no other family even thought of putting itself forward: the folk of Keltia—both those who came on immram and the first generations born away from Erith—knew very well what their Astrogator and his Danaan mother had done for them, and they were by no means eager to change swords in mid-fight.

In the Brendanachta, therefore, lay all their trust and hope and love; but Fionaveragh, eldest child of Brendan and Etain, had little interest in ruling, being devoted only to the holy order of the sisters of the Ban-draoi that her grandmother Nia had founded. Though all Brendan's grandchildren and cousinage were well loved and respected, it was Sithney, eldest child of Fion-averagh and Donn, who had over the years and through the outfreyn wars emerged as the best general, and a brilliant one at that; and, queen or king, a warrior ruler was what nearly all Kelts, given the choice—with the memory of the Coranians and Fomori and Fir Bolc still a raw aching scar, and fully expectant of fresh wounds in the future—wished to lead them here and now.

So by acclamation Sithney was named to succeed Brendan, and she carried on his policy and work; though like him, she refused a royal styling, insisting upon the name of Taoiseach and no more. She had wedded Morragh mac Lassra, the young lord of Galloway on the newly claimed and settled planet Caledon, who for his bridegift had commissioned Kerredec, son of Grad-lon, to build Sithney's Keep, a great stronghold on the western marches of his own lands, near a long finger of sea-loch. From Sithney and Morragh descended the Aoibhells of Findhorn, while her brother Kiaran and his wife Lorn, heiress of Benderloch, began the line of the Thomond Aoibhells—so that no royal branch in Keltia, however slipped and grafted, would not come of the scion-stem of Brendan and Etain.

Thus did Danaan blood and magic infuse Keltia's families, great and humble alike. And blood of the Gael likewise among the Sidhe: for Morna daughter of Rohan was queen of the Sidhefolk of Erinna, as the wife of Kelver Donn Midna; their son was Allyn, of whom, it has been said and Seen, shall come one of Keltia's glories. But that is another tale…

On his homeworld Erith, which though he left forever he never ceased to think on, Saint Brendan the Astrogator is remembered not at all, save in tales and myths the wilder the better, and perhaps that would please him best and most. By order of Rome itself he was concealed out of existence in the monk-written, or monk-ridden, history of Tir Gaedhil, his deeds and his very name conflated with those of another Brendan who came a half-century later.

This second Brendan, a worthy monk who followed the Tangavaun's teaching—though Pátraic was long dead before this other was even priested—not only carried the Astrogator's name but bore credit for his deeds: deeds for which, strangely enough, he too received the name of 'saint'. Deeds scaled down, though still great enough in any telling: a crossing not of space in a mighty silver ship but of the Western Ocean in a tiny boat of leather and ashwood—a brave voyage. But no Immram Mhór.

In the secret records kept by the monks of Éruinn, it was set down that this monk Brendan was the youngest son of the holy nun Bríd, own niece of Pátraic, born late in Bríd's marriage with a Christom chieftain whose name has not come down to us. When

her lord was slain in battle, she notably refused to foster out her four children but raised them herself; then,
on the death of her own mother, the undoubtedly
sainted Darerca, Bríd had gone to her mother's
brother in his church at Ard Mhacha, and Pátraic had
wedded her as a nun to the White Druid of the Tree—
which was her uncle's victory over her father.

Bríd had had two sons and two daughters with her
chieftain mate, and though this second Brendan followed his great-uncle's calling, the other three made
marriages among the lordliest clans of Éruinn and
Aulba; one daughter even wedded King Laoghaire's
grandson and was queen at Tara herself in time.

But strangely enough, the name of Bríd's father—
the mariner-monk Brendan's grandfather, the lord who
had wedded the holy Darerca to become own brother-
in-law to the great Pátraic himself, presumably worthy of
celebration if not veneration even as the rest of his
saintly kindred—his name was nowhere set down. The
recorder-monks, most unlike themselves and their otherwise scrupulous careful attention to detail, preserved
on this matter a tight unbroken silence—on their own
account, or maybe it was that they had had orders to do
so. But perhaps it was simpler still: perhaps it was merely
that they knew that silence here would best serve other
scruples; and of course they lived to serve.

For all her pious Christom faith, though, Bríd kept
the Old Ways in her own way—and that was her father's
victory over her uncle. It was her fate also to be well
known to history, as Saint Bríd of Kildare—called 'the
Mary of the Gael', which might not have displeased her
Draoícht father as much as her Christom uncle might
have thought, or hoped. She kept alight the sacred fire

in the oak-clad hills of Éruinn's north, though none
save she perhaps knew for whom that Fire truly
burned, and even she herself would likely not admit it.

But where nineteen priestesses once had tended
the holy Fire for Bríghid Rhên, mate of the Gabhain
Saor, now nineteen nuns tended it for Mary Virgin,
Mother of God; and the difference was—well, was
there in truth a difference at all?

The Christpriests conceal all this from the people, of
course, as they have concealed so much else, and will
conceal so much more. But those who are meant to
know, who are strong enough and worthy enough to
know, will puzzle it out for themselves—and instructions were left in many places for heroes to decipher.

For stories are still told—round the hearths on
dark rainy winter nights at Tara, or as travellers' tales
shared with strangers over supper at lonely bruideans
in the deep woods, or sung at splendid bardfeasts
beneath the faerie hills—that every now and again,
some will go to the secret crossroads, the stone circles
and alignments, the holy hills and sacred places; and
sometimes, if the stars are right and the petitioner
versed in the correct means of summoning, a silver
ship comes down from the heavens on a road from the
moon, or sails across the green hills out of the eye of
the sun, and those who step aboard her are seen on
Earth no more. Or so at least it is sung.

Laoghaire Ard-rígh died some years before Pátraic: the
monkish historians viperishly report that the king, who

was never the same after Brendan went, was killed by
his own pagan gods for breaking the heathen oath
which he had taken. He had sworn by sun and moon,
fire and water, earth and air, night and day, sea and
land, never to abandon the Shan-vallachta; and perhaps he was indeed forsworn, for the monks gleefully
recount how he was struck by lightning from a clear
sky, or died in some other sudden dramatic manner,
after at last allowing Christom rites to be celebrated on
the Hill of Tara—a punishment dealt him by the Goddess, some said, though other some said it was rather a
much-deserved punishment from the Tree-druid for
his unregenerate pagan ways.

After him, as his grandmother Cairenn had predicted, all the kings were Christom kings—at least on
the outside. But a strange thing: Laoghaire's body was
never found, and his queen Duvessa vanished also, one
night of storm and thunder; and the only word the
bards had on it—though just how they knew this they
kept secret as well, and certain it is they never told the
monks—was that King Laoghaire had gone laughing.

The tiny Christom contingent that had begged to sail
with Brendan, the Celi Dé, the Friends of God, settled
down at once, quietly and happily, under the rule of
Dorren and Malise, to follow their Way and Path in
peace and trueness as it had never been properly followed before. Brendan gave them a small island on the
giant planet Caledon—which was in great need of
good strong colonists—and they built a clochan community there, named Ionagh for the holy isle they had
left behind. They and their descendants troubled no

one, and no one troubled them: they attempted no
conversions, they showed full respect for the gods of
others—as others did for theirs—and they enjoyed full
protection of law and Crown like any other Kelts; and
like any other Kelts they fought in Keltic wars, preferring their Iosa's doctrine of bringing not peace but a
sword over his more-quoted preaching of turning the
other cheek. And in that they were true Kelts indeed.

Though they would not know it for many centuries,
their tiny tribe was to find its own share of high destiny,
though it lay a long and weary way down a hard road.
But that road would lead to glory in the end.

Two Brendans certainly, possibly even two Pátraics—
who is to say which of these was the true explorer, who
the veridical apostle to the Gael? But in Keltia there is
no doubt: the son of Fergus Fire on Brega and Nia the
Golden is known forever as Saint Brendan the Astrogator, honored as founder and patron protector of the
Kelts and their new home among the stars.

Though many down the ages have laid words upon
him and put speeches into his mouth—some good,
some less so—Brendan himself never made any personal record of his story, apart from the logbooks and
rutairs of the Great Immram. That is fascinating read-
ing, most carefully set down; but it is by no means all
the story, or the best of the story, or even the truth of
the story. Some folk say his choice should be honored
by silence, since he himself chose not to speak: but others say history and art are owed and must be served,
and Brendan mac Nia's tale recounted.

I hold with those latter; but perhaps I have better

cause and claim to do so—I, his many-times descendant Lassarina Aoibhell, of the Findhorn line of the family. And therefore have I presumed to tell it for him. I have done my best, and only hope he approves my poor effort—hard it is to write of your kinfolk, easier far to write of yourself!

But it is a fine, grand, high story, and I am by no means alone in the telling: my late beloved lord, even, most beautifully did frame the tale in song. There have been others, of course, who made songs of it before, and will again after; but his song has become a wonder—and this is the bard speaking now, not so much the loving wife... Word and music, it catches at the heart: folk sing it at dawning in the deeps of Westmark woods, and in the noon on the heights of the Long Hills, and at sunset on the shores of Glora; they sing it at evening in the Mardale Road.

And they will always sing so.

> *For I and mine have fought our way*
> *'Cross fateful gulfs and stranger,*
> *And gained a new and fairer day*
> *Past any fear or danger.*
> *We shall not be the last who leap—*
> *Many will follow after.*
> *Though even the sternest spirit weep*
> *All tears shall turn to laughter.*
> *We have the Highest's promise won,*
> *Upon our hearts engraven:*
> *'All gods and folk in peace shall come*
> *And all souls find safe haven.'*

> —from *'Brendan's Voyage'*,
> by Séomaighas Douglas Ó Morrighsaun

APPENDICES

GLOSSARY

The Celts of Earth did not call themselves that, nor did they think of themselves as we think of them today—a homogeneous and culturally consistent ethnic group. The Greeks gave them the name Keltoi *for convenience's sake, when classical writers needed to refer to the non-Teutonic tribes that ultimately settled in northwestern Europe. We don't really know if the Celts even had a general name for themselves, or if they used only the many tribal appellations that have come down to us—Thracians, Galatians, Milesians, Galicians—or if they even knew they were all related. We only know they didn't call themselves Celts. We think.*

Wherever possible, I have tried to dodge this difficulty by relying on those tribal names—and it doesn't help, either, that the ancient Irish were historically 'Scotti', or Scots! But when I couldn't avoid it, I have in this book used 'Celt' to generally denote the insular or peninsular peoples—the folk of Ireland, Scotland, Wales, Cornwall, Man and Brittany, and the words, terms and concepts referring to them—on Earth.

'Kelt' is used of them only after they get the hell out.

a chara: 'friend, dear one; used in the vocative (**a charai**, pl.; **m'chara**, 'my friend')

Abred: 'The Path of Changes'; the visible world of

everyday existence within the sphere of which one's various lives are lived

Aengus: one of the High Dânu; god of love, journeys and the winds

Afferic: the continent of Africa, of which, in those days, only the northern coasts were generally known

alanna: 'child'; used in the vocative; an endearment used chiefly to girls, not necessarily only one's own daughter but to friends as well

Alemaenna: the regions later to be known as Germany; the lands of Teutonic tribes often at war with the Celts

Allfather: title and attributive for Othinn, king of the Northing gods

Alterator: one of the three High Powers of the Draoícht pantheon; neither male nor female, the Alterator works with the Mother Goddess and the Father God to effect the changes they decree as the will of the Highest, forming the Holy Triplicity of the Draoícht faith

amhic: 'son'; used in the vocative, not necessarily only to one's own male child but to friends as well

an-da-shalla: 'The Second Sight'; talent of precognition

Annir Choille: the Maid of the Woods; an aspect of the Goddess, when as the Young Queen She weds the Young Lord at Midsummer

Annwn: the equivalent in Draoíchtas to Hades, the underworld, ruled over by Arawn Lord of the Dead; lowest of the Three Circles of the World. Though sometimes the word 'hell' is used to describe Annwn, that should not be read as the

Christian concept but merely as a chthonic descriptive. Annwn is not a realm of endless punishment but of endless peace and learning, and includes Moymell, the fair and pleasant place where souls contemplate their physical incarnation just past and prepare for their next (*Annoon*)

Aoroth Kalerri'aren: the royal flagship that led the fleet that brought the Danaans from Núminôrë to their new home on Earth

ap: 'son of'

Aquae Sulis: the Roman-built city in southwest Britain, with hot medicinal springs sacred to the Romano-British goddess called Sul Minerva; latterly, Bath

Arawn: god, highest below the Three; known as the Doomsman, Firstborn of the Absolute; lord of the High Dânu, ruler of Annwn, mate of Malen Rhên; Danaan astronomical name for the planet Saturn

Ard-rían, Ard-rígh: 'High Queen', 'High King'

Argetros: among the Sidhe, another name for **Caer Coronach** (q.v.)

Argialla: the white moon that is the smaller and inner of the two satellites of the planet Tara

Arianvron: 'Silver Breast'; Danaan astronomical name for Earth's moon

ashling: waking wishful dream, daydream

asthore: 'darling'; used in the vocative

athair: 'father'; a formal style; **athra**, 'father', an informal usage

athiarna: 'high one'; address of a subordinate to an officer

Atland: the great island realm destroyed in the conflict between the warring tribes of Telchines and Danaans

Aulba: that part of the island of Britain now known as Scotland; **Aulbannach**, the people now known as Scots

Avilion: mythical island in the Western Sea, one of the Otherlands; the prince Connla and the Sidhe maiden Eithne, lovers of legend, sailed there in a crystal ship with silver sails

Avon Dia: in Keltia, the great central river of the Northwest Continent of the planet Tara

banaltrach: 'other woman'; a wife wedded in a lesser form of marriage; not a chief-wife

ban-charach: 'loved woman'; term for a woman formally and legally associated, short of chief-wife status, but above that of banaltrach

ban-draoi: 'woman-druid'; order of priestess-sorceresses in the service of the Ban-dia, the Great Goddess; in Keltia, when Brendan gave state religion status to the Shan-vallachta, the order was formalized, and the word capitalized; **Mathr'achtaran**, Reverend Mother, title of the head of the order; Brendan's daughter Fionaveragh was the first

Bannaventa: Roman settlement in northwestern Britain, in what would be known as the Lake District, probably located between the extremely beautiful lakes Windermere (**the Long Lake**) and Ullswater

Ban-Nighe: the **Washer at the Ford**; spectre that washes war-shirts at a river-ford where a battle is about to take place

bannock: thick, soft bread or roll; a biscuit or muffin; by extension, a thick, dull, lumpish person

bansha: female spirit, often red-cloaked, that sings

and wails before a death in many families of the
Gael; often seen as a wild rider in the air or over
water

ban-sidhe: generally, a woman of the Sidhefolk

bards: Keltic order of poets, chaunters, musicians and
loremasters; they often function as teachers,
mediators, marriage brokers and spies; the Order
was officially founded in Keltia in the year 347 A.B.
(Anno Brendani) by Plenyth ap Alun, known as
Pen-bardd. On Earth, it was rather different: bards
were simply poets, later musician-poets, and the
lowest order at that; masters were known as *filidh*,
and music played no part in what they did.

Bellendain: the red moon that is the larger and outer
of the two satellites of the planet Tara

Beltain: 1 May; beginning of summer, one of the two
holiest days in the Keltic (or Celtic) calendar

Bluestack Mountains: in Ireland, an indeterminate
mountain range of the east or southeast, probably
the Wicklows

the Boarholms: the Orkney Isles, north of Scotland

bonnive: little pig, piglet; of persons, used in
affectionate exasperation

brehons: order of judges and lawyers, who practice
the extremely comprehensive and compassionate
(and astoundingly modern) system of brehon law

Brigantes: in Britain the More, a tribe living just south
of what would later become Scotland

Brighid of the Flame: goddess of fire, artistic inspiration
and smithcraft, spouse of Gavida, the Gabhain Saor;
one of the High Dânu; **Brighnasa**, her feast, is
celebrated on 1 February (and was known as Imbolc
to Celts of Earth) (*Breed; BREE-nuh-suh*)

Briginda: an aspect of the Goddess, as Lady of Spring

Britain the More: at this time, pretty much limited to the area later known as England; to the north and the west were independent kingdoms, often extremely hostile ones

brugh: in Keltia, a fortified manor house or town-house of elegance and size; on Earth, any permanent residential dwelling

bruidean: inn, roadhouse or waystation, where any traveller of whatever rank or resources is entitled by law to claim hospitality free of charge

Brython: dweller in Britain the More

buidhe-chonnaill: see **yellowstalk ill**

Cabarfeidh: the Antlered King; aspect or person-ification of the God, the male principle of the universe and the Goddess's mate; as the Hornèd Lord, a tall dark-haired man with the antlers of a stag, blasphemously demonized in Christian mythology as the Devil (*CABBER-fay*)

Caer Coronach: 'Castle Lamentation' or 'Crown of the North'; the silver-walled castle behind the North Wind, to which souls journey as the first stop after death, on the road to Annwn; a place of joy, light and peace, to which the newly dead soul is guided (and guarded en route by the living who love it) by those who have gone before who were loved or admired by that particular soul in life (also **Argetros**)

Caerdroia: 'Spiral Castle'; the capital of the new realm of Keltia; founded by St. Brendan the Astrogator; its walls were raised by his mother, St. Nia

Caersalím: Jerusalem

Caledon: another name for the area also known as Aulba, now Scotland; in Keltia, the fourth planet and system settled by Kelts of the Immrama

cam-anfa: 'crooked storm'; an extremely violent localized weather disturbance of the sort known on Earth as a tornado

cannauns: onions

Caomai: the Armed King, the constellation Orion; a beautiful winter constellation of the Keltic zodiac, equivalent to Leo

carán: 'darling', 'dearest'

catbears: appealing, red-furred creatures, very similar to pandas, native to the planet Tara

ceili: party or revel with dancing, feasting and music (*kay-lee*)

Celi Dé: the Friends of God; a small sect of Christian mystics that, revolted at the tactics of Pátraic and other missionaries, begged Brendan to be permitted to join the Immram Mhór; he allowed it, and they went to Keltia, where a tiny community of their descendants has thrived and lived peacefully ever since; indeed, some of the Celi Dé sided with Aeron Regnatrix and Gwydion Imperator in the Fírian Wars, fiercely supporting them out of deep conviction or long loyalty, while others turned against them, betraying them out of greed and fear and hate

céo-draoíchta: 'druids' fog'; a magical spell

chief-wife: in ancient Irish marriage law, a woman married 'on terms of equals', in **launamnas** (q.v.), where she is of equal rank with her husband and brings to the marriage as much property as he does; usually, though by no means always, the first

wife a man weds (if a woman brought more to the
marital contract than a man, she was the one—
legally—who called the shots in the marriage)

Christom, Christery: colloquial terms for the
Christian religion

cithóg: lefthandwise, counterclockwise; also, the port
side of a ship

civis: 'citizen'; legal designation of a freeborn Roman,
a title rather jealously guarded

Clanadon: the maenor of Brendan Aoibhell and Etain
nighean Gwastor, in Fanad; it was given them as
dower on their marriage

claymore: huge two-handed broadsword

cliamhan: in-laws; any sort of kin by marriage for
which another word does not exist

clinker-built: a ship or boat built with timbers
overlapping downwards

clochan: small beehive-shaped stone construction,
built entirely without mortar; the stones are
shaped and fitted

coach-a-bower: ghastly portent, invariably seen before
major disasters, of a red war-chariot pulled by four
headless black horses; if you hear it in the street
and go to look out your windows or door a basin
of blood will be thrown in your face

coire ainsec: 'the undry cauldron of guestship'; the
Celtic tradition of universal hospitality to strangers

Coranians: the ruling race of the Cabiri Imperium,
hereditary enemies of the Kelts; they are the
descendants of the Atlandean Telchines, as the
Kelts are descendants of the Atlandean Danaans

Corca-Vaskin: in Ireland, an area of the lush central
southeast

Cormac mac Art: king at Tara, c. 227–266 C.E.; **as blank as King Cormac's shield**, Cormac bore a white shield without device or charge; a popular idiom for utter vacant amazement

Cornovia: Cornwall

Corryvreckan: the huge and very dangerous whirlpool off the western coast of Scotland

covin-tree: large tree, often an oak or yew, planted outside a country maenor, under which the head of the family traditionally welcomes visitors

craivahans: basically, hash; made with salt beef (though other meats may be used as the cook pleases), onions and potatoes all chopped fine and mixed together into a thickish flat cake, and then fried to crispness in a pan

Crann-draoi: 'Tree-druid'; name given to the god and teacher Jesus Christ by those of the Gael who do not profess the faith named for him

Creavanore: maenor of Fergus Aoibhell, known as Fergus Fire on Brega, lord of the province of Fanad; **the Creavanore**, 'the Golden Bough', a name for the sacred World Tree known in other cultures as Yggdrasil or Hethel or even the Cross; also a name for the sacred plant mistletoe, which grows as the crown of an oak tree

Cremave: the magical clearing-stone given by Gwastor to his daughter Etain and son-in-law Brendan to take to Keltia in the Immram Mhór

Criosanna: 'Woven Belts'; the beautiful rings that circle the planet Tara (*criss-anna*)

crómag: 'crook'; shepherd's crook; later, the crosier that Pátraic and others carried as symbol of their authority, and the fact that they considered their followers sheep; **Crómmaun**: 'crooked one'; contemptuous term applied to those who carried such staves

Crown of the North: the aurora borealis, also called **the Dancers**; **the Hollow Crown**, the opening in the electromagnetic field surrounding Earth, or any planet, through which entrance from space is most safely effected

Cruach Aogall: the hill upon which is delved Sidheanbrugh, or Newgrange

cuach: the cuckoo bird

curragh: a small leather-hulled boat, sometimes masted, rowed with oars

Dagda: title and attributive for the God, in His aspect as the Great Father, the mate of Modron; Danaan astronomical name for the planet Jupiter (also **Iau Rígh**)

Dahût: one of the Dânu, goddess of springs and wells; Danaan astronomical name for the planet Neptune

dama-wyn: 'grandmother', 'great-grandmother'; respectful address to any very much older woman, kin or not

dán: 'doom'; fate or karma (*dawn*); **dánach**, one who is so fated

Dâna: goddess, one of the High Dânu; sister of Dôn Rhên; patroness of the Keltic people, particularly well disposed to the Erinnach, those descended from the Irish Celts of Earth; one of the names for the Sidhefolk was **Tuatha De Danaan**, Tribefolk of the Goddess Dâna

Davan Water: the river running through Fanad, near Brendan's home at Creavanore

Daynighting: the spring or autumn equinox; the ceremonies held at those times

Deer's Cry: the Faedh Fiada; a powerful rann, or prayer, to the God in His aspect as Fionn; Pátraic seized and desecrated it by Christianizing it and using it to work magic against Brendan on the hill of Tara

deosil: righthandwise, sunwise; the starboard side of a ship

Diníosas: the god Dionysus

Dord Faunya: the great rann or spell that Brendan used to counter Pátraic's magic in their duel on the Hill of Tara

dorter: large common sleeping room or hall, found in garrisons, colleges, large households or travellers' halts

Dragon's Spine: in Keltia, a mountain range in the southwest of the Northern Continent of Tara

Draoíchtas: the generic term for the native religion of Ireland and other Celtic nations of Earth; **draoícht**, those who practice it, or the practice itself (*dreekht*)

dreefolk: contemptuous Christian term for those who follow the Old Ways

dromond: a class of starship large enough and swift enough for interstellar travel

Dromore: in Ireland, maenor of Coll mac Gréine in Corca-Vaskin

druids: order of sorcerer-priests; in Keltia, when Brendan gave state religion status to the Shan-vallachta, the title was capitalized

Drumnadarroch: a hill in Corca-Vaskin, beneath which is the dún of the Sidhefolk known as Rinn na gCroha

dúchas: lordship or holding; usually involves lands and titles

duergar: a spirit of mischief or even malevolence

Dún Aengus: in Keltia, the chief stronghold of the Sidhefolk on the planet Tara; located in the pathless Hollow Mountains, far in the northeast of the main continent

dún: a stronghold, usually of the Sidhe (also **liss** or **rath**)

Eastern Sea: the body of water lying between the islands of Éruinn and Britain the More

Eastern Shore: in Britain the More, the area of east-coast lowlands infiltrated by the Sassanaich incomers allowed in by Vortigern, originally to protect his own interests; they ended up by taking over the country; for this deed he is regarded in the Keltic Triads as one of the Three High Betrayers

Ebbrow: Israel

Éigipteach: the Egyptian people

Eirias: literally, a great white flame; the Sacred Fire of the Goddess and the God

Emain Macha: the ancient capital of the Ultonians, in northeastern Éruinn; it was destroyed in a great exploit by King Niall Nine-Hostage, Laoghaire's father

éraic: 'blood-price'; the honor payment exacted for a murder by the victim's kin, in lieu of killing the offender (which is also a perfectly lawful option)

Erinna: in Keltia, the first planet and system claimed by Kelts after the founding of Tara, chiefly settled by those from Éruinn

Erith: ancient Danaan name for the planet Earth

Éruinn: name among the Sidhefolk for the island
     later known as Ireland
Eye of Fire: the red star Betelgeuse

Faol-mór: 'Great Wolf'; the famous wolf fetch of
     Clann Aoibhell; Brendan mac Nia was the first to
     whom it appeared, and it has been the Aoibhell
     guardian spirit ever since, most notably favoring
     the renowned bard Lassarina Breastknot of Poetry,
     Queen Athyn Blackmantle, Brendan Mór Ard-rígh
     and the Queen-Empress Aeron Regnatrix, all of
     whom were of one or another line of the Name of
     Aoibhell
faunt: a child when he or she becomes a walker and
     talker; a sentient intelligent being of any race,
     conscious of self ('human' as opposed to 'animal')
fetch: the visible form, usually an animal of some sort,
     taken by the spirit-guardian of a Keltic family,
     clann or individual; totem or power animal
Fianna: warrior class; an organization of military
     supremacy that originated in Éruinn, some say
     founded by the god Fionn himself; hence the
     name
fidchell: chess-style game played on a round board
Fields of Súl: in Danaan astrogational terminology,
     the system that contains Earth, or **Erith**; the other
     planets, in order outward from **Súl**, the Sun (Sol),
     are **Lugh** (Mercury), **Gwener** (Venus), **Malen**
     (Mars), **Dagda** (Jupiter), **Arawn** (Saturn), **Midir**
     (Uranus), **Dahût** (Neptune) and **Síon** (Pluto)
Findhorn: in Keltia, a region of Erinna; descended
     from Brendan's eldest grandchild Sithney, the
     Findhorn Aoibhells were one of the most ancient

noble lines in the new kingdom; the line is
thought to have died out with the High Queen
Athyn Blackmantle and her consort King Morric
Fireheart (see *Blackmantle*)

findruinna: a silvery, superhard metal used
abundantly in Keltia; on Earth, an alloy of white
bronze and platinum, the secret of which the
Danaans brought from Atland. There is no
platinum in Ireland, though the element has often
been found in metal objects dug from mounds
and sites, because it was all mined out and used up
in the making of the Hui Corra and the other
ships of the Great Immram

Fionn: also **Fionn the Young**; god, one of the High
Dânu. Fionn is problematic in that he is a god in his
own right, but he is also the vehicle by which others
of the High Dânu (Gwydion, Mihangel, even
Arawn) on occasion choose to make themselves
known; the Cabarfeidh, the God Himself, Kernûn
Rhên, often aspects as Fionn to interact with
mortals, as the Young Lord. For this, Fionn is known
as Friend-to-man, and is much beloved by Kelts; his
feast of **Fionnasa**, celebrated on 29 September, is a
day of revelry as well as worship (*finn*)

fíor-comlainn: 'the truth of combat'; legally binding
trial by personal combat either magical or military

Fir Bolc: in Ireland, a predecessor race to the
Danaans; the name means 'Folk of the Bag' (*feer
BUH-lug*)

Firvolgi: an alien race nicknamed 'Fir Bolc' by the
Kelts for their similarity to the old enemy and for
their love of their purses; **Firvolgior**, their
homeworld

fith-fath: spell of shapeshifting or glamourie; magical illusion

flett: a structure or dwelling common among the tribes of Britain the More, made of woven wattles, daub and thatch

Fomori: another predecessor race to the Gael; they were directly displaced by the Danaans on the arrival of the latter from Atland. Later, the Kelts would give the same name to another enemy alien race, formerly known as the **Oyarzün**, with such insistence that eventually the Oyarzün would adopt the name as their own; **Fomor**, their homeworld

Fomor-summer: unseasonally hot weather that comes after the first hard frost; cf. Terran 'Indian summer'

force: a waterfall, especially in hill-country

fosterage: *an-altram*, the Celtic custom in which children of all social classes are usually exchanged between sets of fostering parents, beginning at the age of five and continuing in most cases to age thirteen; reciprocity is not always necessary, especially among the very highest social classes

foumart: weasel, polecat, skunk; any of the mustelids, known for their fetid scent and furtive ways

fox in the grain-kist: dog in the manger; a selfish person who grudges things to others that he himself cannot make use of or benefit from

Gael: Milesian Celt; at the time of this tale, the predominant and pre-eminent race inhabiting Ireland

Gaeloch: the official language of Keltia, a
   combination of Old Irish, Old Scots Gaelic and
   Old Welsh; **High Gaeloch**, the ancient formal
   tongue, kept linguistically pure by the Sidhe,
   whose language it is among themselves
gammon: ham or salt pork
garron: breed of small sturdy coldblood horses, 13–14
   hands high, usually gray or dun in color
Gavida: the Smith of the Gods, one of the High Dânu,
   god of crafting and magic; his spouse is Bríghid;
   very well disposed to mortals, he is also known as
   Gavannaun, the Gabhain Saor, **the Forgelord**;
   Gavida's Smithy, in Keltia, a volcanic island many
   miles out in the bay from the newly founded
   capital of Caerdroia; also, the Otherland seat and
   forge of the god himself
geis, pl. **geisa:** command or moral injunction placed
   upon a person, often at birth or other significant
   moment, to do or not do certain things, some of
   which are ridiculously arbitrary (certain kings were
   prohibited to 'incite their horses' while crossing
   certain fords, for example, or to drive their
   chariots righthandwise round the hill of Tara; the
   great hero Conaire Mór was forbidden to enter
   North Teffia on a Tuesday); geisa are broken at
   great peril, resulting in certain ill-luck and
   misfortune for the one who breaks them, if not
   worse (*gesh, gesha*)
gens: in Roman society, the equivalent of a clann or
   noble house; the notorious Claudians are an
   example of a gens
ghostfires: the electrical or astromagnetic phenomenon
   later given the name of St. Elmo's Fire

the Giants' Dance: see **Stonehanger**

glamourie: small magical spell of altered appearance
or disguise

glib: fringe or forelock of hair; bangs

goleor: 'in great numbers, overabundance'; root of
the English word *galore*

gort: open space between outbuildings and chief
structure of a country maenor

grafaun: double-edged war-axe, very nasty; the
preferred weapon of Coll mac Gréine

Grecaia: Greece, Hellas

Grian: in Keltic astronomy, the sun of the
Throneworld, Tara

grieshoch: embers; low-smoldering hearthfire

gúna: long straight shift-like garment worn by women
and sometimes by older men

Gwalia: Wales, in general; the various parts of Wales
had specific names and were settled by very
different peoples (among them, **Gwynedd**, the far
northwest; **Caradigion**, the midsouth; **Gwent**, the
southeast)

Gwener Fairface: goddess of beauty and insight; one
of the High Dânu, whose mate is Midir and whose
lover is Aengus; Danaan astronomical name for
the planet Venus

Gwenhidw Cloudherd: sky goddess, mate of Manaan
Sealord; she is frequently invoked by those who
herd domestic beasts; **Gwenhidw's sheep**, the
small white fleecy clouds seen running on a high
wind before a storm

Gwyddel: Kymric word for 'Gael'

Gwydion Rhên, Gwydion ap Dôn: god of writers and
sorcerers, one of the Dânu, son of Dôn Rhên;

extremely well-disposed and helpful to mortals, he
is often aspected as Fionn the Young

Gwynedd: on Earth, northwest Wales; in Keltia, the
third planet settled by Kelts of the Immrama, the
chief planet of the system called Kymry

handfasting: rite of religious marriage according to
the Shan-vallachta; on Earth, this style of union
was recognized as lawful from the earliest days well
into modern times; then it became a form of
private ceremony, and now it is again being
openly, and legally, acknowledged

Hethel: name among the Sassanaich folk of the
Eastern Shore for the World Sacrifice Tree known
to other peoples as **Yggdrasil** or **Creavanore**

High Danaan: name given in Éruinn to the unmixed
line of the people commonly known as the Sidhe;
descendants of unions of High Danaan and Gael
were referred to as simply Danaans, though this
was by no means consistent, and **Danaan** was also
used to describe this folk when they dwelled in
Atland or, before that, in their original homeworld
Núminôrë

Hill of Slane: in the east of Ireland, a hill that lay
across the valley from the royal Hill of Tara;
Pátraic kindled a fire there before King Laoghaire
lighted the fire on Tara itself, and thus set the
stage for fifteen hundred years of an unparalleled
theocracy's oppression of an appallingly priest-
ridden people; Edeyrn himself did not come close
to this achievement

Hispania: Spain

Hui Corra: the great starship that was the flagship of

Brendan the Astrogator, in the Immram Mhór, the
first journey of Celts of Earth to discover their new
homeland of Keltia

Idris: the Marshal of the Stars; a god, one of the
Dânu; also aspected as Fionn the Young

Imbolc: in Celtic lands of Earth, the name of the
feast later known in Keltia as Brighnasa, the holy
day of the goddess Bríghid, and celebrated on
1 February

imda: 'bed-nook'; a small alcove, just large enough for
a bed and clothes-kist, in a common dorter or
sleeping-hall for slaves, students or travellers

immram: 'voyage'; **Immram Mhór**, 'Great Voyage', the
first historic journey of migration from Earth to
Keltia (**immrama**, pl.)

ingheann: 'daughter', 'girl'; used in the vocative (cf.
amhic, alanna); form of affectionate address to a
girl or woman; not limited to one's own female
child

Iosa Chriesta: Jesus Christ; also **Iosa Crann-draoi, the
White Druid of the Tree, Iosa mac Mhúir** ('son of
Mary')

Ísais: the Goddess Isis

Isca Dumnoniorum: in the southwest of Britain the
More, the small Roman-built city later known as
Exeter; the Dumnonii were the Brython tribe
dwelling in that area

Joussef Saor: Joseph the Carpenter; father of the
historical Yeshua (Jesus); in Christian mythology,
the platonic spouse of Mhúir and fosterfather of
Iosa the god

keeve: beaker or barrel

Keltia: the name of the interstellar kingdom founded by St. Brendan the Astrogator; it consists of seven star systems—the Six Nations of **Erinna**, **Caledon**, **Kymry**, **Kernow**, **Vannin** and **Brytaned** (or **Arvorica**), and the Throneworld system of **Tara**

Kelu: 'The Crown'; that One High God above all gods, held by those who follow the Shan-vallachta to be both Mother Goddess and Father God together, or neither, or beyond such distinctions entirely; the will of Kelu is manifested in Abred by the Goddess and the God, and brought about by the Alterator, who is also Initiator and Completer (these comprise the **Holy Triplicity**)

kethern-a-varna: 'the fighter in the gap'; the one who sees danger coming, the warrior who holds the pass against all comers

Killary: the maenor of Brendan's grandparents, in the province of the Laighin, in southeastern Ireland

King of Winter: a title of the God, the Cabarfeidh

kist: metal, wood or stone trunk or chest for storing clothing, grain, weapons or other such things

Knavogue: the Road of Cinders; the asteroid belt lying between Mars and Jupiter in Sol system

Knockfierna: the palace of Donn Rígh Midna, high king over all kings and queens of the Sidhefolk in Éruinn; in Keltia, the palace of Donn's son Kelver Donn Midna, one of Brendan's dearest friends, who accompanied him on Immram Mhór and who wedded his granddaughter Morna

lai: in Keltia, a unit of distance measurement, equal to approximately one-half mile

the Laighin: province of southeastern Éruinn
Lannabrachan: river in the Laighin province; in its
 valley the maenor of Killary was located
lasra: laser
launamnas: 'marriage'; specifically, in brehon
 marriage law, the first-form marriage, the union
 between equals, in which both partners are of
 equal social status and bring equal property to
 the partnership, and have union on equal terms.
 On Earth, launamnas—indeed, formal legal
 marriage of any sort—was contractable between
 man and woman only; but when Keltia was first
 established, Brendan decreed that marriages
 between man and man, and woman and
 woman—unions virulently condemned by Pátraic
 and the church of Rome—should in Keltia be
 given full standing before the law; the Kelts
 found this perfectly natural, moral and logical,
 and of no concern whatsoever to anyone save the
 parties involved
leinna, pl. **leinne:** loose, long-sleeved shirt of linen,
 usually worn under a tunic or plaid (*LEN-ya*)
levin: a lightning-bolt; also **skyfire** and **fireflaw**
Londinium: chief city of Britain the More, on the
 banks of the river Tamesis
lorica: a war-shirt, a mail tunic; a breastplate made of
 metal, leather or both
Lugh: god, one of the High Dânu; Danaan
 astronomical name for the planet Mercury;
 Lughnasa, Lugh's feast, celebrated on 1 August
Lúndaigh: the island of Lundy, off the north coast of
 Cornwall, renowned for its tin
lymphad: a war-ship; *the Lymphad,* a Keltic

constellation and sign of the Keltic zodiac,
equivalent to Pisces (also known as *the Moonboat*)

Macha: title and attributive name of the Great
Mother, the Goddess

machair: sea-meadows; wide tracts of salt grassland
bordering on the sea and running down to the
highwater mark; in Éruinn and Aulba, certain
reeds that grow on the machair are often
harvested for bedding and floor-covering

maenor: hereditary dwelling-place, usually a family
seat, estate or farmhold

Magheramorna: maenor of Coll mac Gréine, friend
and swordbrother to Fergus Aoibhell, father of
Brendan

Malen Rhên: goddess of war and love, one of the
High Dânu; mate to Arawn Rhên and queen of
Annwn; in battle she rides in her chariot above
the field, and her two ravens, **Brónach** and
Lanach, choose the slain; also **Malen Ruadh, the
War-red War-queen**; Danaan astronomical name
for the planet Mars

malison: a curse or black working

mamaith: 'mama' or 'mommy'

Manaan Sealord: god, one of the Dânu; his crystal
ship that can sail both land and sea is known as
'Wavesweeper', as is also, rather confusingly, his
beautiful white stallion; his wife is the sky-goddess
Gwenhidw

Mari Llwyd: the **Ghost Mare**; a giant horse all of
bones, with fire for her eyes; an omen of the most
dire and desperate sort

Mathr'achtaran: 'Reverend Mother'; title for the head

priestess of the Ban-draoi order; first given, in
Keltia, to Fionaveragh the daughter of Brendan

mether: four-cornered drinking-vessel, usually of
pottery or wood

Mhúir: in Christian mythology, Mary, the mortal
woman who gave birth to the god Jesus; she was
later effectively elevated to goddesshood herself,
by the Church who at the same time insisted she
was nothing of the sort, and a virgin to boot

Midhchuartaigh: the banqueting hall at Tara; **Mi-
cuarta**, in Keltia, the banqueting hall in the palace
of Turusachan

Midir: god of meaning, healing and plan, one of the
High Dânu, whose mate is Gwener; Danaan
astronomical name for the planet Uranus

Môn: on Earth, the island of Anglesey; a holy island,
the last retreat of the Druids when the Romans
invaded Wales

Morimaruse: dead sea of space; also **Morasaluran,
Maru-sha-sharru, Masu Sar, Merizalda**

Moruadha: the **merrows**, the seafolk; green-haired
and red-skinned, of lithe and graceful build,
completely amphibious; they came to Keltia in the
first Immram

Moymell: 'the Pleasant Plain'; region of Annwn, the
Otherland, where souls between lives spend time
in contemplation of the life just past and the life
they will choose for their next incarnation

nemeton: sacred circle of stones
Newgrange: modern name for **Sidheanbrugh** (q.v.)
nic, nighean: 'daughter of'
Northings: the Nordic peoples

Núminôrë: the name of the original star system from
which the Danaans and Telchines, among other
nations, set out for Earth when their sun went nova
[and yes, it's an *hommage*, even if differently spelled;
if C. S. Lewis can do it, so can I—not to mention the
fact that in their book *The Eternal Man*, Louis
Pauwels and Jacques Bergier speak of Numinor as
"the Atlantis of the North, the Celtic Atlantis"—so
maybe Professor Tolkien was into more than he let
on, or maybe even knew—*P.K.M.*]

orm: huge amphibious water-beast found in
deepwater lakes and oceans; the species was
known to Erithfolk as the Loch Ness monster

Ósirais: the God Osiris

Otherlands: the magical realms, of death or beyond
death

Othinn Allfather: the great King of Gods of the
Northing people, who hung nine nights on the
tree Yggdrasil as a sacrifice to himself, to obtain
the knowledge of the Runes for his people

Ottermoon: in the Keltic calendar, the month more
or less corresponding to August

outfreyn: outland, foreign; in Keltia, offworlders (also
outfrenne)

owl-time: the hours between one and four in the
morning

Oyarzün: the alien race that the Kelts will later come
to call Fomori (these people are no connection to
the Fomori that dwelled in Éruinn before being
displaced by the Danaans, merely named after
them)

People of the Star: another name for the Sidhefolk

piast: another name for the orm, or a similar species

Pict, Pictoi: the pre-Celtic people of eastern Scotland (also **Crúithin**); **Pictavia**, their ancestral lands

Pillars of Herakles: the Rock and Straits of Gibraltar

pishogue: very simple spell or minor magic

plaid: the shoulder-swash formed by the free end of the great-kilt; it can be used as a cloak, hood or pillow at need (*plade*, not *pladd*)

porrans: potatoes, usually baked, pan-fried or roasted. Common wisdom has it that Celts were not blessed with the mighty tuber until it was introduced from the Americas in the 17th century, but this is a lie. In fact, the Danaans of Atland, who had extensive trade with their kin in lands all over the planet— including the great nation that would later be known as Peru, potato homeland—acquired it early on, and may even have brought it with them from their former homeworld of Núminôrē; along with chocolate (shakla), the Danaans carried it with them everywhere, to Ireland when they fled Atland's destruction and when they left Earth for Keltia in the immrama

Portingale: Portugal

quaich: a wide, shallow, double-handled drinking-vessel, usually made of silver, pewter or pottery, often ornamented with knotwork or jewels

quaratz: the mineral quartz

rann: chanted verse stanza used in magic; spell of any sort; sometimes, a poem or song-story

rechtair: steward of royal, noble or wealthy

households; on a farm, the rechtair attends to
crop management and animal husbandry

reivers: thieves, bandits, raiders

Rheged: an area of midnorthern Britain the More

Rhenia: area of Germany, or Alemaenna, around the
Rhine River

Rhian: the Maiden, the Young Goddess; an aspect
assumed by the Great Mother, when She appears
as a young woman, usually with long brown hair
and gray eyes

Rinn na gCroha: in Éruinn, a liss or fort of the
Sidhefolk, in the Bluestack Mountains; the home
of Nia before her marriage, and of Brendan after
his; the rulers there are her parents, Calatin and
Súlsha (*rin-na-GROW-huh*)

Rómanach: 'Roman'

ruddenwood: giant long-lived tree native to Keltia,
tough and resistant, very similar to the sequoia of
Erith

rutair: ship's sailing manual, containing navigational
directions and information

Saighvildanach: a title used in prayer to the Young
Goddess, in Her aspect as **Saighve**, mate of Fionn;
it means roughly 'Saighve All-making' or 'All-
fating' (*Saighve* to rhyme with *thrive*)

Samhain: the all-important feast marking the Celtic
New Year and the beginning of winter; celebrated
on November Eve (**Great Samhain**) and continuing
to 11 November (**Samhain the Less**) (*sah-win*)

sark: Sassanaich word for 'shirt'; usually refers to a
mail war-shirt rather than a leinna

sarsen: dolmen; a great upright stone often found in

conjunction with or near nemetons, usually of rough granite

Sassanaich: the influx peoples of Teuton race from northern Europe coming to settle—and conquer—Britain the More

(take) seizin: to make a formal lawful claim on land, demonstrated by cutting a turf and removing it, and putting a little salt and water on the bare earth by way of return offering

sett and flett: literally, family and dwelling; an expression roughly equivalent perhaps to 'hearth and home'

sgian: small black-handled knife, worn in sleeve or boot-top

shamrogue: small green three-leaved plant of the white clover; trefoil; a sacred symbol of the Goddess stolen, like so much else, by Pátraic and the Christom

Shan-vallachta: 'The Old Ways'; name for the spiritual practices followed since time immemorial by those Celts known to Pátraic and his ilk as pagans

shavepate: mocking name for a clerical tonsure, or the one so barbered; the peculiar tonsure favored by Pátraic and those who followed him was not the familiar shaved circle atop the head of later monks but a shaving of the entire front of the head, from a line drawn ear to ear over the crown of the head, with the rest of the hair allowed to grow long in back

shieling: on Earth, a herding hut up in the hills; in Keltia, a mountain cavern where grazing herds are stabled against rough weather

Sidhe: the Shining Ones, the People of the Star; the magical High Danaan kindred that came to

Ireland and other sea-lands of western Europe
when their home of Atland was destroyed by civil
conflict and resultant cataclysmic earth changes,
including a massive tidal wave

Sidheanbrugh: 'palace mound of the Sidhefolk'; in
Ireland, the great chambered tomb now known as
Newgrange (at other times known as **Ros na
Ríogh**, **Achadhalla**, **Cashel Aonghus**)

Sinan River: in Ireland, the River Shannon, named
for a goddess

Síon of the Storms: a goddess, one of the High Dânu;
Danaan astronomical name for the planet Pluto
(*Sheen*)

Síreach: the people of Syria

siriac: a fine, costly satin-like fabric

sky farmer: a dreamer and wisher who never
accomplishes anything; his farm is in the sky

skyhook: an ominous cloud formation that presages
the cam-anfa

the Sleeve: the body of water lying between France
and England

Slemish: a hill in the northwestern province of Fanad

Sluagh-rón: the Sealfolk, the **silkies**; a phocine race
that came with the Celts on the immrama; many
Celtic and Keltic families alike proudly claim
silkie blood, and some individuals are even
phocimorphs, shapechangers capable of
assuming seal form at will

snowstones: hail, sleet, frozen rain

Solas Sidhe: the Faery Fire; a natural phenomenon
similar to the will-o'-the-wisp but occurring over
rocky ground; usually seen in the spring and fall;
also, the magical silvery light or aura sometimes

worn by the Sidhe themselves in the presence of mortals (*sullis shee*)

stipendium: in Rome, a fixed fee for labor, usually a very modest one (also known as *salarium*, the money allowed Roman soldiers to buy salt)

Stonehanger: the great bluestone and sarsen circle on Salisbury Plain (**Great South Plain**) known as the Giants' Dance and, latterly, Stonehenge

Stone of Fál (or **Falias**): the Eye of Balor, one of the Four Chief Treasures of Keltia (the others, which do not figure in this book, are *Birgha*, the Spear, of the holy city of Findias; *Fragarach*, the Sword, of Gorias, also known as Retaliator or the Answerer; and *Pair Dadeni*, the Cup or Cauldron of Rebirth, of Murias, also aspected as the Graal)

Strath Mór: 'Great Valley'; in Keltia, the broad, glaciated valley on Tara through which runs the Avon Dia; the Hui Corra landed her boats there in the first immrama

Strivellin: a mountain in the province of the Laighin

Struell-wells: sacred springs in the province of Fanad; Brendan performed a mighty cure there in Pátraic's despite

sulter: oppressive, unnatural heat and humidity

Sulyonessa: great island off the extreme southwestern tip of Britain; it was broken and inundated by a tidal wave at the launching of one of the ships of Immram Mhór, so that only a few mountain peaks showed above the surface as the **Sullia Isles**; now known as the Scillys

Summer Queen: a title of the Goddess

sun-sharks: a species of dolphin that went on the immrama to Keltia; they were faunt to begin

2222

232232222222

472 PATRICIA KENNEALY-MORRISON

with—intelligent and self-aware—and in Keltia
they grew more so. They enjoy all the protections
and recourse of any other Kelt, and the
punishment for killing a sun-shark is the same as
for killing a human, silkie or merrow

Sunstanding: the summer or winter solstices; the
festivals held at these times

Swanmoon: in the Keltic calendar, the month more or
less corresponding to May

tagget: a yearling sheep, either male or female

Taghnavalla: 'landfall'; place in Strath Mór where first
the Keltic ships touched down

Tangavaun: 'white tongue'; in the bardspeech, 'word
of death'; name by which Pátraic mac Calprin was
known among Gaeldom; also, name for the Christ
cult's holy book, the Bible

Taoiseach: 'Chief'; title assumed by Brendan and his
first four successors, although they are counted as
kings and queens by Kelts, and were invariably
addressed so, especially by foreigners; later, the
Prime Minister or First Minister of Keltia (*TEE-
shaakh*)

Tara: in Ireland, the sacred hill upon which is built
the High King's palace; in Keltia, the double-
ringed Throneworld planet first settled by the
emigrants from Earth

Teffia: in Ireland, region of the central east; in Keltia,
a southwestern area of the planet Tara

Tha fios fithich aige: 'Thou hast raven's knowledge';
clann motto of Amris mac an Fhiach

thole: to endure, to bear a grief or burden, to stand
what is thrown against one

Thomond: in Ireland, a western region; in Keltia, a lordship on Erinna, ancestral dúchas of Clann Aoibhell

thoughtspeech: telepathy

Throne of Scone: the great white granite chair brought to Keltia from Pictavia in the third immram; symbol of the royal authority of Ardrían or Ard-rígh over all Kelts; it is carved with mystical and magical symbols, many of which have never been successfully interpreted

thunderhelves: cumulonimbi; the anvil-shaped thunderclouds that reach to the borders of space

tinnscra: the marriage portion given to a couple by their families, clanns or friends, or, for those of particularly high rank or note, the king or queen

Tir Gaedhil: name for the island later to be known as Ireland

torc: heavy open-ended neck ornament of gold or silver, worn by almost every Celt of rank on ceremonial occasions or in battle (sometimes the torc was the *only* thing a Celt would wear in battle...)

torse: wreath or garland, often of twisted cloth, worn to keep the hair out of the eyes, or by a warrior beneath his helm to ease its weight and absorb sweat or blood

traha: more than simple arrogance; overweening wanton pride, hubris

triskell: three-armed device, often spiraled, used as a sacred symbol of the Goddess

tuath: 'people'; tribal kindred; any group larger than a clann

tundish: common household funnel; by metaphor, applied to the cam-anfa, the terrible stormcloud formation known on Earth as a tornado

Turusachan: 'Place of Gathering'; on Earth, the great stone circle of Callanish, on the island of Lewis in the Outer Hebrides; in Keltia, the palace and seat of government at Caerdroia on Tara

Ulidia: in Ireland, the province Ulster, in the northeast quadrant of the island; in Keltia, a region of the planet Erinna

Unensouled: name Pátraic and his followers use for the Sidhefolk and those who consort with them

vails: scraps or leftovers, given as charitable handout to beggars or travellers

vaward: the vanguard of an army (*VOW-erd*)

Voclut: an oakwood on the slopes of the hill Slemish, in Fanad; sacred to the Goddess, it contains a miraculous spring and well

Wainlight: the star Sirius; so named because the Celts of Earth fancifully saw it as a lantern hanging on the Chariot or Wain (their name for the Dipper)

Warrior: the constellation Orion as seen from Earth; in Keltia, the polestar of Tara

Welland's Smithy: a souterrain, a chambered tomb near the White Horse Vale, long held sacred to the Smith-god under the name Welland or Wayland

wether: castrated male sheep; **wetherlamb**, young male lamb not yet a year old

White Druid of the Tree: Gaeloch name for Jesus Christ

Whitetongue Book: name given by the unimpressed to the Christom Gospels

yellowstalk ill: the terrible plague that descended on Ireland around 440 C.E., having killed a full third of the population of Europe; it must have been a bacterial infection of some sort, as the herbal cure Brendan distributed for it was completely effective once applied

Yggdrasil: Northing name for the Holy Tree, the World Sacrifice Tree

yowes: female sheep, usually three years of age or older, who have lambed at least once

Yr Mawreth: 'The Highest'; Kymric name for that supreme Deity known also as **Kelu** or, to the High Danaans and Atlandeans, **Artzan Janco**, the Shepherd of Heaven; the One God who is above all gods, neither male nor female, or both male and female, or beyond both male and female

CHARACTERS

Allyn mhic Midna: Sidhe lord; son of Brendan's granddaughter Morna and the Sidhe lord Kelver Donn Midna (*allen vhick MEETHE-na*)

Amris mac an Fhiach: 'son of the Raven'; close friend of Brendan, a druid and general; with his wife Arianwen, built Ravenspur on the newly colonized planet Caledon

Aoifa Fínneachta: Fergus's mother; a warrior in the service of King Niall Nine-Hostage (*EE-fa*)

Barinthus (Barrind): a lord of the High Danaans; the last starfarer left on Earth; he and Brendan worked together to build the ships of Immram Mhór, including the great flagship, the Hui Corra

Beirissa: Coll's Brython wife; a lady of the Brigantes tribe of Britain the More

Brendan Aoibhell: also known as **Brendan mac Nia, St. Brendan the Astrogator;** the leader of the great Immrama and the founder of Keltia (**Aoibhell**, *ee-VELL*)

Bríd: Brendan's second daughter, by his Christian 'wife' Darerca, Pátraic's sister; known to history as Saint Brigid of Kildare, foundress of the Brigidian order of nuns (*Breed*)

Cairenn: mother of King Niall Nine-Hostage, grandmother of Laoghaire; daughter of a king of Cornovia

Calatin: Brendan's Sidhe grandfather; father of Nia

Celestine: the Christian pope who sent Pátraic to convert the Gael

Coll mac Gréine: friend, neighbor and swordbrother of Fergus Aoibhell; he lived at Magheramorna, with his wife Beirissa

Conn Kittagh: friend of Brendan; he married Shane Farrant in Keltia, and they were among the first to settle the planet Gwynedd

Corlis Typhult: priestess; Danaan leader on Immram Mhór; her mate was Breos mac Machaire

Darerca: Pátraic's sister, Brendan's Christian 'wife'; mother of his daughter Bríd

Domhnall Avarcagh: Fergus's father, lord of Killary (*DOWN-ull uh-VAR-ka*)

Donn Aoibhell: a distant cousin and clannsman of Brendan; he was one of Brendan's chief captains and friend to Brendan's son Rohan; in Keltia, he married Fionaveragh, Brendan's daughter; he and his wife were co-founders of House Aoibhell in Keltia

Dorren nic Cána, Malise mac Guaire: leaders of the Celi Dé, who went with Brendan to Keltia, and who founded a tiny Christian community that is still happily thriving in Aeron's day

Dúnomaglos: Pictish leader, mate of Kunera of the Boarholms

Duvessa nighean Suibhne: wife of Laoghaire mac Niall; queen at Tara

Etain: Sidhe lady; Brendan's only wife, and queen in Keltia; mother of his children Fionaveragh and Rohan (*eh-TAWN*)

Fergus Aoibhell: Brendan's father; also known as **Fergus Tinne fo Brega**, Fergus Fire on Brega

Fiaren of Clannrannoch: daughter-in-law of Brendan, wife of Rohan; mother of Morna (*FEE-uh-rin*)

Fionaveragh: Brendan's eldest child and first daughter; wife to Donn Aoibhell, and, with him, founded House Aoibhell in Keltia; mother of Sithney, Tiaquin, Kiaran, Breila; first Ban-draoi Mathr'achtaran (*finn-uh-VAIR-uh*)

Gradlon of Ys: Brendan's master-builder; architect of Caerdroia, Caer Dathyl, Ardturach and the Nantosvelta, among other great works

Gwastor: Etain's father; gave her the Cremave as a gift on leaving; her mother was **Liriagh**

Kelver Donn Midna: son of the Sidhe king Donn Rígh Midna; he himself became king of Knockfierna (named for his old home) on the Keltic planet of Erinna; he was mate to Morna, Brendan's granddaughter, and father to Allyn who will figure so prominently in these tales

Kiaran: third child of Fionaveragh and Donn; husband to Lorn of Benderloch; they were the founders of the Thomond Aoibhells (*kee-AH-rin*)

Kunera: Pict leader, a princess of the Boarholms (Orkney Isles) wife of Dúnomaglos; led her folk on Immram Mhór

Kynmarra of Templarian: friend of Brendan; on

Immram Mhór, the Cornovian leader; lord of
Cantire in Keltia

Laoghaire: high king at Tara, son of Niall Nine-
Hostage; his queen was Duvessa (*leary*; **Niall** is
pronounced *NEE-ill*; **Uí Néill**, of the kindred of
Niall, is *ee-NAYLE*)

Lorn of Benderloch: wedded Kiaran, Brendan's
grandson; together they founded the line of the
Thomond Aoibhells, pre-eminent royal house of
Keltia

Lucet Mael: Druid to Laoghaire; died at Tara in
magical combat with Pátraic

Morna: Brendan's granddaughter, only child of
Rohan and Fiaren; she wedded Kelver Donn
Midna, and by him was the mother of Allyn mhic
Midna—therefore Brendan's granddaughter was
Athyn Blackmantle's great-grandmother!

Morragh mac Lassra: wedded Sithney, Brendan's
granddaughter; they were the founders of the
Findhorn Aoibhells

Nia: a princess of the Danaans; wife to Fergus Fire on
Brega, mother of Brendan the Astrogator; also
known as **Nia the Golden**, **Saint Nia** (*NEE-uh*)

Niall Nine-Hostage: Laoghaire's father, son of King
Eochaid and his Cornovian ban-charach Cairenn
Chasdubh; he was one of the great rulers of Irish
history

Pátraic: Patricius Calpurnius; a North Brython of a
Romano-British gens; captured as a slave and sold

in Tir Gaedhil; escaped, and ordained as a
Christian priest and bishop, he returned to begin
the conversion of the Gael; Brendan's great
enemy; also known by the slavename **Ferganam**,
'Nameless', and as **Maughn** in his homeland
(*PAW-drick*)

Pyllas Nadron: Brython; evil monk who tried to
assassinate Brendan; spy for Vortigern of Britain

Rohan: Brendan's second child and only son

Scathach of Lochaber: friend of Brendan; on
Immram Mhór, leader of Caledonian clann
alliance

Shane Farrant: Fian and scientist, he was the spouse of
Conn Kittagh; they were among the first founders
of Gwynedd

Sithney: eldest child of Fionaveragh and Donn; wife to
Morragh mac Lassra; she was the founder of the
Findhorn Aoibhells, and followed her grandfather
as Sithney Ríghan (or Taoiseach, as she preferred)

Súlsha: Nia's mother; daughter of the great Danaan
queen Maeve of Connachta(*SOOL-sha*)

Vortigern: High Lord of Britain; a Welshman, he
opened the door for the Saxon invasion of Britain,
and was deemed a traitor to his own people
forever after

ROYAL AND DANAAN LINEAGE OF THE BRENDANACHTA IN KELTIA

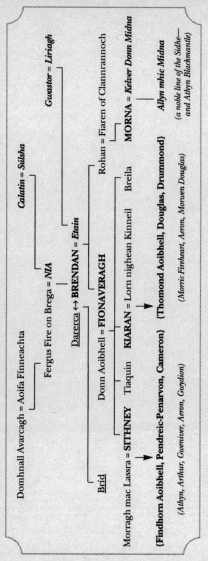

Domhnall Avarcagh = Aoifa Finneachta

Calatin = Sulsha

Gwastor = Liriagh

Fergus Fire on Brega = **NIA**

Darerca ↔ **BRENDAN** = *Etain*

Rohan = Fiaren of Clannrannoch

MORNA = *Kelzor Domn Midna*

Donn Aoibhell = **FIONAVERAGH**

KIARAN = Lorn nighean Kinneil

Breila

Allyn mhic Midna

(a noble line of the Sidhe— and *Athyn Blackmantle*)

Morragh mac Lassra = **SITHNEY**   Tiaquin

{**Thomond Aoibhell, Douglas, Drummond**}

(*Morric Fireheart, Aeron, Morwen Douglas*)

Brid

{**Findhorn Aoibhell, Pendreic-Penarvon, Cameron**}

(*Athyn, Arthur, Gweniver, Aeron, Gwydion*)

BOLD CAPITALS denote individuals through whom pass the chief lines of ancestry and monarchy.

Regular roman type denotes mortals and those of mixed Cael-Danaan ancestry; *bold italics* denote High Danaans (pure Sidhefolk).

Bold roman denotes some of the many noble Keltic houses that can trace direct Brendanacht lineage, usually in several lines of descent; names of a few notable descendants who might be familiar to readers are given in *regular italics*.

Brendan's Christian 'wife' and their daughter appear underlined.

At this period, surnames are not yet standardized family names, but rather bynames: matronymics, patronymics, toponymics, taken from notable deeds or other attributes, or general names of clanns or tuaths.

NOTES ON THE TEXT

I finished writing *The Deer's Cry* on 17 March 1998: St. Patrick's Day to the amateurs, but a day of infamy to true Celts—or, indeed, Kelts—those who are loyal to the great and ancient spirit that Patrick and those who came after him suborned and co-opted, battered and raped and castrated, until today it is but the merest travesty of the powerful vital presence it once was.

This strange and felicitous timing was not intentional—well, at least it wasn't intended by *me* (bring back those snakes! Right now!)—but now that I think of it, it does rather seem like karma; or dán, if you prefer...

The native Irish are still perceived by far too many as the Stepin Fetchits of Europe, grinning and shuffling in greenface, priest-ridden from here to eternity. Some of us even shamefully collaborate with the cultural bigotry, while our proud history and spiritual heritage, our brilliantly humane brehon law system and long-ago-enlightened attitudes toward women (equality) and children (no bastardy), our ancient art and literature and warrior past, all continue to be dissed as heathen barbarism or caricatured as demeaning shamrockery (everything from "The Quiet Man" to Lucky Charms cereal).

Well, I swear by the gods by whom my people swear,
THAT'S going to change! And THE KELTIAD is meant,
among other things, to serve that end: one more nail in
that leprechaun-infested coffin. I know it's pathetically
little, in the face of fifteen hundred years of sneering
and defamation and cultural imperialism and spiritual
genocide and actual persecution; but, you know, it
feels really, *really* good to hit back. (Celts don't turn the
other cheek, we rip off both of yours...)

And by making the Celts free of the stars I can
bestow, if only in fantasy fiction, the rightful dominion
they—we!—should have been enjoying all along. Cel-
tia an uachdar!

(And oddly enough, even as I was handing in the
final draft to my editor, peace seems to have broken
out, however tenuously, in Northern Ireland—coincidence? Or Brendan at work?)

In *The Deer's Cry* I have made Patrick, Brendan and
Arthur contemporary on Earth. I can do this because
my Keltic Brendan is not the historical Navigator-saint,
my Keltic Arthur is not the historical king, and my
earthly Pátraic may not even have been the historical
'saint' known as Patrick.

In any case, there's a lot of sword-room: the dates
claimed for even the three historical individuals vary
wildly from source to source, sometimes by as much as a
century; and I am by no means the first writer to suggest that there may well have been stunt doubles—two
Patricks, two Brendans, *many* Arthurs—for all these guys.

*   *   *

Priestly self-castration among early adherents to the Christ cult is well documented, and it is quite likely that the true founder of what we know today as orthodox Christianity, Paul of Tarsus, was a subscriber to the practice (as was possibly even 'Saint' Patrick himself; and, yeah, okay, some Pagan religions were into it too)—to recompense what perceived or actual inner insufficiencies we can today only guess at. Or maybe he was just, uh, nuts…

Lastly, I have allowed Pátraic to claim the birthday of Jesus Christ as taking place at the Winter Solstice. This just might squeak by, although the historical Yeshua ben Yussef was most likely born in the spring and there is no evidence of *any* formalized Nativity observance, let alone on December 25, before the fourth or fifth century—though in 534 C.E., as one sourcebook puts it, "Christmas Day and Epiphany were reckoned by the law-courts as *dies non*." (Other sources give other, sometimes very much later, dates—as late as the twelfth century, in some cases—for the codifying of Christmas.)

But either way, a winter birthday for Jesus was purely and solely opportunistically established to compete with that darn Solstice those pesky Pagans just couldn't seem to stop celebrating (come back, Sun!!), the way other Pagan feasts and holydays (Samhain, Imbolc, Midsummer…) were also cynically shanghaied by the Christian Church. (The historical Jesus, if he ever even existed, is of course to blame for none of this, and the Christian Church itself was more Pagan than not for the first few centuries—and, to an extent it'll never EVER 'fess up to, it is Pagan even today.)

Not to mention the fact that the god Jesus was competing for attention (and the affections of worshippers) with a passel of other divine birthday boys and light festivals: most notably Mithras (born a few centuries earlier, in yet another cave, and of a virgin too, while shepherds watched their flocks by night and angels sang—hey, what a coincidence *that* is!), *and* the Roman Saturnalia, *and* the Greek Helia, *and* the Jewish Hanukkah, *and* the Norse Yule (birthday of the god Frey), *and* the Midwinter natal days of all those other mankind-loving sacrificial Solar Hero/Sacred Kings also miraculously or divinely born, also in caves, also heralded by cool celestial phenomena, who later also died on, amongst or in close proximity to trees and who also rose from the dead anywhere from immediately to nine days later (what *do* you figure those odds are??!!)—guys like Dionysus (hi, honey!), Kernunnos, Osiris, Tammuz, Adonis, Attis, Krishna, Syrian Baal, oh, and lots more—all of whom were also known as Savior, Divine King, Light of the World...

Well, you get the picture—though the early Church Fathers (and I do mean FATHERS) laid it all on the Devil making a *really* diabolical pre-emptive strike. They actually claimed that centuries *before* Jesus even made the scene, Satan arranged this big divine copycat scam, causing the gullible Pagans to fall for all these other "fake" gods so that when Christ finally did show up the heathens would be *soooo* confused that they wouldn't buy into his trip—yeah, right—which incredibly naive (read 'cunning and disingenuous') apologia

I have reflected in the merry doctrinal confabs Brendan and Pátraic have on Slemish.

Anyway, ever mindful that, as the Emperor Julian put it, "There is no wild beast like an angry theologian," I wish you all the Happy Sacrificed Sacred King's Birthday/Festival of Light Returning of your choice, whatever!

—*P.K.M.*